THE

BOOK

OF

RACHAEL

Leslie Cannold is a researcher, ethicist and columnist. She is a regular commentator on commercial and ABC TV, radio and the web. Leslie is the author of the critically acclaimed *The Abortion Myth* (2000) and *What, No Baby?* (2005), which made the *Australian Financial Review*'s top 101 books list. In 2005, Leslie was named as one of Australia's top twenty public intellectuals and in 2011 she was honoured as the Australian Humanist of the Year. Leslie lives in Melbourne with her partner, two teenage sons and French bulldog.

www.cannold.com

THE
BOOK
OF
RACHAEL

LESLIE CANNOLD

TEXT PUBLISHING MELBOURNE AUSTRALIA

The paper in this book is manufactured only from wood grown in sustainable regrowth forests.

The Text Publishing Company
Swann House
22 William Street
Melbourne Victoria 3000
Australia
textpublishing.com.au

First published by The Text Publishing Company 2011
Reprinted 2011

Cover by W. H. Chong
Page design by Susan Miller
Map by Guy Holt
Typeset in Bembo Book by J&M Typesetters
Printed and bound in Australia by Griffin Press

National Library of Australia
Cataloguing-in-Publication entry
Author: Cannold, Leslie.
Title: The book of Rachael / Leslie Cannold.
Edition: 1st ed.
ISBN: 9781921758089 (pbk.)
Dewey Number: A823.4

To the women of my family, and to every woman
still struggling for a place in history.

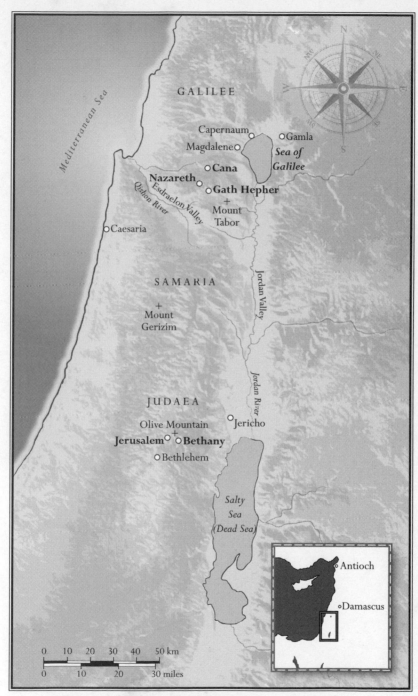

Ancient Israel
c. 3790 (30 AD/CE)

When I was five years old, our ewe gave birth to a lamb. He was white and had eyes as black as olives. Shona and I named him Timba. Two weeks later my eldest brother Joshua held him down, and Papa slit his throat.

The place was Galilee, the fertile northern province of the land of Israel, and spring was in the air. It blew in from the deserts to the east to dry the mud beneath our sandals, and gave life to the sudden profusion of wildflowers blanketing the rolling hills. In the valleys, geometric plains stretched as far as the eye could see. Soon the grain harvest would begin and Israelites of all but the highest stations would swarm—babes strapped to their backs, sickles held high—across the fields. They would reap and gather the browning sheaves of barley, oats and wheat until the last shard of sunlight fled from the sky, then fall to their knees to offer praise to God.

In the hilltop village of Nazareth, grapes ripened on the vine and in the groves nearby, visible from the roof of our house, figs, apricots and almonds swelled like expectant women on the boughs of ancient trees. In the months that followed, we highlands people would join the ingathering, filling woven baskets with fruit, nuts and olives before the rains of winter fell again.

It was a time of promise: of warmth and plenty after the hungry wet. A time of temporary truce as the Galilean resistance fighters, dug into a hill shaped like a camel's hump in the nearby town of Gamla, crawled from their caves. Tired, hungry, in need of a woman's love as well as a bath, the rebels slouched towards their homes in the upper and lower reaches of Galilee. They would linger there for weeks, joining the work of the harvest; later, they would travel with the other men of the village, their kin and clansmen, to Jerusalem as God commanded they do for the Passover Feast. The Roman legionnaires, relieved at the break in the Jewish rebellion, withdrew too—to Caesarea, their Mediterranean capital in our occupied land. There they would promenade on the boardwalk of the majestic harbour, recline in the healing waters of the bathhouses and cheer on the champions who raced, wrestled or fought to the death in the newly built Forum.

It was a time of prayer and purification, as my mama sanctified her soul by baking tiny loaves of bread and lighting candles to cleanse the hearth of leavening for the coming Passover. A time when Papa hurried to complete orders at the woodshop before the pilgrimage to Jerusalem intervened. It was a time when my eldest brother Joshua still took me on his knee and told stories of Jewish trials and triumph. Tales of the strongman Samson, who lost his strength when his woman betrayed him by cutting his hair; of the prophet Daniel whose faith in God saved him from the lion's den. And the wondrous tale of my papa's ancestor King David, the shepherd boy who killed the giant Goliath with a single stone from his slingshot. I liked that one the best.

It was a time, for a child, when the texture of life in the small farming village of Nazareth was still filled with the wonder of surprise: the piquancy of food after fasting, the throb of the new-moon drum in my breast, the dance of the oil lamp's light against our whitewashed walls as we lay down to sleep on Sabbath eve.

It was a time, so many years ago now, when I learned in no uncertain terms what it meant to be a girl.

∽

'Quick, Shona, hurry! The mother ewe! It is time!' I shook my elder sister awake. It was late at night. Moonlight streamed through the uncovered window of our mud-brick house, its back end snuggled into the hillside like a sleeping cat, its tall face overlooking the square. Dutifully, my sister made haste to rise, then paused.

'Rachael,' she began, 'you mustn't. You know what Mama said.'

I knew. My eyes darted to my mother but she, Papa and all five of my brothers were asleep on their mats. Buried beneath several threadbare blankets, my mother's short, slight figure looked like a corpse. I returned my gaze to my sister and shrugged, eyes wide with innocence. Helpfully, from below in the stables, the ewe bawled again, her pitch making clear that the matter was urgent.

'Come on,' I ordered my sister. She stood and, with a resigned sigh, submitted her hand to my outstretched one.

With one last backward glance at my mother, I began picking my way through the sleeping bodies, leading my sister down the run of stone steps that led to the lower floor of our house. There, in the low-roofed, straw-scattered space we called the *oorvah*, the animals were stabled. Beside the ewe were a cow, two goats and a handful of chickens. Alarmed at the ewe's bleating, the cockerel clucked and strutted while the hens flapped about the room. The cud-chewing creatures turned to us, doe-eyed and panting. As I strode across the floor, towing Shona behind me, they shifted and murmured, then parted like the sea to let us pass.

The sheep's liquid eyes were dark and wild. Her grey sides heaved. When she saw us, she tried to rise despite her bulk and desperate condition, but the tethers held her fast.

'Oh!' Shona was dismayed by the ewe's suffering. She sank to the labouring one's side, smoothing her white nightdress beneath her knee, and placed her ear against the ewe's belly, listening. Then she beckoned me towards her and pulled me on to her lap.

We waited. The cow lowed and shifted, dancing candlelight across the room. The cockerel, rebuffed by each of the hens, withdrew sulking to his perch. The sheep bucked and thrashed, her ears twitching as my sister whispered words of comfort. But no matter how many times Shona looked, the folds between the ewe's legs remained sealed.

I wriggled with impatience. Laying a hand on my sister's arm I spoke solemnly. 'We must hasten her trial before she loses heart.'

Despite her unease, my sister smiled. My words, their cadence, were unmistakably my mother's; but when she replied it was with Mama's words too. 'It is not in our power to save her, Rachael. If she is deserving, God will deliver her. If she is not, He will cast her aside.' She stroked the sheep's side and gave a sigh at the weight of her helplessness. 'There is nothing to do but wait and pray.'

Wait. Pray. Even on their own, these words vexed my spirit. Taken together, they made me feel like I'd been chewing sand. I stood and stamped my five-year-old foot on the stable floor. 'I hate waiting! I hate praying!' I declared. 'Why can we not *do* something?'

My beautiful sister Shona. Heart like a split melon, back ready to bend, robes wafting the cinnamon-scent of her skin. Though six years my senior she was a follower by nature, not a leader. She had never sought to thwart me, but admired my wit and spirit. Her willing submission throughout my short life had encouraged me to trust my instincts; to step forward and assume command.

Now she turned her gaze to me. Her eyes were velvet brown and wide, fringed by lashes thick as fur. 'What would you have us do, Rachael?'

And, somehow, I knew precisely what to do to save the lamb's life.

'Sit there Shona, by the ewe's head,' I commanded, and assumed my own place at the sheep's hindquarters. 'Now hold her head still, as still as you can.'

I pushed up the sleeves of my nightdress and took a deep breath. Then I plunged my hand deep into the sheep's birth canal. Paying no heed to the blood and spongy membranes, I took a few moments to explore the terrain. I could feel bone and sinew, flank and cartilage but, it seemed to me, all in the wrong places. At the end of the passage, where there ought to have been a head, two cloven hoofs and a damp fetlock were wedged instead. The lamb was stuck.

Crying out to Shona to comfort the ewe—Talk to her! Sing!—I sought to ease the newborn's way. Scrabbling for purchase on the straw, I wrestled with the tiny body, rolling shoulder and arm this way and that to obtain leverage. I pushed and slid and tugged and eased while the ewe bucked and mewled, and Shona, hanging on to the poor creature's neck, did her best to hold her until at last the errant limbs gave way. Working quickly, I pushed them into position and reached for the lamb's head, tugging it into place. I gripped the tiny muzzle, braced myself and dragged it towards the light.

The ewe's shriek would have been heard in Jerusalem. But with it came a torrent of blood and water and, finally, the pleasing bump and weight of a sodden lamb, still tethered to a pulsing membrane.

Shona was jubilant and threw her arms to the heavens. But this was no time for praise. The newborn had yet to draw breath; it was still and sallow. Lifeless.

Without thinking I bent to the lamb and sucked the muck from its nose, spitting it to the ground like a curse. I laid my head on its flank to listen. Grabbing a tiny leaf-shaped ear in my fist, I shouted into it, then cupped my lips around the muzzle and offered several of my breaths. When this failed to draw a

6

response, I placed both hands on the body and rocked it, gently at first and then harder. Nothing. I looked at Shona helplessly, at a loss about what to do next. My usual wellspring of ideas and plans was exhausted. My sister gripped my hand and squeezed it and we both turned back to the lamb, hearts pounding, breath trapped in our throats. We waited.

Finally, the lamb's tail twitched. It sneezed—once, twice—then began flipping like a fish to escape its caul.

My sister and I rejoiced. 'You did it, Rachael!' Shona exalted, throwing her arms around me. She kissed each of my cheeks over and over while repeating her words of praise. 'You did it! You did it! You did it!'

But the ewe could not be saved. Her body leaked blood in waves that would not stop, soaking the straw and the hem of our nightdresses. Horrified, I looked at Shona, then myself. We were covered in it.

'Oh no!' Shona cried, throwing herself on the animal's neck. 'Don't die! Don't die!'

But she did die. Touching her tongue to Shona's nose, she twitched her tail and was gone. Shona threw herself into my arms and wept. The lamb, heedless of the sacrifice that had blessed it with life, shook free of its caul with a satisfied bleat. It flicked its ears and began the work of standing.

He was perfect. Frankincense-white, unblemished, male: everything the Law said a Passover lamb must be. Mama would be so pleased. He bawled and teetered towards me, exploring the blood and brine on my outstretched fingers, his suckling causing something wonderful, terrible, to bloom in my breast.

'We shall call him Timba,' I proclaimed and Shona, her face streaked with blood and tears, nodded and said, 'Yes.'

Before we slept, my sister squeezed some milk from the teat of a pregnant goat and showed me how the lamb could be made to swallow it. She dragged her fingers through the tangled skein of my hair and poured water from the stone jar to wash my hands and feet. Usually I would squirm and scowl beneath such ministrations. But now I accepted them without protest, my mind absorbed by thoughts of Mama. What would she say, what would she do, when she heard the good news? I imagined Shona recounting my triumph at first light.

'You should have seen her, Mama,' she would say as she laid wood on the fire. 'That lamb was stuck fast. He would surely have died had Rachael not seen the danger and averted it. She saved that poor creature's life! And a Passover lamb, too. Now we need not trade our eggs or the honey Papa brought from the wood the other day to get one at market!' I could see my sister's cheeks, the shape and colour of plums, draw skywards with her smile.

Mama's eyes would fall on me, her lips turned upward in a rare show of pleasure. 'Hosanna! A miracle!' she would cry, her hands lifting in praise of God. Later, when I woke and came to sitting, rubbing my eyes, on my palm-leaf mat, she would say, 'What a good girl!' She might point to a spot beside her at the hearth, and tuck a corner of dough in my mouth. 'What a blessing to have a daughter, so sure in command,' she would say. Or perhaps, with a glint of pride in her eyes, 'Now there's one who uses his head,' just as she had when Joshua arrived home from Papa's shop with a mortar he'd carved from the antiseptic wood of the almug tree. She might even flutter her tongue noisily, her mouth shaped in a circle, to ensure my father and brothers, the whole village of Nazareth, were alive to my triumph. I hugged myself with delight and drifted off to sleep, smiling in the dark.

But when dawn broke, nothing went to plan. I woke to the sound of slaps and women's cries, to pots smashing and doors being kicked in, to the bray of fearful mules and the thud of cargo being loaded on to slave-drawn carts. My mother was kneeling by the hearth, a hole in our dirt floor surrounded by stones, while Papa, his eyes bleary and long white beard uncombed, stormed up and down the stone steps connecting the lower and upper rooms of our house: pushing animals aside and ransacking the hen's nests in the *oorvah* and, upstairs, pawing through the jars around Mama's hearth like a honey-seeking badger.

It was the tax collectors. At first light, the ram's horn had wailed from the watchtower, announcing their descent on the village to garner the seemingly endless tithes we owed to our many masters. Rome, King Herod and the priests of the Jerusalem Temple all held out their hands for payment from the men of Nazareth: a yearly tithe on the first fruits of both field and grove; a tax on the first born from every stable; sales taxes, land taxes, export and urgency taxes. Tax collectors were the most hated men in the land. Not only were they Jewish traitors, suborned by the Roman overlords to fleece their own people, they were cruel and corrupt too: their own extravagant living underwritten by what could be skimmed from the monies they amassed for priests and kings.

'You have it all, Yosef. I told you this already,' Mama was saying. She was gnawing at her lips, tearing small shreds of skin with her teeth, just as she always did when she was worried and fretful. Her mouth, usually so pretty, was now little more than a patch of blood.

'But it is not enough. It is not what was there,' said Papa. He was a giant of a man, nearly twice Mama's size, and his voice barrelled from his chest like a new-moon drum. He was angry now and his fury was surely the cause of Mama's distress. Her eyes fixed on his towering form, I watched as she tore another strip of skin from her lips, then blotted the blood with the back of her hand.

But while my mother sought to please my father, she did not fear him. No one in Nazareth did. Despite his impressive stature, Papa had never been one for spears or bonds or vengeance. Instead, his faith was in books and God and the power of prayer. When the elders called in search of men to raid our enemies, or to carry out sentence on a woman judged a whore, Papa always said no.

'These are not the causes of darkness,' he would insist, dismissively waving his hand—the size of a laying hen—at the wickedness of the world. 'They are signs. The evil is here.' He would tap his broad chest. 'As is the good. So here is where we must look to know our sins, and repent them.'

Now he paced back and forth from the hearth to the square of light beneath our lone window, which overlooked the square. My brothers squatted around the eating mat, marking his strides with wide eyes. Shona, returned from the well, eased the stone water jar to the floor as quietly as she could and leaned against the wall to catch her breath. My mother pressed her frayed lips together and returned pointedly to her baking, briskly shaping chunks of dough into tidy balls. The silence, punctuated by the muted slam of her fist against the oven wall, seemed to offer the chance I had been waiting for.

'Mama,' I said, starting towards her, 'do you know what I did last night?'

She shooed me from the hearth as if I were a fly. 'Not now, Rachael.' Her gaze flickered momentarily towards me before returning to Papa. He was still pacing our packed-earth floor with a thunderous tread, his long legs making short work of the distance between the far ends of the house. Joshua reached out and snatched me from his path. Unseeing, Papa spoke his thoughts aloud. 'If we cannot find the coins, perhaps they will take more of our harvest?' He fretted at his chin with his fingers, muttering. 'Another homer of barley, perhaps, and two measures of oil—'

My mother shrieked as if she had been stabbed, and scrambled to her feet. 'Another homer of barley? Two measures of oil? Two *full* measures? Have the demons got hold of you, Yosef? What shall I cook with? What will the children eat? It is all very well to distribute our food like blessings, but I have nine mouths to feed!'

Papa sighed, the purity of his rage corrupted, as it was always, by my mother's excuses and special pleadings. He was, in this way and others, a man divided. A man who despised the tax collectors as much as any poor peasant, but who saw little purpose in railing against one's fate. His life, his prospects, were as they were: so they would stay until God made them different. He shook his head and told my mother. 'We must give over the portion demanded, Miriame. It is the law.'

'Yes, but how will they know?' Her voice was so low it hissed. 'How can they know what is owing unless we tell them ourselves what we've sold?' Emboldened by his hesitation, she pursued him, her small, pert nose almost touching his chest. 'Our share of the village harvest, yes. This all eyes can see. But your takings from the woodshop? Who knows whether you

11

have built nine ploughshares or ninety-nine? Hewn seven cedar chests or seventy-seven? Only you, Yosef,' she darted her chin in the direction of my eldest brother, who at age fourteen had only just become a man and begun working with Papa in the shop. 'You and Joshua.'

I watched my father's expression change from surprise to anger, before coming to rest in sorrow. He dragged his massive hands through the greying remains of his hair and spoke in a way intended to make my mother feel shame. 'You know the truth, Miriame,' he said. 'And God. God knows it, too.'

Silence again, though this time punctuated by my mother's mouth opening and closing like a fish. No one moved. My brothers and sister were agog, their gazes moving back and forth between Papa and our red-faced mother.

This was my chance. Heedless of the gravity of what had passed between my parents, I struggled free of my brother's encircling arms and rushed towards my mother, determined to tell her my good news. 'Mama! Last night I—'

'Not *now*, Rachael!' she cried, shoving me aside with a force that made me stumble and fall. As my knees scraped the floor, I let out a cry. But Mama never glanced my way. Instead, eyes brimming with tears, she dug in her belt and extracted two precious silver coins. She walked towards Papa, her palm extended. 'Here Yosef, take them. Take it all. But do not blame me when the winter rains come and our daughters are crying from hunger.'

The coins clinked as they fell into his palm. He closed his fist around them and headed for the door. But before he left he turned back to face her. 'Trust in God, Miriame,' he told her softly. 'Never doubt that He has a plan.'

In the days that followed I shadowed my mother, silently mouthing her name. I prayed for her to stop seething and sulking, and for the Mama of my imagination to materialise and attend to the story of Timba's birth.

But Mama, the real one, had other plans. 'Do it properly now, Rachael,' she would say whenever I drew near, shaking her head at the state of our floor and pushing a broom into my hands. Or, stilling my arm as I peeled apples, 'Away from you Rachael, not towards!' She soaked and beat flax to prepare it for spindling, gathered up the sleeping mats to spread on the roof terrace so they might freshen in the sun, scrubbed the hearth with tallow and sour wine. She ordered Shona to collect herbs to season the meals, sewed new robes and repaired others for my careless fast-growing brothers. Still, there always seemed to be more to do, and never time to listen.

My sister watched me being scolded and dispatched until, finally, she could bear it no longer. It was now the day before Passover, and the three of us were busy around the eating mat. Shona and I were shelling almonds while Mama sewed the cushion on which Papa would recline for the festive meal. The air smelled of turned earth and poppies. Through the uncovered window, the shrill voices of boys too young for school could be heard. They were in the square, organising themselves into teams for a tug of war.

'Mama,' my sister said softly. 'Rachael has something to tell you.'

Mama was squinting at her stitches. She sighed, picked up her knife and began ripping them out.

'Mama?' Shona said.

'Yes?' Mama's gaze followed my sister's to me. She pursed her lips. 'What is it, Rachael?'

'Mama,' I began, but then hesitated.

'Yes, Rachael.' She was impatient now. Her hazel eyes were so flecked by orange they often looked the colour of rust. They grazed my face, but her mind was elsewhere. I could almost hear her listing off the tasks that remained to be done before the feast began at sundown the next day: the candle-pilgrimage through the house to eliminate all traces of leavening; bitter herbs—dandelion, chicory, hawkweed—to be collected from the meadow just beyond the village gates; the large jar to the grape press for...

'Timba,' I blurted. 'Mama. I want to tell you about Timba.'

'Timba? Who is Timba?' She looked to Shona but my sister, not wanting to thieve my glory, looked to me. She nudged me with her eyes. *Go on.*

'The lamb, Mama.'

'The lamb?'

'Yes.'

'What lamb? You mean the one born at new moon?'

'Yes, him. I—I did something wonderful, Mama.' The pride-filled words gushed from my lips like water. 'He was stuck, you see, and I saved him. Shona did not know what to do, but I did. I stuck my arm inside and pushed his legs backward and,' demonstrating with my hands, 'pulled him around and forwards and he came. Out. Alive. Saved!'

There was a cold silence.

With a terrible deliberateness my mother set her stitching down and gave me her full attention. 'You mean to tell me,' she

14

said, 'that you attended a birth I said you must have nothing to do with?'

'Yes, but—'

'A birth that, when you asked me, I said that Shona should manage on her own?'

'Yes, Mama, but—'

'But nothing, Rachael. I told you plainly not to go near that animal when her trial began. I explained that with Passover afoot we could not risk misstep. I said that Shona should carry on alone. Do you recall my telling you all this, Rachael?'

From the corner of my eye, I saw Shona swallow. My own mouth was as dry as a potsherd. 'Yes, but I wanted—'

'You wanted.'

'I thought—'

'You thought.' Each retort was a slamming door. I could not make my mother proud. I could not even make her listen.

Mama smoothed both hands down the cloth of her veil, from the top of her head to the knot at her throat, checking for any hairs that might have escaped; ensuring that the tie of the scarf was tight and firm. It was a familiar ritual, one that often accompanied explanations and demonstrations of what was required of a girl. Both her veil and tunic were the palest blue, like the sky after it rained.

'I understand you far better than you know, Rachael. But commands are not for you to consider. They are for you to obey.'

I stared at her through a shimmer of tears.

'Do you understand, Rachael?'

Shona dug her elbow softly into my ribs.

'Yes, Mama,' I whispered.

The following day at dawn, the strangled cry of the ram's horn sounding from the village watchtower summoned my father and brothers from their mats. Splashing their faces with water from the jar by the door, they trudged to the square to join the other men in the rituals and prayer that would occupy the morning.

Mama had been up since first light, moving about the hearth with frantic paces, her face creased with worry. She ground and sliced and grated, filling the air with cassia and the sharp scent of horseradish. Shona arranged bowls of salty water on the mat and rummaged beneath the hens for eggs. The Passover had begun.

I wanted to be a good girl like my sister, and to help too. Mama was still angry about Timba, her rust-coloured eyes hard whenever they found mine, and I tried to make her smile. Instead, I wound up straying too close to the hearth, where I singed my tunic. Then I shattered a pot of olives. When I tripped over the broom, Mama screamed, clutched the sides of her head with her hands and ordered me out from underfoot.

But Shona would not see me cry. Bowing to my mother, who was cursing and muttering as she swept up the shards, my sister snatched my hand and raced me down the stone steps into the *oorvah*. Past the lowing cow, the chickens scattering in our path, she urged me out the back door and into the forest.

The wood beyond our house was lush and dense. Mint and myrtle huddled near the weathered trunks of silver-bark trees, while evergreen shrubs of laurel and poplar trees blanketed the earth with green as far as my eyes could see. The air smelled of new life, too: of turned earth and moulting fur and blossoms unfolding their petal wings in search of the sun. To our north, about an hour's walk away, was the city of Sepphoris, where Mama sometimes ventured to buy dyes or rare spices, and Papa went regularly in search of work. On good days, he might return from city with commissions to build three-legged tables, paw-footed sofas or any number of Greek-styled luxuries demanded by the wealthy Jews who lived there, and who Mama condemned as worse than the Greeks themselves for the way they flouted God's Law.

To Nazareth's west lay the Qishon: the White Nile, a river seen as miraculous by the people of our arid land because it never ran dry. Its headwaters ran down from the ridge of Gilboa in the east and across the Esdraelon Plains, to meet in the west before emptying into the Mediterranean Sea. To the east, between Sepphoris and Gilboa and less than half a day's walk from Nazareth, was the inland Sea of Galilee. Crowded from first light to sundown with tiny fishing vessels, its shores littered with grim-faced fishwives and their many children casting out threadbare nets again and again in hope of procuring their supper. But it was only through the gates of Nazareth to the south that the thicket of surrounding greenery grew thin enough for us to actually see our Israelite neighbours, the Esdraelons, tilling and tending their grain in the fecund valley below.

'What I need you to do is simple, Rachael,' my sister said. We were at least twenty paces from the house now, though the door to the *oorvah*, with its rotten wood and sagging frame, was still visible through the branches and leaves. She bent and rummaged beneath a moss-covered stone the size of my head, then returned to standing. In her hand was a narrow white shard. 'Do you see this? It's bone, from some animal. A coney or bird or squirrel,' she gestured at the surrounding trees where a bevy of flying and

17

leaping creatures were shivering leaves and bending the branches as they went on their way. 'Your job is to find as many of these as you can, and put them in a pile over there,' Shona pointed at our house. 'Right at the base of the *oorvah* door. I'll grind and sharpen them into sewing needles later.' My sister bent at the waist so our noses were level. Picking up the corner of her robe, its colour the grey of undyed wool, she swabbed at my tear-stained cheeks. 'Don't cry, sister. You will enjoy this task, crawling and scavenging in the dirt. But you must keep your mind on the work, and not get distracted or wander off.' She traced a fond finger down the uneven ridge of my nose.

'Shona!' Mama shouted.

'Be good,' Shona pleaded before she fled.

The next few hours, alone in the wood behind our house, were the most contented of my life. Turtledoves cooed in the trees and the air was thick and pleasantly scented from Passover fires in the square. Scrabbling about on hands and knees, I made a game of the chore. First, I fancied myself a squirrel, imagining that each shard of bone I uncovered was a precious nut to be tucked away for the winter wet. Then, having unbound my loincloth and tied it round my waist, I filled it with scraps, singing and swaying like the women in the vineyard as they bent to gather grapes. When I stumbled upon the remains of a dead bird, I mimed wrapping the dry, crumbling body in linen, then mourned like a keening woman, scratching my arms and tearing at my hair.

'Quiet those women in the back!' I scolded aloud, switching to the role of an officiating elder. In my mind's eye I saw the upturned faces of the villagers, rapt at my every word. 'The wages of sin is death,' I intoned in the deepest voice I could muster, recalling the words I had heard usher forth from the lips of an elder at an interment several months earlier. 'Death is how God punishes each of us, and all Israel, for failing to heed the Law.' I was just accepting praise for my wise words from the dead bird's family when I heard footsteps and a scuffle inside the *oorvah*. Papa's low-pitched prayers followed, and Joshua's broken-voiced reply. Then, more scuffling, a curse and the alarmed bleat of a lamb.

'Timba!' I shrieked. Leaping to my feet I ran towards the house and began pounding and beating on the *oorvah* door, trampling beneath my sandals the mound of fragile bones. Until suddenly I realised the door was not barred and, throwing it ajar, rushed inside.

It was nearly done. Joshua was on the straw-covered floor with his knee on Timba's chest, his hands working to expose the lamb's throat. Timba's spindly legs pawed the air uselessly while Papa, on bended knee, loomed over the beast. One of my father's long arms reached out to one side, restraining a restless mill of goats. In the hand of the other, raised high overhead, a knife glinted.

'No! Not Timba, Papa!' I ran towards my father, skidding and sliding on the hay. Danced around him with arms outstretched, reaching for the blade.

'Rachael! Come away from there!' Mama scolded from the top of the steps.

Ignoring her, I leapt and strained towards the knife. But it was no use. Even when he was kneeling, the length of Papa's body kept it well beyond reach.

'Rachael!' Mama growled, making her way quickly down the steps. I saw her eyes register disgust at the grime on my face and the makeshift tie of my apron. 'This is men's business! The lamb's throat must be slit for the meat to be pure! Kosher! Take hold of yourself and move out of the way.'

'No!' I searched for Papa's eyes, blue and—as they found mine—shadowed with pity and doubt. His hand trembled. 'Please, Papa,' I whispered. 'Not my lamb.'

'It is the most painless way for Timba to die, Rachael,' he tried to explain before, with an indignant cry, Mama stretched out her talon fingers to grab my arm and yanked me away. She ordered Papa to carry on.

The blade descended in a neat arc. There was a rip of flesh, a gurgled bleat, the scent of blood. Joshua, ready with an urn, collected the first scarlet spray. He scattered some in every corner of the barn while Papa begged and pleaded with God to forgive our sins. The goats clamoured around the still body of the lamb, bleating piteously. I buried my face in my mother's belly and bleated, too.

I sensed rather than saw the hesitation in Mama's hand as it hovered above my head, before finally landing in an awkward pat. 'Oh Rachael,' she murmured, the sadness in her voice unmistakable. 'How hard the world is for you.'

⁓

It was time for the feast to begin. The sun fell to the horizon and in the twilight, my father marched from the square, my brothers scurrying behind. Joshua, short and slight, his movements neat and his manner diffident; the next in line, Jacob, with close-cropped red hair and the diamond eyes of a snake. Tubby Simon came after, followed by the eight-year-old twins, their skin sallow and hair like matching bowls.

Mama scanned the Seder mat, gripping the knot of her headscarf like a raft, her worry evident, as it always was when she faced a test of Jewish womanhood, that she might stumble. But everything was there, and in its proper place. The date and nut paste and two stacks of flat bread. At the top of the mat, the cup of wine customarily left for the Prophet Elijah, whose arrival would herald the Messiah, the man God said should be king. A space had been left vacant in the centre for the platter Papa now held aloft in his hands: a plate of roasted lamb. My Timba. A lump formed in my throat but my tummy grumbled its yearning for a taste of the flesh or fat on the bones.

Papa cleared his throat, preparing to tell the story of Passover. Mama lit the candles and poured the wine. 'Passover commemorates the journey of the Israelites from slavery to Freedom,' Papa began, and the story flowed from there. The bread of affliction, Moses' plea to the Pharaoh, the ten plagues from God and the terrible death of every one of Egypt's first-born sons: Papa's voice waxed and waned with the familiar liturgy.

The twins fidgeted and fought beneath their breath while my second brother, the red-haired Jacob, utterly uninterested, let his chin droop to his chest. I stood between my mother and sister with our backs pressed to the wall, separated from the men as tradition dictated. Shona nodded off too, clearly unable to grasp the special language that Papa used to tell the Passover tale. Mama, her rust-flecked eyes open, was also miles away, no doubt calculating the effort required to clear the mat and tidy the hearth when the ritual meal was through.

But as the deep rumble of my father's voice filled the candle-lit room, I was rapt. I lifted and swayed to the sound, eyes peering through the gloom at his long arm as it lifted and fell, pointed and quailed with each twist and turn of the epic tale. Stuck to every word.

Then it was question time. 'How do you teach a wise son the story of Passover?' Papa asked Joshua.

Joshua's response was quick and sure. 'You should reply to him with all the laws of Passover,' he told Papa, and Papa nodded before turning to Jacob, 'And a wicked son?' he demanded of my second eldest brother in harsher tones. Jacob, just woken from his nap and still groggy from sleep, nonetheless managed to give the right response. My third brother, Simon, knew the answers, too, but the twins were a disgrace. Granted the two easiest questions of the night in deference to their youth, they stumbled and blushed, their reply an incomprehensible mash of notions and tongues. Even when Papa spooned them the first, then the second, of the Hebrew words needed, they could not find their way.

How could the silly things not see the answers? I was bouncing around on my toes, unable to contain my excitement. Mama saw the warning signs and put out her arm to restrain me, her eyes sparking daggers, but it was too late. I had already stepped into the halo of candlelight surrounding the mat and opened my lips to speak.

'*Ba layla hazeh ha yehudim ochlim matzah.* On this night Israelites eat matzah,' I told my assembled family. 'The Jewish people did this because we had to flee our bondage so quickly, there was no time for bread to rise. We recline on this night so that we might recall that at his own Seder mat, each man is king—'

Mama grabbed my arm and shook it. Papa stared as if a monkey had just popped out of my mouth.

'Rachael,' he said, 'where did you learn to speak Hebrew?'

I had spoken Hebrew? My stomach lurched; I felt my lips

22

bend and quiver. Even I knew it was forbidden for female lips to shape the language of the Law.

But Papa called me to his side and lifted me into his lap like a kitten. He smoothed my covered head. 'You must be honest, Rachael. Has someone taught you the Temple's tongue?'

'No, Papa. No one.' I spoke the truth. I understood as little about how I had just spoken Hebrew as I did about why I usually spoke Aramaic. I only knew that when I had reached for words, those were the ones that came.

'A miracle,' Papa breathed and lifted his awe-struck countenance to Mama's face. But the sour expression he found there saw him turn to Joshua instead. 'She is a mime,' he told my brother proudly. 'My daughter is a mime.'

The twins looked at me as if I smelled of goat dung. 'What is a mime?' asked one.

'A mimic, a reflector. An…impersonator,' he explained, until their dull eyes made him sigh. 'She sees it once, or hears it and—' he twisted a pretend key near his ear, 'she remembers.' He looked at me, shaking his head, 'A miracle.'

Joshua's dark eyes met mine and quickly, one winked. But the rest of my brothers were churlish. They muttered and spat, their eyes fixed on the ground.

My mother's gnawed lips shone with blood in the dim candlelight. 'What are you talking about, Yosef? A mime? Rachael? Who would think such a thing,' she dismissed the possibility with a flick of her wrist, 'because of a few Hebrew words? Just a few words of Hebrew only and you in a froth like a boiling pot, insisting we have a miracle on our hands?'

Papa turned back to my mother and protested, 'She understands it, Miriame. She is not just spitting up like—' His eyes fell on the twins but his tongue went no further. 'Those words were chosen, pulled together to answer the questions I asked, not just repeated by rote, from memory.' He slapped his brow with his hand, aghast at his failure to have parsed the clues and knitted them together before. 'And it makes sense, Miriame. I should have seen it before. Say something near her and back it comes with the same words, same tone. Show her something, and she remembers every detail.'

'Except if it is how to sweep a room properly, or to peel apples or—'

Papa batted these objections away with the back of his giant hand. 'Too simple. She is not interested. She needs more—'

'More?' My mother's pretty mouth twisted in an ugly way. Both my parents seemed to have forgotten the Seder meal. 'Yes, let us encourage her to want more. To think she needs it. That she deserves it! Here is a sound plan. Oh Yosef, how can you be such a fool?'

'A fool?' my father spat, but then it was there. The pity that swelled his eyes whenever she advanced claims that appealed to propriety. The pity that restrained his anger, no matter the strength of his conviction, or truth of his case.

She moved to finish it. 'Girls do not belong at the Seder table, Yosef.' She snatched me from his lap. 'This is the way of our world. The sooner she accepts this, the better. Trust me, I—'

'No!' Twisting from Mama's grasp I opened my lips and let the words pour forth. 'Seder means order. The Passover meal must be done in the right order, nothing left out, nothing new. When we do as God commands us, we honour the covenant He made with Abraham. God commands us not to bow down to

24

idols or to worship Gods other than Him. He says we must obey His Law. If we do, He will keep us as his Chosen People, blessing us with the land and the freedom to live on it according to His word. But if we fail—'

All eyes were on me. 'A miracle,' Papa said again.

But Mama clicked her tongue with impatience as she moved back towards the shadows, knowing better.

When the Seder was finished, I stood near the hearth, my face pressed against the wall. Taking my punishment. Mama and Shona moved about, tidying up, while Papa and my brothers rose from their places and wound their arms about each other. Chins lifted to God, they danced in a circle while Papa sang the traditional songs of Passover.

No one saw when I took the knife from its place by the hearth and slipped it in my belt. No one noticed when I stole down the steps and made my way towards the dying fires spattered across the square. I was alone. Even the watchtower was empty as every man, no matter his caste or fortune, reigned at his own Seder table. Somewhere in the boughs overhead, I heard a cat's frenzied song.

Standing at the edge of the closest fire, I fumbled at my throat, my child's fingers struggling to unpick the knot of my veil. When, eventually, I pulled it off, I stood for a moment, smoothing the cloth with my hand, just as Mama did each night when she removed her headcovering before lying down to rest. But I did not fold the cloth carefully and reverently set it aside. Instead, I cast it to the flames.

The coarse grey fabric flared, curled and shifted, then flew off as ash into the night. Drawing the knife from my belt, I grabbed a handful of hair and cut. Grabbed and cut, grabbed and cut, until the thick black clumps formed a halo around my feet.

I felt light, and free. A girl no longer.

No longer a girl.

What happened then?

What do you think happened? In the wake of my fire-side rebellion, Mama took to me like a demon possessed. As Papa stood by, disapproving, but chastened as always in the face of her fretful chagrin, she scoured me daily in tones loud enough for the lowliest trader in East Nazareth to hear and chased me about the hearth with a wooden spoon. At night I would wake with a fright to her shouting right in my ear: harsh, hissing rants that meditated on each act of my rebellion and the countless ways I brought her shame. She urged the girls of the village, from those even younger than me to ones on the verge of their first blood, to trail us as we went about collecting provisions for the day of rest, which would begin that evening when the last ray of light left the sky. As we moved from baker to wine-maker, then across to the stone vats of the olive-press, with me scurrying in front like a prize duck while she prodded me with a stick, she encouraged the entourage to find new ways to punish me.

'Pinch her,' she would cry. 'Why not a little slap?' She laughed when one of the girls, eager to please, ran behind me and, before I could turn, grabbed the neck of my robe and dropped a handful of biting insects down my back.

On the day of the Sabbath, she would hold out her hand to demand my veil, hands on hips and foot tapping impatiently as I struggled to loosen the knot. Then she would parade me in the village market, driving me from stall to stall and into each coven of gossips so all might witness the ruins of my scalp, with its bald patches and tufted clumps of hair.

But most of all, she encouraged the woman of the village to chatter. To mince and sashay and tell and re-tell with a titter the tale of my downfall to every villager in Nazareth and every peasant, taxpayer and pilgrim who happened past on their way from Jerusalem to the north or from the Sea of Galilee in the east across the Esdraelon valley to the Mediterranean. Urged them to recall how I had crept like a thief from the house in the dead of night and stood over the Passover fire as a witch does her cauldron, hatching my plan of rebellion. Then, brazenly bared my head to God, not just once when I threw the veil aside but again, when I hacked off the thick rat's nest of black hair that covered my head. The immodesty! The shame!

Beneath the hand of such careful tending the story of what I had done, and what this revealed about who I was, flourished. It grew grander and more florid with each repetition and, as it did, made my insurrection seem increasingly churlish and absurd. But as my standing in Nazareth declined, the stature of villagers who repeated the story budded, then flowered. Those who claimed to have witnessed the events first hand were the most feted of all.

Soon, everyone had. Everyone in Nazareth just happened to have been passing through the square or glancing through their window arch on that fateful night; just happened to be watching, aghast, as I stood by the fire and cast my modesty to the flames. I had become a siren, a warning chime, a cautionary tale for every woman and girl in the village.

Mama made little effort to conceal her pleasure. When I returned from the well or the press with pinch-marks on my arms, a torn robe and bloodied knees from where I'd been tripped and fallen, my tear-stained cheeks burning with humiliation, her tone was rich with wrath. 'That will teach you to overstep yourself,' she would say. 'That will teach you to disobey!'

But apart from the pleasure she took in both orchestrating and witnessing my shaming, she paid me no mind, tending my brothers and moving through the housework as if in a world quite separate from mine. If I spoke, she ignored me; if I reached for her, she turned away. In the weeks and months to follow I began to wonder what was worse: to be paraded and shamed by her in the manner of a harlot, or treated as though I were dead.

Then came the afternoon when I could stand no more of it. It was several months later and the season was hot and dry. For days, every spare hand in the village—men, women and children—had been in the vineyards, singing psalms as they carefully packed what Papa said was the best grape harvest in years into hand-held baskets. My hair was growing back now, though I could see in Shona's fretful look as she spat on her fingers and fussed at my skull whenever my veil slipped, that the history of damage was still visible.

That morning, I had joined my mother and sister amid the vines, moving up and down the rows, discerning which bunches were ripe for picking and clipping them from the vine. But soon, Mama was sniffing and frowning at the fruit in my basket and, having decided I was 'far too clumsy to carry out such careful work,' sent me packing. I was to sit beneath the shade tree with the other girls, taking turns fetching water from the well. My disgrace ensured not a single girl would talk to or even look at me. Quickly recognising this as an opportunity, not a torment, I waited until the bevy were deep in conversation and slipped away unnoticed.

I knew exactly where I was headed. Hurrying up the hill-side I crossed the square, flew down the path towards our house and circled around the back, to the wood that lay outside the door of our *oorvah*. I sprinted the final cubits and fell to my knees beside the rough and fissured trunk of an ancient poplar. I began to dig and moments later my fingers found a hollow. Scratching and clawing, I pushed the last remnants of dirt aside. There, before me, lay the prize. I leaned in to brush the dead bird's skeleton with a gentle finger and watched it collapse in a jumble of bones and dust. Sitting back on my heels, I considered.

The bird looked like a dead thing; nothing more, nothing less. This was what Timba, my lamb, would look like now, even if he'd been mourned properly and laid in the ground to rest. Not much different from what had been left on the Passover plate: a pile of lonesome bones.

But what if it were possible to put things to rights? What if the bird could be made to live again? If its bones could be assembled and re-ordered, each rib and vertebra set securely in place? Might she sing and beat her wings once more? And if it were possible for a bird to be reborn, why not a sheep? If a lamb's bones could be gathered all in one place, instead of burned to cinder in a Passover flame, might he come to frolic and bleat again? Suddenly, urgently, I needed to know.

I set to work directly. Swiping a place on the dirt clean with my hand, I reached again and again into the shallow grave, extracting the ribcage, the femurs, the delicate bones of the wings and fitting them into place. I worked confidently from the image in my mind of the intact skeleton asleep in its earthen nest. Slowly, the puzzle drew together; the creature began to take shape.

'Rachael!' My mother's voice was like a bark; her pinching fingers bit my ear. 'What are you doing?' Mama cried. 'Get up! Get up!' She hauled me, painfully, to my feet. Then her eyes fell on my project, only half completed, on the ground. She squinted at it and chewed her lip. Examined me up and down for clues. 'What's this? What's this?' she said at last. 'I have no need of needles.'

'They are not bones for needles, Mama,' I told her. 'I was just wondering if—'

But she had heard enough. Grabbing my shoulders roughly, she turned me towards the *oorvah* door and pushed me in that direction. 'Home, Rachael. You have no business here. You should be at the hearth, preparing the midday meal. Or in the fields with the other girls, fetching and carrying water. Not out here in the wood, alone, indulging your, your *curiosity*.' This last word, as it fell from her lips, was laden with contempt. Beneath the weight of her indifferent sandal, I heard the bones crackle and snap.

I began to cry, my stumbling step slowing with the burden of my grief. I was nothing, no one! No matter which way I turned, or how hard I tried, I could do little right in my mother's eyes. I had not asked to be born as I was, but this was my fate, and I craved for her to accept it. To accept me as I was, and to love me for it. But she would not. Instead, she had castigated me for my failings as a girl—my inability to be a good girl, the right sort of girl—then scorned me all the more when I had tried to be other.

The thought of my failed attempt to make myself male, and the scorn and shame that had followed, only made me sob harder. I was now at a standstill, standing amid a tangle of pink rockrose and spiny evergreen shrubs, sobbing as if my heart would break. I had failed, I was a failure. I could not gain my mother's love on my own terms; I could not shed the femaleness that made all that I wanted, all that I was, so wretchedly wrong. And what had my desperate quest for recognition brought me? Not Mama's love, nor Papa's protection. Nothing but dishonour, and the sharp-clawed ridicule of the entire village.

I heard her approach and in a different tone, softened by unaccustomed compassion and pity, she said, 'What are you standing there for, Rachael? Nothing to be gained by wailing about what is done and what cannot be changed. You will survive, daughter. All of us do.'

'But Mama, I—' I whirled around, provoked by the surprising gentleness in her voice to make one last try.

But while her tone remained kind, the hardness in her eyes did not abate. 'But nothing, Rachael. There are no buts, no exceptions: there is nothing else to say. Get home now, daughter. Go home. And do not walk this way again.'

My neck bent and my chin fell to my chest; beaten. The membrane of my resistance, having thinned, now split and the girl I had been—Old Rachael—spilled to the forest floor. She lay there, stricken, quivering like entrails. I observed her indifferently then gave her carcass a kick, and walked away. I did not look back. That girl was dead to me now.

I chose instead for my mother's love.

☙

Having acquiesced to my mother's demand for obedience, and passive acceptance of my female fate, I became a new girl. That girl—New Rachael—sought only to sweep.

Just days after New Rachael's capitulation in the woods behind the house, Papa presented her with a new tool of trade. He turned the cedar broom handle in the shop and Joshua bound the stiff splay of pine needles with leather. Mama bestowed it on New Rachael like a present and she accepted it in the manner of her sister, Shona, her head modestly bowed, her mouth shaped in an O.

New Rachael was nothing like the old one. She understood that sweeping, done properly, was a grave and monumental chore. To sweep a room properly, one must begin from the far corner of the upper room and work outwards, walking backwards, in increasingly broad triangles until one reached the door at the room's far end. It was through this door that the sordid accumulation of one's efforts was disposed. New Rachael quickly noted that a failure to conform to such work practices caused all manner of strife. It meant finding oneself at the centre of the upper room of the house at the conclusion of

33

the morning's work with no clear pathway for the removal of the dirt, dust and dung acquired. Then one must lower one's broom to the floor and search for a cloth, which must be dampened in the wooden bucket kept on the terrace roof and applied to the pile for purposes of collection. This must be done several times, each attempt interspersed with a further rinse in the bucket, until the last of the mess had been gathered, the cloth rinsed once more and hung out to dry. Only then might one realise that the effect of the entire process was to drip water and distribute fresh dirt and dust across the newly swept floor.

But even where such mishaps transpired, New Rachael did not complain. In her new incarnation, she was determined to maintain a bright face at all times and to make old wine into new. She decided that it was precisely the challenge of keeping both the upper room of their house and the lower one, where the animals were stabled, tidy and clean that made the task so engaging. Consider, for example, the difficulties of sweeping hay stained with animal dung of the looser variety; or the issues involved in removing all traces of dirt and dust from the ridged and uneven surface of a packed-earth floor. For the latter task, New Rachael discerned that a smaller brush might be superior for the task. She requested such a tool, which Papa and Joshua were quick to provide, and…victory!

Now, if only the problem of the men tracking dirt up the steps from the animal stalls, or from the woodshop, square, grove or other parts of the village into the upper room when they returned home for the midday meal or at the end of the working day, could be so easily solved. Of course, she would plead with them to shake the dust from their robes, to remove

34

sandals before crossing the floor, but only Joshua and Papa, and sometimes Simon, would do her bidding. Carrot-topped Jacob and the dull-witted twins would simply spit on the ground at her feet and laugh as they strode indoors. They would stop at the water jar, lift the dipper to their lips and slurp noisily, then shake the excess slobber to the floor, eyeing her with amusement all the while. She tried not to find their behaviour so vexing, even tried to laugh with them, her heart seeking the humour they so clearly saw in her predicament. After all, why be vexed? She had little else to do—no; there was little else she *desired* to do—but sweep and set things right again.

And so went the sweeping years, six of them, spanning the fifth to the eleventh year of my life. I gripped the cedar stalk of my broom and held on tight. The first bloom of blisters on my fingers and palms quickly gave way to hard, yellow layers of callused skin. The push of my palm against the wood wore grooves as soft to the touch as the cups for Mama's knees by the hearth.

These were the years of looking at the floor and holding my tongue and counting my blessings. The years of focused, committed effort to please my mother by remaking myself in my sister's image so that I might finally find love when I looked in those rust-coloured eyes. Occasionally, I was rewarded: with a small smile on rose-coloured lips unmarked by blood or scabs; with an absent-minded pat on my tightly veiled head and a muttered, 'Good girl.'

Mostly, however, my mother remained an unrelenting

taskmaster, distracted or squint-eyed as she surveyed my efforts day after day after day. As slow to forgive my past insurrection as the villagers of Nazareth were to forget it; as suspicious of my sincerity as she was certain that the way to prolong my efforts was to withhold the prize.

Of these years, little is left to me by way of coherent memory. Instead, what I recall is like a mosaic, vividly coloured tiles affixed at different points on a large white wall: discrete scenes of colour and movement floating in a sea of empty, whitewashed space.

◜

I am eight years old. The wife of Jonah the baker surveys New Rachael then says to Mama, 'You should be proud of her, Miriame.' She pinches my cheek. 'You're a good girl now, aren't you?'

'Proud?' Mama tosses her head like a stallion, unconvinced. Jonah's wife sighs. She puts down her broom and comes to take the coins, smiling as if it hurts. She is a comfortable woman, fat and round like the braid of bread we are buying for the Sabbath, but she does not care for Mama; none of the village women do. But still, respect must be shown. Papa's family is a long time in Nazareth and we are descended from King David; also Mama has birthed many sons. I duck my head, caught between the baker woman's kindness and my battered hopes for the same from Mama, a pained smile on my lips too.

My two eldest brothers fight. They fight about everything, circling one another like cocks set free from their cages, a cacophony of bluster and blows. They argue over Jacob's harsh treatment of the simple-minded twins, which Joshua does not like. They contest for the place beside Papa in the woodshop, where there is room for just one son: the eldest, Joshua, not the next-in-line. They bicker about who will accompany Papa when he travels to Jerusalem for the most important Jewish feasts: Passover, Pentecost and Tabernacles.

But today the contest is particularly fierce. Jacob has just been turned out from the orchards belonging to Simeon of Iscariot, one of Nazareth's wealthiest men. More time on the ground than in the trees, Simeon told Papa when he deposited my red-haired brother—pustule-pocked and sullen—at our door. 'I am sorry for it, Yosef,' Simeon said, chins and thorn-scarred hands flapping. 'But I pay taxes, too.'

Still stewing from the shame, Jacob insists it is his turn to travel with Papa to the Temple. Men are required to appear there, before God, three times a year, but Mama decrees there must be a man in the house at all times, so Joshua, Jacob and my brother Simon take turns. But now Jacob says it is his chance to visit the Holy City for Pentecost, even though he made the journey just a few months ago.

Joshua is bewildered. 'But you just went Jacob, at Passover. Surely you recall the tales you told? The priests who let the unleavened dough ferment so it had to be made again? The sacrificial sheep that jumped their stalls and nearly trampled you?'

But try as he may, neither Joshua nor anyone else can get Jacob to see reason. The next-in-line turns his back on Joshua, huffing, his ears sealed shut.

But I know that it *is* Joshua's turn to travel to the Holy City. The way Shona presses her lips together tells me she also knows this, although she pretends to have interest only in her sewing.

So I carefully sweep my pile of dust out the door and press my lips tight, too. It is not for us to interfere.

The day of rest. No smiths at the forges or women by the hearth. Children tumble like brushfire through the square while Papa, Joshua and my brother Jacob rest with the other men on tree stumps. Heads bent closely together, they crack seeds between their teeth and speak in hushed tones of rebellion.

Six centuries after Moses led the Jewish people from slavery in Egypt, we still yearn for freedom in the Promised Land. Perhaps we have already had our golden age under the great kings David and Solomon; if so, it did not last long. One after another the empires of Assyria, Babylon, Persia vied for the spoils. Since the great general Pompey entered the Temple three generations ago to claim Jerusalem for Rome, the empire has ruled through puppet kings. The Herods: opportunist converts to the Jewish faith who make no pretence about the power to which they answer.

Always there have been overlords, with their sackings and taxes and foreign deities. And in reply, always some measure of resistance. Sometimes sullen and covert, at times breaking out into armed rebellion.

As pigeons and doves pick over the hulls with noisy precision, the men issue their ritual appeals to the Lord for deliverance. They rejoice at the exploits of the current strain of rebels, some from our very own village, dug in as soldiers in the Galilean village of Gamla to the north and the Roman capital of Caesarea. Just two days ago, the beloved stallions of the Roman cavalry were poisoned and the building holding tax records set alight. The men chuckle at the thought of the inferno; the scraps of papyrus floating back to earth like gentle rain. But they are soon beating their breasts again. Why has God forsaken us? When will He deliver us? When will a leader like Moses or David—the Messiah promised by God—make himself known and help us free the land?

By the well, the women preen like geese. Spear-carriers in the whisper wars, they praise and fuss over New Rachael's veil. It is more than four years old now, but this shows they don't forget. As for messiahs and revolution, they do not care a fig; they know that whoever rules, their lives will alter little. There will still be animals to keep, cloth to weave and men to comfort. And floors to be swept.

⌒

When I was eleven years old tragedy struck. The sweeping years drew to a close, suddenly and forever.

It was late spring, the season neither too hot nor too cold, the cool rains of winter more than two moons behind us, when Shona came back too quickly one afternoon from her private business in the wood. The men were away from the house: Papa and Joshua returned to the woodshop after their midday rest, the rest of my brothers were in the hills pasturing the herds. Shona pulled Mama aside to whisper in her ear but, having seen the berry-coloured smear on the back of my sister's gown, I already knew the truth. Shona was a woman now. It had come late to her, but at nearly ten and seven years old, she could finally be wed.

Mama was ecstatic. She waved her arms in the air and shouted, 'Hosanna!' She raced to the window and leaned out as far as she might without tumbling to the ground, ululating so loudly that even the tanners in East Nazareth could hear.

The women of the village came from all over, as if drawn by threads from her sewing basket. Jonah the baker's wife like a moving ball of dough; the one-toothed crone waddling like an uneven load with her basket of secret herbs and balms; the fat wives of the elders filing from their stone houses on the hill, jars of wine and fragrant crocks of nard balanced on their heads.

The women flooded the house shouting words of praise while the crone banged a tambourine. Surrounding my sister, they passed her from woman to woman, disrobing her with gentle hands. Turning her in circles as each piece of clothing was removed: soiled robe, child's belt, veil. Snapping her fingers, the wife of an elder called for my sister's sleeping mat and Mama bustled off to get it. The women spread it before the hearth and my sister was laid upon it, a swathe of white cloth tucked between her legs.

The women cursed and spat upon Shona's soiled clothing and her other childish things. Chanting songs of life and love, they cast them to the fire, singing and swaying as the room thickened with smoke.

I saw it all from my place by the wall, my mouth agape at the sudden crowds and rapture, hands gripping my broom. The crone, who went by the name of Bindy, beckoned me towards the circle of ceremony for a look. She removed the cedar handle from my grip and set it to one side, brushing women away to make room for me by her side. She pressed a gnarled finger to her lips, a warning not to speak. 'The sacred prayers are for women only,' she said and I nodded, wide-eyed, impressed by the rivers of age on her cheeks.

Kneeling by Shona's side, the wives of the elders patted rosemary oil on her brow, her nipples, the top of her sex. They soaked her chestnut-coloured hair in wine. They called my sister to dance to the beat of the cymbal. And so Shona danced, naked and free, the stain of life on her thighs, a strange mixture of fear and pride on her face as the women cried for joy and heaped praise on Mama's head. *Hosanna! Hallelujah! Mazel tov, Miriame!*

Mama stepped forward with Shona's new robes. She smoothed my sister's hair and pinched her cheeks before presenting the woman's belt and freshly stitched veil, the one Mama had been squinting over for so many months, with eggs and fish and vine leaves etched in precious purple thread. The women shouted and stamped as Shona drew each new item on. They cried out to God to open my sister's womb and bless her with sons.

Then did they all dance to the shivers of the tambourine, snake-lines of women winding their way around the hearth and across the terrace-roof, laughing and shouting. Mama clutching Shona's waist, her face broad with pleasure, her slim hips swaying like a girl's.

Like dust in the wake of a caravan, Shona's ripening stirred up a flurry of offers. Heralds arrived with proposals from an aged cousin in Legio and one even less spry from Gath Hepher, a hamlet just south of Nazareth. Mama sniffed the proposals like rotten fruit before dispatching the messengers empty-handed. She waved off Papa's persistent pleas to consider the village potter, a young man of just thirty years, with no brothers to contest his claim to the business or the modest home he shared with his soft-spoken mother.

Instead, like a cat ready to pounce after an age of patient stalking, Mama waited until the house was free of men. When Papa and Joshua had departed for the woodshop and the rest of my brothers had gone to Mount Tabor with the flocks, she hurried off to East Nazareth, determined to find a way of sending word to my Aunt Malcah. Arms outstretched, voice pleading, she would hail travellers heading south. 'Brother! Begging your pardon!' 'Sisters, a kindness?' Until at last someone agreed to take a message to her ancestral home of Bethany on the outskirts of Jerusalem.

Mama's message dispatched, she returned home to wait, passing the intervening weeks until my aunt's reply arrived in a state of fretful distraction. She shredded her lips and cursed the beasts in the *oorvah* for their failure to produce enough milk or eggs, for the noise of their lows and bleats. She tripped up and down the front steps and bumped against walls, her glassy gaze blind to all matters not concerned with Shona's future.

Then, at last, a reply arrived, the words of her elder sister Malcah, spoken through the dry lips of a dust-coated tent-maker or merchant as they journeyed north to Tyre or Tripoli. Mama worried the knot of her headscarf impatiently while I invited the messenger inside and proffered hospitality: a dipper of water, a handful of grapes. Then, as the news was delivered, she swooped, alighting on certain words, insisting the offer be described over and over again, her lips moving silently as she tallied and apportioned, weighed and measured.

Shona feigned indifference to the proceedings, so I did the same. Until the cold morning in Kislev when Mama climbed the front steps and crossed the roof terrace to the hearth, clapping her hands of dust, a satisfied look on her face. She dripped honey from her secret store over a quartered fig to tempt my sister from the loom, then settled herself beside Shona to lay out her plans like jewels: her plans to marry off my sister to the wealthy Bethanian merchant my Aunt Malcah said was in need of a second wife.

'Poor man,' my mother continued with all the compassion of someone listing the contents of her larder. But she became animated when she came to the bride price: her arm indicating the depth of Shona's cooking pot, fingers wheeling as she numbered the promised servants. Not to mention the silver! Enough to clear Papa's debts and for Mama to hold her head high again in the square, as well as repay Aunt Malcah for her efforts in securing the match.

But I don't want to live so far away! When will I see you? And Papa and Rachael? And who is this man, Mama? Is he old? Short? Fat? What if he's too fond of wine? Or smells like a goat?

My sister said none of this, of course. But I saw the doubt that shaded her eyes and dampened the corners of her mouth as she gave all that Mama wordlessly demanded. Appreciative murmurs as Mama produced each benefit of the match for inspection like eggs from a basket; vigorous bobs of the head when, spent at last, Mama asked, in the way one does when there really is no question, is there a match? I never will forget the look on my sister's face as she brought forth the required assent in response to Mama's prompt: like a woman accepting last rites before the noose slips over her head.

So it was agreed. Mama sent a final messenger with careful instructions to my aunt to remove her sandal for the giant pot, three slaves, five cubits of linen and fifty silver shekels promised by the merchant. Once my aunt had these treasures securely in hand, she would bring them to Nazareth on a donkey colt, also furnished by Shona's suitor. When Malcah returned to her home of Bethany she would take with her, tethered to the colt's back, the aloe-wood chest Papa had built for the groom. Sitting astride the beast would be Shona, her face obscured by the long hang of a white wedding veil. The deal would be done.

The haste and secrecy of the nuptial transaction infuriated Papa, who in any case had never much liked Malcah. Mama delivered the news upon his return home with Joshua for the midday meal, her pride undisguised. When Papa began to shout, she barely marked him. Humming beneath her breath, she bustled about the house, full of plans.

'But she is so young,' Papa cried, pacing after her. 'And only the second wife? The second wife, only? Surely a real matchmaker could have done more for the price.'

'I was just a baby when my father promised me to you. And the same age as Shona when we wed.'

'But to go and live in Bethany!' Papa stuttered. His long arm measured the miles. 'And the man is so old and—'

'Rich?' Mama threw a handful of the pistachios Shona and I were shelling into a bowl and whirled around to face him. 'Pious? Close to my sister if there is trouble? Blessed are we that she is so fair, Yosef, or we might never have caught such a fish.'

'But we've not even met the man, Miriame, and the potter—'

'The potter! The potter!' Mama pressed her hand to her brow in agony. 'He has no name, Yosef! And his father—a drunk! What would people say?'

This brought Papa up short. 'A boy doesn't choose his father,' he said at last, and Mama's cheeks flushed, though she did not turn away.

They stood, face to face, in silence for a time before Mama said quietly, 'This is Shona's chance, Yosef. The potter's son, the baker's,' she shrugged. 'Good men, I am sure. But is this the reach of our dreams for our eldest daughter? That she wed a village boy and pass the rest of her days in the boot heel of the empire, far from cultured society and people of stature and means? That she spend her life *here*?'

The silence that followed lived and breathed. She had wounded him, though that did not seem to have been her intention. Despite the harshness of her words, her tone was earnest. Matter-of-fact. As if such truths, long known but unacknowledged, must now be faced squarely for my sister's sake. I saw Papa struggle to recapture balance, so he might view these new considerations with clarity. To set aside his injured pride so he might ponder anew what would be best for Shona.

At last he said, 'Very well, Miriame. As you will it, so it shall be.' Nodding stiffly, he moved towards the door. Joshua, refusing to meet Mama's eyes, turned on his heel and followed, leaving us women alone.

Mama sighed. She took the broom from my hands and went to the roof to sweep. Gossips, drawn by Papa's shouts, lingered at the gate in hope of more action. Feigning solicitousness, they called up to Mama with offers of help. She paid them no mind. Instead, palm shading her eyes, she scanned the horizon where the two men had disappeared.

'Shona,' I whispered.

45

But my sister would not let her gaze meet mine. And though her eyes shimmered like marrow jelly, they refused to shed tears.

⌒

My Aunt Malcah arrived two weeks later bearing gifts from the merchant. She also brought with her an unseasonable storm. The harvest season was close to an end and in the arbour, vines and bowers were denuded of fruit. Only the darkest-skinned olives, the last of the season, remained to be picked.

But instead of bathing in rain, as was usual at the start of the winter season, Nazareth was drowning in dust. Without warning, dry gusting winds from the wilderness to the east had begun blowing in. They eddied ephemeral tops across the square and sent women scattering to retrieve fruit and freshly washed clothes left to dry in the sun. They pasted desert sand into folds of skin and blurred eyes with tears. They turned our house into a tomb, the door slammed shut and plugged with rags, the window draped with cloth.

Mama failed to notice. Neck bent and brow fierce with concentration, she dyed, ripped and fitted as if the vibrancy of her hues, the strength of her stitching, might safeguard Shona's future. She read tea leaves, sacrificed twists of bread, prayed for auspicious signs and acted the slave to her sister Malcah, dispatching Shona and me to get ale and manna seeds to flavour the stew, petrified that any breach of hospitality might see the match undone.

Malcah both did and did not look like my mother. She had rust-coloured eyes, like her younger sister, that were widely spaced, giving her a perpetual appearance of surprise. But where

46

Mama was slim and handsome, my aunt was like a badly stuffed doll. Her extremities—face, hands, feet—were pointed and narrow, her midsection thick and blowsy. Despite this slovenly appearance, Malcah had an imperious nose that she liked to peer down at all who dared open their mouths in her presence. She preferred to hold court uninterrupted and her sense of entitlement—not just to rapt attention, but to Mama's servility and the best morsels from our paltry larder—gave her a regal air.

One week after Malcah darkened our door, Papa and Joshua arrived home with the aloe wood chest promised to the merchant. Shona's wedding preparations were nearly done. At first light, she would leave for Bethany with my aunt.

Now Mama, Malcah and Shona were clustered about the eating mat doing the last of the embroidery and Malcah was recounting, not for the first time, the events leading up to my sister's betrothal. 'So I said to her, you mean the merchant called Lev, who sells rugs from Tarshish? And she said to me, none other. So I said to—What the devil is wrong with that girl, Miriame?' Malcah's eyes fell on me, hovering near the eating mat with my broom. 'She's as sour as a camel.'

Mama did not look up from her needlework. 'She is sad to lose her sister. Though grateful, of course, for Shona's chance at happiness. Is this not so, Rachael?'

'Yes, Mama.'

'Well then.' Malcah sniffed, before making to pick up her tale. But her eyes fell on the length of white linen in Mama's hands and, with a sharp intake of breath, she turned almost the same colour. Her lips began moving but no sound issued from them. Her work-wealed finger pointed accusingly at a spot on the cloth, her mouth gaping uselessly, her eyes wide with horror.

47

Mama paused, looked, and gave a short yelp. She leapt to her feet and ran to the window, lifting a corner of the curtain for more light, gesturing wildly for Malcah to follow her. The two women exclaimed and bickered in the dusty wedge of day, pointing and staring at the mark on the cloth. Malcah called it soot; Mama thought it was oil. Malcah said Papa was at fault ('The weave was pure when it came from Bethany, Miriame! Yosef must have set the basket on the ground when he unloaded the mule!'), while Mama accused Malcah ('The merchant swindled you, sister! Sold you damaged goods!') But soon the shouts gave way to weeping and gnashing of teeth because, whoever was to blame, the truth was plain to see. Shona's wedding sheet was stained.

Mama was the first to swallow the bitter pill and to chart a path forward. She pushed the sheet into Shona's hands. 'Frankincense will whiten it,' she told my sister. 'Scrub the sheet with it, then soak and scrub again. If it bleaches, good! If not, we start again.'

Malcah staggered and moaned, but Mama turned on her. 'What choice do we have, sister? We will sew all night to make a new one if need be. But you will leave in the morning as planned,' Mama's eyes narrowed. 'And the means to prove Shona's purity will go with you.'

Shona's eyes, too, were wide with fear. Mama pointed her towards the door. 'Go!' she ordered, before turning to her sister. 'Sit, Malcah. Rest. I will brew the tea while we wait to see if the cloth comes clean.'

Mama was a woman who only saw what she wanted to see; she did not notice what she hoped was not there. So it was that as

48

she and her sister Malcah sipped their tea, the falling shadow of dusk escaped her. She did not hear the chatter of roosting ravens in the chestnut tree beyond our window, nor the sound of tools being set aside and men wearily ascending the terrace steps. Only when Papa and Joshua came through the door, shaking dust from their robes and calling for water, did she look up and realise Shona was not there.

My sister was not a wanderer. There was nowhere she would go without saying. She would have understood Mama's order to run to the washing point, work the stain free, and return straight home, and would never have thought to disobey. Yet, here it was time for her and Mama to prepare the evening meal, and she was nowhere to be seen. As alarmed looks spread from one adult face to the next at the speed of contagion, I heard myself start to whimper.

We set out after her, torches blazing, peering and calling, moving through the forest in the direction of the washing point. Papa shepherding Simon and the twins, Mama leaning on Jacob and Malcah bringing up the rear, moaning about her knees and back. But I knew the short route that Shona took to the stream. Without a word I broke away from the group and pulled my eldest brother through the trees in that direction. This was how Joshua and I found Shona first.

Leave me. Don't touch me. Turn away.

My sister was wedged in the knothole of the ancient willow not far from the water's edge: a large grin of rot that had sheltered me as a child when I would run off as she beat the washing, daring her to chase me. As Shona spread sheets on the ground and over bushes to dry, she would call to me in a sing-song voice, 'Where are you, Rachael! Come out, Rachael, wherever you are!' while I kept still and hidden, giggling into my fist.

Now my sister's eyes were like Old Noah's mule, cowed and wary. Obsidian pupils overlarge, lashes like frenzied wings, awaiting the next rise of Almighty anger, the next unstoppable blow. Her robe was torn and streaked with dirt, her limbs cast asunder to reveal the secret openings of her body, each of them weeping seed and blood. *Leave me. Don't touch me. Turn away!*

A low, shivering moan escaped my brother and his head fell to his hands. He turned his back to protect her modesty, his body bent with grief. With both hands, he tore at his robe, the rip of cloth the sound and symbol of mourning. Dropping to his knees my brother raised up his hands in prayer.

But I was still frozen, unable to accept the truth of the scene before me: that the shattered woman struggling to pull herself to sitting was my beloved sister. I continued to stare, bewildered, as if I had somehow stumbled off the path of my life and into someone else's: a foreign land where the divine scales of justice had become unbalanced and character and deserts bore no relation. For surely it was plain to see that, more than anyone else in the world, my sister deserved the Lord's blessing?

But this was my world: my sister clawing at her face and biting her arms; my brother howling at the heavens, his anguished pleas sailing beyond the forest's height into the star-flecked dome of the night. The rest of my family, summoned by Joshua's wails, blundered towards us through the trees, the shadows from their torches waving like angry clubs across the land.

'Turn away,' Shona snarled at me with teeth bared. I had never seen her angry. 'Turn away, Rachael. I am unclean. Save yourself and walk away from me.'

Papa burst into the clearing, followed by Jacob. Mama came next, my younger brothers clustered about her like litter-bearers. She raised her torch and shrieked, reeling back from the sight of my ruined sister lying on the ground. Shona tried to hold her robe together with both hands, but it was no use. The gown was a rag. She turned her shoulder and curled in on herself like a snail, shamed beyond endurance.

'Joshua.' My voice held both warning and entreaty. 'She needs—' But he had seen already. He pulled his cloak from his shoulders and dropped it on the ground, motioning me to bring it to her, the flow of his prayers uninterrupted. Mama and I bent to my sister, covering her as best we could before heaving Shona to her feet. We drew her arms around our shoulders and began the long walk home.

Behind us, Papa and my brothers staked their torches and fell to the ground beside Joshua, baying like wolves. They prayed the way our people had prayed through the ages. Remonstrating with God; affirming their faith in him. *O God, you have forsaken us! O Lord your strength will rescue us!*

And Shona with every step: *I wish I was dead. I wish I was dead.*

We arrived home. Mama pressed her back against the *oorvah* door to open it and slowly, we dragged my sister up the steps. Mama set a cauldron of water to boil, working quickly to beat the return of the men, helping Shona to undress. But like a child hoarding sweets Shona held her ragged robe tight to her breast and fought Mama with her elbows. 'Let go of the robe now, Shona,' Mama chided softly. She prised my sister's fingers open one by one and, with a cry of disgust, hurled the filthy garment to the fire. Chewing her own lips ragged, she bathed my sister's wounds with tender hands.

⸙

Like fire through dry wheat, word of Shona's fall swept through the village. At first light, men began to gather outside our house, kicking dirt and hefting stones. When the sun showed its face, so did the elders. Arms laden with scrolls, they waddled down the hill in black robes belted around bellies round as cooking pots. At the mob's edge they halted to confer amongst themselves before arranging the speaker's box beneath our window so the Law could be read.

This would be done by Sirach the Ancient. With the aid of one of Jonah the baker's young sons, the Ancient limped to the platform and hoisted himself onto it, huffing and groaning. The elder's mouth was a sinkhole, falling in on itself from age and want of teeth. His eyes, which must once have been blue, were now leached of all colour. As the oldest man in the village and the most senior of the patriarchs, this moment was his due and he intended to savour it. He cocked his brow at the chattering mob, his dry tongue moistening what remained of his lips, and waited for the villagers to notice him; for them to nudge one another and pay homage to his years and presence with rapt attention and, where required, rapid agreement with everything he said.

When finally the crowd had settled to his satisfaction he extended a skeletal hand. A scroll made of stretched goatskin was placed in it. Sirach the Ancient unfurled it, cleared his throat and read verse twenty-three from the Law of the Jews:

If there is a young woman, a virgin already engaged to be married, and a man meets her in the town and lies with her, you shall bring both of them to the gate of that town and stone them to death. The young woman because she did not cry out, and the man because he violated his neighbour's wife. So you shall purge the evil from your midst.

'Verse twenty-three? Verse *twenty-three*?' Papa was appalled at the error. He paced up and back behind the bolted door of our house railing at the heavens and tugging worriedly at his beard. 'It is not twenty-three you want!'

He went to the window and leaned out. 'Twenty-five!' he shouted. His panicked gaze swept the crowd, alighting on the elders he knew best. 'Yonotan! Eliazar! Please! She…it happened in the fields. Surely it is verse twenty-five that…?'

The elders looked up from the parchment and acknowledged his pleas with a nod, before burying their faces again.

I was pressed against the wall to one side of the window, daring the occasional peek at the restless crowd below. Mama was on the window's other side, her back pressed to the wall. I waited for her to chastise me, to demand that I cease all my ducking and weaving and be still. Law and justice were men's business and the very sight of a female at such times would be unwelcome. But instead, and for once, she seemed to appreciate my daring. She even encouraged it.

'Look again, Rachael,' she said in a whisper strained with fear. 'How many men would you say are gathered there? Is it the entire village? Have they also come up from the plains? Do they have stones in their grip?'

At Mama's feet was Aunt Malcah, draped across the aloe-wood chest and sobbing lustily. On her mat, Shona shivered,

53

a fresh robe on her back and her clean, wet hair uncovered while my white-faced brothers stood guard by the doors. All my brothers that is, except Joshua, who had moved to sit as near as he could to my sister without touching her. He seemed to want to comfort her with his presence, resting there beside her, making occasional shushing sounds though he kept his ear cocked to listen to developments outside.

The decision took hours. The elders, scarves hauled up over nose and mouth to defend against blowing dust and sand, retired to the tree stumps beneath the knobbly fig tree in the square to deliberate. The mob did not budge, maintaining their menacing vigil outside our door, though occasional emissaries were dispatched to discover the rate of progress and bring back reports. The elders, too, sent men to the scene of the crime, to take readings and gather evidence.

As morning turned to afternoon, the men below swarmed and hovered like flies, cursing the strange wind and scratching. They beat their breasts and yelped dirty laughter while distances were measured, recorded, then walked again.

Finally, the judgment. A ripple of quiet as faces rose to listen.

'Innocent,' Sirach the Ancient said, and Mama sobbed with relief. Verse twenty-five had been judged apposite, and its specifications applied. Shona had been ravaged in a field; in open country where she may well have shrieked for rescue and pleaded for her virtue, but no one had been near enough to hear. My sister would not be stoned. Her shame was the fault of another, not her own. The man who had done this to her, should he ever be found, would be the only one to die.

Papa sank to his knees, weeping, embracing the air with

grateful arms. Joshua, too, went from sitting to kneeling in an instant, babbling praise to the Lord. I looked to Shona but her face was hidden from view: arms hugging her legs and brow on her knees, her rich chestnut hair covering her like a veil.

Then, down in the square, Daniel the tanner stepped to the speaker's box. 'Wait! Wait!' Voice high pitched and petulant, arms outstretched with palms flexed, he sought to prevent the crowd, already chatting about chores and wagers, from leaving. 'Our work here is not done.'

The elders were impatient. Nose buried in the sleeve of his robe, the one called Yonotan demanded, 'What are you saying, tanner? What grudge must we now hear?' Around the box, a horseshoe of space had cleared, those closest to the tanner gagging and holding their breath.

'There is one more verse to consider,' the tanner insisted.

'Has he considered he smells like shit?' a voice from the crowd asked loudly. The men laughed and made again to leave.

'Verse twenty-eight,' the tanner said stubbornly, his face flushing red.

'Dear God,' Papa said, rising to his feet.

And so it was that verse twenty-eight of Deuteronomy, the fifth book of Jewish Law, stole my sister's chance to regain her footing, to rise above her shame and claim the life she should have had. Because once considered, twenty-eight would not be ignored, no matter how much Papa pleaded and begged.

'But verse twenty-eight does not apply!' he had protested, aghast at the sudden turn of events. 'It has no relevance where there is a contract of marriage, and my daughter—'

'What contract, Yosef?' someone challenged. I didn't

recognise the voice but the heckling tone was hard to miss. 'We've seen no proof of a contract.'

'But there was one, of course there was,' Papa's words jostled with one another in their eagerness to escape his mouth. He looked up at our window, his eyes suddenly alight with hope. 'Miriame arranged it with Malcah, her sister. Malcah took off her sandal, she took off her sandal to seal the deal. They are right here, just ask them. They are both right—' His voice trailed off. Women could not bear witness, a fact Papa knew well.

The elders crossed their arms and turned their backs, while the mob hissed and yowled like cats. 'Submit to the judgment of the Lord, Yosef!' a deep voice cried, and soon they were all chanting, 'Submit! Submit!' Fists pounding on thighs, voices like the marching feet of legions, until Papa's face flashed fear and he turned and ran back into the house, throwing the bolt behind him.

The mob swarmed like bees. They surrounded the house, vaulted the steps, rattled the doors as they tried to get inside. *Submit! Submit!* Stones flew through the window, shattering pots and whistling past heads. I threw myself on top of Shona to shield her while my brothers ran about, waving their fists and shouting. The whole house quaked and so did Mama. Eyes bulging as though she were being choked, she savaged her lips with her teeth until her mouth was nothing more than a wet patch of blood, some of which ran down her chin.

'Relent, Yosef!' she wailed above the din. 'Relent! You will not persuade them! You will not prevail again! I beg you, Yosef! Relent! Relent!'

'Marry him?' I looked from Mama to Papa. I even sought Aunt Malcah's wet eyes when she raised them from her hands. She came from another town, another place in Israel where perhaps they did things differently.

But no one answered. Papa and Joshua were inspecting damage to the walls and searching for stones amongst the bedding, while my brothers sat around the mat, trading tales of near misses. Mama was baking bread, as if this were an ordinary day.

I tried not to whimper. 'Papa?'

Mama's voice was as brisk as her hands. 'Come dish the olives, Rachael, and take this bread to the mat. We have a meal to serve.' Roll, slam. Roll, slam.

I drifted towards the hearth, but had to ask again. 'Papa?'

He straightened from his labours with a grunt of effort. Stilled Mama with a look. 'The elders say there was no marriage contract, Rachael,' he said carefully. 'So the remedy is… different.'

'Different?'

'Yes.' He sounded as if he were choking. 'We must—' He broke off. Bent his giant frame to rest his arms on his knees, his breath short and rapid.

'Yosef?' Mama moved towards him with knitted brow. He pulled himself upright and waved her back to the hearth, nodding at Joshua to finish for him.

'We must find the man, Rachael,' my brother said. 'The one who seized and ravished Shona. We shall leave in the morning. Me, Papa, Jacob, Simon and some of the village men. We must capture him and return with him to Nazareth so he is made

57

to pay. So the stain on our honour and that of our village is cleansed.' Joshua's voice was flat. A dead thing.

'But, Shona?' I looked around the room wildly: at my father gasping for breath, my mother in motion by the hearth, my aunt still draped across Shona's wedding chest in a pose of mourning. 'What about Shona?'

⌒

Papa tried but lacked the fibre, and Joshua was no different. So the lot fell to Mama, with Malcah by her side. It was evening now and Shona's skin had begun to dapple: yellow choke collars on her wrists, a butterfly of sooty fingers around her neck. I hovered nearby, close to the action, clutching my broom tightly.

'Hair?' Mama plied my sister with questions about her attacker. 'Eye colour? Did he wear rings? An armlet? Did he have tattoos?' My sister did not speak, only nodded or shook her head. After each response, Mama would look at my father to ensure he'd taken note. Papa paced by the door, as far from the proceedings as he could get without leaving the house.

'Height?'

Shona flushed and squirmed. Hesitated.

'How tall was he, Shona?' Mama repeated.

Again, no response from my sister, who suddenly became absorbed with a pull in the weave of her sleeping mat. I saw a tear splash on to her hand.

Mama sighed. 'Papa cannot track him if we do not know his features,' she said. Shona bowed her head again. She cleared her throat, but no words came. Mama lifted my sister's chin with her finger. 'Height,' she repeated.

'I did not see him upright!' Shona burst out at the same time as Papa cried, 'That is enough, Miriame!'

But Mama raised her finger, shushing him. Her eyes were still on Shona, who was weeping now without restraint. 'When he lay on you, where did his head come to? When you kicked, did your feet find sandals or shin?'

'Sandals,' Shona cried. 'And he forced me to look in his cold eyes the whole time!'

Mama turned triumphantly to my father. 'A short man.' But Papa had fled, the door banging behind him. Joshua touched my sister's elbow before following, his gaze passing over Mama without seeing her.

I felt hot all over. My breath grew short and blood pulsed in my ears. I tried to swallow and turn away, but my throat buckled and would not obey. I could not swallow any more. 'How could you?' I shouted, launching myself at Mama.

If Mama was surprised at my outburst, she did not show it. She moved past me on her way to the hearth, hands busy at her scarf: checking the knot, tucking in hair. 'I am sorry for it, Rachael, but judgment has been passed. We must submit and hope God will reward our faith. This is the only way. Trust me, I—'

'No!' My shriek was like the death-cry of an animal in a snare. I gripped the broom like a weapon. 'You said! You said, Mama. And now look! Shona was a good girl. A *good* girl!'

At least she had the decency to look ashamed, though her reply, when it came, was crisp. 'Yes. Yes she was. But sometimes this is not enough.'

Through my mind flashed Timba. The scrape of Mama's brow each time the village women recalled Old Rachael's shame. The look and texture of the wall as I had stood facing it that

Passover night six years ago, my clumped scalp like a badly-sown field, taking my punishment as I schemed how to win her love.

'No.' Not shouted this time, just firm. The word feeling full and right in my mouth. I said it again. 'No.'

And dashing the broom to the floor, I ran from the house.

Three days later, the men of my family drove Boaz into the village: whip-marked, arms roped behind his back, his smock stained with tears. They paraded him through the square, let the villagers hiss and spit, before the elders forced him to stand on a box. There he would remain all night, bound and guarded, awaiting the finger-pointing that would begin at dawn.

The next morning, as the sun teased the horizon, my sister limped down the steps and braved a choppy sea of whispers to declare that yes, it was he—Boaz the field hand with his pock-marked skin and broad, short stature—who had defiled her. Seized and injured her. Stolen her name.

They were wed on the spot. Mama keening and clinging to Jacob's arm. Papa and Joshua as stiff and unseeing as soldiers. Later that night, my brothers would see to it that Boaz slept in the *oorvah* with the beasts, tethered like a ram to a post while the fowl, sensing sport, roosted on his head.

But the next day they were forced to set him free and by afternoon, the pair had left for Cana: the groom's ancestral village and my sister's new home.

I am sure Mama was as stunned by my sister's downfall as I was. I am certain that, just as I did, she mourned my sister's sudden loss from our lives without remit. But whatever the internal workings of her grief, Mama did not want pity. Not from me. What she sought, what she saw indeed as her due, in the wake of Shona's departure with her new husband to Cana, was for me to assume my sister's household burdens.

It was late summer and the square was overflowing with baskets of grapes, figs, pomegranates and walnuts. Soon, the Esdraelons would climb from the valley to collect their share, but the rest must be pickled, dried or pressed. The pitch of Mama's barked orders grew shrill as she plotted every movement of my waking hours. 'The well first, Rachael. Then the washing point. Get the salt and visit the bee-keep while things dry, so I

can start the curing and laying out of trays. Then I'll start the…
Rachael? Rachael!'

⌒

The first 'no' is always the hardest. After that, they fell from my
lips with increasing ease. As the months since Shona's departure
creaked past—eight, ten, the twelve that meant she'd been gone
a year—more and more, I did as I pleased. Disappearing with
neither apology nor excuse to return hours later, stinky and
breathless, my veil untied and feet black and tacky from running
through the woods without sandals. I stole drying fruit or sweet
Sabbath dough left to rise in the sun from the terrace roofs of the
far-flung cottages at the furthest ends of the village and, when
the urge overtook me, yanked my robe to my waist with barely a
glance around me so I might relieve myself with a boy's upright
form.

My rebellious attitude and unexplained absences agitated
my mother beyond endurance. Where had I been? What was I
doing? How dare I wander the land like an untethered goat? But
when neither hounding nor scolding brought about the conversation she sought, Mama plucked up her wooden spoon and
chased me about the hearth, swearing like a drunk.

'I'll lash you to a tree in the square! Strip you bare and
stable you with the goats, that will teach you. And don't you
think you'll be having any dinner. Not this week or the next.'
Collapsing in sobs at the foot of Papa's mountainous form,
'Yosef, I beg you. Do something!'

But Mama's vexation seemed only to soothe Papa's spirit; to
somehow rebalance the cosmic scales of justice so overweened by
recent events. Or perhaps he had just aged beyond the rigours of

battle. Whatever the truth, the singular air of pity or compassion that, in the past, had moved him to intervene on Mama's behalf when she and I crossed daggers, was gone. Now, he considered her distantly, as if they stood, finally and forever, on opposite shores.

'She's run wild, Yosef!' 'The whole village is talking, Yosef!' 'The demons have got her. We need to cast them out.'

Slacker of shoulder, greyer of hair since the day he had lifted my sister to sit behind Boaz on our only mule—given so she was not forced to cross the gates of her new home burdened like a beast—Papa's reply was simple. Turning to gaze on Mama with eyes that had once been blue and sharp with wit but were now vacant and rainwater grey, he unrolled his mat and fell instantly asleep.

But it was not long before I realised that 'no', however satisfying—necessary even for the forward-footing of claims—was insufficient on its own. To ascend beyond youthful petulance, I had to find some manner of life, some way of being in the world, to which I could say 'yes'.

I dreamed without cease of ways I might to get to Cana to rescue my sister. My longing for Shona was like a hunger. I craved the cinnamon scent of her skin, yearned to see her cheeks rise in a smile. I imagined stowing away on a tax cart heading north with its bounty of oil and food collected from the Jews for the empire and king. I considered simply waiting until my family was asleep, then filling a goatskin with water and heading north. I would take a clay oil lamp with me, filled with as much beaten oil as it would hold, to guide me across the rocky way at night. In the morning, Shona would find me at her door, bedraggled but strong and unbowed. The relief in her eyes would be my reward. *Thank God you've not forgotten me, Rachael. Thank God you have come to save me.*

But when my brother Joshua divined my nascent travel plans, he swiftly forbade them. 'It is not safe, Rachael,' he said, shaking his head. It was early morning and we were standing at the foot of the terrace steps. I had just returned from the well with a full jar of water on my head, while he had clearly delayed his departure for the shop, letting Papa go on ahead so he might speak to me alone.

His insight into my plans mystified me. I had spoken of them to no one.

'I have not been resting well at night either,' he said, reading my face. 'And you talk in your sleep.'

I felt the heat rise to my cheeks. 'But Joshua,' I began, deciding in an instant to take the setback in my stride and turn it to my advantage by enlisting his support. 'If I can only get—'

'No,' my brother's voice was low but unusually firm. He repeated the command, to ensure I was in no doubt. 'No, Rachael, you may not go to Cana. And if I learn of any more such wild ideas, Papa will hear of it. We know now how Boaz takes a wife. Why would he not see you, pure and young and Shona's kin besides, as ripe for the picking?'

His tone grew more sympathetic as he watched my face fall. 'I know how heartbroken you are about Shona, Rachael, and how desperately you miss her. I swear to you that as soon as her waiting time is through, we men will go to Cana to see how she fares.'

The waiting time: the two years after the nuptials in which a bride was forbidden contact with her family. In that time her new husband's headship, and that of his kin, would be fixed in stone. It felt like a lifetime since I had watched Shona, her back straight, yet somehow broken, sway with the lumbering cadence of the mule as she disappeared into the northern wood, but Joshua corrected me. 'Just eight months left now.'

So I waited, doing my chores sullenly or not at all and disregarding the drill of Mama's commands whenever the spirit took me. I was not patient, but nor was I idle.

Some days I would stroll past the well and into the woods at the far end of the square as if I had urgent business there, but then circle back with stealthy steps to huddle at the back of the schoolroom.

The schoolroom was a low building with a peaked roof and broad eaves made of mud bricks, like most common buildings in Nazareth. Unlike the others it had just one room. No animals were stabled at ground level, the rising heat from their bodies warming the people living in the room above. Instead, or so I'd heard told, a large circular hearth was buried in the centre of that single room in which a blaze burned merrily throughout the cool, damp months of winter. This fire was not fed by kindling collected by girls of the village, but by wood provided by the elders, offered as a gesture of respect for the sacred work of learning undertaken there. Every morning except the Sabbath, as the sun began its climb in the sky, a gate could be heard creaking high on the hill, and a servant would descend from one of the fine stone residences of the elders on his way to the schoolroom, a basket of wood roped to his back.

Pressing my ear against the rough, damp-smelling bricks I would strain for the voices within: the honking tones of the rabbi, who had a large nose that always seemed to be sneezing, and the hum of the boys as they chanted their response to his stern Hebrew questioning. The boys studied numbers, letters and, most importantly, the Law. The eldest of them, close to my age of ten and two years, had been engaged with such subjects since the age of five, though you wouldn't know it from the alacrity or accuracy of their replies. They were such dolts! Even through the dense, musty walls you could hear the lassitude in their voices as they repeatedly offered up incorrect answers to the teacher's pointed enquiries.

'*Ma?*' the rabbi would honk incredulously. 'What? But we have been studying this all week.' Then, when the dimwits answered wrongly again. '*Ma? Ma?*'

I always had the right answer or, at least it seemed so when, ear pressed to the wall, I could discern the reply that finally summoned a relieved gasp from the teacher's lips and a honk of praise, '*Yoffee! Tov! Nachon!* Correct at last!'

'Good work, Rachael!' I would mutter to myself, reaching an arm around to pat myself on the back. If I were allowed in that classroom, I told myself, I would be the cleverest pupil the rabbi had ever seen. Well, maybe not the cleverest, but next in line behind my brother Joshua.

This thought often comforted me as I crept from the woods in the same circuitous fashion that I had entered them, to complete whatever errand Mama had sent me on in the first place. I would return home with my head in the clouds, my sandals barely anchored to earth, absorbed by whatever new titbit of knowledge or insight was contained in the day's lesson.

On bad days, such comfort was elusive and I would find my eyes streaming unbidden tears. Resting my brow against the schoolroom wall, I would grieve silently over the injustice of my predicament. Then, quite suddenly, I would feel compelled to leap to my feet and begin running. Sometimes I'd flee out through the groves in the opposite direction to Nazareth, running through the forest as fast as my feet could carry me, dodging the trunks of the towering silver-bark trees and leaping over the hump-backed roots of figs that rose from the ground, my tears flying off in the wind. Sprinting as if it could possibly be true that if I ran fast and far enough, I might never have to go back.

On other days despair made me mean and I'd charge across the square shrieking like a fishwife and scattering the gossips like chicks before bursting through the town gates. Moving past the tenterhooks of the fuller and the cloud of stink from the tannery to the crossroads of East Nazareth, where the widows gathered to sway to the sitar and lift their veils, tempting the tax collectors and soldiers stumbling from the inn. East Nazareth, where animals brayed for water and men swilled ale, and the false climb of female laughter mixed like water with the unctuous cant of the merchants hawking their wares.

This was where Bindy, the one-toothed crone who had shivered the tambourine at Shona's first blood, did her business. More than once I saw her return from Nazareth proper in the wake of some errand or another, her distinctive gait more uneven than usual and eyes hooded with tiredness, robe spackled with nameless stains and basket stuffed with soiled sheets. She conferred regularly with the harlots who knew never to cross the town gates. In the dank, foul-smelling corridor between brothel and inn, Bindy would palm their coins in exchange for small, roughly tied cloth parcels, the contents of which were mysterious to me but for which the cast-outs seemed truly grateful.

I never said a word to Bindy, nor she to me, until the day in early spring when I stopped to watch a cockfight. I often did so. I enjoyed the spectacle: the almost maternal care the cock-masters—men who looked as if they could tear a lion apart with their bare hands—offered their prize pets; the simpering of women hollow-eyed with hunger as they rushed toward the victor to purr and praise; the loser, forlorn in the blood-strewn dust, clutching the limp carcass of his bird.

Usually I kept my distance for the one-eyed viciousness of the crowd was not to be treated lightly, but on this occasion the mob was larger than usual. Women thronged the edges, standing on their toes as they peeked and peered through the jostling bodies. Children ran about excitedly, pointing and clapping. What was happening? I had to know. At twelve I was tall for my age, but still smaller than most adults, so it was easy to worm my way through the crowd, ducking beneath waving arms and even bending to crawl through a tunnel of legs.

When at last I stood, breathing hard, at the rim of the fighting pit, the cause of the fuss was apparent. A gamecock of outstanding shine and stature was strutting the perimeter, his black and gold plumage deep and regal, wattle waving as he turned his head this way and that, acknowledging his admirers. There were two men in the ring, but judging from the matching strut of Micah the smith's son, this was his bird. Bought that morning, I heard a man behind me tell his fellow, from a prize breeder in Sepphoris city. The other fight master was crouched in the dirt, his head in his hands. Even through the tight weave of his closed basket you could see it contained a much smaller bird. As the wagers flew in favour of the new contender, the outmatched cockfighter in the ring rose to his feet and began to protest. He would not enter his bird in such an unfair fight, he told the crowd. He knew not what evil had given rise to the monster before them, but he would not allow his prize game-cock to be laid to waste by such unnatural forces.

The roar of the crowd was like a clap of thunder. They had come here for a cockfight, and a cockfight they would have! Pushing turned to shoving and soon a punch was thrown—a terrible exhale as a man bent double over his belly. Then the mob erupted in a windmill of fists and shouting. I was thrown to the ground, spitting dirt and screaming. I covered my head with my hands just as two rogues rolled on top of me and I was pinned, their bodies crushing me, driving the air from my body. Panic struck. I writhed and fought but the load bearing down on me could not be shifted. My lungs burned, my bones buckling under the weight. Darkness began to occlude my vision. *Shona*, I thought and, astonishingly, *Mama…*

'*Ayyyyyyy!*' The pressure on my chest eased and I heaved a loud lurching breath. One of the marauders had rolled aside, yelling and clutching his ankle. From the corner of my eye I saw a wrinkled hand withdraw, grasping a bloodied knitting needle. 'What are you doing, you old cow?' the fat man demanded.

The crone looked at him indifferently before raising her weapon again, her gaze directed at the hulk still lying on me. He thrust his hands out, palms towards her in a plea for mercy. 'I'm moving, I'm moving,' he shouted, hurrying to his feet.

Bindy wasted no time. She threw the needle aside, reached in, grabbed my ear and dragged me to my feet. 'Move!' she shouted, and pushed me towards the far end of the fighting pit, away from the rollicking crowd. I was gasping and limping, an unfamiliar pain shooting down my leg, but the old woman had little heart for such troubles. Instead, like a goatherd she drove me away from the crossroads and the feral cries of the mean-eyed mob out to the foot of Deadman's Hill, the most beautiful and terrible spot in Nazareth.

Deadman's Hill. Here did sunshine reflect light off grass shoots of the most tender shade of green. Here did the surrounding forest hum with insect life and the warble of ring-eyed blackbirds. Here did wild flowers—yellow daffodils, asters and anemones of purple and white—thrive on squares of freshly turned earth, fresh coverings for the rotting flesh below. This was the burial site for Nazareth's dead.

For Israelites, the bodies of the dead are profane; an offence to God, who is the giver of all life. Deadman's Hill was full of them. Beneath the strange gaze of the bent-backed crone, I shivered with excitement and fear at finding myself in such a place, and the prospect that Mama might find out.

Bindy peered down her nose at me. It was a substantial one, shaped liked a beak. Beneath it, a chin that was its reflection. She wore a strange, shapeless vest patched with a multitude of pockets made of differently thatched cloth.

'Yosef the woodworker's girl,' she began; it was not a question. She leaned towards me, her nearsighted eyes taking in my slipshod headscarf, the grime on my tear-streaked face, the too-tight cinch of the child's belt at my waist. A laugh like a hawk of spit. 'The recreant.'

I was stunned. How did she know who I was? My perplexed expression saw her laugh again, just as harshly. 'No secrets in this village. Especially when it's Saint Miriame's girl who's run amok.' The old woman cracked my mother's name on her tooth but her bony arm waved, dismissing such gossip as beneath her. One of her pockets bloomed with purple feathers. Another, securely fastened, pulsed with something alive.

The encounter, devoid of all the usual blessings and pleasantries, was unsettling. Who was this woman, and what did she want of me?

'*Shalom*, good woman,' I said with as much dignity as I could muster, keen to return the exchange to more familiar ground. 'I bear you greetings and goodwill,' I continued as I brushed at my skirt with one hand and the other moved to straighten my headscarf. 'I am Rachael. Yosef the woodworker's daughter.'

'Oh,' the crone exclaimed, 'do forgive my lack of form. *Shalom* and blessings upon you. I am Bindy,' she gestured grandly to the small mud-brick house behind her, unsteadily built and overrun with weeds, 'of the Wood.' Another spit of laughter. I turned to leave.

'Mistress of the healing arts and shepherd of new life,' she called to my departing form.

I stopped. Considered. Turned back. I remember the feel of the sun on my face, the way it warmed my skin through my thin woollen robe. 'A midwife?'

'Yes,' Bindy said. She cocked an unruly brow and tugged her pointed chin. 'And word in the village is that you have the gift, too.'

Bindy's house smelled like burnt herbs and loam. Incense and wine-soaked offerings of grain and oil cluttered a small altar.

Shelves lined the walls, groaning with stoppered jars of glass. In a corner, rolls of papyrus were stacked in ramshackle pyramids.

'You can read?' I asked, my tone so accusing and envious that she nearly laughed but, sensing my desperation, did not.

'No. But I have a quill. And record just the same.' The lone tooth made her words whistle.

'Record what?'

She gestured at the jars. Hulls and blossoms were visible through the glass; twisted roots like ancient hands. 'The powers of each element. How they work in unison to heal.' She unfurled a scroll, pointed me to kneel beside her on the floor. The sketches of plant, petal and roots were crude and bold, with crosses to mark where the curative powers lay.

'What are these?' Beside a clump of flowers, drawn roughly in a cramped hand, were several smaller sketches. There was a pot, a jar and a man's head. He was smiling as sweat dripped from his brow.

Like a camel at a watering hole, Bindy dipped her nose to the parchment and moved her head forward and back, seeking focus. 'Hyssop,' she said finally, pointing to the flowering shrub. Then, indicating the pot and jar, 'boiled and mixed with vinegar,' her gnarled finger moved to the face, 'induces the sweats that cool the body and promote good humour.'

'That is all?' I said, surprised.

'No. One must also make drink offerings, and pray for guidance from the Heavenly Queen,' she nodded at the altar, a low-slung platform of wood and brick dotted with mounds of incense and round cakes of dough. The centrepiece was a small terracotta figurine, its rough features female, its unformed hands holding up giant breasts. 'Every morning when you rise up, and before you lie down to sleep.'

I nodded thoughtfully. 'And that is it? All you must know to effect healing?'

Bindy snorted and released the ends of the scroll to curl in on itself. 'No, no,' she said impatiently. She tapped at her temple, 'that is in here.' Then, squinting at me, her finger still working. 'But word in the village is you've got one of these, too.'

⁂

Under Bindy's direction I foraged, unearthed, captured and gathered. I watched breathlessly as the ancient crone soaked, pickled, dried, peeled, boiled and unveiled crocks with a flourish to reveal decoctions left to rise, rind or settle. As she tilted lids to sample smoke and rifled through scrolls to check the formula for one cure or another, I poured libations at the altar and prayed to the Queen of Heaven for success.

'Correct?' Bindy would call me over impatiently, her spoon extended in my direction, her unseeing eyes narrowed as I gasped at the searing of my tongue by a caustic powder, the smarting of my skin from a fermented salve. 'Correct?' she would demand, her thin arm dismissing my protests with a wave. Insisting, demanding, as the days turned to moons and the moons waned and waxed, 'Correct? Correct? Correct?'

So I learned. The number of hours white willow bark must boil to effect a cure for fever, and the portions of sour wine and hyssop required to relieve pain. How honey eases the passage of the finest powder, and apple cleanses a palate made bitter by herbs. The name of the brew that cures dropsy and the vital element in a rub that salves the sores of lepers and knits broken bones.

After I turned woman, an event marked by none of the ceremony that had attended the ripening of my more promising sister, I joined the crone in the birthing room. When babies came—nearly always at night—Bindy would stand beneath the chestnut tree outside our window and summon me from my mat with a hoot like an owl. As I stumbled along beside her, shivering in the night, she would address me as an equal, a colleague and confederate, briskly summarising the woman's previous trials, the breaking of her waters, the strength and space between her pains.

At first she gave me leave only to perform the most modest of tasks: to brew the raisin water that would strengthen flagging pains and to rub balms on aching lower backs. Swept aside as the crown came into view, I would watch Bindy and the penitent grasp one another's forearms, sitting on air, and join silently in the urging as the midwife trumpeted the age-old cry. *Push! Push!*

After nearly a year of service, the earth scenting spring and preparations for yet another Passover due, Bindy briskly declared me ready and began allowing me to catch the slippery bundles myself, as well as to examine the afterbirth and tie the cord. With belly-pressed ear and palm, she taught me how to find the heartbeat, and how to wield the knife to ease the passage of the head. When all hope of new life was lost, she made me assist with the loathsome task of clearing the womb, limb by broken limb, to try and save the mother. She encouraged me when I had ideas of my own, too, displaying a waspish sort of pride at each success: applications of olive oil in the months preceding the birth to prevent tearing; the trick of persuading an infant lying wrong-way in the womb to turn by having the mother crawl on all fours; the administration of watercress juice for loss of blood.

This last innovation came to me during a particularly long and unyielding labour. The initiate, less than two years my senior at ten and five years, bled so much that my only task to that point involved bucket and mop. Her mother and elder sisters shouting encouragement, then frenzied with prayer and, finally, prostrate like slaves across her failing body as word of the tragedy spread and the village prepared to mourn. But then I remembered something; I saw a chance and took it. Throwing aside the sponges and leaving Bindy with the unfolding tragedy and mess I walked, then ran, from the room straight to a ditch by the crossroads where I had noticed the growth of watercress. I grabbed some and ran back to administer it. Bindy gave an acquiescent shrug; the girl was as good as dead.

But the cure worked. The women were astounded as poppies returned to the girl's cheeks and light to her eyes: as she quickened and recaptured the will to endure. 'Saved! Saved!' they cried, falling to their knees, their arms wide with love of God. Afterwards, they pressed coins to my palm and whispered words of thanks.

'I had not mentioned cress,' Bindy said later when the baby, a boy, had finally been delivered and the young mother had fallen asleep, her lips pressed to his gourd-sized head.

I shrugged. 'It was in the scroll,' I said, referring to the one she had unfurled for me the very first day we met.

Joshua was in love. I could tell by the way he ducked his head at the sight of her, stammered through his *shalom*s if their paths crossed as he and Papa traversed the square, making their way home from the woodshop for the midday meal.

Soon Mama knew and she was not pleased. Not one little bit. She warned my brother not to make promises. It wasn't the girl, she said, who was fair and virginal, her kin hailing from Magdalene where they had prospered from the salt trade. No, the problem was the timing. The rains of winter had been poor and the harvest was set to be thin, while Papa's shop was struggling in the wake of another tax increase from the Temple and Rome.

'A time and a place for everything,' she would natter like a jay as Joshua, still downing his last morsel, strode into the night.

Papa refused to meet her accusing eyes. Rising from the meal, he clapped imaginary dust from his hands. 'It is spring, Miriame. And he is a man.'

'Some man,' she snorted, hastening to clear the mat so that she and I could eat. 'With what to support a wife?'

'It won't be long,' Papa said mildly. As if to emphasise the point he shuffled to the jar with the gait of an old man. Poured the water. Began to pray.

I watched Mama chew her lip. It was true Papa would not live forever and his portion had always been thin. How much poorer might we be with him gone and Joshua in his place, with both wife and children to feed?

The following morning I was in my usual place in the wood at the back of the schoolroom. It was spelling time for the boys trapped within, and I was bent to the same task. On my lap, the wax tablet that Nahum's heedless son Malachi had left the previous week on the schoolhouse steps, and that I now kept carefully hidden behind a loose brick in the crumbling school-house wall. The rabbi's voice swelled and ebbed as he paced

76

the floor, and I bore down on the twig used to mark the wax, recording his words.

A looming shadow blocked my light. Irked, I lifted my chin to discover the trouble.

'What on earth are you doing, Rachael?' Papa said.

My heart pounded but I said nothing. Papa lowered himself, knees and throat groaning with age, to examine my slate. He turned it this way and that, moved it closer and further away, before scratching his head, his expression perplexed. 'What is this, Rachael?'

I hung my head in shame. Whatever my imaginings, it was clear the reality was different. That the markings I had so painstakingly transcribed on my tablet were not words, but more like the random scratches of a hen. 'Nothing, Papa.'

We sat silent for a time. Shadows crawled across the forest floor as the sun continued its rise in the sky. Inside the schoolhouse, the boys chattered, re-ordering their mats to study numbers. Papa placed the tablet on the ground and wiped it clean.

'Writing words made of letters one has never seen,' he mused, as if speaking to himself. 'How to conquer such a task, even approach it, is hard to fathom. As is the depth of character of she who dares it.' Removing the twig still clutched in my fist he employed it to impress the wax with several lines and a scatter of points and waves.

'Now,' he continued, pointing. 'If I were teaching someone their letters I would start with this word. A word of sanctity and meaning. For Israelites, the most sacred and secret word in the world.'

Not long afterwards Shona's waiting time finally came to an end. At last the men could journey to Cana to see how she fared.

The night before they left I barely slept, considering and reconsidering my contribution to the gifts and messages they would deliver, and imagining the look on my sister's face as she removed each one from the travel bag and unwrapped it. Mama had baked a cake stuffed with precious figs and dates while weeks earlier I had taken up the hated needle and, night after night by the dim flickering glow of the oil lamp, stayed awake late to sew my sister two cloth dolls. I had made one in my likeness, with long tresses of dark curly hair, and the other in hers, its brown eyes wide and densely ribbed with an embroidered row of lashes. The heads of both were stuffed with rags, but the small arms and legs were filled with bones and small stones so they could twist and curl with ease. I had arranged them in my favourite pose before packing them carefully into the cloth carry bag that now stood, ready for travel, by the door. Both dolls turned to face the same direction, the Shona doll clasped the Rachael one to her chest, as if whispering her a story at night as they lay on their mats awaiting sleep.

But it was not at all certain the journey would be successful. Before we had unfurled our mats for sleep, Jacob had announced he would not be coming.

'Not coming?' My eldest brother had replied, incredulous. He had been checking his travel bag, but now looked up to meet Jacob's eyes. My eldest brother's tone was rare but familiar, one he reserved solely for Jacob: suspicious, and laced with disgust.

Jacob was now, like Joshua, a full-grown man, as impressive

in height and breadth as Papa. Despite that, he was still a child: still a bully towards my younger brothers; still unable to keep his hands from picking at a face that now, at the age of four and twenty years, was a lunar landscape of pockmarks and fresh red pustules; still unable to see the world through any eyes but his own. The evening meal was finished but Jacob had remained at the mat, his lanky frame stretched insolently across the flat, well-worn cushions surrounding it, making it impossible for Mama and me to brush the crumbs away and re-set the space for our own dinner.

He sat up abruptly, always ready for a fight. 'Not going Joshua, you heard me.' He stuck his chin out. 'I. Am. Not. Going. To. Cana.' My other brothers, in various states of undress as they readied for bed, turned their attention to the impending brawl.

But Joshua held his temper. I saw him open his lips to argue with Jacob, to call the next-in-line a coward, which was what everyone in our family—not to mention the village—thought about him. But then he shook his head and kept his mouth shut. A lifetime of Jacob had taught him there was little point in naming his younger brother's faults and Joshua remained a person loath to waste words. Instead, in a manner that made his vexation plain, he began knotting the leather ties of his travel bag.

Papa, however, was not so reticent. Sitting on his mat preparing for sleep, his travel bag tied and resting beside him ready for the morning, he let his voice roar from the barrel of his chest, loud enough not just for villagers in East Nazareth to hear but possibly even some down on the Esdraelon Plains.

'You must be too *busy* to make but a few hours journey to see your sister, torn from us in the most terrible of circumstances and gone without word these last two years,' Papa mocked, his

79

tone sharp and terrible. 'I know, Jacob, how much there is in Nazareth for a man of your mettle to do. You have fights to pick—then run from—in the square. Women's bodies you must examine with impertinent eyes as they come and go from the well,' Papa was listing on his fingers. 'Evil, or just plain inept, plans to discuss with the winemaker's boy, Ruchel. What do they call him again? Ruchel…Ruchel,' Papa pretended to rummage in his memory, tugging on his beard as if deep in concentration. 'Oh, I remember now. Ruchel the brainless.'

'Papa,' Joshua said quietly. 'There is no point.'

'That's precisely right Joshua, there is no point,' the gaze Papa shot across the room at Jacob was blistering. His eyes roamed the next-in-line's large, lounging frame with contempt. 'No point reasoning with a whining child. No point cultivating goodness in a man without a heart.'

'Yosef, stop!' Mama, who was kneeling at the hearth, finally found her voice. 'Lower your tone at least. You are shaming us.' She pointed through the window at the crowd gathered below.

'I think not, Miriame,' Papa replied, though he did speak more quietly. He considered for a moment, then shook his head. 'No, this I no longer accept. I know this is what they say is true, what is taught, but I say it is not so. Every family has a bad apple, but that one does not spoil the rest. Nor is the rot the fault of the tree! I wash my hands of the boy, Miriame.' Papa got to his feet, bones creaking, and made his way towards Jacob. Standing over my brother, who stared up at him open-mouthed, he clapped and cleaned his hands. 'Responsibility for Jacob now rests with him.'

Mama made to protest again but, seeing the look on Papa's face, reconsidered. She pressed her lips shut.

I watched these proceedings slack-jawed, both thrilled and aghast. Delighted that my sour, snake-eyed brother was finally being dressed down in the manner he deserved, but worried that without him Papa and Joshua might have less chance of crossing Cana's gate to see Shona. Not for the first time in my life, I wished I were male. Then I could step into the breach and save the day. But I was not a man, and if there was one thing my life had taught me so far it was that this deficit was not easily overcome.

⌒

'Bindy, who is she?' I gestured at the round-bellied figure on the altar. 'The Queen of Heaven?' It was late afternoon three months later, a day when the warm winds of summer brought the scent of ripe fruit from the grove and women bustled to the square to shop for the Sabbath that began at nightfall. A day when I needed to be occupied, because that morning Joshua and Papa had once again set off for Cana to see my sister.

This would be their third attempt in as many months. The first and second efforts, both of which my brother Jacob had scorned to join, had fallen victim to precisely the forces Joshua and my father had feared. Both times they had been outnumbered: gangs of chanting, foul-tempered, spear-carrying men—kin to Boaz through blood or marriage—had met them at the village gates and forbidden them to pass. Both times Papa and Joshua had been forced home, downcast, having failed even to lay eyes on my sister, much less deliver greetings and pass packages.

The Cananite fury was payback for the humiliation

Boaz endured at the hands of the men of Nazareth, who had pursued him like an animal and forced him back to our village at spear-point to marry my sister. Beyond that, Papa and my brother could expect no help from the men of Nazareth in their efforts to see Shona. She remained sullied and covered in shame, and the village men would extend no effort on her behalf.

But Papa and Joshua were determined to find a way. Joshua grew so desperate he even went down on bended knees to Jacob, pleading with the next-in-line to join them on this third and final trip. 'We need you, Jacob. With another man of your size and strength we would have some hope of reaching Shona,' he implored. But Jacob said no, just as he had the two previous times Joshua had asked him, in sullen tones and without giving reasons. So disgusted was Papa at this third refusal that he spent the following day in mourning, donning sackcloth and smearing his face with ashes: declaring to anyone who would listen that in his eyes, his second son was dead.

My eldest brother's response was more practical. He went to the crossroads of the caravan routes at East Nazareth and hailed passing travellers until one agreed to take a message north to his childhood friend, Judah. Judah was now a rebel soldier with Judas the Galilean's rag-tag army in the town of Gamla. My brother asked if his old friend would meet him and Papa in Cana to help them enter the village and see Shona. Judah's reply came at once. Yes, he would be there. Papa and Joshua need only name the day.

That day was today and, at first light, both men were gone, leaving me to help Mama feed and dispatch my other brothers to their various occupations.

'Bindy?' I tried again. I was used to her hesitation in the face of my persistent inquiries about the Queen of Heaven. It was only the possibility of mercy on this difficult day that had prompted me to try again.

She sighed and put down the spoon she had been applying to a hissing cauldron of roots. 'The Queen of Heaven is Sophia. Sophia is the One God. The One God is the Queen of Heaven. The Queen of Heaven is Sophia, Sophia is—' She chanted the words so quietly, her nearsighted eyes lost in the distance, that I had to edge closer to the hearth to hear them. She repeated them three times, reclaimed the spoon and returned her attention to the pot.

'Bindy!'

She shook her hands at the heavens but, eventually, relented. Abandoning the spoon once more, she lumbered towards the mat and settled herself upon it, then waved me to sit across from her. She reached for both my hands and held them tightly in her own. Her skin felt smooth and oddly tender, like very old leather. 'It is forbidden, Rachael. The Heavenly Queen is forbidden.'

'By who?'

Bindy's sightless eyes rolled, and she snorted, though beneath this rough-edged reply I sensed emotions less constrained.

'The elders?' I persisted. 'Why?'

She ignored me, determined to tell the story her own way. 'It was in my mother's time that they banished the Queen. Struck her name from the Law and forbade devotions to her in the square. But Mama would not have it. She was like me, a healer. But a leader too and clever. Very clever.' Insight sparked her eyes, followed swiftly by concern. 'Like you,' she said slowly.

I chose not to let the comparison distract me; I wanted to hear the end of this tale. But Bindy had fallen silent.

'And?' I said finally.

'And what? She knew. Knew how to save the Queen. No,' Bindy stilled the rising question with a bent finger to her lips. Her voice slowed and deepened. 'Keep her by the hearth,' the crone nodded at the altar, 'praise her through your lips.'

'Praise her? When? Where?' I had never heard the name of the Queen spoken beyond Bindy's door.

'Always and wherever you go,' she replied without hesitation. It was a verse learned by heart, spoken in a manner not her own. 'At the well, in the field. At the side of a woman in labour and the deathmat of the crone.'

'How?' I whispered, my heart pounding to the distant drum of rebellion.

'By speaking the truth. That all Gods are one, and in being One are All.' As Bindy channelled her mother's voice through her withered lips, I saw her as the young girl she must have been. Rapt. Admiring. Filled with dread at her mother's mutiny. 'In that way shall we remember because—' Abruptly, the girl disappeared and the exacting crone, my teacher, returned. She lifted a brow in my direction. Waited.

'Because in praising One God we praise them all,' I said.

'Correct.' She listed and seemed to sag, waterlogged—I recognised it then—by sadness.

'What happened to your mother, Bindy?' I asked. But she was lost to me, ears as well as eyes. Two oily tears navigated a trail down her furrowed cheeks. I sat with her in silence for a time before rising and slipping away, closing the door quietly behind me.

Three months later I emerged from the wood behind our house to see Joshua ahead of me, hurrying along the path to the square. It was unusual for him to be abroad at that hour when most men, having finished the noon meal, were patting their lips, mumbling blessings and preparing to rest. It was the day before the Sabbath, with summer coming to an end, and the air was thick and weighty, pregnant with the promise of rain. Insects shrilled and chattering conies, rabbit-like creatures with yellow-flecked coats, foraged fearlessly for grass. The Esdraelons had just returned to the valley with basket-laden backs, signalling the end of the matrimonial bargaining season. In the square, mothers of newly ripened girls elbowed one another aside, each after the plumpest fowl, the finest wine for her own daughter's wedding feast.

Far away in Cana, Shona's time was nearing, but I would not be there to count through her pains or wipe her brow.

I followed my brother, keeping distant enough to avoid notice. I trailed him past a water jar abandoned by the well and into the northern woods, where he paused to pluck several blooms of rockrose. He patted his head, trying to impose order on his lank, dark hair before forging onwards, a tune on his tongue, his footfalls exploding dust in tiny clouds. The tread of my sandals found his and my heart thumped a tattoo in my chest, rebelling against the pace of his stride. Then, a murmur of voices brought me to an abrupt halt. I slipped into a stand of poplar trees to listen. The grunts and rustles were as familiar as the wind in the trees, or the tinkle of bells as animals shifted in their sleep: the sounds of night I had known since before I knew anything at all. The sighs and gasps, the billow and flap of robes, the slap of bodies, the wet sound of mouths. Joshua's voice scaled her name and she replied from deep in her throat, barely audible but in words that left no doubt. 'Oh yes, beloved. My love, my love, yes.'

I could see only movement through the welter of branches and jagged sunlight. A discarded scrap of clothing dripped from a branch. But my flushed cheeks and pounding heart, the cleft between my legs, knew what was happening. Knew that what I was witnessing was not the mindless rutting of animals or the routine coupling of the marital bed. It was the fervent clash of souls about which Solomon wrote in his songs. The tender, savage coupling of two people in love. I moved my hand between my thighs.

Joshua's passion was mounting. He was gasping, choking, dying: dying of love. She panted and strained and mewed and as my own rhythm took my mind and body to the same still yet falling place, something—his hand?—stifled her peaking cry. Then, all three of us, coming back and down, panting like dogs to the shrieking pulse of insects and the sweaty heat and green of the wood.

She whispered something. He replied and they both laughed softly. The way lovers do. And suddenly, I thought of Shona. How this would never be hers. How she would be buried alive in the stale, dark home Joshua had described to me—little more than a cave really, its only opening a door and animals and people thrown together like soup—where she toiled for Boaz and Boaz's pinch-faced mother. A widow who could never have raised the price for a girl like Shona, and so had encouraged her son to take what he wanted by less honourable means. And now my sister was bound, trapped, like a beast in a stall. Tethered to her fate by her condition, and all that would come after.

'I tried, Rachael,' my brother had said of their third journey to Cana, the movements of his slight body as contained and deliberate as always, the anger fierce only in his eyes. 'It took all morning to soothe the mob and persuade them to let us pass. And Judah! Every time Papa and I calmed the waters he would begin frothing again, and rile them up.'

'But did you get through, Joshua?' I was in agony. 'Did you see her at last and—' I gestured at his belt where I had seen him tuck a roughly tied cloth parcel, one of my gifts to my sister.

'When at last we arrived at Shona's door,' he shook his head, 'she was already swollen. Like a grape.' His voice whispered like the powder in the cloth he held out to me. 'Too late.'

'Could you not have left it with her?' I cried, refusing to reclaim the cure. 'To defend against his seed taking root in her again?'

'You do not understand, Rachael.' Joshua sighed as if the world was heavy on his chest. 'She is not like you. She is resigned. Resigned to her fate. She told us not to return.'

'What?'

'She said, "The fact that you've come will make things worse."' Joshua paused. 'I would swear at that moment I heard Papa's heart rip in two. But she did not relent. She drove us through the door and slammed the lock shut, leaving the three of us—Papa, Judah and me—on the dusty road.' As he spoke, I pictured them there, open-mouthed and staring.

'But what about me?' I cried, ashamed, even as the words left my lips, of the self-love propelling them, but needing to know.

'I asked her,' Joshua had replied, his eyes downcast. 'She said, "Tell Rachael I am sorry. That I wish I were stronger. That I wish I were like her."' He looked up at me. '"But I am not."'

Now, in the forest, Joshua's breath was slowing, along with that of his lover Maryam. There was some shuffling, followed by his deep mumble. Then Maryam, plaintive. 'Don't, you must not. It is I who gave over—'

Joshua again, too soft and low to hear. Then Maryam's reply, in a tone that made me see her shining eyes, the heave of her breast. 'And he will! He will!'

But Joshua doubted. 'We have risked everything, Maryam. Your virtue, and your name. I should not have—'

'Held me like a jewel in the light?' she interrupted fiercely. 'Claimed me so I might bear children for the man I love instead of being bartered like an ox for the highest price?'

Joshua startled. 'Your father has plans?'

'Yes, yes,' Maryam shushed him like a child. 'But he will change them. When the time is ripe, I will ask his leave for us to marry and he will not deny me. I will ask him, and he will say yes. Fear not, my love.' A pause. 'My love,' murmured this time as the heat rose and the slap of skin and wet sounds began again.

Their passion blurred my vision. I stumbled back towards the well.

⌒

Having abandoned hope that Papa would take a harsh hand to my absences, Mama pursued Joshua. 'An iron rod to the back, that will fix her! Or a flogging, then soot rubbed in the wounds!' Desperate to whet my eldest brother's appetite for the task, she proffered a new means of straightening me each evening. But

88

Joshua never replied. Instead, he would simply look past her, as if she were not there, his eyes shaded with contempt.

They were not kindred spirits. For as long as I could recall, the mere sight of my eldest brother caused Mama pain: her breath would catch and her brow collapse. She would chew savagely at her lips. It was highly unusual for an Israelite son, never mind the eldest, to be so unlovely in the eyes of his mother; even harder to fathom what a boy of my brother's gentle nature could have done to cause such a gap in Mama's affections.

Whatever it was, the facts were plain: Mama favoured Jacob. She favoured him with soft eyes, steady praise and the tenderest morsels heaped on his plate. She favoured him with urgings towards greatness and excuses for his every fault and blunder. Shona and I had never discussed this perplexing state of affairs. Nor did any of my brothers as far as I knew. This was how things were in our family, what was there to say?

But the women of Nazareth were not so circumspect. Joshua's habitual reticence, combined with his sympathetic recall of even the most trivial triumphs and miseries of others, endeared him to all in the village, from those of the finest blood to the ear-pierced slave. While Jacob! The women grubbing at the well for gossip hissed and spat. They pressed their palms to the heavens in search of sense until someone would conclude at last, 'Miriame.' The rest would nod, as if Mama's very name captured the essential problem with her: the fractured, secretive part of her nature that challenged both pity and sense.

One afternoon, as Mama ruminated on my obstinacy and disobedience, and a fresh roster of punishments offered my brother to break my rebellion, Joshua rose from his sleep to reply. The wet season had begun and the world outside was cold and sodden. For days, water had been sleeting from a colourless sky, logging the spaces between stones in the square and creeping beneath the door of the *oorvah* to rot the hay. Papa was on his mat, silently picking his toenails, though from the looks he and my brother exchanged, it was clear he was in on Joshua's plan.

Mama heard my brother out in silence, but when he finished she looked up, indignant, from the flour she was grinding between two flat stones. 'You want Rachael to come to you? To bring the midday meal to you in the shop instead of coming home?'

My brother shrugged. The late afternoon sun through the window revealed variations of bronze in the charcoal black of his beard. It was as long as Papa's now, though his aversion to strong emotion and unnecessary words remained his own.

'It is well you have so much work to do,' Mama ventured, trying to draw him out.

Joshua nodded.

'But if you don't return home to eat,' my mother persisted, 'when will you and Papa rest? When will you sleep?'

Joshua shrugged, his face a study in neutrality.

She tried once more. 'Can it not wait? The Dedication Feast is near, and now with just one daughter to prepare…Could you not wait until the feast is done and—'

Joshua shook his head impatiently, crossed his arms and waited. Dedication was mainly marked by the lighting of flames in the square, one for each of the eight nights it had taken our ancestors to cleanse the Temple of pagan stain after they drove out the apostate Greeks two hundred years ago. The role of women in commemorating a rare Jewish military triumph was minimal. We need do nothing more than cook meals in oil to fulfil our obligations to God. In any event, it was not as if I would be gone from Mama's hearth all day. More likely, from the sound of it, an hour or so.

Fortunately, there was much in my brother's plan that suited Mama. The potential benefits arched provocatively before her, like a cat in the sun. If I attended Papa and Joshua in the woodshop each day at noon, I would have less chance to roam the alleyways of East Nazareth. Less chance to keep company with that witch, the only name she ever gave Bindy. Here was a chance to restore my family's reputation and propriety.

So she agreed. Appraising me slyly, she beckoned my brother's ear to her lips and cupped her hand to her mouth. 'It is a clever plan,' she whispered in audible tones. 'But will she do it?'

Mimicking her secretive gesture, Joshua's reply was loud in her ear. 'I don't know. Ask her.' My brother moved towards Papa and helped the old man to his feet. Without a backward look the two men left for the shop.

The next day, as the winter sun peaked in the sky, I crossed the square with a linen-draped basket in my hand: delivering the midday meal to my busy father and brother in the woodshop.

Like the eight flags of flame in the square at Dedication, that day shines in my memory. Papa's shop was near the village gates, a square room in a longer building with a shared thatched roof. Befitting the higher status of woodworking among the artisan trades, the shop was at the western end, next to the potter's place. This gave the woodshop the luxury of a single, roughly hewn window that looked over the forest to the north and east. The walls were lined with narrow workbenches heaped with tools and clay-fired pots overflowing with dowels and differently sized nails. Stacked in the corners and beneath the benches were planks of various lengths and thicknesses. There were sections of tree trunk on which to sit, or rest a knee while sawing.

As I moved to dust off the small, squat workbench at the room's centre so I could set out the meals, Papa's hand stayed mine. Joshua bolted the door and lowered a threadbare cloth over the window. Papa looked at my brother and nodded his permission, before setting himself heavily on a tree stump and rifling through the basket for bread.

Joshua moved to the workbench and spread the scatter of wood dust evenly across the rough surface. He began to draw. He drew for a long time, lips moving in concentration, before stepping back and summoning me.

I stepped closer, a throat full of beating heart. Markings: wavy lines and angled ones like ladders; scattered flocks of birds. The secret word Papa had drawn on my wax tablet that day outside the schoolroom sprang to mind. 'Words,' I guessed. 'These are Hebrew words, yes?' I gazed up at my older brother, wanting desperately to be right.

But Joshua shook his head. 'They are not words, but the… materials,' he gestured at the stacked planks and pots of nails on the workbench, 'we use to build words. They are letters, Rachael. The letters of the Hebrew alphabet.'

The alphabet! I dashed over to one of the tree stumps and shoved it closer to the bench so I could look properly at what my brother's hand had set out. 'How does it work? How does it work? Tell me, tell me!'

Joshua explained how letters made words and words, in turn, made sentences, which were the basis of verses. And verses—here he looked up to smile into my eager face—were the foundation of books: the wondrous scrolls kept with such care by the rabbi and the elders, and read from with such solemnity in the schoolroom and the square. He pointed to each letter in turn and announced its name. Aleph. Bet. Gimmel…When he arrived at the last, a crooked shed-shape called Tav, he began at the top again. 'Aleph. Bet—'

'Gimmel,' I interrupted and then continued on, pointing to each of the letters and announcing their names until I arrived again at Tav.

'Correct.' My brother was open-mouthed. 'Not one error.' His voice inflected with pride he turned to my father for confirmation. 'Not one, was there Papa?'

Papa agreed with shaking head, his beard shedding crumbs. 'Not one. I said this about her. I have been saying so for years.'

The shifting shadows in the room said time was moving on. I tapped a frantic finger on the bench to recall my brother's attention. 'More! What comes next?'

But Joshua was hungry. He must have his own meal, then open the doors for trade before the men began returning to the surrounding shops. Mama would be expecting me home soon, too. The next lesson must wait until tomorrow. Ignoring my scowling face, Joshua wiped the bench clean with his sleeve and placed his meal on it—bread spread with olive oil and herbs, a handful of dried figs—before returning the basket to me. He crossed to the door, unlocked it and wordlessly waved me through.

I heard the bolt drop behind me. I tripped home happily, basket empty and mind full. For the remainder of the day I scrubbed and swept with precision, lips moving silently to sounds my bewildered-looking mother could not hear.

By the end of the first week I could voice each aspirating and guttural note of the twenty-two Hebrew consonants and every vowel sound. I could knit some together to form words. If I put ב and ן together, they formed the word 'son'. גדי fashioned 'lamb' and זית spelled 'olive'. Pointing at every object in the woodshop, Joshua would ask me its name in Hebrew, then command me to spell it. Table was *shulchan* (shin, lamed, chet, nun!). Saw was *masor* (mem, samech, vav, resh!). Beckoning me to the woodshop window, we did the same with all the objects in our purview: Bucket! Wood! Shop! Scrub! Manure!

The tedium of my days became a blessing. Chore time provided the perfect chance to spell the words in the daily prayers, the ones we chanted at feasts and fasts (Bread! Earth! Justice! Truth! Wrath!), and the word for every man, woman and child in the village, including my own, Rachael, which was the Hebrew word for ewe.

At night, I was restive, my mind—now wakened—reluctant to sleep. The darkness behind my closed lids an irrepressible slate on which the letters of a word would appear, then shuffle about to form a different word. The letters of the Hebrew word for *innocent* reforming to make the word *dead*; the word *bad* becoming, when the first and last letter were transposed, *awake*.

I ceased disappearing for the day when Mama dispatched me to wood or well; ceased caterwauling and heel-dragging when told to muck out the animal stalls, or oil and scrape my brothers' feet. I even ceased moving beyond the village gates to see Bindy, a fact about which the crone complained bitterly when she saw me next. Mama was thrilled.

But knowledge was like a sorcerer's supper, the more I ate

the hungrier I felt. Having quickly grasped how one built and recognised words, I wanted to write them down. To summon objects and ideas—like my brother did—with the touch of my hand. Joshua was pleased to guide me, but I was dismayed to discover that my fingers, which had struggled to embroider and unpick threads from even the most slackly strung looms, lacked skill here, too. They jarred and juddered through the sawdust-scattered bench, leaving rivers of scribble in their wake. Ashamed, I persevered, lying awake beside Shona's missing form each night with my arm aloft, carving letters into the blackness long after the rest of my family was asleep.

It took a lifetime—more than three weeks—before matters improved. Before my brother's head nodded and Papa, polishing a ploughshare in the background, struggled to his feet to assess my efforts and grunt his assent.

I drank like a wanderer at a desert oasis, greedily and with undiminished concentration. Joshua was pleased, but no longer surprised. 'You are special, Rachael,' he said one afternoon, after examining line after line of my handiwork but finding no errors. 'Papa is right. God has given you the soul of a male.'

They may have been right. Certainly it was the only hope for eternity that a woman might be offered: that we should receive God's blessing and enter His kingdom by making ourselves male. And I might have gained sustenance from this idea, embraced it as my philosophy, too, if not for the distraction that came soon after. The rattling of the barred shop door, followed by the noisy breach of the window.

It was just before Passover in the Hebrew year 3785 and I was ten and five years old. The intruder was a man, his hair a long mane of kinks, his powerful body as graceful as a cat's. But the dust-covered floor saw him slip, sending the plank Papa was cutting in two, and the jagged-toothed saw he was employing to do it, crashing to the ground.

'Judah!' Papa cried, throwing his hands to the sky.

I looked up from the words I was forming and fell in love.

The lines of his body made me sweat. Dry tongue, neck glowering beneath the wrap of my headscarf, stumble-footed whenever he was near: all the usual signs were there. Signs that I had noted with amusement in those maidens of Nazareth I considered to be the most flighty and simple-minded, but was now discomfited to find were plain for everyone to see in myself.

Judah appeared not to notice them. Or to notice me, the sister of a friend who had been no more than a child when he first left for war. His attention was with the young men. His star shone brightly with those like my brother Jacob and the low-caste workers trudging home from the east at day's end, who would linger shyly at the rim of the crowds until someone hailed them with a cry of 'brother' and drew them into the fold. The elders, sensing the threat to their authority, strutted past more often than necessary, affecting the air of one late for an audience with the king. If they paused, Judah would lapse into contemptuous silence as they rapped like knuckles on a desk the names of those surrounding him: 'Jonah, son of Micah the weaver! Were you not on your way to deliver that rug? Zechariah of Tabor! The pleas of your herd for milking can be heard from here!'

When at last they waddled off, Judah would slam his fist into his palm and take up the thread of his story, the throb of veins that mapped the muscles in his upper arms visible through the thin weave of his summer robe. With vivid pantomime he chronicled his life for them, brandishing shields to hold imaginary hordes at bay, pelting flaming spears into buildings the size of mountains, heaving himself atop rock ledges to spy on the centurions as they laid out their plans to rout the zealots once and for all. He was a zealot, a rebel, a sworn enemy of Rome: a man who lived his convictions in actions, not words.

The fierceness in his eyes, the Samsonesque length and swing of his abundant hair, the constancy of his convictions, transformed the square into a battlefield and captivated Nazareth's young men. They jostled to be near him, pushing one another aside and back to clear space for his fulsome slides and parries. Vowing that when the harvest was in or next year, or the one after that—yes!—they too would join the Galilean rebels in Gamla and lay down their lives for God.

Judah of Iscariot was larger than life. His galloping maleness made me feel oddly, though not unpleasantly, female. I watched from afar, swooning inside.

Judah's return to Nazareth had been prompted by his Papa's poor health. Plagued by boils on both hands and feet and persistent unexplained fevers, Simeon of Iscariot feared his end and summoned Judah back from the war in Gamla so he might confer his blessing—which belonged by right to the elder son, Gideon—upon the younger and braver.

At first, all had gone to plan. Just days after Judah returned to Nazareth his corpulent father, short of breath and fading fast, laid both hands on the curly lion's mane of his younger son's head and named him as heir. Gideon protested, but the rebellion finished moments after it began, a jeering crowd bearing witness to the knife Judah held at his older brother's throat until Gideon swore acquiescence to their father's will.

Then, in the shining hour before death and the eternal sleep that lies beyond, Simeon of Iscariot balked. Abandoning his piety, he banished the muttering fugue of anointing elders from his bedside and summoned the witch of East Nazareth.

Bindy and I arrived that night, laden with baskets filled with dried herbs, barks for brews, salves and clay-fired cups for extracting fever. Simeon's condition was woeful. The lesions on his palms and soles had begun colonising broad swathes of the skin on his arms and neck. His eyes were bright with fever but he lacked the sporadic energy that sometimes comes with it. The elders' repeated application of leeches had drained his vigour along with his blood.

We set to work, taking readings of the humours through pulse and palpation, examining the stools and the markings in the eye. Simeon's sweat- and pus-drenched mat was replaced with fresh bedding. Every day we stretched and rotated his heavy limbs to forestall wasting. We strewed garlic around the house and hung it from the doorposts to repel contagion. Once in the morning and again in the evening, two steaming bowls of water were set by the door. In them, roasted corms of crocus flower were steeped to summon the healing breath of the Heavenly Queen.

It took us months to unseat the rot. To cleanse the air of incense and the stench of animal blood; extract heat from Simeon's body with vinegar baths and fever cups; replenish the old man's blood with marrow soup and seal his weeping wounds with salves. Bindy was never much for praise but during this time she made plain, in her own tart and irascible fashion, her satisfaction with my contribution to the healing work. Some heirs took years to attain the required level of skill, if indeed they ever did, but I had proved as quick a study as she had hoped.

But when Judah entered the room, I was suddenly silly and dense. Kneeling by the hearth over a boiling cauldron, I would forget the ingredients I had already added, and those to come next. In the midst of a spirited debate with Bindy about Simeon's prognosis or changes needed to our cures, my tongue would fall still, the words that had been pouring forth from it melting away like honey, leaving no trace of their shape. One afternoon, I even fumbled one of the fever cups bequeathed to Bindy by her mother. It tumbled to the floor but thankfully did not break.

'What ails you, Rachael?' the crone snapped, her forbearance at an end. With her deadened sense of smell and poor eyesight she could make no connection between the scent of Judah rising up behind me as he woke from his afternoon nap, or a glimpse of him through the window as he strode through the square on his way home from the groves, and my abrupt descent into addled lunacy.

I prayed that Judah would notice me. I prayed that he would not. At one instant I would be confident that a man like him would be drawn to a woman of similar strengths: a tall, independent-minded creature like me, ahead of the more diminutive and commonplace females of Nazareth. The next moment I would gaze down the length of my body in despair at the barely noticeable cinch of the woman's belt around my barely noticeable waist, the angles and planes of hips and belly where voluptuous swells should be. 'Please God,' I whispered to the heavens each night before falling asleep, as exhausted from my inner turmoil as the challenging work of curing Simeon of Iscariot's ills. 'Please make me lovely in his eyes.'

But although I was a constant presence in his household, Judah paid me no mind. He was distracted by his brother Gideon's incessant provocation and undermining. He was preoccupied by the persistence of the illness plaguing his beloved Papa and the hovering possibility of Simeon's death. He was disturbed by thoughts of the war in Gamla going on without him and absorbed by the self-imposed obligation to recruit more able-bodied men. Judah was a soldier with no doubts about the importance of his quest or his centrality to its success. He had no time for love or romance, and no interest in the thick-fingered, tongue-tied apprentice of the near-sighted witch hovering by his father's side. Bindy and I were but minor players in the drama of his life.

But one morning Judah did see me, if only momentarily. Showing early signs of illness, he had remained asleep on his mat that day and away from the groves. The favoured son slept behind a tapestry in a small space of the central upper room where Simeon's sick bed was arranged. When he emerged just before midday with a red and weeping nose but his vitality intact I saw straight away that the malady would be passing.

I took care to keep veiled the relief that spread like sunshine through my body and busied myself with the task at hand. Bindy and I were kneeling by Simeon's side, burning a thick braid of herbs over his bulbous chest in hope that the dense, musky fumes rising from the smouldering sprigs would disperse all lingering congestion. Suddenly the patient, who had been resting peacefully with eyes half-closed, started with a cry.

I knew instantly what had happened. Watching Judah emerge and cross to his mother's side at the hearth, I had forgotten to tap the burning ash into the small, water-filled dish by my knee. Instead, I had allowed it to fall on to Simeon's chest. I ducked my head with shame at my ineptitude, and the terrible fact of Judah's presence to witness it.

But if Judah had taken note he gave no sign, and nor did his mother Olivia. Mother and son stayed as they were by the hearth, heads bent together, lost in conversation. I was spellbound by the intimacy between them, and by Olivia, who seemed an entirely separate species of woman to my own mother. Large-boned and ample-fleshed, at ease with the demands of the world and her capacity to meet them, her lips tipped skyward in a perpetual smile.

'Rachael!' The bark of Bindy's voice brought me to attention. She might be blind, but her timing was impeccable. The ashen rind of the burning herbs that I continued to hold in my hand above Simeon's massive chest was ready to be tapped away again. 'Put it out,' Bindy growled, and waited with folded arms for the hissing sound as the burning leaves met the water. 'Now, stand the bowl aside,' she continued testily. 'No, over there so you don't upset it. We shall turn him now.'

I swallowed a sigh. Shifting the sick man's position was crucial to avoid the resting sores that afflict the chronically sick, but Simeon's bulk made it a fearsome task. It had begun to dawn on me that such unpleasantness, and others like it, formed a large part of a healer's work. Reluctantly, I took up my position on the other side of the bed and we began to struggle and strain.

Suddenly Judah appeared at my side. 'I'll do it,' he said. As if Simeon weighed no more than an empty basket, he gathered his father to his chest as a mother does her baby. Cooing in the sick man's ear and pressing his lips to Simeon's cheek, he reached out a hand to plump and arrange the cushions, then gently settled his papa face down on the mats. For a time he knelt there, neck bent and eyes full of tears, a hank of thick hair obscuring each cheek as he stroked his father's sweaty bald head.

Then Judah turned to me. 'Will he die?'

The intensity of his gaze, the suddenness of the question, were unbalancing. I looked to Bindy for guidance, but she was groaning her way to her feet and shuffling towards the hearth with a pinched look of intent, as if the sorrel and vinegar cure we were preparing for Simeon's remaining lesions was her only care in the world. I turned back to Judah, forced myself to breathe and spoke with all the calm and sincerity I could.

'He is unwell,' I said, thankful my voice did not shake. 'This you can see for yourself. But he is improving. With God's grace he will—' From the corner of my eye I saw Bindy shake her head. 'He may,' I corrected myself, 'be fully restored to health.'

Judah nodded absently. He was listening but his gaze was

inward-looking, roaming a landscape I could not see: the terrain, perhaps, of future prospects and possibilities in a world without his papa. Signalling the end of the conversation with a nod, he made to stand up. Simeon jerked and moaned in his sleep and without thinking I reached out my hand to comfort him.

The impulse to offer comfort seemed to make an impact on Judah. He hesitated. For the first time since he'd stumbled into the woodshop, altering my world forever, he looked in my direction and actually saw me. His eyes, the rich brown of fertile earth, scanned my face and his brow creased with a question. 'You are Joshua's sister, yes? The daughter of Yosef the wood-worker?'

I acknowledged these designations with a nod, then looked into his eyes. 'I am Rachael. Rachael of Nazareth.'

His lips twitched with the start of a grin. 'Ah, *shalom* then, Rachael of Nazareth. Peace be with you.'

My face was like the desert sand, radiating heat; the place between my legs an oasis of desire. I dropped my gaze to the floor and battled to contain the heaving of my chest. 'And upon you be peace,' I whispered. But when I found the courage to look up, Judah was gone.

Mama soon noticed my befuddled state and her scorn was predictable. Unexpectedly, however, Papa took her side. 'All this breast-beating and talk of war,' he lamented in the shop one afternoon. 'God's hand will not be forced at point of sword. Not Judah Iscariot's, or those of the brigands. The Lord will send his Messiah when the Jewish people live as He commands. Each of us, submitting to every decree of the Law. And not one moment sooner.'

He was measuring a door with a length of string but, noticing my impassive expression, sighed and sought another tack. 'The man's a fool, Rachael. Not a bad man,' he continued, as my mouth opened to protest, 'but rash. Your mother is right to recall his form as a boy. Charging off that rooftop after your brother!' Papa dismissed the air with both hands, his tongue clicking with chagrin.

'He was trying to break my fall, Papa,' Joshua corrected quietly. This was an old argument, based on an even older event. Like most village boys in Israel's north, Joshua and Judah had been enthralled by the exploits of Judas the Galilean and his revolutionary zealots. When school let out for the day, the two boys would race up the steps to the Iscariots' roof and hurl pretend rocks and spears at one another. 'No Lord but God!' the boy playing Judas the Galilean that day would shout in Aramaic. 'Hail Caesar!' his opponent would retort in Latin.

During one such game my brother, that day a zealot, tripped over a tray of dates that Judah's mother had left to dry in the sun. Joshua tumbled over the parapet and hurtled towards the ground. Judah issued a blood-curdling war cry and lunged after him, skinning both knees and spraining his wrist in the fall. The collective judgment the villagers of Nazareth formed of Judah's character that day proved as hard to shift as resin on a sandal's sole. Papa repeated it now: 'Long on passion. Short on common sense.'

Joshua had a more charitable view, cemented one afternoon a few months later when Ruchel the winemaker's son and a handful of his feral, broken-toothed kin filled their fists with stones and pursued my unsuspecting brother through the woods. Joshua had no idea that he had insulted the bone-headed Ruchel that day at school by offering, in the hearing of others, to help the older boy with his sums. But Judah, high in an apricot tree in his father's grove, spied the threat. Stuffing his belt with hard, green pellets of unripe fruit, he shimmied down the tree, hit the ground running and slowed, as he approached the louts, to fire a perfect shot at the back of Ruchel's head. Then he ducked behind a bush and emerged moments later, wielding a garland of burning brambles. 'I am the burning bush, sent to you by God,' he told the terrified gang in the most booming voice he could muster. 'Joshua of Nazareth is innocent. Leave him this instant and flee! Flee, or endure the Almighty's wrath!' They fled.

Joshua never doubted that Judah's intercession had saved him that day. Nor that the qualities the people of Nazareth disparaged—Judah's impetuousness and reckless disregard for his own safety—were but courage and loyalty by other names. He said as much to Papa now and my father fell silent, considering, before he grudgingly conceded the point.

It is a truth widely known that the desire of the amorously infatuated to hear their lover's name, to speak it and hear it spoken aloud, makes them tiresome company. I proved no exception.

'You would have seen Simeon of Iscariot's son Judah in the square of late, Bindy? Urging the young men to cast aside excuses and join the insurrection in Gamla?' It was now many months since Judah had made his bumptious entrance into the woodshop, and the crone and I were having a rare day away from Simeon's bedside. It was midwinter and had been raining for days. We had come to the grassy shores of the washing point, burlap sacks in hand, to track frogs.

Bindy did not reply. Scarf flapping low over her brow to shield her weak eyes from the winter sun, she squatted by the water's edge, ear cocked to the cold mist rising from the rushing stream. 'Blessed is he who returns from battle with nary a chink in his armour,' I intoned, oblivious to her silence. 'For truly has he found favour with the Lord.'

'Blessed is she who keeps her mind on her initiation,' the crone returned tartly, clearly as unimpressed as Papa with Judah's lust for liberation, 'lest she humiliate herself by failing.'

Initiation. My heart, already in an uproar since Judah came to town, put on another burst of speed. Initiation would be my trial: an appraisal, by senior women of the craft, of my worthiness to become a healer, midwife and anointed servant of the Heavenly Queen in my own right. As the appointed time drew closer, I quailed at the rigours of the test, which was to be conducted in the moon of Adar at a secret, sacred place—the house of a priestess no less—in the lands surrounding Gath Hepher. Yet I yearned for it too. Yearned for the chance to justify Bindy's quiet confidence that I would not only pass, but do so as none had done before: triumphing without a single error.

Now the old woman shushed me harshly. Her arm shot suddenly from her side, like a lizard's tongue, towards a tussock of grass. She lifted her hand victoriously to reveal a moss-coloured frog twisting around its trapped leg. But the creature was not captive for long. Bindy's grip was insecure and the frog bounded free, springing from earth to river-rock to water, where it disappeared without a ripple. She scowled and, beneath her breath, took the Lord's name in vain.

'Did you know the zealots search for one of my tribe? A

descendant of David to reign as Messiah and king over the land given to us by God.' Of course she knew; I was simply babbling my way towards an occasion to say his name. 'Judah says the Herods are Rome's puppets, as good as Greeks the way they behave. And converts besides. Not really Jews at all.' Bindy, bent on getting another frog, growled low in her throat, her irritation plain.

'He has much to say that draws others near,' I prattled on, but then fell silent, pondering the image I had conjured of those drawn near to Judah Iscariot. In particular, those of distinctly female proportion, including a cloister of chittering, tittering virgins that included the elder Sirach's daughter Sarai, whose woman's belt—safflower yellow and sewn of silk—displayed her hips and bountiful bosom to devastating effect. Frowning at my image in the water, I tried to arrange my hair more fetchingly beneath my slackly tied veil.

Bindy noted my frantic ministrations and burst out laughing. But when she spoke, her words were soothing. 'Do not lament this union, Rachael, nor eye the vixen with envy. Sarai's fulsomeness is much like his. It is of body, not wit, and dims when raised to your light. You are a sight to behold, my girl. No longer the awkward yearling you imagine yourself to be, but a graceful gazelle. But more than this, you are a woman of spine and subst—'

'Union? What union? He has not chosen her!' I cried, with a shrillness that surprised even me. 'And you have no call, no call to know my thoughts as you do!' Bindy looked as if she had been slapped, but recovered quickly.

'Please yourself.' She returned to the frogs with a shrug. 'Perhaps the match between you and Judah would be a good one after all. Two stubborn mules galloping along on their own trail.'

~

Did Joshua speak of me to his friend? In a whisper, perhaps, when the men huddled in the square on the day of rest? Or on the rare evening when my eldest brother spurned his lover Maryam's embrace and ignored the sentries' clicking tongues to follow Judah beyond the gates to East Nazareth; returning at dawn smelling of women and wine?

At first, it appeared not, or not with any success. For while I continued to gaze rapturously upon Judah as he came and went from his papa's side, and vaulted and sparred in the square, he did not look upon me again. Once, perhaps—to this day I am not sure—I thought I felt the weight of his stare as he stood beneath the fig trees in the square, amid an adoring round of men. He may even have taken a step towards me, as if to speak, when Sarai moved in front of me, blocking my vision. Her expression was mocking. The usual cluster of virgins was assembled behind her, squawking like a flock of birds.

'And who might you be gazing on, Rachael,' she sneered, her arms crossed beneath her munificent chest. 'Look girls,' she cried, before I could answer. 'Mad, bad Rachael is in love!'

It was an old jibe, the hurt worn thin, but it caught the followers' simple fancy. They shrieked with laughter. I swore beneath my breath and ducked my head, racked by conflicting impulses. I wanted to punch Sarai in her beautiful face and run, but feared returning to Bindy's side without the full jar of water she had demanded.

'As if,' Sarai continued, her voice low and ruthless, casting a glance over her shoulder to ensure her followers were still paying attention, 'a man of Judah Iscariot's calibre would look twice at the likes of *you*,' she spat the word like it was foul-tasting.

At that moment, a shout rose up from the throng of men. It was Judah. Having turned in our direction he mimed the dangerous throw of a spear. There he stood, a Greek statue of beauty, his arm still poised above his head in the position of final release, as the imaginary weapon sailed in our direction. Obligingly, the women squealed and scattered, including Sarai who giggled ostentatiously and mimed terror as she cowered behind the well. Judah muttered something beneath his breath and nodded, clearly satisfied by the disruption he'd caused to proceedings. He may even have turned to me and winked before turning back to the men; or perhaps it was just the sun in his eyes.

Not long after, as preparations for the spring feast of Pentecost began, Simeon rose from his mat, ordered it burned and declared himself clean. The elders shuffled into the house and pushed us aside. Painstakingly, they inspected every handsbreadth of the old man's skin and conferred in murmurs. Ultimately, they were forced to agree: Simeon of Iscariot was cured. That night in the square, a fire was raised and a fatted calf slaughtered. The villagers heaved the elders to their shoulders and paraded them before Simeon, who fell on his face before them, praising their power to heal. Then, with light feet, the men danced and sang to the glory of God.

I turned from the revelry spitting with rage and sought out Bindy. The elders had not beaten the drum by the sick man's mat night after night to steady a heart made frantic by fever. God had not dug for serpent's root in the swamp near Deadman's Hill and returned spackled with mosquito rash for His trouble. I had.

The crone, drinking tea on her mat, sought to smooth my feathers. 'You and I know the truth, Rachael. God healed Simeon of Iscariot, but He worked this miracle through us.'

'Then why must we stay silent while the elders claim the prize?' Kneeling across from her, I scratched viciously at the bites on my hands. 'Why should we give credence to the lie that only they can channel God's healing love?'

My vinegar features made Bindy frown. She snatched my thumping fist from the air and made to smooth it in her palm. 'Seek it in the work, Rachael,' she urged. 'The reward. Find it in the work.' But I snatched my hand back and turned my face away, distraught. It was not just the injustice of it all, but the unwelcome news that in light of Simeon's recovery, Judah had begun making plans to return to Gamla. Soon, he would be going away.

⌒

Papa looked up from the log he was sawing, alarmed. The bolted door of the woodshop was being pummelled by what sounded like a water-wheel of fists.

Joshua and I were quick. As my brother swept the embossed wood dust from the bench with his cloak, I bent to the basket at my feet and began setting food on the bench.

Above the clamour, a bear's bellow. 'Joshua! Brother!' Recognising the voice, Papa sagged with relief. Joshua did, too. He crossed the room and threw the door ajar.

The force of his blows no longer meeting resistance, Judah

stumbled into the room. My brother's lips rippled with amusement while Papa made show of removing the saw from Judah's path.

Judah did not notice. Recovering his balance, he trained the full force of his energy on Joshua, striding towards him with outstretched arms to pound his old friend's back and pinch and pat his cheeks, his voice full of wonder. 'You were right, brother!' he repeated over and again. 'I saw her! You were right!'

Abruptly, he turned to me. His eyes took in the woman's belt and veil, the lanky protrusions of arm and leg from every corner of a robe that, despite Mama's efforts, failed to disguise the ramshackle growth Bindy had called graceful: seeing me for the first time. The words from the canyon of his mouth wending their way towards my ear in slowed motion. 'Rachael! Rachael of Nazareth, a miracle! A miracle!'

And eventually, through the volley of exclamations and praise, I came to understand that he had been watching me. Peering beneath the window-covering while I laboured at the workbench, bent over my letters like a scribe, taking dictation from Joshua with swift-flowing finger and graceful arcing arm.

A woman—reading and writing! Who could believe such a thing? Yet he would stand on a box in any square, before any elder or priest, and attest to it, having seen it with his own eyes!

And then he allowed them, his eyes, the sacred colour of fertile earth, to search my face. His silent lips to shape my name. *Rachael*.

It was then that I knew, hearth stoking in my belly, gooseflesh stippling both arms, that he would be for me as I had been for him, from the very first moment I saw him. The words of

King Solomon humming in my ears as I met his gaze with mine. *Sustain me with raisins, refresh me with apples, for I am faint with love.*

⌒

But while Judah's and my promise had been wordless, the price of my virtue must be agreed by our fathers. Papa still was not persuaded and, in any event, any marital bargaining must be delayed until Simeon of Iscariot was restored to full health.

Suddenly time, which to that point had been careening at an unseemly pace towards the day of Judah's departure from Nazareth, seized to a crawl. Each moment was an agony as days, hours, moments we should have had together were spent apart. Our hearts and minds possessed by longing, we were nonetheless prohibited from touching, speaking, even looking upon one another without a third party present. Joshua usually drew the short straw.

'Peace be with you Rachael of Nazareth, Joshua of Nazareth.' Judah greeted us as we moved through the square, his chest heaving with exertion. He was schooling a group of wide-eyed village men in the tricks of urban warfare: in particular, how to dispatch a Jewish traitor on a crowded city street without attracting notice. His unsheathed dagger glinted dangerously in the sun. Noting my attention, he hastily hid it behind his back.

The day was warm and Judah steamed with sweat, the muscles of his arms straining against the fabric of his robe. I swallowed hard. 'Peace be with you, Judah of Iscariot.'

'Peace be with you, Judah,' Joshua echoed, before moving discreetly aside and feigning interest in some distant happening in the grove.

'It is a beautiful morning, Rachael,' Judah continued. He

ventured a pace in my direction. 'Beautiful,' he repeated softly, his gaze lingering on my face.

My breath jammed in my throat, while the hammer in my breast plunged between my thighs and began beating there. I did not trust myself to speak.

'Off to market?' Judah said finally, nodding towards the empty basket on my arm. He was close enough for me to feel the warmth of his body, the heat and spice of his breath on my brow. Behind a sinew in his strong neck, a pulse winked. I tried again to speak but failed. I began to feel faint.

'Rachael?' he said softly.

'Yes!' I said, too loudly. Then again, quietly this time. 'Yes!'

By now, a crowd had formed. The waiting youths, whose eyes had never strayed from our tryst, stood smirking and lewdly scratching the front of their robes; labourers and women drifted in from the grove and well.

Joshua had no choice but to act. Acknowledging the growing assembly with a pleasant nod he farewelled his good friend. '*Shalom*, Judah,' he said, gripping my arm firmly and dragging me away. 'Upon you be peace.'

The next day at Bindy's, I acquitted myself poorly. My initiation was now less than two years away, and preparations had begun in earnest. Each Sabbath day Bindy insisted that I escape the restful quietude of my own home to prepare.

The morning would start with devotions to the Queen of Heaven. Then we would settle, steaming cups of tea to hand, facing each other across the mat. First, Bindy would review the week's deaths and infirmities: the loss of Leah, the winemaker's wife, to diseases of drink, the stillbirth of the ironmonger's wife, the failure of another salve to ease Daniel the tanner's rotted crotch. Then the questions would come thick and fast. What were the signs that announced the afflictions? Given the cure had failed, had it, or the diagnosis, been in error? What steps should now be taken to vanquish the condition and restore health?

Taking counsel from experience, common sense or the scrolls—the complete content of which I had long carried in my head—I would proffer answers, gauging my success by whether Bindy nodded or frowned. Then the crone would call on me to make up the potions we would need in the days ahead, her cane thumping behind me as I roved among the racks of bottled roots and powders in search of the required herbs. Shaking the right proportions into a bowl, I would hand it to her, to sniff and sift before judging it pass ('Correct, Rachael, correct') or fail ('No! Try again, Rachael').

But when I arrived that morning, having tripped my way along the path, lost in thoughts of Judah, Bindy was already bent in worship, her offering to the Heavenly Queen aloft on the altar. 'You're late!' she said, without lifting her brow from the packed-earth floor. She sat up on her heels and began the painful work of standing. 'No excuses!' she snapped when I parted my lips to speak. 'They reveal weakness,' she settled herself on the mat, 'and they never help anyway.' I hastened to pour the tea, which she accepted with a curt bob of the head.

Moments later, however, her discontent surfaced again. 'Hyssop for nose bleeds? It is a colic cure, Rachael! What ails you, girl?' She repeated the plaintive cry again and again as I stuttered and blinked through the lesson, failing to recognise ailments 'even an infant could spy'.

I begged her pardon profusely, and bowed my head in

shame, but a slip of a smile remained on my lips. *I am Judah's and he is mine. Soon, we shall know each other and be wed. He will smooth my hair and cup my chin, looking deeply into my eyes. His lips will find mine as his hands—*

'Rachael!' I was swaying as if in a breeze, the contents of my thoughts revealed in my heaving breast and dilated eyes. Bindy was aghast. She was not one for passion, not with men anyway. And marriage! She spat over her shoulder. 'Steals your health! Rots your talents!'

Her certainty grated. 'Bearing does, Bindy. Not love. Nor marriage.'

She rolled her sightless eyes. 'Same difference. You marry, you bear.'

'How astonishing that you, of all people, should say that! There are herbs—'

'—and draughts and potions. All of them forbidden to a woman wed,' she chided me with clicking tongue. 'You know as well as I the fate of barren women.'

I did. Set aside and left to beg outside the city gates if fortunate; if not, accused of infidelity and forced to drink poison to prove their innocence. Refusing marriage, as Bindy had done, was the only means for a woman to avoid children, but spinsters drew their own kinds of danger and strife.

I tossed my head. Such problems were for other women, they would not impede me. I would avoid or circumvent them... somehow.

My distraction and intransigence enraged Bindy. She railed at the walls like a jealous lover, then clutched at her belly, bent double with misery. '*Ay-ya-ya*,' she mourned, casting off her veil and tugging cruelly at her few remaining wisps.

I pitied her, but I would not agree; would not submit to the choice she said I must make. I would neither waste my talents nor relinquish my passion for Judah. I would be a wife and serve the Queen of Heaven, too. Somehow I would find a way.

'Bindy, stop!' Her keening hurt my ears. 'I am not lost to you, Bindy, I am here, right here! Don't cry. Don't despair!' But no matter how I pleaded and tugged at her sleeve, she refused to listen. Lurching towards the hearth, she clutched the breast of her robe as if she'd been stabbed. 'Stupid girl! Fool!' she ranted before falling about mourning again. 'What a waste! What a waste!'

I showed her my eyes, blazing with determination, but she refused to see. So I seized her hand; ran it around the determined thrust of my chin. 'Believe in me,' I whispered.

But how could she, when ever since Judah's arrival in the village I'd been as aimless as a moth? Dismayed by the morning's performance, she continued to doubt. Snatching her hand from mine, she limped to the door, opened it and ushered me out, her gaze downcast and heart hardened.

⁀

'Rachael!' The call through the window was whispered, as coarse and grainy as the moonless night.

I slid from my bed. It was him! He had said he would come; had whispered his intention when we passed in the square earlier that evening as I returned from Bindy's. Now he was here.

As I moved towards the window, Judah called my name again, more insistent this time. 'Rachael!'

I looked out, then down, and into my beloved's upturned face, its features lost to darkness, but for the crescent of his smile.

It was bright and broad and full of love. I gripped the ledge for balance.

'So?' he said.

'So what?' My unbound hair formed a curtain about my face. Behind me, Jacob snorted and murmured in his sleep.

'So, we'll go,' said Judah. 'I will take you.'

'Take me? Where? What are you speaking of, Judah?' I tried to sound vexed, but knew I had failed. Even his name on my tongue—*Judah!*—was like a celebration. I inclined towards him further, leaving only my toes on the ground: as close as I could get without falling at his feet.

'To see your sister, of course. To see Shona. This is what you wish? What you want, no?' My silence forced a note of uncertainty into his voice.

I was overcome with emotion. Here was a man who not only knew the yearning of my heart, but strove to satisfy it. I felt I might explode with gratitude, and passion.

'Rachael?'

'Yes. Yes! Yes!'

I heard rather than saw his little smile, his shrug. 'So, we'll go. I'll make the arrangements and tell Joshua. He will let you know the plan.'

'But how can we? How can we go together? We're not even free to speak in the square,' I said plaintively. 'They will never permit you to escort me to Cana. Never allow—'

He smiled again, a spreading stain of brightness against the dark. 'Because you want it, Rachael. And I shall make it so.'

Judah worked quickly. By the time I arrived at the shop the following afternoon, a deal had been done between the three men, Papa, Joshua and Judah. As I cleared the workbench of dust after my lesson and reached into the basket to begin setting out the meals, its terms were explained.

'We shall leave on the morrow. All four of us: you, me, Judah and Joshua,' Papa said. He was putting the finishing touches to a Greek-style chest ordered by a wealthy Jew from Sepphoris, and did not look up from his labours. It was an intricately carved piece, with lions on all sides and gemstones rimming the lid. 'Where the path divides, you three shall turn off for Cana while I continue to the city to deliver this piece. At day's end, well before dusk, we shall reconvene at the same spot, returning to Nazareth together. 'Do you understand, Rachael?' he asked.

I did. Not just the words spoken, but also what remained unsaid. Papa approved of my attempt to see Shona, and would allow Judah to take me there as long my brother was on hand to guard my modesty. Mama was not to learn of Papa's dispensation. She must believe he was taking me to Sepphoris, a journey of which she would disapprove in any event.

'Sepphoris is a town of great splendour, the ornament of Galilee,' Papa stated forcefully, as if making his case to Mama. 'The colonnaded streets and new amphitheatre built by the king are wonders all Galilean Jews should see. A woman, in partic-ular, before she is wed and unable to—'

I shook my head, as if to clear it, unsure I had heard him correctly. 'Wed?' I ran towards him, my hands clasped to my breast. 'Did you just say that Judah and I have your blessing to marry?'

My father shrugged in the way he had of implying that such a thing had always been known.

'But why, Papa? What led you to change your mind?'

In reply, my father ran his hand through his grey wisps, taking time to formulate his answer. 'Because everyone wishes to try their hand at love, Rachael,' he said at last. 'Why should you be any different?'

I turned to my brother, astonished at such unfamiliar sentiments. Joshua was working a file over a rough piece of board. He winked and laid the tool down, then turned to my father with one more question. 'But what about the potter, Papa?'

I stared at my father hungrily, as curious as my brother about the answer. Papa's preference for the potter had never been a secret. Just the other night at the dinner mat, he had sung the man's praises. Yet here he was risking Mama's wrath and the whole family's reputation to allow Judah and me to be together.

Papa gave a long sigh. 'I was awake last night,' he finally admitted, 'when Judah came to the window.' He swiped a rag with bee's wax and began polishing. 'I heard the way he spoke to you, Rachael.' A pause as he worked a corner of the lid to a shine. 'Judah loves you, Rachael. He loves my daughter. A man can't thank another man enough for that.'

☙

We left at first light the following morning in a hail of Mama's complaints. The well! The kindling! From two daughters to none in the blink of an eye, and this being washing day! And what of Papa, who was no spring hen? He should not be straying from the village, he should send Joshua to Sepphoris, with Iscariot's son if need be, while he took his rest.

But once out on the trail, the outlook cleared. At the fork in the road to Cana, Papa made his farewells, embracing each of us in turn, but leaving Joshua for last. 'Tell Shona she is in our hearts,' he told my eldest brother. 'That we mourn and pray for her daily. Return Rachael to me as I have vouchsafed her to you: her virtue intact. On this her future depends.' The reference to the brutal cause of Shona's lost promise could not have been clearer. Papa smoothed my brother's hair aside to bless his brow with a kiss, 'I am counting on you, son,' he said, before setting off in the direction of the city, while the three of us turned towards Cana.

Judah and I walked and talked, while my brother trailed behind at a discreet distance. We walked and talked and battled.

We did not begin by rowing, of course. In those first tightly strung moments, freed at last from the shackles of supervision. I found it hard even to meet his gaze. In reply to my shyness, Judah's eyes trailed me like I was royalty; or so fragile, perhaps, that I might break. It was spring, and the climate was a cradle, the outside air a perfect match for the heat in our blood. The trail was a narrow bridal walk, strewn with the season's flowers: cyclamen of every shade and explosions of white hyacinth. Strangers trudged past from the opposite direction, Assyrians and Phoenicians, their eyes downcast, backs and beasts burdened with sacramental wares for the Temple market in Jerusalem. We neither greeted them nor spoke to each other. So long did the stilted silence between us prevail that the skin beneath my arms and woven belt began weeping with uneasy sweat.

Finally Judah cleared his throat. 'Rachael,' he began, his voice cracking. I turned as if admiring a rolling hill of wild-flowers to hide my smile. He was nervous, too.

Shyly at first, but then with increasing boldness, he began speaking of our future. The joy and comfort we would give each other, the bounty and pride the union would offer our families, all he would promise to win my hand: golden bracelets and silver rings, countless pots to clutter my hearth. Now in stride, he began to wax lyrical about my beauty: the strong rounds of my calves, my berry-stained lips, the perfume and glory of my tresses.

At that, my hands rose to my hair, sun-warmed and largely visible beneath my badly tied veil. 'Now I know you are jesting,' I said coyly. 'I have never had pretty hair.'

'Pretty?' he showed me his eyes, flexed wide with surprise. 'Pretty is for primping, simpering women. Women like Sarai, whose wealth allows the extravagances required for such praise.' His disdain for my rival made me smile. 'You are a woman of substance, with glorious tresses to match. Thick and abundant and the rich dark colour of fertile earth—'

'—and tangled and far too wayward with curls, especially when the damp sets in—'

'Too wayward? *Too* many curls?' Judah gave a showman's gasp, a passionate hand pressed to his heart. 'I have never heard of such a thing, nor knew it existed.' He patted the mayhem of his own springy tresses. 'Do you not favour curls, Rachael?'

'Well...no,' I stuttered, stumbling to retract. 'Not mine I don't. But yours are far more ornamental and defined in their descent. And the shade is far prettier—'

Judah let out a laugh, then stopped. Tenderly, he reached

out his hand, his fingers brushing my face. 'Ah, Rachael,' he whispered. 'My soul, my heart, my eyes.' And there we stayed, swaying towards one another, doe-eyed, mawkish and lost to the world until Joshua caught up. '*Yallah*,' he said gently, herding us forward like sheep, before falling back to grant us solitude again.

Judah continued. 'Once the marital bargain is sealed, we shall be free to lie together behind the tapestry that marks off my bed-place. It is small space, but big enough for us. You would know, from the weeks you spent at my father's sickbed, how kind my mother is, Rachael. She has promised already that you shall not be made to rise from your bed while unclean from bearing. She says she will take a servant to aid her by the hearth instead, while you recline like a queen for the full allotment of days the good Lord grants you. When—'

My pleasure in his words evaporated. Bearing was a subject I had no wish to entertain, even if talk of the delights behind the tapestry door that would precede it made my breath come fast. In my mind's eye, I saw my sister shuffling at Boaz's hearth. His violence had made her fate but it was her swollen belly that sealed it. I remembered Bindy's pursed-lips and shaking head: *Marriage! Steals your health. Rots your talents.*

Suddenly, I wanted to scream and sob and rage; to grab Judah and fall to the ground with legs spread and hips thrusting; to knee him in the groin and flee from him as fast as I could. The conflicting impulses, their brutal and forbidden nature, confounded me.

I picked a fight. 'Why is it,' I asked, cutting across Judah's lovesick cant, 'that a female infant renders the mother more unclean than a male?'

'What?'

'Forty days confinement if the child is a boy, twice this time for a girl,' I said, rattling off the well-known rule.

The peremptory challenge had taken Judah by surprise but he was an insurgent, with an insurgent's quick wit, and was not wrong-footed for long. 'I have no idea, Rachael.' He scratched his angular jaw before trying for something better. 'Because it is the Law and the Law is what we live by. *Nachon*?'

What a woefully feeble reply. Ill-tempered and mulish, I pressed Judah for a more compelling answer and refused to be drawn on other matters until, at last, he abandoned hope of distracting me and returned to the question. Hemming and hawing, he cast furtive glances behind him, in hope of rescue by Joshua.

He was disappointed, for my brother had left the trail and was relieving himself, with some urgency by the sounds of it, against a skeletal carob tree.

'The cause for difference,' Judah ventured hesitantly, 'could be the labours. The distinct way that women labour when bearing a boy as against a girl. And the difference in the burden of guilt they acquire.'

'What?' Distinct labours? Different guilt? Since my own flowering I had attended dozens of births. My preparation for initiation had required I listen to Bindy describe hundreds more. Not once had I even heard it suggested that an infant's sex deter-mined the severity of the trial faced by the mother. 'Whatever are you talking about, Judah?'

But Judah mistook my confusion for a confession of ignorance and a request for enlightenment. Relieved to have been restored to his accustomed role of authority, he set forth confidently to explain. 'Everyone knows, Rachael, that in her hour of suffering, the mother is desperate and swears she will not live in intimacy with her husband again. If a boy is born, she repents this vow sooner because he occasions such rejoicing. But with a girl, all is gloom. Many women feel their failure keenly, so the mother's return to her husband's arms is delayed.'

It was the silliest thing I had ever heard. And from a man! A man who knew nothing of monthly cycles and giving birth, yet had no hesitation in describing—explaining!—the features of that experience as if they were his own. A man, like the Great God Almighty, who had no right to say!

The blasphemy sprung into my head full-blown, like Chavah's body from Adam's rib. Like something I had always known was true, just never stated. Judah, having seen his misstep in the blaze of my eyes, took a step backwards and swallowed audibly, a stone of discomfort moving between the cords of his throat.

Then my brother was there. He looked back and forth between us, his features brushed with mirth. 'A spat? Already?'

In the face of my fury Judah was a study in dismay. 'There—we—disagreement about labour—' he stuttered.

'Labour?' My brother looked back and forth between our faces, sizing the situation.

'Yes, labour,' I said through gritted teeth. 'The life-threatening work undertaken by women to give men heirs.'

Joshua had heard enough. Throwing his arm across his old friend's shoulders, he dragged Judah away 'You are mad to argue with her about this, brother,' I heard him advise his old friend confidentially. 'Mad. Birth is women's business and Rachael would know more about it than a thousand men joined together.'

By the time we reached Cana, harmony had been restored. Judah had Joshua and me hiccupping with laughter about a scrape he had got into the previous spring involving a Roman soldier, his white stallion and a bucket of cochineal worms, used by Israelite women to dye thread crimson.

The laughter sobered and the atmosphere tautened as we rounded the last bend and trudged towards the gates of the town. But when we drew close the three of us were struck still. We stood gaping with open mouths. In place of the locked doors and feral swarms of kin and clan that had greeted previous attempts to visit my sister, the gates were wide open and unguarded. Even the crumbling watchtower perched atop the cobbled village wall was empty.

Judah had fallen silent as we'd broached the village, drawing his dagger and adopting a prowler's stance; now he seemed almost disappointed. But he did not falter. Seizing the moment, he moved quickly across the village threshold and, having surveyed the surrounds to left and right, waved us through. He set off at a pace, Joshua and I hurrying behind him: down a deserted path and across an empty square, similar in size to that of Nazareth, heading in the direction of Boaz's house.

Where was everyone? Cana slept in a notch of rolling hills, overlooked by a scatter of elders' homes perched on the ridge. Goats grazed on the slope, dining on crocuses and virescent, low-lying shrubs, but there was no sign of human life.

As we crossed the village, however, I realised I could hear voices somewhere to the east. Faint shouts, bossy exclamations and the purr and murmur of a milling crowd rose from a distant cluster of limestone dwellings. Such sounds were familiar enough to anyone who had grown to adulthood in a small town: the sounds of an entire village drawn to a happening even slightly out of the ordinary—in this case, we would learn later, the failed birth of a calf. The wretched creature had become wedged in the birth tunnel and ceased breathing. To salvage the cow, on whose milk several families depended, a hook with a rope had been inserted so the village men might tug to remove the corpse.

Shona! Judah marched to her dwelling—Boaz's dwelling—without hesitation, recalling its location from the visit years earlier when he had arrived at her door with my father and brother, only to be ejected. This time, my beloved rapped on the door and I waited, heart skittering in my chest. Movement could be heard within; then, one by one, various bolts and latches were undone. The door swung wide and there, facing us, was my sister.

She was much as I remembered her: her tawny skin and animal grace; her tiny frame made to seem even smaller by an apron tied twice around her and knotted at the front; the cloud of pleasant spice that always surrounded her. But as she stood in the shadows of the cave-like dwelling that was her home, the mouth of the open door breathing dampness and ancient cooking smells, I saw differences, too: a dryness of skin as if the succulence of life was slowly being leached from her; a flintiness about the eyes and mouth. As she turned, her unbelieving gaze traversing all our faces, I saw a sleeping infant tethered to her back. 'Rachael?' my sister said, incredulous. 'Joshua?'

I could wait no longer. Elbowing the men aside, I raced into her arms.

This was an embrace I wished to savour forever. I longed to collapse at my sister's feet and clasp her knees and weep while she comforted me. I yearned for her to take me indoors and offer me tea while I made memory of each square of the room: here was where she kneaded bread, this was where she slept. I wanted to gush about every detail of my courtship with Judah and to unswaddle her babe—a girl called Chaloum—while we both looked on, clucking and cooing. But such small pleasures were impossible: taunting shadows of a life that never was and never would be Shona's.

Having kissed my head and caressed my face lovingly, Shona pushed me away. Her face was etched with fear. She stuck her head out the door and glanced up and down the lane, sucking on the plum of one cheek, wizening it. My sister had not been a girl since the day Boaz had violated her; but nor did she seem the shattered, shame-filled woman my brother had described after his one brief visit to Cana. It was clear as she clucked and frowned, trying to fashion a plan, that she had become someone else.

Shona made her decision. Disappearing indoors, she returned in a trice with a bulging cloth bag on her shoulder. She stepped into the light, revealing one eye black and swollen, and turned to pull the door shut behind her. '*Yallah!*' she said, grabbing my hand and moving down the path in the direction of the town gate. 'Follow me.'

He was an old man in a scruffy, embroidered robe. He had a white beard and, it immediately became clear, a pressing need to relieve himself. Shona helped him to his feet with an ease that implied experience and together they lumbered towards the tall grass, he leaning heavily upon her, she listening with head cocked to the stream of unintelligible chatter pouring from his lips.

The three of us stared after them, swallowing our astonishment. A man who dwelt out on the plains like a den animal, living in a shallow hole with a woven roof on tent poles overhead, was one thing. That he seemed to be in my sister's tender charge was quite another, for this man was an alien and impure. As his robes made clear, he was not a Jew at all, but a Samaritan.

The Samaritans were a people who thought themselves Jews. They claimed to be descendants of the lost tribes of Ephraim and Manasseh: tribes that had escaped Israel's exile to Babylon centuries ago. The Temple priests, whose ancestors had been deported, saw it differently. They said Samaritans were foreigners: colonisers brought by the conquerors to thieve Jewish land. When Persia overran Babylon and we Jews returned home, our priests sought to rebuild the Temple but would not accept help from the Samaritans. Insulted, the Samaritans turned their backs. The ancestors of the high priests did the same and five hundred years later, the hatred between our two peoples still simmered.

The old man, had he ever been a thief or a coloniser, was long past this now. Now, he was an invalid in clear need of help. Still leaning on Shona, he returned to his makeshift camp, breaking off his insensible prattle momentarily to meet our startled eyes and display his gums in a smile. When Joshua stepped forward to assist Shona, the Samaritan beamed again and mimed a blessing. The authority with which he described this gesture—one strictly reserved for priests—stilled Judah's half-formed protest against my brother's certain defilement by the old man's touch.

'What is your name, brother?' Joshua asked the old man,

helping him to ease his frail frame back into his lair. The ancient flashed his gums again, but gave no answer, as if the question had been put in a foreign language.

'I call him Benny,' Shona said as she drew a pot of porridge from her bag. 'His full name is Benyamin bar Honi. He hails from a small village midway between ancient Shechem and the foot of Mount Gerizim.'

Shechem, where Jacob the patriarch's daughter Dina was defiled; Mount Gerizim where the Assyrians massacred the ten lost tribes. Both names rolled off Shona's tongue with ease, despite being places of Israelite torture and disgrace. I saw Judah's hackles rise but she took no notice. With the brisk manner of an experienced mother, she prised the pot open and began spooning its contents through Benny's lips. There was silence, punctuated only by the rattling songs of an unseen nest of warblers.

When the meal was through, Shona pulled Benny's robe from his back and used it to swab his face and beard. She was smiling. 'It's good to see you eat,' she told him. She stowed the soiled garment in her bag, withdrew a fresh one and manoeuvred it over the old man's head. By now the infant, who had been asleep in its sling the whole time, was awake and fussing. Shona untethered the child, sat herself on the ground and, adjusting her cloak for modesty, offered the child her breast. Throughout she chattered to Benny, relating news from the village, including that of the unfortunate cow, and her own joy at receiving an unexpected visit from her kin and clan from Nazareth.

'Hef yoothee tof,' Benny exclaimed, beaming at us three strangers like we were freshly baked cakes. His open gaze lingered on my face. Embarrassed, I turned to Shona, not certain how to respond.

'No,' Shona told him, her loving smile caressing my face. 'She is far lovelier than I. She is in love.'

Eventually, having fed from both breasts, the infant returned to slumber. My sister stood and adjusted her robes, making clear it was time to leave. But before we did, Shona gave over the child to my uncertain arms, then knelt and bowed her head before Benny to receive his blessing. The words of the prayer he canted were unintelligible, but the tune of the psalm, one that the elders used each week on the Sabbath to bless the men, was as familiar as my mother's hand:

May the Lord bless you,
and keep you.
May His face shine on you,
and be gracious to you.
May the Lord lift up His countenance to you,
and grant you peace.

As we made our way back to the village, the afternoon sun warm on our backs, my sister seemed loose and free: momentarily relieved of her burdens. Baby Chaloum was still in my arms and Joshua toted the bag full of the old man's linens. Having passed the visit with Benny in stunned silence, I was now quick to catechise my sister. Who was the man? How had Shona come to know him? Why was she nursing him in his final days; did he not have his own kin and clan? Did Boaz know of this and if not, what might befall her should he find out?

The barrage of questions made Shona laugh. She drew me towards her in a hug. 'It is a joy to see you Rachael, and to see you unaltered. She's a gem, my sister. An uncut diamond,' she threw her words in Judah's direction. 'See that she is treasured!'

Her praise pumped heat to my face. 'Sister, keep still!'

'Why? Why should I?' Shona gestured at the shrub-strewn plains to left and right of the narrow track, vacant but for grazing goats and, at the base of a myrtle bush, a social cluster of conies. 'No one is near. Why should I not boast of my sister's successes to the two men in Israel who might care to listen? Of her ability to read and spell and—' At my staggered expression, Shona laughed again and gestured towards my brother. 'What did you think we were talking about on the way to Benny's? Mama's new broom collection?'

I cringed, awash with pleasure at my sister's pride, and with guilt. Would such masteries seem indulgent, cruel even, in light of Shona's plight?

But my sister, comprehending my worry, quickly waved it past. 'I am well, Rachael,' she took my hand and squeezed it. 'Very well, truly. Let me tell you why.'

She began to speak of Benny, who had been a man of wealth and station before the Samaritans cast him adrift the previous Passover. 'He is an elder, Rachael, a Samaritan elder. Or was, though what he did to be shunned by his people he will not say. I found him two months after he'd been thrown from his village. Wandering without direction, drifting east, disgraced and alone, he was begging scraps, meeting with violence and growing weaker and more forlorn by the day. Then he collapsed and would have died, had I not found him there,' she gestured to the west, 'and taken pity. The birds were already circling overhead.'

'You should have left him,' Judah said bluntly. He was whittling a branch he'd picked from the ground with aggressive cuts of his knife. 'He is not your kin, not your kind, and he is an enemy of the Jews. We have troubles enough—you have troubles enough—without helping yourself to theirs.' It was an uncharitable thought, but one with which I found myself reluctantly agreeing. Surely, Shona had enough problems of her own.

But Shona disagreed. She stopped short and turned to face Judah, boldly standing her ground. 'I am more of a stranger to elders of my own tribe than I am to Benny; and he is less strange to me. We are both outcasts: those who know well what it is to suffer while our betters look away. I helped Benny because he needed my help,' she told Judah stoutly, 'and because I could.' She turned to Joshua and me then and added, almost as an afterthought. 'It was a clever choice, too, as it turns out. Benyamin bar Honi is a wealthy man. There is gold buried in the hills surrounding his Samaritan home that he never had time to dig free. He has told me where it lies, and that when he dies wealth will be mine.'

My sister squinted into the diving sun and pointed at two distant figures, picking their way across the hills. 'That is Boaz and Jemina, making their way home. She turned to me. 'Your other young niece, Aunt Rachael.'

It was time for farewells. As Shona revealed matter-of-factly, sending a shiver up my spine, she did not like leaving Boaz alone with the girl in the house. Nodding at Judah, my sister threw her arms passionately around my brother. Then she came to me. Gently she lifted the sleeping infant from the crook of my arm and, clasping the baby to her breast, pulled me close and awkwardly cradled me there, too.

Then she disappeared, hurrying down the path under the watchful eye of the sentry and through the gate before disappearing from view. I watched her go, swaying and moaning in the ancient way of women, buffeted by unspeakable grief. I collapsed in sobs to the ground and neither Joshua nor Judah could comfort me.

I wept for a long time. Only when I could mourn no more did Judah whisper to me softly and haul me to my feet. He spat on a cloth dug from his belt and scrubbed the tears from my face. Then, limping and sniffling, I leaned on both men and we turned towards home.

The dream came—or rather, I sought the dream—months later. After I had shivered and moaned through the midnight of my loss, and allowed my tears to fall to the sacred earth from where such prophecies come.

It was a hot night in Elul; I had arrived at the cavern of firs, a secret ritual site known only to women, in search of a sign. I came with my sleeping mat, a blanket, Bindy's advice, Olivia's blessing and cassia bark, which I scattered about the woodland cave to infuse it with Shona's scent. I had been fasting for days. Falling to my knees I keened and mumbled devotions to the Heavenly Queen into the early hours of morning. When I could no longer keep my eyes open, I fell to my mat and pulled the cover over me, praying to summon in dream form the shape of my sister's fate.

A woman nurses her infant. Moving closer, I see it is Shona. I know this, though a veil obscures her face. I move closer, calling to her, wanting her to see me, wanting to help. But the closer I come, the louder I call, the more insistent the hand I extend, the deeper my sister retreats into the folds of her veil.

I see Shona's child. But the face of the infant is not that of Chaloum, but of Shona herself. My adult sister is cradling, tending, comforting herself. So absorbed is Shona in this task that, without realising it, she is emerging from her veil. The tip of her nose and eyelashes appear first, followed by the familiar rounds of her cheeks. She is crooning a lullaby, something about a rat that gets trapped in a well.

The sky opens, but instead of rain, it is gold and silver coins that fall from the heavens. They collect in bowls at my sister's feet. The babe in her arms sheds its swaddling and sprouts wings. These she flaps, tentatively at first, then more strongly, before flying off without a backward glance. The elder Shona waves her child goodbye. She is unclothed now, her tunic, cloak and veil discarded on the ground, the mantle of scabs and bruises on her skin an accusation in the unflinching light, until my sister turns to a pillar of salt and collapses to dust on the ground.

I woke to darkness. Insects covered my blanket and crawled across my face. I was alone. Yet, within my breast surged lightness and hope. The revelation before my eyes was still vivid, and had the solid feel of truth. Shona would escape. She would find her way to Benny's fortune and use it to flee Boaz's home with her daughters. Her love for her girls had already tempered her passive form into something far more resolute; soon it would spur her to action. Because whatever cruelty my sister might accept for herself, she would not allow Boaz to inflict it on them.

So when the news arrived, weeks later, I was pleased but not surprised. *Yes, remember her? Yosef and Miriame's girl? Vanished one night, with her little ones. Neither hide nor hair of her seen since. The man, what was his name again?—ah yes, Boaz—has sworn his vengeance should he ever catch up with her. Though some say that she is surely*…and the gossips would hush their voices to make their grisly speculations.

It kept them occupied, but I knew better; or thought I did. Years later, I would come to question whether I truly knew anything at all about my sister's fate beyond two certain facts. That it seemed a lifetime since I had seen her last, and would feel that long until we met again. And that during that time I missed her every day, as indeed I miss her still.

The elders finally declared Simeon of Iscariot fully recovered and Papa approached him to discuss my bride price. For more than a month, the two men bartered in secret. Then, one afternoon, Papa returned for lunch to say that a deal had been done. 'It is settled, Miriame,' he said, signalling me to bring water. 'Simeon of Iscariot has agreed.'

Mama was not surprised. Just disappointed, although in a way that seemed to speak more of habit than circumstances. Having muttered something about the lowborn soiling our name, she turned to more vital matters. 'At least he can pay. What did you get?'

'The final sum has not been agreed. Yet. We shall continue our talks on the way south to Jerusalem for Tabernacles. But it will be enough, Miriame,' his tone a warning as she opened her mouth to complain. 'Enough.' He eased himself to the eating mat, the furrows in his face so grey they seemed to be lined with dust. 'Small wonder Iscariot is rich,' he muttered. 'He steers a steep bargain.'

He waited until the angry slam of crocks and pots had settled back before clearing his throat to speak again. 'About the approaching feast, Miriame. Tabernacles.'

Standing by the hearth Mama turned, hands on hips, waiting. 'Yes?'

Papa swallowed. 'This year, Rachael will join her brothers and me in Jerusalem.'

I was stunned. The look on Mama's face made clear she was too. 'Jerusalem? Why?' Wordlessly she indicated the household chores awaiting my attention: the barrel of olives for pickling, the woven basket heaped high with mending, the oil to be beaten for the lamps. We were barely keeping ahead of the housework together. How would she manage alone?

But Papa's jaw was set. 'Why?' he answered in a cantankerous tone. 'Because she has never had the chance to move from this village and meet the Lord at His Temple, an honour that all Israelites deserve.' He was listing on his fingers, well-armed for this fight. 'Because if she fails to go now, the chance will be lost. She will marry, grow ripe with child and,' he shrugged, 'that will be that.'

Mama continued to stare at him, plainly unconvinced.

Papa shook his hands at the rafters with exasperation. He moved towards the door but before he left he turned to add this: 'Because she is my daughter, Miriame,' he said, his voice low but resolute. 'And I say it shall be so.'

I had packed for Jerusalem many times before, equipping Papa and my brothers for the three-day journey by scouring their travel bags for unclean food and animal skins that were forbidden entry to the Temple, then filling them with clean robes and food. I would wipe the men's goatskins, then fill them at the well.

But now, with my own bag to prepare, I was racked with joyful indecision. What blanket to take: blue or grey? Should I pack the bedding first, or wrap it about the food to preserve freshness? Would Papa buy me a goatskin, or need I share with my brother? I must have been humming to myself as I laboured because Mama looked up from her weaving to remark on it.

'Bound for adventure, Rachael?' she said. Her eyebrow was cocked and a small, stiff smile shaped her lips.

'Yes, Mama.' The snake-whisper of the shuttle through the warp filled the room as she continued to work. I crept towards her, like a deer sensing footfalls in the forest, needing to see her face. What did she want from me?

But she waved me back to my task. These words were difficult to birth, and she had no wish to have her labour observed. 'I wanted to say—to tell you—' She broke off and fussed with her veil before trying again. 'I thought to say that—' But it was no good. However hard she tried, the words would not come. The pride in her throat could not be swallowed.

Instead, she dug in her belt and, beckoning me towards her, placed an object in my palm. It was a scapegoat, a small cloth replica of the sacrifice animal the elders released to the wild each year, burdened with our people's transgressions and carrying our hopes for forgiveness.

I stared at the small figure in my palm, unsure what to say or even how to look. She wanted something from me. Perhaps even wished me to forgive her something, but I did not know what. I had no idea what to do next: what gestures to make to avoid misstep; which words to speak to avoid giving offence. It seemed I had waited my whole life for this moment—for Mama to admit guilt and plead for pardon—but now that it was upon me, I wanted only for it to end. Through the window, two crones could be heard comparing pains and eagerly anticipating the Sabbath. A runaway toddler squealed devilishly and squirrels bickered as they leapt from branch to branch in the chestnut tree.

My confusion seemed only to provoke her. Mouth and brow pinched, she huffily withdrew and returned to her task. 'Perhaps one day all will come clear to you, Rachael,' she said, mouth pressed in a line. 'When you are not just a daughter, but a mother, too. Water jar's empty,' she continued, dismissing me with a wave of her hand. I stuffed the scapegoat into my belt.

'And bid that witch farewell!' she called after me as I crossed the terrace towards the steps. 'I want you within the gates before sunset.'

To visit the Holy City! To set one's own feet inside the Temple that King Herod built, and let one's gaze ascend the majestic colonnades to the portico made of gold! Like me, Bindy had heard of Jerusalem's grandeur and like me, she was thrilled that I would see such wonders for myself. She also assumed that the journey would take me far from Judah, who she wrongly believed would not be joining us, but returning to Gamla before the pilgrimage commenced. I did not correct her. Since my return from Cana, relations between us had recovered themselves. I was more attentive to my lessons and we spoke often of my initiation, though not at all of my impending marriage.

'The Temple of the Israelites is the grandest in all the Lands, Rachael. From Egypt to the Aegean Sea,' Bindy told me, limping from the room to make tea. The house was dark and airless. Window covers were dropped so the leafy branches and freshly-harvested roots hanging from the rafters could dry. 'They say it took more than one thousand masons and wood-workers to hew the stones and carve the Temple altars!' she exulted from the heart.

'Have you not seen the Temple, Bindy?'

Gripping the steaming pot with a rag as she entered the room, the old woman scowled. 'With these eyes? Already I was old when the plans were drawn. And I was not blessed with a papa like yours: a man who knows the hunger of your heart and travels lengths to feed it.'

Taking the pot from her hands and setting it carefully on the mat, I helped ease the crone to sitting. 'But why are women not obliged to present at the Temple three times a year in the manner required of men?' I asked. 'Why are they free to either make the journey or to remain at home?'

'Because "Thou Shalts" are not for children!' she shouted abruptly, in the commanding voice of a father. 'Light the candles! Bake the bread! Stay clear of men when you have blood! But do not think the Lord will bless you, girl!' Her voice thundered and finger wagged. 'Only men are sanctified by God!'

Wiping her hands of dust, Bindy reached for the pot. 'Tea?' she inquired. I nodded meekly.

It was unusual for Bindy to pull back the curtain of her childhood and offer insight into the events that had made her as she was, but as quickly as the storm had stirred, it subsided. She began to speak of the roots and blossoms of the south for which I must keep watch, and gather for her should I spy them. 'Balsam gum, camphor and rock aloe,' she listed on her fingers. 'Oh, and locust pods!' her eyes misted as if beholding a lover. 'Nothing better for red and raw throat. When you return I shall teach you a cure of my own invention better than all others known,' her pride was unmistakable. 'Should the priestess call for it at your initiation, and you brew it correctly, she will gasp with awe and pass you through at once.'

At the mention of my trial, my belly clenched. I must conquer this test. I must make Bindy proud.

'Ach,' Bindy cried, having sensed rather than observed the furrowing of my face, 'not today, Rachael! Today is a day for rejoicing! Go! Pack your things! Have your adventure. Return to me with all I've asked for, and a heart and mind ready for work.' I rose uncertainly, wanting to kneel and kiss her withered hand before I left. But she lifted the cup to her lips with one arm and waved me off with the other. I was dismissed.

I was awake before first light the next day. I sat on my mat and waited for the first streaks of light, intimations really, to colour the sky. Lips moving soundlessly, I spoke to my lost sister about my excitement, my hopes for the coming adventure. I described the lightning that seemed to crackle and race beneath my skin; the towns and buildings and oddly dressed people I had heard others describe in detail so often, but would now finally get to see for myself.

'I wish you could come with me, Shona,' I told her silently. 'I hope you are safe.' Touching my head and breast in a gesture of reverence to the Queen of Heaven, I rose to light the hearth for the morning meal.

A short time later I was standing on the rim of my world, just outside the town gates of Nazareth at the summit of the steep, rocky path that descended to the plains. The crowd of pilgrims shivered as one with excitement. To the rhythm of tambourines borne by ululating village women, the elders were being helped on to their mules by servants. One even knelt beneath the skittering hooves so that Sirach the Ancient could use his back as a footstool.

Judah watched this scene with disgust from his place at the front of the assemblage. I caught sight of him—belt dripping with weapons, hair barely restrained with a loose tie—from my place with the other women at the rear, and tried to catch his eye. But he didn't see me. Fretful and impatient, he smacked fist into palm and pointed at the sun, his meaning clear. Already the procession was delayed by last-minute offerings deemed essential for our safe passage, and the varied physical requirements of so many doddering and infirm elders. As one of the young men charged with defending us, Judah thought we should make haste, to use the remaining daylight for travel. If we were caught afoot at dusk, the chance of mishap or ambush was greater.

Right before the caravan shifted, shuddered like a boat leaving its moorings and began moving towards the south, I lifted my eyes to the heavens and offered up thanks. For it was in this moment that I knew that the open space in my breast radiating through my limbs was peace. The rope-burn of anger, the louse-itch of discontent was gone. Bindy's apprentice, my brother's student, Judah's betrothed: my portion was rich, my cup overflowing, and I was fat and full with life.

At every turn, Judah was recruiting. As the pilgrimage shuffled south, the fertile rocky hills of the Galilee giving way to the sparse, dry flatlands of the south, my beloved leavened his task of guarding us against rogues and robbers by haranguing the young men to join the war.

By noon of that first day, his show of deference to the mule-bound elders had worn thin. He danced and ducked between the legs of their beasts, coaxing and cavorting the men to rebel and take up arms against Rome. Judah's hunger for revolution was like a lust, his hands endlessly scolding the air as he stoked the men's fire for war. 'Ravaged! Misused! All that was given to us by God stolen by Rome! Our land. Our crops. Our hard-earned coins!'

'Our women,' grumbled another, as an Israelite woman passed our cavalcade from the opposite direction, her head uncovered and robe draped in the more revealing fashion of the Greeks.

Judah's blunt fingers poked the chests of the men encircling him, his face a mask of scorn. 'Their idols sully our land. Their handpicked Jewish king, the puppet Herod,' he spat, 'reclines on the throne, the throne God gave to David's heirs. When will we stand tall and say no? No to occupation and the insult of our faith. No to the desecration of our land. When will we defend the promise that Abraham made to God?'

'No Lord but God!' A voice from the crowd.

'Yes! No Lord but God,' Judah scanned the faces and found its owner, a gangly youth with down on his upper lip. 'That we

Israelites will accept no Lord but God.' His let his gaze remain on the youth, clearly grasping for a name.

'Baruch,' the young man offered helpfully. 'The weaver's son.'

'Baruch,' Judah affirmed. He beckoned Baruch towards him, enfolding him in a bear's embrace. 'Do you want freedom, Baruch?'

'Yes!'

'Justice?'

'Yes!'

'Will you come to Gamla to fight for it? Join the zealots and take up your spear for God?'

'Yes! Yes!'

'Good man.' With the youth still tucked beneath his arm, Judah addressed the others with scorn. 'If someone like Baruch, barely quit of boyhood,' Judah broke off. 'How old are you, Baruch?'

'Ten and four years.'

'Fourteen years only,' Judah lingered on this fact, before turning back to the men. 'If Baruch can pledge his life for God, right here and now, then what ails you? What a-ails you, O bra-a-ve men of Galilee?' He drew the words out, taunting them. 'How long shall we be slaves in our own land? How long shall you damn the empire, whining like old women, yet do nothing to make yourselves free?'

Joshua listened quietly. His eyes were bright and his gaze respectful as they traced the pitch and roll of Judah's restless form, the peaks and troughs of his relentless rhetoric. But he would not be persuaded. My brother's loyalty to his friend was born of shared history, but their attraction was that of opposites: Judah's brawn to Joshua's litheness; Judah's untrammelled enthusiasms to my brother's considered faith; Judah's boundless vigour to Joshua's reserve.

And behind the fond amusement, my brother was distracted. He had his own passion, his own sacred path, and she was waiting for him back in Nazareth. Digging into a dank cave in the hills of northern Galilee, emerging only for periodic harrying raids to challenge Rome's iron grip on power in a campaign certain to last for years, was the furthest thing from his mind.

I strained for every word of Judah's entreaties, and the shouts and disputes among the men that mushroomed in the interstices between them, but caught only snippets. The elders and their well-fed beasts—strategically positioned between the younger men and the mute scatter of women bringing up the rear—absorbed sound like overstuffed pillows.

'Can't afford one? Can't afford a bullock for sacrifice at the Temple?' cried one elder in querulous tones. 'He might have considered this before trespassing against God.' The elder was aggrieved, perhaps as much at the coinless sinner as at Judah who, despite having been commanded several times to fall still, continued to agitate among the men.

'A face like a horse? Yes, I suppose this is true,' another voice said a short time later. Daniel the tanner, perhaps? 'But she's as willing as a sheep's arse!' The other men brayed with laughter. I glimpsed my father flush and turn away.

Then Papa's voice, at a time later again. 'Yonaton the Baptiser, now there's a righteous man. Sanctifying souls in the desert by the mouth of the salty sea.' He sounded unlike himself; breathless, I thought. I peered through beasts and baskets to catch sight of him. His colour seemed odd, papyrus-pale with two flushed smears high on each cheek. But whatever the costs of forcing his older bones to keep pace with the procession, Papa seemed determined to be heard.

At the Baptiser's name, the elders recoiled as if slapped. 'Blasphemer!' one hissed, his voice like a death rattle. 'Yonaton the Baptiser is a blasphemer! He scorns the One God.' It was Sirach the Ancient, his bloodless fingers twisted cruelly into the ruff of his mule.

'Blasphemer?' Papa did nothing to hide his outrage. 'Because he preaches that all Israelites must repent? Because he offers redemption, through the cleansing rite of baptism, to all who transgress, no matter the bloodline or size of the purse? No Sirach, the Baptiser is no blasphemer,' Papa wagged his head. 'It is not *God's* power to heal that he disputes.'

The slur on the legitimacy of the Temple priests could not have been clearer. This was dangerous talk. The elders were low-ranking kin of the priests, whose claim to pardon sin on God's behalf was being, questioned. My brother looked worried. He tugged at Papa's robe to silence him. But my father waved him away, his face wearing the same expression he had worn that day Mama chased me about the hearth, then pleaded with him to straighten me with rod and soot: the look of a man fed to the teeth with injustice, and too old to care about consequences anymore. Sirach the Ancient said haughtily, 'The priests you decry are appointed by God, Yosef. Appointed by God to pardon our sins.'

'Appointed by God? By *God*?' Papa was purple with rage. 'Yonaton the Baptiser is heir to the high priest who served King David himself. It is to his kind, down through the generations, that God gave the high priesthood, not to Rome to auction to the highest bidder!'

The villagers were now stunned into silence. Having been invited to retreat from his provocative claims that the Jerusalem priesthood was illegitimate and corrupt, Papa had refused. Instead, he had chosen to expand on them, gesturing at a link between the profiteering of the priests and the greatest of Israelite betrayals: collaboration with the pagan occupier. The young men of Nazareth turned and drew closer, their eyes bright with excitement, their gaze shifting from Sirach to Papa and back again, like boys watching bulls in a paddock. But it was on them that Papa turned next.

'And all of you, with your cocked spears and arrows, your ceaseless thirst for war!' I saw Judah, who was roughhousing with another young man, draw swiftly to attention. 'Prepare the way for God. Repent your sins and follow the Law. Remain good and pure of heart,' Papa thumped his chest, his breath laboured. 'Good and pure of heart,' he repeated. His gaze fell on Judah. 'Then will God vanquish the Romans. And send us a king, the Messiah descended from David, to reclaim our land.'

We had arrived at the caravanserai, the roadside campground where we would pass the night: a dusky clearing by a slim tributary of the Jordan, choked with oleander and tamarisk. Already it was crowded with Jews from the Galilee and lands further north, from Lake Huleh near Assyria and as far south as Nain: all on their way to the Jerusalem Feast. Women spread blankets and set out food while men tethered beasts before trailing their elders to the water for prayers. Insulted by Papa's public chastisement of his son, Simeon of Iscariot stormed off, pausing only to collect the bag, belt and sheath Judah had cast to the ground as, whooping loudly, he had raced towards the water with the other young men in close pursuit.

There was much riding on the successful conclusion of my marriage negotiations. My happiness and, with the coins from my bride-price, my brother's chance to secure Maryam. Was it really necessary to provoke Simeon of Iscariot? Joshua and I addressed Papa with stern gazes.

But the old man was all innocence. Face restored to its normal hue, eyes as bright as I had seen them for years, he shrugged his shoulders helplessly and wandered off, whistling tunelessly between his teeth.

The following morning passions at the caravanserai ran high. The mules had been watered and the packs made ready at first light. But then our departure was delayed while travel plans were thrashed out between the different tribes and clans. Elders from places I'd barely heard of congregated by the stream, speaking in heated tones. They railed and debated, arms hurtling and throats clutched for emphasis, while the rest of us clustered together, grouped by village, waiting. At last it was decided. Having travelled to this point as separate villages, we would now unite as Israelites. The next leg of the journey, through the territory of our ancient enemies the Samaritans, we would traverse together.

And so, amidst the braying of strange beasts and the scents of unknown women who, like me, were required to travel at the rear of the procession, I began picking my way down the trail behind what seemed like hundreds of beast-bound elders. The village men, eschewing their place at the front of the procession, surrounded us. Daggers drawn and footfalls deliberate, they herded us towards the natural boundary of the mighty Jordan. The river would do half the sentry work, guarding us from the east so the men might turn both shoulders westward, towards the sheer, barren cliffs where the true danger lay.

'Judah,' I whispered. For the first time on the journey, he was close. Close enough for me to have tasted him on the air, to have felt the heat of his presence as he moved into view, to have reached out to touch him as he hunted the seemingly empty landscape and scanned the cliff tops, his knife held aloft. My heart galloped, and the place between my legs grew wet. 'Judah!'

He did not turn around.

'Judah!' More insistent this time. I cleared my throat, coughed as if choking and finally, in desperation, contrived to stumble and fall, crying out loud as my knees and palms meshed with gravel. But to no avail. His cheek never turned, his lashes did not stutter, his concentration on the task at hand never wavered as I thrashed and flailed about. Until, finally, he left to defend another section of our column, leaving me to ponder the cause of his brutal rejection, and to the mercy of the women, tittering behind their hands at my foolishness.

The shame forced heat to my cheeks and germinated bitter thoughts in my heart. I fumed. Even when an unexpected fall of rocks threw up a dust cloud in the dry ravine through which we were gingerly making our way, I continued to ruminate on my grievances, barely marking the shouts of the startled men around me as they fell into position and took aim.

Until at last we crossed into the Israelite province of Judaea and the caravan dissolved. Villages and clans reassembling with backslaps and muted cries of relief even though the next cara-vanserai—where we would pray, eat and sleep together once more—was only hours away. The relief of tension granted me broader scope to consider the day's events, and the humiliation I had endured, and allowed my fury to bloom.

That evening I spied Judah cooling himself in the shallows as I made my way to the spring to refill our goatskins and veered towards the far end of the water, as far from him as I could get. I felt the weight of his stare as I knelt by the water's edge, the heat of it on my back as I made my way back to the tent, but would not lift my chin or turn to meet his eye.

While Papa chewed Joshua's ear during the evening meal, testing strategies to increase Simeon of Iscariot's bid for my hand, I kept silent, tending my rage like a garden, encouraging it to send down roots and sprout several heads. I became a fire-breathing monster: a vengeful demon from hell.

My eldest brother sought my attention at first light. He wanted—judging from the looks he and Judah exchanged as Judah approached to help us pack up our tent—to salve my injured pride by offering excuses for his friend. But it was too late.

As we descended the sandy trail to the Jordan Valley, passed beside the palm-lined walls of Jericho and began our final ascent to Jerusalem through winding ravines walled by sheer sand-coloured cliffs and bereft of all vegetation but thistle-whirls, Joshua sought my ear again and again, or tried to. First he must get past the elders, who kept barring his way.

'So tell me Joshua, eldest son of Yosef the woodworker,' wheezed Sirach the Ancient turning his beast into Joshua's path. 'What possessed your sister to join us this year? Or should I inquire, what gripped Yosef,' he hurled Papa's name like an insult, 'to allow her?'

Another elder called down from on high when my brother

tried again a short time later. 'And what is your position on this question, Joshua? Yossi the weaver says women are a distraction on a spiritual journey. Do you agree?'

I knew my brother well enough to recognise his anger. A certain rigidity across the shoulders, a leaping muscle in one cheek. But he gave way each time without protest, meekly rejoining the men at the front of the group.

Then our lumbering caravan staggered to the crest of yet another summit and, for that moment, all our grievances fell away.

There it was. Perched on a hill and enclosed by walls, encircled by springs and olive trees and wreathed with smoke from fires just visible behind the ramparts to the south: Jerusalem. The holy city of the Jews.

The men fell to their knees and began to pray. *If I forget thee, O Jerusalem, may my right hand wither. May I never speak again.*

'Look!' cried a woman in front of me. 'The Golden Gates!' The other women stopped and pointed, too, before falling on their faces like scythed wheat, granting me a clear view: of two majestic doors pressed with vine leaves and leopard lilies that glinted in the sun. The stone wall surrounding them hung heavy with signs forbidding any but Israelites to pass through the gates and into the Temple.

Abandoning their protected position at the group's centre, the elders assumed the lead. They coaxed their mules along a path that wound through a primordial tangle of olive trees. Gethsemane: the ancient garden on the mountain's western face, where stone walls crumbled from the weight of years, and the branches of olive trees straggled towards God like a hag's withered arms. The garden where, with sunset only hours away,

Israelites laboured—men felling trees from the forest to the east, women with baskets of snake-curled vines—to raise up the thatched-roof dwellings that would shelter us for the seven days of the harvest feast.

The two patriarchs had finally concluded the marital bargain as they struggled to the summit of Olive Mountain. They had sealed the deal in the way of our ancestors, Papa and Simeon of Iscariot each placing a trusting hand on the other's thigh, as the rest of the village pilgrims streamed past in the rush through Gethsemane towards the Temple's Golden Gates.

I would learn of it later that afternoon when discussion of our group's sleeping arrangements commenced. Astounded and then overjoyed, I listened as our two fathers agreed that three booths would need to be built to house us for the duration of the feast. One for Papa and Joshua, one where Simeon would dwell with other important village men and one…well, that one was for Judah and me.

It would be dusk by the time the sawing and raising was done and the trumpets heralded the start of the feast. Before Simeon, Papa and my brother blessed us and, with knowing eyes and smiles, retreated to their own dwellings, leaving my beloved betrothed, Judah, and me alone.

But now we continued to make our way through the Gethsemane gardens behind the elders, on our way to the Temple. The elders had dismounted. They called for the men to tether the beasts. Smoothing their robes over their bellies, spitting on their hands to tidy their beards and clearing their throats, they prepared to descend by foot towards the Temple. 'Over here! Over here!' they shouted above the clamour of saw and mallet, their stout arms flailing wildly as they urged us forward.

This signalled to the women to break ranks. We moved quickly through the advancing wall of men in search of husbands, fathers or brothers: the men whose escort and imprimatur we needed to enter the shrine. Papa, his grey head towering above the rest, beckoned me and I hastened to his side.

But the crowd moved slowly and our progress was soon halted, too, by the mountainous accumulation of pilgrims awaiting entry to the Temple. Sweating and swearing, they seethed like infested flesh, spilling down the marble and halfway up the path.

The source of the blockage soon became clear. It was a cordon of armed soldiers and officials. Pilgrims were being forced to submit their belts and bags for inspection firstly to Rome's soldiers, who searched for weapons, then to the Temple police, low-ranking priests of the Levite caste who scoured each person's belongings for unclean food and skins. Only when the supplicant was cleared could he proffer his tithe to the priest, receive a cursory blessing and be pushed through the golden doors.

Atop the Temple walls more soldiers paced, aquiline noses wrinkled beneath their helmets in seeming distaste at the restless crowd below.

The elders were no longer among us. The Temple police, their distant kin, had summoned them forth from the crowd and waved them through the gates, unmolested by either search or blessing.

In my mind, I sifted through the contents of our bags once more. 'What if I have missed something? If I still have some-thing unclean?' I worried aloud to Papa.

'That's a simple problem to fix,' a voice said snidely. 'You simply pay a tax to the priests to cleanse it.' It was Baruch, Judah's young disciple. The remark was barely audible in the babble and bray of the crowd, but a look of fear flitted across Papa's face. He pinched the youth's ear and pulled him close. 'Not here,' he hissed. 'Such talk is dangerous enough in Galilee! Here, you'll wind up dead.' Dropping the ear as if it burned, he turned away.

Or tried to. The honey trickle of pilgrims through the gates was no match for the successive waves of villagers cresting Olive Mountain from the north and tumbling through the Gethsemane garden towards the Temple. Solid walls of humanity hemmed us in on all sides. As the crowd thickened, the heat and din increased, people and herds pressing in upon each other like stacked cords of wood. I streamed sweat and fought for breath.

Then, there was a shout. The mob convulsed and I was hurled into the wall of bodies before me, which fell into those before them. Men cursed. Women screamed and shouted for their children, who wailed in reply. Amid the tumult, I struggled to stay upright. To stumble would see me trampled. 'Papa!' I cried.

But he was not there, and neither was Joshua. I looked around wildly. On every side were faces, but not one that I knew. 'Papa! Joshua!'

Nothing. Somehow I had become separated from them and the rest of my village. I was lost and drowning in a sea of wretched strangers. Even the new faces of the women I had walked among for so many miles to get to this place had fallen away. Frantically I scanned the throng but recognised no one. The crowd reared and bucked, then pressed in upon me again.

'Papa!' I screamed as my foothold slipped and I began to fall. 'Joshua!' I cried in terror as the crush closed in. I clawed and thrashed like a cat, struggling to stay upright, to keep my head off the ground and avoid being trampled in the dirt.

Then Judah's voice sounded in my ears. I heard him in the distance roaring and snarling as he tore through the crowd, dagger drawn, scattering bodies before him like an enraged lion. I felt the pressure ease as he hauled the weight of strangers off me and threw them aside like twigs. Saw the light grow above me as he reached down and plucked me to safety, like a flower from a tomb.

He cradled me to his chest in his strong arms, his eyes searching my face for answers. 'Are you all right, Rachael?' His ear bent to my lips to catch my reply. 'Are you all right?'

I hadn't the strength to answer. Instead, I went limp in his arms; let my head fall against the muscled armour of his chest. The thud of his heart offered comfort as he waded me through a sea of curses and rattling fists to safety.

Jerusalem. I had arrived at last.

After Judah extracted me from the mob and carried me out of harm's way, he charged up Olive Mountain, my limp form still in his arms, and set me beneath an olive tree with the tenderness owed to ripe fruit. Then he rushed back through the crowd to recover Papa and Joshua. On his return, my beloved held water to my lips and waited until I deemed myself recovered, a conclusion that may have taken me longer to reach than absolutely necessary. I was enjoying the profusion of his attentions, which I saw as my due: the whispered endearments, the worried looks, the territorial baring of teeth at any stranger who dared come too close.

When Judah finally led us back down the trail to endure the wait before the Golden Gates once more, he shielded me from harm with his outstretched arms, and periodic beast-bellows designed to keep the throng at bay. When at long last we were searched and declared clean by both Empire and Temple (Judah had retained his weapon without difficulty by offering a bribe to the Levite guard), then waved through the yellow doors, it was a shock to find our purity being questioned again.

'All Galileans must bathe!' The high priests were pacing to and fro, garbed in long, white robes embroidered with pome-granates and swinging ropes attached to bells. The brow plates beneath their tall turbans were graven in gold with a word I knew. It was the one Papa had taught me that day in the woods by the schoolroom. The secret, sacred, unpronounceable name of God. 'Papa, look!' I nudged him but he shook his head with a warning glare and turned away.

The bathing vats, twice the size of a grain mill and shaped like a box, were sunk deep into the ground. Papa, Joshua and Judah were ushered towards one while I was pushed towards the one reserved for women. The journey down one flight of steps and up another was overseen by unsmiling, low-caste priests who seized and submerged us with a casual efficiency that left me slack-jawed and gasping at the indignity. Papa, similarly drenched, pinched my elbow and led me away.

I had been expecting a holy place—majestic, serene—but instead found myself in a market. Both sides of the broad court-yard swarmed with pilgrims who clustered like bees around tables draped in blue cloth. Some of the tables groaned with leaning stacks of coins and broad-plated measuring scales, others displayed mounds of salt or tiny loaves, arrayed by the dozen to evoke the twelve Israelite tribes. Above the cries of Greek and Arab merchants hawking wine and oil, doves flapped in gilded cages and beasts lowed in cavernous stalls. The air was ripe with incense and dung and, from somewhere inside the Temple itself, the stench of blood.

Even Joshua seemed ruffled by the mayhem though Judah appeared not to notice. His hand pressed to the side of his face against the sun's long rays, he gazed north towards a fortress just beyond the Temple walls, bristling with Roman mail.

'Why so many?' I asked quietly. As we watched, more soldiers appeared in the circular watchtower, their gaze and arrows trained on the riotous pilgrims below.

'Large gatherings always set Rome on edge,' he replied. His jaw was tight. He passed his hand absentmindedly over the knife concealed in his belt, as if seeking assurance it was still there. 'Large gatherings of *Iudaei* in particular.' His use of the Latin was heavy with mockery. 'Such a volatile people.'

Papa shushed us, then turned to the business at hand: Temple business. Frowning at the modest collection of coins in his palm, he calculated beneath his breath.

'Judah, you come with me,' he announced at last. 'We will trade our denarii for Temple money over there,' he pointed at the stalls, 'then purchase some beasts for sacrifice.'

'Why must you change money, Papa?'

'Because Roman coins bear the Emperor's image,' he waved them beneath my nose, 'which is profane. King Tiberius on all of them, worshipped by the pagans as a God,' his nose wrinkled with displeasure. 'False idols have no place in the Temple.' He turned to my brother. 'Take charge of Rachael while we are gone.' Papa gestured towards the shrine, a regal ascension of oblong blocks with blue-painted archways at the centre of the square, the pride in his voice unmistakable. 'Show her the house our People built for God.'

There was much that astounded. At the far end of the court, scribes and their bickering disciples littered a dazzling fall of cream-coloured steps. To the west, high priests and their silk-clad families strolled from the Temple to Ophel, the quarter of Jerusalem built just for them, where single homes filled entire streets and the tiled floors were heated. To the east was a majestic gate, donated by a wealthy Alexandrian Jew named Nicanor, made of pure Corinthian brass.

'Am I permitted to enter the Temple?' I asked my brother. In answer, he took me to the doors of the Women's Court. Through it, he explained, the sanctuary's higher reaches—the Court of Men, Levites and High Priests—could be reached.

Large signs posted on the barrier walls detailed in Hebrew who might enter the building, and how deeply they could penetrate its sanctums. I began to read, but when two men marked my flickering eyes, Joshua stepped before me. He read the injunction aloud:

Warning! No Gentiles to enter the fence barrier around the Temple. Anyone caught is answerable to himself for the ensuing death.

Warning! No woman in menstruation or other blood impurity to enter the fence barrier around the Temple. Anyone caught is answerable to herself for the ensuing death.

Warning! No Samaritans to enter the fence barrier around the Temple. No one possessed by demons, afflicted with lesions, paralysed, crippled...

The list went on. My brother fell silent. He took a draught from his goatskin. It was more than he usually spoke in a week.

But I had to ask. 'The High Priests. Can they really order death?'

'No.' Joshua shook his head. Wiping his mouth with the back of his hand, he motioned towards the Roman soldiers visible in the fortress towers beyond the Temple walls. 'But they can.'

⌒

In the end, what I remember most about that day in Jerusalem was not the honey and pomegranate juice Papa insisted on buying me with the last of our Temple coins, nor the backs of the men receding as they left me in the Women's Court and ascended to the next level, Joshua and Papa holding sacrificial doves and Judah driving a sheep. Nor was it the look of pity that crossed my brother's face as, our penance duly offered, we hurried back towards Olive Mountain, passing a widow trying to pay her tithe. A fat woman once, she rummaged for her belt beneath folds of hanging flesh, but could produce just two copper mites.

Instead, what shines in my memory is how the steady stream of Judah's enthusiasms made my older brother smile as the two men worked together to build the tabernacle—the makeshift dwelling—in which soon, so soon now, Judah and I would retire together for the night. I recall the way the horns the high priests trumpeted from the Temple ramparts gleamed in the sun's dying rays. I remember how Papa looked standing beside me in Geth-semane. Rocking and bowing, his lips knowing every word of the priests' chanted prayers, as darkness took over from day.

And there are other moments from that night, when at long last Judah and I lay down together and he made me his wife, that I can't stop remembering.

The litter of moonlight through the thatched vine roof on the neatly spread blankets, and the baritone whisper of

Judah's voice as he beckoned me towards him, gently, gently, as if seducing a cat from a tree. The way Judah's arm reached out to me and his rough palms caressed my cheek, murmuring his love, promising to stop the moment I felt pain. The way my flushed skin dimpled in the cooling night air as Judah came towards me and touched my lips with his own, feather-light at first, then stronger, insistent. Nibbling and sucking my ears, my neck—and finally, finally—my breasts, until I was whimpering with longing and pleading for release in whatever form it might take. 'Come my love, come,' I begged, lying down on my back and pulling him to me, my breath catching in my throat as passion overtook him and he moved above me with crocodile speed. Kicking my knees apart, all promises of restraint thankfully forgotten, as every part that made me woman—hips, lips, breasts, cleft—swelled and opened. I remember how my hips lifted, pleading to receive him again and again, even as the pain fanned through me like ripples on a pond. His thrusts driving everything, everything but him and the mounting urgency in my blood, from my thoughts.

These are the moments, the Judah—my name on his lips as his face contorted and he filled me with his seed—I wish to remember.

Crabbed tentacles invaded my sleep. Lying in the tabernacle in the hours before dawn, wrapped safe in Judah's arms, I felt them poke at my ribs, my arm. I tried to evade them, to swim away, but they reached for me again and again. Shook and rattled at the gates of my resting place. 'Rachael! Rachael! Wake up!' Joshua's voice but different, wrong. Too busy with words, too tightly strung with emotion. 'Sister, please. It's Papa!'

'What?' I threw aside the dead weight of Judah's arm and sat up, my tongue thick with sleep.

Words poured from Joshua like wine. 'He was fine last night. Stiff and tired from the journey, yes; but who would not be at his age? He may have cried out, but I did not hear, I was too deeply asleep. All I know is that I woke to blankets wet and thick with—' he mimed the disgust of someone finding himself shrouded in human waste.

From somewhere outside my body, I heard my voice calmly enquire if Papa was dead.

'No. Yes. I don't know!' Joshua raked a hand through his hair. 'He was alive when I woke, this is certain, one eye open and seeing. But not able to move. He tried to say something but—' Joshua shook his head. 'Nothing but a gurgle. But now the eye is closed and though I shake him and shout, he—' Emotion swelled my brother's throat and fell from his eyes as tears. 'Papa!'

Judah finally stirred, then bolted upright, a dagger in his fist. 'Who's there!'

'Papa,' I said. 'He's ill.' Pushing aside the blanket we had slung across the open wall of the tabernacle for seclusion, I crawled from the dwelling on all fours. I stood and brushed the dust from my robe as I waited for Joshua to follow.

'The breath,' I said the moment he appeared, noting again from that external place the serenity of my manner. 'We must seek it. In Papa's throat and breast.'

I kept pace with my brother as he raced across the garden towards the tabernacle that sheltered Papa, ducking and weaving through the thicket of makeshift dwellings from which sleepy pilgrims were emerging into the breaking day. But once within, and kneeling by Papa's side, I realised I was woefully unprepared to remedy his suffering. Even if Bindy's entire dispensary had been laid before me, with every herb, root and bark easily to hand, I would never have been equal to the malady that was draining his colour, drying his tongue and slowing the wind in his throat. The disease of age, Bindy would confirm when I described the symptoms to her later.

And so Papa died; may even have willed his failing body to do so. To breathe its last when—one eye opening in response to the slap of my hand on his cheeks, the splash of my grief on his brow—he saw my pain and determined to bring it to an end. The light fled his eyes, his body went still, the flesh turned grey and slackened.

I passed my hands across his eyes to close them. It all happened so quickly that by the time Judah found us on the crowded hillside, his breathing heavy and blade still drawn, Joshua and I were already on our knees, our robes rent in mourning, praying for forgiveness and praising God's holy name.

We were not alone long with our grief. A death far from home brought procedural problems, problems of funerary law that the elders must solve. Huffing and puffing, their skin still creased with sleep, they congealed like old blood near Papa's tent, conferring in self-important tones about the fate of Papa's body. It must be buried without delay in Jerusalem, they agreed, among the ocean of tombs just beyond the city walls in the Valley of the Dead.

'No!' Joshua's head snapped up. He had been weeping silently at the edge of their expert circle, waiting for judgment to be passed. Now he looked Sirach the Ancient in the eye. 'My father deserves to be buried in the place he called home his entire life. Not left like filth to lie in foreign soil.'

They battled. The elders arrayed against Joshua, with Judah standing right behind my brother, his fists clenched and powerful jaw jutting. My brother pleading with the elders to give us both mule and blessing so we could take Papa home. As the light from the rising sun spread like butter across the mountain, and priests roamed among the waking pilgrims dispensing branches of palm and goodly fruit for the day's rituals, the contest escalated. Voices tumbled over one another and men, drawn to the noise, flocked from all parts of the garden to observe and make comment. Even when the ram's horn sounded from the Temple, summoning the faithful to prayer, the crowd held fast, refusing to disperse.

'His entire life was lived in Nazareth,' Joshua was insisting for what seemed like the seventy-seventh time, my usually taciturn brother now hoarse with entreaty. 'He is from the north, not from Judaea. He must be laid to rest in the hills of Galilee.'

The elders were unmoved. 'It is the Law! The body must be buried without delay,' one shouted at Joshua, his rolling eyes making plain his dismay at my brother's foolishness. 'Already death's stain is upon you. And her.' His arm flung in my direction. 'Yet here you stand, begging blessings! Have you not done enough already?'

'It is impossible, Joshua!' averred another. 'Impossible. Mules don't grow on trees. How will we get back to Nazareth if we give ours to you?' The rest of the elders liked this argument. Huddled together like beetles, they murmured and bobbed their heads.

'To walk, it seems, would kill them,' Judah muttered and

165

the crowd, astonished at his brazenness, nudged one another and laughed.

'Be sensible, son.' It was Eliazar, the elder Papa had begged for mercy the day of Shona's judgment. 'You are struck by grief and burdened by guilt. This we comprehend. But we must decide with our heads, not our hearts.' His tone was soothing. Conciliatory. 'Yosef was not a king. Not a priest or sage. Not an elder. What claim can be made on God to bend the Law?'

Already something had given way in my brother. Clearly, Papa's suffering and sudden passing had disturbed the still waters of his nature and unseated his reserve. Now, as Eliazar spoke, Joshua's astonishment at mercy's flight, at the self-serving nature of the elders' claims, moved across his features, transforming them. I witnessed the world shake and crumble beneath my brother's feet, saw him pitch and rear, then scrabble for purchase on firm earth again. I gripped tighter to my new husband's arm.

Quite suddenly the expression on my brother's face re-arranged itself, setting in lines I had not seen before. Without warning he spun, turning his back on the elders, and appealed directly to the crowd instead. 'If my father were an elder, it seems he would have his final rites read in the village of his birth. But no; he is just a simple man, a common man like you and me, so they mean to leave him here, to lie for eternity in a stranger's grave.'

There was no mistaking the 'they' to whom my brother was referring. The elders sniffed indignantly and put their heads together, buzzing like flies in a jar. 'Who among you,' Joshua continued, his eyes scanning the mass of upturned faces, 'who among you has heard tell of the good Samaritan?' A murmur went up from the throng as men hoisted shoulders and shook heads.

What was he doing? I looked up at Judah for answers but my husband's gaze was elsewhere, fixed on the soldiers crowding the turret of Antonia's Fortress. Rome's centurions were no longer peering into the Temple, but staring at the crowd around my brother, their bows and slings in hand.

But the mob saw only Joshua. They hung on every word of my brother's tale of an injured Israelite left to die by a Temple priest on the dangerous and deserted road to Jericho, but rescued by a merciful Samaritan. The parable's thinly veiled meaning—about the fate of Israelites without money or breeding at the hands of the holy—was quickly grasped.

There was a beat of silence as the last of my brother's words died away. Then, a voice rose up from the throng: 'Send him home!' The cry rippled through the gathering: 'Send him home! Send him home!' Fingers curled into fists and fists pounded on thighs while the chant continued and Joshua spun around amid a sudden sea of kin and clan, his face a study of light and surprise at the force he had unleashed.

Send him home! Send him home! My brother fell to his knees before Eliazar and made his case again. 'Mercy,' he said, so quietly I almost missed it. 'Have mercy on Papa and send him home.'

They relented in the end. What choice did they have? Clicking their fingers to summon a boy leading the beast that would bear the body to its last resting place, the elders waddled off. Noses stuck in the air, shooing the now-docile crowd before them in the direction of the waiting Temple, they departed, leaving Joshua, Judah and me alone. With the crowd's dispersal went the interest of the soldiers. Judah heaved a sigh of relief and sheathed his dagger.

A few hours later we were on our way out of the city, heading back to Nazareth.

❧

The days that followed are like a dark, tangled skein of wool. A knot that, however much I pick and peer and card, reveals only scattered images, sudden flashes of light and sound. Papa's massive form hastily wrapped in linen and tethered to the mule like a sack of wheat; Judah's sleep-fogged face lit by the flicker of a single torch as we journeyed, knowing ourselves in a race against heat and time, through the night. The sound of Papa's name on Joshua's lips—demand, plea, prayer. Until, worn by grief, my brother pulled back within himself and spoke no more. Then, as we made our final ascent to Nazareth, the mournful notes of the herald's horn warning the village of death at our door.

Mama was there as we reached the plateau. She barrelled through the gates with veil askew, hurling herself at Papa's swaddled corpse, dragging it, still partly bound and tethered, to the dust. His name from her lips like a severed vein pumping blood: *Yosef! Yosef! Yosef!* Until at last she could keen no more and curled instead atop his mountainous, dirt-streaked form to mew like a kitten: 'My God, my God, why have you forsaken me? What have I done? What have I done?'

How could I not have known how much she truly loved him?

The rites of death bound and swaddled us, allowing clarity—the gift of faith and purpose—to illuminate the dark despair. Mama and I washed Papa's lifeless form, then wrapped him in sheet after

168

sheet of linen gummed with aloes and myrrh. Joshua looked on, heaving silent sobs as he sheltered beneath the protective arm Judah slung across his shoulders. My brothers heaved Papa's body to their shoulders and paraded him, first to the square, then through the gates to Deadman's Hill, while my eldest brother mumbled prayers and the keening women writhed and moaned and the earth made wide its throat for Papa to begin his forever rest in Sheol. *Ashes to ashes. Dust to dust. May peace and life be upon all Israel. And so we say Amen.*

Then we must sit at home for seven days on wooden planks and mourn, our bodies draped in sackcloth, brows smeared with ashes. Respite was granted just once on the third day and again on the last for Joshua—the head of the family now—to purify us from the pollution of death by sprinkling all corners of the house with water mixed with the ashes of a red, unblemished cow. All of us bent to the task of mourning, none more earnestly than Mama, surrounded day and night by the wives of the elders who took it in turns to witness her agony and place morsels of bread soaked in egg in her mouth.

I also had tasks to perform. Prayers I must chant, sacred oils of regret and penance—myrrh and spikenard—to touch to my brow. I performed each of these rituals dutifully, in the precise manner commanded of women for generations. But my thoughts were with Judah.

When we had departed Nazareth, Mama knew Papa's intentions to conclude my marriage deal and, amidst the chaos of our return, had discerned what had come to pass. Acknowledging the consummation of Judah's and my union with a vague nod, she made way for my new husband to sit as family at Papa's *shiva*. But although Judah rested beside me on his own hard pallet, we were forbidden to touch. Not during the day or at night. Such was God's requirement of those touched by death.

As the fifth, then sixth, day of mourning crawled past, I could think of nothing else. I began dreaming with eyes open of Judah throwing me down and pushing my robes aside and—as we panted and rocked and he looked deeply into my eyes—of being known again. Seen and loved for the Rachael I was, and was becoming; as Papa had seen me, and Shona once, too, so that as I came to accept all I had lost, I would not feel abandoned, and so terribly alone.

'Maryam?' The faraway sound of my brother's voice exploring space with his lover's name. Puzzled. Desperate.

The mourners at our house, mesmerised by the steady beat of psalm and prayer, startled at the sound. The drone of their invocations dribbled to a halt as eyes turned to Joshua's empty pallet. Until that moment no one had noticed he had gone, that he had slipped the knot of obligation to discover why, on the seventh and final day of our lamentations, there was still no sign of his beloved, nor Abraham or Shula Magdalene, either. Not at the burial march nor the *shiva*.

'Maryam. Maryam!' Joshua's call was now a dog's howl, lush with dismay. We heard the sound of wood—her door?—being kicked and pounded, followed by the thud of running feet.

My brother, flushed and breathing hard, burst into the room. 'Where is she? Where is Maryam?' His eyes passed over Judah and me—what would we know?—before coming to rest on Mama and the wives of the elders, none of whom would meet his gaze. The girl was not kin and this made the question, quite apart from the passion with which it was charged, highly irregular.

But Joshua did not care. He moved towards Mama. 'Where is Maryam, Mama?' His voice was high-pitched and cracking with emotion. 'Her house is stripped bare. The stables are empty. Where is she? Where is she?'

Mama blinked, like a mole exposed to light. Her mouth moved soundlessly as she surfaced from the fog of grief and self-pity to which she'd abandoned herself. 'Maryam?' she croaked at last. 'Maryam?'

Joshua was unmoved. She knew. No one could have nested in the bosom of the wives for as many days as she had and not known something. Yet to him, not a word had been said. He dropped to his knees before Mama, scattering the women like pigeons. Leaning towards her face, each word hissing danger-ously through his clenched teeth. 'Don't. Play. With. Me. *Where is Maryam?*'

He was frightening. Someone I was no longer sure I knew. Mama started as if slapped and began to gabble. 'She is gone. Not long after you departed for Jerusalem: her father clinking with every step from the weight of coins in his belt, their mules piled high with pots and bedding. Sheep and goats trailing behind.'

My mind reeled. Had Abraham discovered—in ways too terrible to think about—Maryam and Joshua's secret love? Or had Maryam pleaded with her father to bless their union and received this, his sudden, wordless desertion of Nazareth with every possession in tow, as the old man's reply?

Joshua, perhaps countenancing similar thoughts, turned

green. 'Gone?' he spluttered. 'Gone? Where?' He leapt to his feet, as if to sprint away in whatever direction Mama pointed.

But it was not in Mama's interest that Joshua career off in pursuit of Maryam. She needed him to complete the rites that would cleanse us from death's corruption. When the *shiva* was done, he must return to the woodshop, earning the coins she required to feed herself and my brothers. Mama shook herself like a wet dog, commanding herself to stay alert. This must be managed carefully.

'Did I say everything?' She spoke slowly, the wheels turning visibly behind her dark eyes. 'This is not correct. In truth, the mules were loaded with essentials for no more than a month or two.' She looked to the elders' wives; they obliged with nodding heads. 'They will return,' Mama said. Then she corrected herself, 'Maryam will return.'

'The house is boarded shut,' Joshua said, still poised to depart. 'Which way did they go out?'

'Joshua, see reason,' Mama remonstrated. 'You don't know where she is, or how to find her. If you charge off in one direction, she's certain to return in another.' Seeing my brother's face soften with doubt, Mama pressed forward. Her voice was low, rich with assurance like Eliazar the elder's a few days earlier on Olive Mountain. 'But she will come back. Of course she will, and soon. For now, I need you here, son. To sprinkle the house when the sun sets tonight. To earn the coins that will save us from pity and ruin.' Mama's hands smoothed her veil, starting from the top of her head and ending beneath her chin, where she clung to the knot for dear life. 'Your debt is to me and your brothers, to your family honour and name.'

The speech was soothing and Joshua seemed lulled by it.

His jaw loosened and his shoulders fell slack.

But then Mama overplayed her hand. 'If Papa were here, this is what he would tell you. I know he would say the same thing.'

Joshua started, like he'd been flicked by a whip. As if, in the face of the lie, he suddenly knew the truth. He moved towards the holy water. It had been prepared earlier that day for the *shiva*'s closing prayer, and was resting by the door in a special urn. Grasping it, he began sprinkling drops in each corner of the room, speaking to Mama all the while.

'Papa was nothing like you,' he said, 'bound by the call of others, deaf to the truth in his heart. If Papa were here, if he were here now—' Joshua's voice quavered and tears fell from his eyes. He swiped roughly at them with the heel of his hand. 'If Papa were here he would say, "You have other sons, Miriame." He would tell me to be true to myself, and to make good my debts to the woman I love. He would say I must do what I know to be right because God is my only judge.' Having completed his tour of the room, Joshua came to rest beneath the lintel. He set the empty vessel down. 'Papa would tell me to trust in God because He has a plan, and that is what I intend to do.' He nodded, as if affirming to himself that this was the correct course of action, before saying again, 'Yes. That is what I shall do.'

And with that my eldest brother was gone, the crunch of his sandals on the path quickly lost to our hearing as he hurried towards the village gates. Judah, casting a helpless glance in my direction, leapt to his feet and ran after him.

It would be months before I saw either one of them again.

The imperatives of my new situation were delayed until Simeon of Iscariot returned from the Tabernacles Feast in Jerusalem with the rest of the village men. But when he did, a few days after Papa's *shiva* ended, Mama's eager fingers took payment of my price and, Judah's absence notwithstanding, I was ordered to roll my belongings up in my sleeping mat and take up my place with the Iscariots.

Judah's mother Olivia welcomed me with a kindness I had no right to expect. Mothers could be wary, even hostile, to the new daughters with whom they were expected to share their hearth, their confidences and their son's favours. Olivia might have seen cause to worry about me: my well-known rebellious streak, my low standing as the crone's apprentice. She could have met me with rod in hand, hoping to break me to her stride before Judah returned. Instead she proved solicitous. She was tolerant of my reputation and missteps, and the shyness brought on by an unfamiliar hearth and the absence of my family.

Like Simeon, my new mother was round from lack of want: her eyes lost to cheeks, her body to belly and breast. Her skin's perfume was dry and pleasant, like freshly milled grain. Some days, after Simeon and Judah's brother Gideon had finished their midday meal and settled to sleep on their mats, Olivia would wave me away from the hearth towards the small, windowless room I was to share with Judah. 'You rest too, Gazelle,' she would say comfortably. 'I have lived this long without daughters. One more afternoon won't hurt.'

Lying huddled on my mat beneath several blankets, my nose buried deep in an unwashed robe I'd found of Judah's, I would listen to her sweep and tend her pots: a song beneath her breath, her step a contented shuffle.

I would listen and think of Shona. What would the first weeks of her new life in Cana have been like? Trapped amid the sounds and smells, the rhythms and demands of a new family and, just beyond the door, a foreign village? What would it have been like to spend the day cooking, carrying and cleaning beside the pinched-face widow my brother Joshua had described? The woman who had raised Boaz to be the violent lout he was? My sister knew nothing of life in Nazareth. She did not even know, I realised, that Papa was gone. Why, in these ways and so many others, had I been blessed and Shona cursed?

I turned this last question over and over again, like a squirrel with a nut, but never found an answer. All I knew was that my sister's absence leaked like a wound, and that I would happily have given an arm just to see her again.

⌒

Pestilence had come to Gath Hepher. All morning, wild-eyed women had flown down the trail from the north with crying babies on their backs, looking for cures. Bindy shuffled and ground and, when her stoppered jars became empty, cursed. Her list of necessaries was long. 'Half a pot of coriander seeds, and a bushel of passionfruit. And half a bushel of lemons. When you have returned with this I need you to—'

Standing by the door, arms wrapped about the woven basket she had pushed in my arms, I hesitated. It was late spring and the Pentecost Feast was just weeks away. Since my marriage at harvest time, my visits to the crone had been brief and infrequent. If I did as she was commanding now, I would be absent from Olivia's side all afternoon, far longer than I had ever stayed away. Would my new mother be angry?

'Olivia will manage.' Bindy knew my thoughts, but her compassion lay elsewhere. 'Look at this child!' She pointed to a babe, red-faced with fever, squalling in his mother's arms. Pressing her nose to the tiny skull she sniffed deeply and shook her head. 'Trouble is brewing, Rachael of Nazareth, and you are needed here!'

So I stayed, hard at work in the meadows and orchards for the rest of the afternoon. Returning to Bindy's with plump pouches of seeds and baskets full of fruit. Then I hurried back to Olivia just as night overtook the sky. I managed to arrive home just moments before Simeon and Gideon returned, knocking loam from their sandals and calling for wine to moisten lips made parched from shouting orders to men high in the trees of the orchard.

The floor had been swept, the jars were full and the hearth was fat with kindling. 'Gazelle!' Olivia exclaimed as I raced through the door. Unruffled by my lateness, she appeared pleased to see me. Dipping her spoon in a pot, she held it out towards my lips. 'More salt?'

Bindy was not surprised by my new mother's attitude. 'Olivia's grandmother worshipped the Heavenly Queen,' she informed me when we next met. It was a week after the sickness began in Gath Hepher and the flow of supplicants down the northern trail had finally begun to slow. 'The Queen who is All and in being All is One.'

I nodded. This explained much. No matter how ill Papa might have been, Mama would rather have slit her own throat than allow Bindy and me to care for him.

Bindy continued. 'Of course they all know what we do. They just choose not to speak of it. Of us. To us,' she snorted. 'Until they are ill, of course. Then they come running. Healing women are like the harlots and fishermen. Reviled but necessary. Correct?' She answered her own question, 'Correct.'

I frowned. However correct she was, it always stoked my fury. But seeing my expression, Bindy threw up her hands. 'Do not start, Rachael. Please. I have too much to do today to fret about worldly injustice.' Standing at the hearth, she lifted a lid. Steam billowed, wetting her face and painting it red.

'You raised the subject,' I said stiffly.

'And now I am letting it drop.' She clanged herself on the brow with the heel of her free hand. 'I forgot who I was speaking with.' Still holding the lid high, she plucked up a spoon and prodded the cauldron's contents.

'But it is not right, Bindy. It is not just and I do not see why—'

Bindy slammed the lid into place and threw down the spoon. 'Why? Because it will not be changed. Not by one woman alone. Not in my lifetime, or in yours! You will rage and kick and struggle, and for what in the end? For nothing. Nothing, or a noose about the neck!'

Her thin voice was pitched with emotion. For once I managed to stay silent, sensing I was not the sole object of Bindy's ire. Not for the first time, her mother's ghost was in the room.

'Do not swim with rocks in your pocket, Rachael. Smother your rage. Dedicate your wit and passion where there is hope. And finish preparing this cure,' she said, storming from the room. 'I have other work to do!'

Mama had gone grey. Wiry strands of white sprang from beneath her slovenly veil; her sleepless eyes were bloodied yolks. The weight of washing on her back had bent her nearly double. 'Have you heard from him yet?' she whispered.

We were at the washing point, surrounded by the slap and song of the other village women. It was Pentecost and most of the men were in the Holy City, feasting and praying. 'No,' I said, knowing she was speaking of Joshua. 'But Judah has sent word to say he is safe. They both are, though still searching for Maryam.'

Mama's appearance frightened me, though I was alive to its cause, and my contribution to it. Papa's death was only the start; then there had been the loss to her hearth of the last pair of female hands and, at the same time, Joshua's abandonment. How much more could a mother bear? But now my brother Jacob seemed determined to strike the fatal blow. The shame the next-in-line was causing Mama was clear to anyone with eyes. In the event I was suffering difficulties with mine, however, Sarai— still livid at having lost the battle for Judah's affections—was more than willing to assist.

'Right there in the woods, he was!' she had exclaimed the other day by the well, as I waited my turn with the dipper. 'That Jacob, son of Yosef the woodworker,' she looked around and dropped her voice to a penetrating whisper, 'rutting a goat from his flock!' She was holding court with the usual herd of gossips, and had pretended not to see me at the back of the line. 'If only that man would do an honest day's work,' she continued, smoothing her yellow belt with both hands and tossing her head like a horse. 'The woodshop is there, ready for use, yet it lies idle day after day, while his poor mother starves and battles the shame. So many sons, but not one to defend her name. Poor Miriame.' Sarai's sigh was long and billowy. 'She'll be on the widow's wage before long. Oh, Rachael, I'm sorry!' Her pretty hand flew to her mouth. 'I did not see you there.' She turned back to her entourage and they collapsed together in giggles.

If only Joshua would come back, and bring Judah with him! Return to save Mama from her shame by taking Papa's place at the workbench and bringing Jacob to heel. I knew that Mama had asked my second-eldest brother, begged him on her knees, to cast off his pride and pick up hammer and saw for the time that Joshua was absent. But Jacob refused.

'Papa blessed Joshua, not me. I would not dream to thieve my brother's place,' Sarai had him saying, the palm at her chest, the expression of aggrieved injury capturing Jacob so well that I had no trouble believing it was true. Of course, when other matters were at hand, my older brother displayed no such reverence for tradition. When I left Mama's hearth for Olivia's, Jacob observed barely a week of my waiting time. For him, my marriage into a family of means was an opportunity he would waste no time in exploiting. Loitering outside the Iscariot doorway, he assailed me each time I came or went. 'Sister,' he would cry, his robes dishevelled, his breath soured by wine, 'have you any money?' Or, when his half-wit friends were present, he would demand an audience with Judah. 'I must be informed when he returns from war, sister, so I can speak with him at once,' Jacob would slur importantly. 'The men and I want to sign up.'

Though I refrained from revealing it to my intemperate brother, I too was keen to know when Judah would be back.

Five moons had waxed and waned since last our eyes met, since I had heard his voice, since his callused palms had caressed my cheek and, when we were alone, much, much more. I could still remember every moment of our first—our only—night together: the trepidation, the longing, the urgency.

Then, early one evening not long after Pentecost Feast, I went to the well. It had been a long day. I had spent most of it in East Nazareth which is why I was mixing cures for Bindy, heaving the dipper from the stone-lined depths at an hour when I would usually have been serving the evening meal.

I watched the man descending the trail from Sepphoris, encrusted with dirt, armed but alone, and wondered at his purpose. I can still hear the creak of the cogs, taste the metallic tang of stone and water on my tongue as the traveller approached, the shape of his frame, the rhythm of his gait growing sharper and clearer with each passing moment. My nipples hardened, my thighs sweated, my pulse raced: all clear victors in the race with my lumbering mind to recognise the broad, strong body and the swinging line of hair. To know that it was Judah, picking his way towards Nazareth, returning to me at last.

As he crashed from the woods into the square I heard myself yip like a puppy. The forgotten jar crashed to the earth as I ran towards him. It was then that he saw me, his lips—a pink slash in a canvas of grime—shaping to a grin as he realised that the lone woman by the well was his wife. Rachael. The smile widening, he barely gave ground as I slammed the full weight of my body into his arms and clung tight, whimpering.

We endured Simeon of Iscariot's formal greetings, and his long-winded inquiries about climate and kin in the far north. We bore Gideon's bitter jibes about the return of the favoured son. We endured Olivia's fussing at Judah's arms and face with a wet, soapy cloth, then at last we were waved from the hearth and through the hanging cloth door of Judah's windowless room, whereupon we fell to the mats and took to one another like animals. Caring nothing about who heard the mewing and growls, the surge and ebb of ecstasy, we found each other again and again.

We stayed for days inside that room, laughing at nothing, crooning endearments, eating from dishes that Olivia left outside the door, relieving ourselves in pots. Enjoying the sequestering that traditionally follows marriage but that we, because of all that had happened since our lone nuptial embrace in Gethsemane, had been denied.

When at last I mentioned Joshua, Judah answered carefully. One foot in front of the other, feeling his way, like a blind man on the rim of a crater. Maryam was still missing. Joshua remained determined to find her and would not return home until he had. That was the sum of it, though the efforts of the two friends over the intervening months had been fantastic. They had covered more distance than an army, spoken to thousands and stopped at every town in the Galilee to make inquiries. They had gone to Magdalene, whence Maryam hailed, but when her kin swore no knowledge of her whereabouts they quickly moved on. Gennesaret. Capernaum, Bethsaida, Hippos: they scoured the hamlets on the shores of the Galilee Sea and spoke to every fisher. On the dusty roads from here to there they questioned each merchant and tax collector they met. Joshua and Judah roamed as far north as Lake Huleh and to the delta of the Qishon River in the south. They scaled Mount Carmel to the east, Gilboa to the south and closer to home, Mount Tabor, where they happened across my three youngest brothers guarding Mama's small flock and shared camp for the night. But no one had seen a gentle-eyed girl and the stiff-necked father who clanked with coins when he walked. Finally, having lost hope of success, Judah announced he was returning home.

'But why did Joshua not return with you?' Judah's tale had gone for hours and it was now late at night. Beside us, on the floor, a single oil lamp flickered while in the rooms beyond the door of our room, the rest of the household dreamt. I was lying on my side, uncovered, my head propped on my elbow. Even at this hour, the air was warm as breath.

Judah had been playing his hand along the tender flesh of my flank; now he moved to my breasts and cupped one, considering. 'He is not himself, Rachael. Has not been since that day on Olive Mountain. First your Papa, then Maryam, one so soon after the other. He is skewered by remorse and grief, is driven by it. His thoughts, his will, are consumed by a desperation to find this woman, who he loves so deeply and fears he may have condemned through his own actions.'

'Condemned?'

Judah shrugged. 'He has not said, but we can guess. What if she is with child? What if Abraham's discovery of this terrible fact is what made him flee, driving Maryam and Shula before him like sheep?'

Bile rose in my throat as Judah continued his litany of doom, for Abraham's options were many. He might have taken Maryam to some foreign land where he could kill her, or simply cast her to her doom. He might have sold her for slavery, to purify the family name.

'Joshua does not know,' Judah went on, 'and it is the not-knowing, the thought that she needs him and he is not there to help, that plagues him. This is why he must find her: find Maryam and bring her home, and why each day that he fails, his guilt and fury grow.'

'But she may never be found!'

Judah turned his attention to the other breast. 'Yes,' he conceded.

I swept his hand to my mouth and kissed each finger. 'So he will abandon hope, eventually. Resign himself to his fate and return to Nazareth. To take up his place and look after Mama.'

Judah threw himself on his back and clasped his hands behind his head. Blew a long breath. 'I do not know, Rachael. He is not the man he was. The quest for Maryam, his rage and frustration, have altered him. He is different: restless, discontented, driven. And so full of words! Men are drawn to his anger—' He thought about this. 'Men enraged by injustices that have blocked their own paths. And there is no shortage of such men, Rachael. At night in the villages, those little hamlets that surround the Sea of Galilee, fishermen would pull in their nets and invite us…invite him really, to share their fire. We would break bread and Joshua would tell his story. About what happened to your sister, Yosef's sudden death and the elders' heartlessness. Maryam's disappearance because Joshua could not marry her—because he was poor and Abraham knew he could get a better price elsewhere.'

I pictured Joshua telling this story: the curves and planes of his bearded face in the flickering firelight; the thickness of night as it fell upon the vast Galilean sea; the smell of salt and sweat on the sun-faded clothes of the seamen who drew close to listen. But Judah was still speaking. '…They, too, have tales to tell.'

'Who, the fishermen?'

Judah nodded.

'What tales?'

'Well…they are similar to Joshua's, now that I consider it.' Judah's frown made clear that it was the first time he had. 'About the trouble and shame that comes with being poor. So poor you must fish from dawn to dusk every day of the week—even on the Sabbath—to feed your children. So poor that it is impossible to meet one's obligations to God by travelling to the Temple, even if there were enough coins to pay for tithe and sacrifice once you get there, which there are not.'

So the poor lacked the means to cleanse themselves of sin at the Temple. They remained polluted and invisible to both God and respectable men. I shrugged: it was a familiar story. Women could never be seen by God, no matter what they spent or offered.

Judah mistook my silence for agreement with him against Joshua and the fisherfolk. He had no doubt that on the central question of our time—who was to blame for Jewish misery and the colonisation of the land given to us by God—I would take his part.

'Joshua can blame the servile, self-serving priests at the Temple, but the Roman Governor of Jerusalem is the true culprit here,' he said, the well-worn polemic flowing easily from his lips. 'It is Governor Pilate who grants the power to reign at will to the most corrupt of the Temple priests. Governor Pilate who encourages their theft from the poor in exchange for forgiveness.' Judah snorted. 'Pontius Pilate wouldn't care if the priests were thieving from God to pay the Devil himself, as long as he got his cut.'

'Whereas a true Israelite king—' I prompted, teasing.

'A true Israelite king would put an end to the corruption and mutual back-scratching,' Judah railed, sweeping aside my attempt at levity. 'He would evict Rome's legions from our land and lay to waste the corrupt Council of Priests and—'

'Yes my love.' Smiling, I pressed a finger to my husband's lips to cut short the familiar tirade. 'He would. But what of Joshua?'

'I left him,' Judah said plainly, clapping the dust from his blunt hands. 'It was time to return. There was no sign of Maryam and no indication where she had gone. We were out of funds and in want of a bath. Most of all,' he continued, turning back on his side to face me. 'I had a woman—a wife—who I had known only once, and who I could wait no longer to have again.' I felt the force of his argument press against my thigh. He nuzzled my neck, his lips sliding across my jaw before forcefully possessing my mouth.

I groaned, rolled to my back and lifted my knees, allowing him to enter. 'But what will he do?' I asked, my breath noisy as he moved inside me.

'Keep looking for Maryam.'

'But he has no money! How will he eat?'

'He said not to worry.' Judah's breath was audible now; his eyes closed and back bent to the task. 'He said. To tell you. God. Would provide.'

Papa's words. So eloquently had they attested to his faith; so rarely were they right. I embraced Judah with my legs and drew him more deeply inside me. 'So, you just left him there?' I whispered in my husband's ear. 'Just abandoned him?' But Judah had gone beyond hearing, or at least replying. A few more strokes and he reached his peak. Back arched, he cried out as if in pain, then collapsed atop me. He rolled off, halfway to dreaming already.

I shook his arm, unsatisfied. 'You just left him?'

Sleepily, Judah agreed, chewing the words like fat. 'Um. Um.'

I put my mouth to his ear. 'Left him? Alone? Just like that?'

Withdrawing from me as if from a bad smell, Judah huffed to the far end of the mat. As far from me as he could get. 'I am his friend, Rachael, not his wet nurse. What more would you have me do?'

Judah could not stay. Less than a week after returning to my arms, he began preparations to return to the rebels at Gamla. He promised to return every few months. Simeon shook his head sadly and tried to persuade his favoured son to stay. 'Just a few more months, Judah! Until Tabernacles, at least, when the year is through.' He was referring to the year the Law grants to newly married couples so they can be fruitful and multiply. Simeon glanced at Olivia, who made no secret of her yearning for a grandchild. 'Consider it, son,' he pleaded. 'For your bride's sake, at least.' But Judah refused and, while I wished it were otherwise, I understood. My husband was needed elsewhere.

'The raids on Caesarea and the Decapolis will fail without me,' he explained as he threw a last blanket into his travel bag and knotted the leather tie. I listened from the floor, my back resting against the wall, knees cradled to my chest. 'I was the one who scouted the terrain, and took the measure of Caesar's men. And no one,' he lunged, needling the air with an imaginary weapon, 'is better with a dagger.'

'Your skills with a sword are indeed unrivalled, husband,' I replied cheekily.

His laugh was a bray, sudden and robust. Lowering the tapestry door with a swift pass of his arm, he tossed his sword aside—the metal one—and came towards me, still chuckling.

At first, I bore his absence well. Indeed, there was little time to brood for I found myself, suddenly and unexpectedly, returned to my mother's service. The grape harvest had begun and the first of the olives would come next. Mama also needed help to prepare for the approaching feasts and fasts. She pleaded with Olivia to release me and finally, although there was more than a year left of my waiting time, my new mother agreed.

It was hard to see how she could have done otherwise. 'What need have you of her?' my mother would demand of Olivia each day at first light. Lying in wait behind bush or rock for Olivia to emerge from her hearth, Mama would rush at her sobbing or berating, her finger wagging. Cheeks flushed as if the knot of her headscarf was choking off air, her voice high and querulous. 'I am a widow with sons to feed!'

It was true. Mama's good name was in tatters, her cupboards close to bare. The twins lacked the wit for any more bountiful trade than shepherding; it would be many years before Simon returned from Tiberius where, in the wake of Papa and Joshua's loss, he'd been apprenticed to a Greek to learn woodworking;

Jacob was useless, full of wine most days, chasing women of ill repute.

'I have nowhere else to turn,' Mama remonstrated with Olivia. 'Who will don sackcloth to mourn the destruction of Solomon's Temple? When the Feast of In-gathering arrives, who will harvest the widow's wage?'

Having relented, Olivia returned indoors with a heavy step. The men were gone and I was finishing my breakfast. 'I am sorry, Gazelle,' she said, her eyes damp with sincerity. 'I could bear her sadness no longer.'

As the dry season ended and the wet commenced, I helped Mama keep pace with the cycle of Jewish mourning and remembrance. Having purified her hearth for Nebuchadnezzar's Fast, I returned to offer blessings for the New Year. Then Mama sent me to the groves. The villagers had reaped the harvest but before the earth was ploughed again it was time for the gleaners. I joined the other outcasts of the village—widows, orphans and foreigners—to gather what remained in field and grove. Working together, we beat the olive and walnut trees, scrabbling in the dust to claim the few fruits that fell. We scraped trampled grapes and rotting figs from the ground to wrap in leaves for stewing or rendering later. At the end of the day, we feigned deafness as we trudged past Sarai and her sneering brood of gossips at the well, baskets of damaged pickings balanced on our heads.

But even when the in-gathering was complete, Mama would not release me. Pressing her advantage against a weaker rival, she secured Olivia's agreement to a permanent loan of my time. So it was that each day, from just after Simeon and Gideon left for the groves until just before they returned to Olivia's hearth at high noon for their meal and sleep, I was sent back to fetch, grade, card, churn and sweep in a house grown still and strangely silent. Shona was gone, Papa, Joshua and Simon too, while Mama rattled around inside, complaining. She complained about Joshua's absence, Jacob's wantonness and Sarai's sniggering pride. 'And you!' she would sigh at the close of this daily recitation, fixing me with the long eyes of a dog. 'Barren as the day is long.'

My lack of fruitfulness was distressing to Olivia, too. Nearly two years after Judah had taken me to wife, my womb remained empty. Unlike Mama, Olivia would not chastise me directly. Instead, she began worrying aloud to Judah on his brief visits home. I remember the first time well. The air that day had been sodden and dense: pregnant with the rains of the new season that had yet to fall. My husband had come crashing into the square from the wood, as he often did, like a wild animal, his hair and robes, even his skin smelling of damp. I ran forth to meet him and we embraced before heading home.

We retired to the mats immediately and remained there until dark, ignoring Olivia's shy invitation from behind the tapestry door to rise for the evening meal. Both of us slept then, but I woke later to find the mat beside me empty. By the hearth, I heard Olivia moving about, making Judah food.

'Miriame was always so fertile,' I heard my new mother fret. 'Even now, so many years after I first laid eyes upon her, I still see her this way. The child bride Yosef brought back to Nazareth: pretty, frightened, and fat and full with child.'

Judah said something and Olivia clucked like a hen. 'I know you are. Everyone knows you are trying. You are a good husband, to come so far and as often as you do, to lie with her. Though, you do know,' I heard rather than saw the shy smile, 'how your

Papa and I rejoice to see you. He has been so ill, and his spirits soar whenever you grace our hearth. You honour us well, my son.'

I heard them embrace and again, Judah spoke in tones too low for me to hear. But Olivia's reply was clear. 'Yes, of course. And as you practise patience, I will do likewise. She is a fine wife otherwise. Clever, dutiful and,' I heard the thump of Olivia's fist on her meaty chest, 'pure of heart.'

Pure of heart. The phrase Papa had used on his last journey to Jerusalem to chastise Judah and the other village men. *Good and pure of heart.*

That night, the words plagued me, jostling for attention in my dreams. In the morning, they were there still, nipping at my heels like a motherless lamb. They bleated for attention as I delivered to Mama Judah's news of Joshua: he was reported to be walking the shores of the Galilee Sea, still searching for Maryam and travelling with two brothers, fishermen, from Capernaum. They nudged me as I raced from Olivia's hearth to Bindy's for the spices I needed to make Judah's favourite bread. I even felt the words turning over, like sunlit petals in the flow of a stream, while enjoying my husband's caresses. The following morning, they were still pressing their case as, my throat closing with sorrow, I bade Judah farewell.

Because I was not pure of heart. If I were, I would not lie to Judah, Olivia and everyone else too. I would not lie, as I did every day, without saying a word, about the fruitfulness of my womb.

Bindy, having foreseen the problem, had little sympathy. She snatched the near-empty herb jar from my hands and returned it to the shelf. 'Not for married women,' she said. 'I told you those vultures would talk.' Cawing and cackling in imitation of the women at the well, she lumbered back towards the sitting mat. 'Why not be done with it, Rachael?' she snapped. 'What are you saving yourself for? You have been little use to me since you married. Here rarely, and when you are, always trying to slip away, to Olivia or your mother, whoever bawls the loudest.'

I was wounded. 'I was never far from your side when plague struck Gath Hepher!' I protested.

'Gath Hepher! Gath Hepher!' Bindy's hands beseeched the sky. 'This was more than a year ago now! I am old, Rachael! Unable to dig, or climb.' She gestured at the rows of jars, many without lids or lying open on their sides. 'Most of them are empty, girl. How do you think I have been managing?'

I did not know. I had not thought. I hung my head as a silence took hold, broken only by the sound of Bindy sucking her tooth. She was right. Ravaged by pity for my mother and burdened with debt to Olivia and Judah, I rarely had a chance to serve Bindy. When I did manage to come, I could never stay long. Even our Sabbath preparations for my initiation, now just weeks hence, had gone by the way. Exhausted by the week's labours, I had little choice on the day of rest but to sleep. Tears welled in my eyes. I would never pass the test now. But when I spoke, my voice held steady. 'It's true Bindy, I am of little use. You are right to question why I continue to fight what will come in time. What you correctly say,' I gazed balefully at my flat stomach, 'is written.' I paused for a moment, searching for the right words to explain the dread that gripped me when I thought about bearing.

'It is not that I don't want Judah's child.' I was still standing by the shelves of jars. 'I do. He is my beloved. My perfect one,' I was speaking to myself now, though Bindy's bearing made clear she was listening. 'It is only that…he *acts*. When he speaks of the brigands, when he arises and leaves me to be with them again, I mark his joy and purpose. I am not green-eyed. I know that he loves me, and I would not have him become less himself, for I love this aspect of him also. It is just that I want…that I wish that I too—' I broke off, knowing myself in sudden danger, at risk of naming the forbidden stirrings of my heart.

But Bindy understood. Stumping towards the shelves she cupped my hands roughly and shook the last of the pregnancy cure into them. A blow of seed and bark and tinder-dry leaf. 'Then we shall continue to strive towards your initiation. To go on together, as teacher and heir,' she said, her milky gaze determined. 'In search of higher ground.'

Two weeks later, the night before my initiation, I woke in a sweat, convinced I'd been weeping and moaning aloud. The pleading words were still loud in my head: *I don't know, I don't know, I don't know!* I lay on my mat, wide-eyed, listening for Gideon's curses, the huff and groan of Simeon's heavy frame as he turned in his sleep, the sweet murmur of Olivia at the tapestry door seeking reassurance that I was all right. But there was nothing but the black silence, throbbing in time with my heart.

That evening as I retired, Olivia had wished me success. I had hoped not to call attention to the trial, and the increasingly frenzied preparations leading to it, by telling both Mama and Olivia I was needed by the other. I may have deceived Mama, but clearly my new mother was less easy to fool.

'You smell beautiful,' she'd whispered, acknowledging the lemon-scented oil with which Bindy had anointed me earlier that day. The crone had pared my nails, too, and shorn every blade of hair from my body, eyebrows included. The hair on my head had been spared: this Bindy washed, then wound into three thick plaits, each containing a thread of gold that she would retrieve when we returned to Nazareth and carefully pack away. For days, I had abstained from meat and egg.

As Olivia and I swept away the crumbs from the evening meal and prepared the hearth for morning, my new mother confided in a murmur that she had dedicated the day's sacrifices to my good fortune. 'I prayed aloud to God, Gazelle, but the Heavenly Queen knew I meant her.'

'I am frightened,' I blurted, surprised even as the words left my mouth by my decision to confess. My mother's distant nature and sister's long absence had accustomed me to bearing my burdens alone. 'I'm worried that I shall disgrace myself. That I will make Bindy look like a fool.'

Olivia nodded, her chins pleating, seeming to understand. Reaching for my hands she drew me to her, her bountiful bosom a place of shelter in a storm. 'You will not disappoint, Gazelle,' she said definitely, placing a kiss on each cheek. 'Not Bindy or me or—' her voice fell to a whisper, 'the Heavenly Queen. You are not one to disappoint and nor is my boy, Judah. In this way you are both so alike! Far too brave and determined to give failure a chance.'

As Bindy and I approached Gath Hepher, a woman with fierce eyes appeared from nowhere. She was heavily veiled and tiny in stature, no taller than a five-year-old. She bade us wordlessly to follow her and so we did: through wood and heath, and across a ravine made treacherous by weeds, until at last we arrived at a ramshackle building hidden from plain view behind a hillock. This was the home of Degania, the High Priestess of the cult of the Heavenly Queen. It was a mud-brick shack as slope-roofed as Bindy's, though better maintained, surrounded by lavender shrubs and garlanded with mandrakes to ward off evil. We followed the midget indoors.

The priestess was propped in the corner atop several thick layers of mats. Little more than dust, bones and brown eyes that were always squinting. She was attended by an unsmiling figure so similar in size and appearance to the one who had guided us from the gate that I started in surprise, until our escort moved to stand beside her and I knew them as twins. When it came time for judging, Bindy had said, two maidservants would load the High Priestess onto a sedan chair and carry her to the hearth, where she would sniff, apply, taste and pass judgment on my efforts. It was hard to believe these two child-sized acolytes could manage the task, but so it proved.

The room was already crowded with midwives and healers from the surrounding towns and villages awaiting the spectacle. More women pushed constantly through the door. The wise-women greeted one another lavishly and offered blessings before presenting daughters and new initiates for inspection, their chatter fierce and loud.

Gripping my elbow, Bindy pushed through the throng, ignoring greetings and glancing neither right nor left. Not without effort, she lowered her uneven frame before Degania and offered formal greetings. Pulling me down beside her, she introduced me to the High Priestess as her heir. 'Rachael of Nazareth, daughter of Yosef the woodworker and of Miriame, a woman lost to the ways of old. May Rachael find favour in your eyes, and those of the Queen of Heaven.'

Bindy's introduction stilled the crowd. The women's chins fell as one to their chests, their palms were pressed together and offered to the sky. 'May Miriame return to the Mother,' they droned. 'May Rachael be found worthy in the Heavenly Queen's eyes.'

'Yes,' Degania told them. The quaver in her voice dragged the word beyond its usual length. She turned to me. 'Your reputation precedes you, Rachael of Nazareth. Bindy's praise, as rare as snow on the plains,' her desiccated lips twitched sardonically, 'has been lavish. Is it deserved? Soon, we will know. Today, your skills shall be revealed. Today, the truth shall be known to all.' A cheer went up from the wisewomen. They beat their mouths and stamped their feet. My belly plummeted to somewhere near my knees and began to thrash like a fish in a net.

'Stand back! Stand back,' Degania ordered. The command needed gesture, but Degania's hands remained collapsed at her side, as if all the life force she had left was required for breath. The fierce-eyed midgets came forward to help, stampeding women away from the hearth and towards the back wall of the dwelling.

'Clear a space so Rachael may practise!' the High Priestess said. 'Clear the door so Bindy may leave. She has no role here. What will be, or won't be, Rachael,' she continued, noting my frantic expression, 'is in your hands alone.'

A well-appointed hearth, scrubbed to gleaming, stood ready. It was surrounded by small clusters of baskets, each brimming with herbs, roots and berries. Without a backwards glance, Bindy left, closing the door behind her.

'I have a lump in my breast, Rachael of Nazareth, and am weary most days,' the priestess announced. 'Tell me, what is wrong, and what shall you do to cure me?' The wisewomen gasped and exchanged looks, before leaning in eagerly, their eyes fixed on my face. I stepped to the hearth. A twin proffered an apron and I put it on, taking my time with the ties as I considered the question. Was Degania describing her own condition or one formulated as a lesson? I shrugged, it made little difference, so instead I asked a question. 'If I palpate the lump, will it be rigid, or move beneath my fingers?' I said.

My trial had begun.

It continued through much of the night. Having pronounced a grim outlook for the woman with the breast tumour, I was asked to address myself to the treatment of numerous fevers, infestations and injuries.

As I questioned, considered, stewed and brewed, I recognised how well my teacher, and my own gifts of recall, had served me. I also seemed to have mastered the measured, methodical demeanour so valued by those in the craft. Even a query about the cure for an early unwanted pregnancy flustered me for no more than an instant.

By dawn the next day, the outlook was bright. Bindy, who had only been welcomed back to the fold when proceedings concluded late the previous eve, was surrounded by admirers gushing praise for my skill and wit as she breakfasted. 'She never hesitated, Bindy! As though everything she'd ever learned was inscribed like...like a doorpost, on her heart. And those roots for red, raw throat; you must tell us where you come by them!'

Bindy nodded but divulged nothing. She was raising

spoonfuls of gruel to her lips, concentrating on not spilling. But despite her gruff manner, when I lifted my eyes from my own bowl, I could see she was pleased. My spirits soared. Perhaps I would make her proud after all.

But then, from outside, where many of the women were eating on blankets, we heard a shriek, followed by many more. A woman's name, or that's what it sounded like. *Naomi! Naomi!*

There was a thunder of running feet. A lone cry of mourning clanged like a bell and then the door flew open. A clutch of wisewomen dragged a foul bundle into the shack and more women flooded in from behind. *Naomi! Naomi!* A terrible crying and wailing sound went up from those closest. I pushed closer as the bundle was unwrapped.

Within shivered a woman's broken body. Naomi looked like a creature torn from a trap: robe shredded, red, raw cuts like bites on her flesh and distended limbs that spoke of broken bones. She reeked, too: of fear and shit.

Pandemonium ensued. The wisewomen tore their robes and staggered about the room. They quivered with prayer. *My God, my God! What have you done?*

Amid the din, Naomi's lips parted. The crowd of mourning women stilled themselves and craned to hear as her terrible tale poured forth. She had been set upon by a pack of legionnaires. They were Romans she recognised, having seen them about her village, taking bribes from the elders. They seemed to have been lying in wait for her at the ravine Bindy and I had crossed the previous day to get to Degania's. 'They knew about the initiation! Knew all of us would be here!' Naomi said, her teeth chattering with shock. The soldiers had ransacked her bags and found her *teraphim*, the idol of the Heavenly Queen all the wisewomen worshipped, which Naomi was bringing to Degania to bless. Holding it high above their heads, they smashed the clay figure on the rocks. They denounced Naomi as a witch and beat her nearly senseless. Then, using their spears as spades, they dug a shallow pit.

'They dragged me to the edge,' Naomi continued, her eyes wide with horror as she recalled the event. 'I was forced to watch as each man walked to the edge, lifted his skirt and fouled it with his dung.' The women shuddered and whispered prayers for mercy. This was a pit of death, the place where sorcerers, necromancers and all others who prophesied or healed in the name of idols met their fate. Laid to rest like a corpse in the filth, the sinner would have a cloth tied around their neck and pulled in both directions until he—or she—choked. Naomi began to weep. 'They laid me there, in the muck and filth. They wrapped the scarf and pulled it tight. But then,' she rubbed her lacerated throat in amazement, 'they let it go. I was brought here and set free.'

The wisewomen figured quickly. This was the work of the elders. Rome might rule the State with an iron fist, but it cared little about the worship patterns of Jewish women. But the elders did care. In such a matter, they would deploy common soldiers as paid lackeys to serve their cause. And every woman knew that the elders gave no quarter to the Heavenly Queen. The manner of Naomi's assault, her release as message bearer to the assembly, was no accident and the warning it issued was clear: those who persisted in worshipping the Queen of Heaven would be uncovered and punished. Punished to the full extent of the law, and beyond. There would be no mercy.

The women flung their hands to the rafters in lavish despair.

The Romans! The elders! The Temple! They were plagued! Cursed! Doomed! Hopelessness rose up from the throng, as pungent as Naomi's stink.

'But this is not just!' I heard my own voice cut through the din, startled as Bindy appeared to find myself on my feet, lips and hands in motion, haranguing the crowd. 'We must make a stand! Resist! Defend the Queen and all who serve her!'

There was a shocked lull in the wailing. 'But how, Rachael?' A puzzled query from a woman of similar years to my own. It was swiftly taken up by other voices. 'How? How?'

'The elders have used the Romans to send a message, have they not?' The women murmured their assent. 'We must send a message back. One that makes our resolution clear.'

'What? What should we say?' The crowd was wide-eyed, every face turned towards me, hanging on each word.

What indeed? In the silence, the weeping intensified. Women began wringing their hands and gouging themselves in despair. I prayed for inspiration. And, just as it had since I was a child, it came.

'We must say no. That we refuse,' I said. 'That we shall not salve wounds, or bind broken limbs or treat fevers and contagion. Nor shall we attend any births,' I was speaking slowly, the words running just paces behind the thoughts blazing the way. 'We tell them that we shall serve no one, heal nothing, until our torment stops. Until we are free to serve and worship the Queen.'

The wailing and gnashing of teeth ceased all together. The women looked at one another, mystified. 'No births?' someone said. 'No cures,' asked another, 'for anyone?'

'No births. No cures. No healing. No exceptions.' A tide of righteousness swept through my breast, buoying my heart.

'They despise us, but they need us. They shun us in the square but at night in their homes, beside the loved ones we have saved, they press coins in our hands. We must stand as one to secure our place in the world, and the place of our Goddess.'

There was complete silence in the room. Looking around I saw brows lift and mouths twist as the midwives and healers considered. I saw the women, young and old, look back and forth between me and the ravaged figure of Naomi, now sobbing as if her heart had been broken as well as her spirit and body. I saw my idea find purchase and start to take root.

But then, a dry, familiar voice piped up from somewhere near my knees. 'And what about the women, Rachael?' It was Bindy. She staggered to her feet, her tone rich with contempt. 'Your anger is virtuous. The sentiment is true. But what of the women who will be trampled in the stampede for freedom? The women who need us to bring their children into the world safely, to save the men they depend on: the women we are sworn to serve?'

'Yes,' a midwife echoed. She was joined by two more. 'Yes, what of them, Rachael? What of the women?'

They will die. We will sacrifice them for the good of ourselves, the good of our Goddess and the good of those who will come after. Resistance demands sacrifice and all victories worth having come at a price. In every war, some soldiers must fall.

I thought this, and I nearly said it. The words rose to my lips and paused there, ready for release. But then I bit down on them, unsure this was an audience I could ever persuade and loath to humiliate Bindy through further contradiction and challenge.

Bindy seized on my hesitation to address the floor. 'Naomi's tragedy is our tragedy, her shame is our shame. But we are healers and midwives,' she glanced at me sideways, 'not rebels of Gamla. We must care for our fallen sister, wash her wounds, offer comfort. We must honour Naomi by pursuing our destiny as the saviours of women, not their executioners. It is not our way to take up some and leave others behind. To refuse care to those who come begging, to decide by ourselves who'll live and who'll die.'

The healers were trading glances and nodding. I had lost them and now Bindy was reeling them back towards the familiar shore. The moment for protest and action—always ephemeral—had passed. Bindy's hand waved me aside. 'Then the case is shut. We shall speak of it no further. Let us pray for Naomi's good health, and the Queen's good blessing on the births and healings we do in her name.'

Bindy turned to the High Priestess, overlooking the scene from her sedan chair. She must have weighed less than a sack of flour: the twins had been holding her aloft for some time, yet showed no signs of strain. 'What will you have us do now, Degania? Continue Rachael's trial, or defer it to another day?'

Degania pressed her lips together. 'I have seen enough, Bindy,' she quavered. 'Indeed, I have seen more than enough. She is quite a woman, Bindy. I fear and envy you both.'

She turned to me. 'Rachael of Nazareth. I judge you fit for the next stage of your journey. Fit and ready to be sworn as a servant of women, a channel of healing for the Goddess, and heir to Bindy of Nazareth.' The High Priestess addressed her small attendants sharply. 'Put me down and bring the sacred oil, so we may draw Rachael into the fold, then return our gaze to Naomi in her hour of need.

'Come hither Rachael and kneel at my feet,' the priestess

commanded. And with no more ceremony than that I bowed my head before the crone Degania and was anointed a healer of the Heavenly Queen.

Bindy was first to offer me her blessings. Her wrinkled face radiated joy and pride as she moved to embrace me. But there was another look there, too. One I knew well, but had never before seen directed at me. It was doubt.

⁊

The arrival of Tabernacles marked two years since my marriage to Judah. In the square, whispers about my barrenness had long since given way to shouts. No longer a matter just for gossips, my fate and Judah's were now subject to the judgment of the elders. They gathered beneath the fig tree in the square, armed with their scrolls. They pondered for many days. Then they laid down the law.

Henceforth, Judah was to return to Nazareth each week to lie with me. Having performed his duties, he would make sacrifice and pray for his seed to take root. I was forbidden to rise from our mats for the duration of his visit and Olivia was ordered to enter our chambers at the conclusion of our coupling, to oversee the deployment of my nether regions upon a pillow, womb open to God.

Bound by such demands and simmering with shame (which I was required to demonstrate) and resentment at the intrusion into my affairs (which I must not); and with all eyes and tongues in the village shadowing my every step, it was months before I could resume my service to Bindy.

But when summer came, and with it the birthing pains of Daniel the tanner's sister, Bindy's summons for me to join her at the mother's side was peremptory and unequivocal. I apologised hurriedly to Olivia and raced towards the birthing house. As I approached, the unmistakable cries could be heard, followed by low, firm instructions in Bindy's weathered tones. Movement could be glimpsed through the window of the one-roomed shack, built of wood and roofed with vines so it could torched, and the site cleansed by fire, at the close of each year.

The tanner paced before the cloth door, blocking my way. He had been muttering to himself but, when he saw me, restraint deserted him and invective flew in a hail of spittle from his gap-toothed mouth. 'My sister is lame!' he shouted, pointing at the building. 'She is lame!' His manner implied this was somehow my fault. 'She ought not be bearing. Should not be bearing at all!'

What to say? I offered what I hoped was a neutral smile and tried to pass. But the tanner crossed his arms before his chest in the manner of a statue and stood firm before the cloth door. It undulated in the gentle autumn breeze while overhead, the silver branches of the evergreen trees quivered too. 'She skewered herself on a winnowing fork,' he complained, 'four months ago now. Made herself lame, the silly cow, so her husband no longer wants her.' Inside, the moan of the suffering woman spiralled upwards. The spasm seemed to go on forever, ending at last in a rush of terrified sobs and a plea to God for mercy.

But the tanner's pity was elsewhere. 'So who was bound to take her? Me!' His voice was rich with invective. '"Send her back to her ancestral home. The tanner will take her. He can feed her and share in her shame."' He spat. 'The harlot! No mention she was quick with child, then!'

I'd had enough of this man, his voice, his views, his stink.

Locking his gaze in mine as if about to challenge him I used my foot to manoeuvre a fallen pinecone into position. Without dropping my gaze, I swung my foot back and, praying for the best, kicked it as hard as I could into the stone water jar standing at the far corner of the birthing house. It connected. The noise of the collision, somewhere behind his left shoulder, turned the tanner's gaze. His head swivelled to locate the source of the sound.

That was the chance I needed. Ducking around him, I fell through the curtain and into Bindy's arms, just as the next of the sister's pains began gathering momentum. 'About time,' Bindy muttered. She handed me the damp cloth with which she'd been dabbing the labouring one's brow so she could dive into her bag for additional supplies.

The hours moved slowly. Day turned to night, then began marching towards day again. The tanner never returned to his bed, nor even rested on a mat outside. Instead, he paced outside the birthing house, ranting and praying aloud for a stillbirth. The boils that peppered his feet and lower legs were much like the rest of him, sweaty and rank in the dusty heat.

The ignorant—of whom there was no shortage in Nazareth—called him leprous, though the tanner told anyone who would listen that the true cause of his affliction was the dungwater he stamped about in all day to soften the hides. Let them judge, he would shrug, feigning indifference. Tanning was the filthiest work known and he had long ago accepted that he would live and die outside the circle of God's concern.

But in Bindy he seemed to have found someone even he might revile. He cursed her freely, shaking his fist at the heavens, hurling her name as abuse. But Bindy knew nothing except his sister's mounting agony, the night of challenges she must face and defy. The crone worked wordlessly: dispatching me for raspberry leaves to make a strengthening brew she spooned through the labouring one's lips; for dandelion root to speed her pains. When the green slime of infant distress appeared, presaging a breech, she stood back as I performed the manoeuvring remedy that forced the infant to turn so it might come into the world the right way around.

At last, just before dawn, it was done. A little girl—too tiny, but clinging to life. I packed the mother with linen soaked in milk-thistle while Bindy rubbed the small body with oil and filled the navel with salt. She wrapped the swaddling clothes tight. Securing the infant to her mother's breast, the crone rose on legs shaking with fatigue to deliver the news.

The hairy mole on the tanner's eyebrow jumped. 'My sister lives? And the child, too? All is well, is it?' He gathered his righteous fury to him. 'For her, perhaps, and her bastard. But what of me?' Each thump of his chest liberated a small cloud of stench. 'Dear God,' he wailed. 'Have mercy on my name!'

I saw the effort Bindy made not to step away or cover her nose. Instead she said, in a flatterer's tongue, 'Long have you suffered, Daniel the tanner. For your kindness, your sister is in debt. May her girl-child grow strong and give birth to kings. May she serve you in your dotage—'

'A *girl*!' This was the final insult. 'The bastard!' The tanner spat, a sea-spawn of jelly that landed on Bindy's foot. 'My sister, the whore!'

And so it went, Bindy's muted words whistling comfort, the tanner snarling with thrusting chest and stabbing finger, threatening violence. Until at last, he seemed to grow weary of repeating his insults. He paused, appearing spent. Prepared to accept his lot.

'I'll bring her and the bastard in. For now,' he muttered turning away, though he offered this final abuse to Bindy beneath his breath. 'Witch's slit.'

And suddenly, before I even knew I had moved, I was there, barrelling through the door of the birthing room after the tanner. Pushing at his back. 'What did you call her?'

'Eh?' Turning with fist clenched, the tanner startled to find himself nose-to-nose with a rangy, arrow-eyed woman of less than twenty years.

'How dare you speak to her like that!' My finger wagged. 'You foul, self-loving, maggot-ridden cockroach!'

'You little witch,' he replied uncertainly, turning so he might strike me with the back of his hand, an insult for an inferior. But Bindy intervened. Pinching my ear, she yanked me aside, her face and palms upturned as she pleaded with the tanner. 'One thousand pardons, Daniel the—' The blow meant for me caught her in the mouth, knocking her frail form to the ground. Her last tooth flew from her mouth and landed in the dust. She grappled in her belt for a nose-rag, pressing it to her face to stem the blood. She tried to rise, but could do no more than rock on her knees, gasping for breath.

The tanner was unrepentant. He took a step closer and spat on her again. Curled a vicious lip in my direction. 'Sorcerer's whores! The both of you, and my harlot of a sister. I wash my hands of you all.' And rubbing his palms briskly to demonstrate the truth of his words, he stormed away.

Bindy wasn't angry. Not then, or a few days later, when I hastened by her home on my return from dispatching a message for Olivia at the caravan trail. The tanner's sister, her sleeping infant bound to her back, appeared at the hearth to serve us tea, then melted away. Bindy flexed the stiff joints of her hands over the rising steam from the cup, her bruised cheek a florid squirrel pouch. The crone had something to say to me, and she delivered the news gently.

I would not be her heir. She was dismissing me, and would seek another disciple. 'It is a pity, Rachael. But this,' she gestured at the scrolls and herbal clutter in the room, her head shaking, 'this is not your way.'

'But Bindy, I have said I am sorry. I did not mean—'

'—to cause harm. To me, or the tanner's sister. Of course you did not. But you could not have done otherwise. I know you, Rachael. If the chance offered itself again, would you not do the same?'

I bit my lip. 'I can be different,' I insisted.

'Different?' Her toothless mouth bent in a smile. 'But why should you be? Daniel the tanner wronged his sister, and before that he wronged yours. He wronged me, just as those soldiers wronged Naomi. Injustice rears its head and you rise to name it. To fight for ways to end the shame. This is who you are, Rachael. You cannot be other. It is I who have erred: in mistaking your true wit for a calling; by misreading, so many years ago, the birth of the lamb. In trying to protect you from my mother's fate by remaking you in my image.'

'Bindy, I…you—' I stuttered, my tone pleading and thoughts in a turmoil. But I could see it was no good. Her mind was made up, her lips shut like a bolted door. 'Then what am I to do?' I wailed. 'Where will I find a place?'

Bindy looked away. Picked up her cup and put it down without drinking. 'I do not know, Rachael,' she said at last.

'The stars do not reveal themselves to me. I do not divine waters nor read the leaves of tea left in the pot. Your fate will probably astound us both. But of this I am certain. Whatever road you travel, however near or far, the words of the Queen in your ear shall be the same.' And beckoning me close, she whispered those words in my ear. '*Speak the truth, Rachael, and fight its foes. Stand firm for all you believe. When doubt assails you, take my hand. I will show the way.*'

The sound of rushing water filled my ears, making Bindy's words, her vow of continuing friendship, seem far away. I had failed. I was a failure. My eyes smarted with tears and a lump formed in my throat, making it hard to swallow. It was a bitter pill to take. But Bindy wanted me to understand: to know that she was not casting me out, but setting me free. She sighed and tapped her chin, rummaging for the words to illuminate her meaning. Finally, she pointed at her sunken old chest, describing a circle with elegant gestures. 'Go around,' she said. Then, leaning forward, she jabbed the air in my direction. 'Go through.'

I grunted with impatience. She often spoke in such riddles but at that moment, my tolerance was thin.

'Always there are walls, Rachael,' she persisted. 'Walls that block our path. Too high, too hard. We stop to rest, to gather strength, and before we know it we have lived whole lives in their shade. In time, we cease to even see them there, casting their long shadows, blocking our path. We cease to yearn for the other side.

'Some don't forget,' she continued. 'They seek to cross over, but not in the brightness of day. In the night's quiet, so daggers stay sheathed and no one gets hurt.' That was Bindy's way. She had sought justice for the tanner's sister and her child, but with bowed head, not drawn spear. I nodded my understanding.

'This is not your way, Rachael,' Bindy said. 'You will never grow comfortable in the shade. You want to pass to the wall's far side, but not just that. You want to condemn the wall and shame those who built it. To stand by the wall in the full light of day and blow your shofar like the warrior Yohoshua and see the wall come tumbling down. That is you, Rachael, and before you can be true to anyone or anything, you must be true to yourself.'

Teardrops streamed from my eyes and stained my cheeks. I stared at Bindy, not wanting to hear the words, yet knowing they were true.

There was nothing more to say. So instead I wept for a long, long time. I bade farewell to the woman I had thought I could be, while Bindy whispered words of comfort and held me tight.

❧

As the months passed, word of my brother arrived more often, usually from travellers who had passed near the Galilee Sea on their way south from Damascus, or moving north-west from Tiberius to Tyre. Joshua's following had grown, the brothers joined by more fishermen, a tax collector and a mute named Nathaniel. Judah confirmed as much on his weekly visit home, not long before the winter Fast of Esther.

'All pursuing Maryam?' I found the faithfulness of my brother's obsession astounding. That men who had never met her would join Joshua's quest was beyond comprehension.

'No. Or not as I have heard it, anyway,' Judah conceded. The day was half-done, but we were still huddled beneath the covers, our breath making clouds in the air.

I hesitated, unsure whether to pursue an old gripe. The Sea of Galilee was less than a morning's walk from Gamla. Why could Judah not desert his post for one day to roam among the fishing villages? To see my brother with his own eyes and discover the truth for himself?

My face must have betrayed me because Judah groaned and pulled the blankets over his head. 'Don't start again, Rachael. I told you! We have been under siege for months. I have lost some of my best men. The officers—the many Davids who would be king—do nothing but bicker over which will ascend the throne, should we ever emerge victors in this endless war. I have no time to wander the seaside in search of an audience with Joshua.'

'But he is your kin. Brother not just to your wife, but to your mission.' Lying on my side, my head resting in my hand, I poked his blanket-shrouded chest. 'They say he preaches bile against the Temple. Condemns it as corrupt. That those who follow him bay for the high priests' blood.'

'And that he is a teacher.' Even muffled, the irony in Judah's tone was clear. 'A prophet, our saviour and the Messiah. Soon, he will be walking on water.'

At last I understood. Grinning, I whipped the cover from my husband's face. 'You are jealous!'

Blinking like a newborn at the sudden cold and light, Judah sought to return to his lair. But when I resisted, battling to hold the blanket at his waist, he graciously gave way. 'Perhaps I am, Rachael,' he admitted. 'But who would not be? For dozens of years the zealots have fought the Romans and seen victory elude our grasp. Time and time again the Jews in the cities side with the pagans and wave the neutral flag. Yet here comes Joshua, roaming the countryside for a few years in search of a woman, hurling stones at the priests with nothing more sharp-edged than a parable, and thousands flock to hear.'

'Thousands? You said—'

Judah dismissed the air with a waving hand. 'Only a handful are true disciples: the outcasts who trail him from town to town with begging bowls in hand, who shelter beside him on barnyard straw by night, and announce him as the Messiah when he crosses the gate of each village. It is they who bang the drums that summon the poor: mallets, forks, nets all cast aside as they draw close to listen.'

'Surely they must also flock to hear the brigands. Your message is the same.'

'No! It is different. Like Joshua, we judge the Temple corrupt, but we know the true enemy is Rome. The brigands say that when the empire falls, the priesthood will too and a Jewish king will assume the throne, ruling over both Temple and State. We say that waiting and praying and repenting our sins is not the way: that God helps men who help themselves.' Grumbling bitterly, Judah rolled over and showed me his back. 'It is not just Joshua's words that captivate, you see. It is the speaker himself. The way he drums his chest, his way with quip and riddle! Who would believe it? Quiet, little Joshua, the fiery preacher of the north!'

'Judah, it was you who said how much he has changed, how his grief and guilt over my sister and Papa and Maryam have transformed him. Stoked his fury, that is what you said. Made him anew.'

Judah grunted, flopping on his back like an oversized fish. 'Made him a teacher? Yes, certainly; already he had such powers. Look how he taught you. Made him a prophet?' Judah shrugged.

'Perhaps. Many hear God's voice in their ear; why not Joshua? But the Messiah? No!' Judah's fist smacked into his palm. 'The Messiah is not a sage, he is a warrior! He does not wield words, but the swords and spears of war. Joshua may be a David—one of many, many Davids—but he is not the saviour promised by God. The Messiah knows that a fish rots from the head down, and the source of the canker is Rome.'

Judah's passion, his certainty about the forces that kept our people enslaved never failed to stir me. Surely, he was correct that the cause of Jewish anguish was occupation, and the key to our salvation the overthrow of Rome. But something rankled. Both Papa and Joshua had heard Judah's account of the curse on our Land, his fervent call to take up arms and fight, yet both had determined a different course. And now, as my brother roamed the fishing villages that surrounded the Sea of Galilee, putting his claims, others were being persuaded to heed his cause.

'You have ears, use them!' Papa used to tell the twins. How I wished I could take that advice now: to see and hear my brother with my own eyes and ears and judge for myself. I said as much out loud.

'Of course you do!' Judah cried in mock despair before throwing himself upon me and ravaging my neck with kisses. 'But this is not possible.'

I smoothed his wild locks, his stubble-rough cheek. 'And why not?'

'Because the back roads and the sandy lip of the Sea of Galilee are no place for a woman in your condition.'

I froze, reminded of our predicament, the one of my own making. Guilt uncoiled itself, hissing in my gut like a serpent. 'What condition?' I parried.

'The one I seek to get you into,' he said, before possessing my mouth with his own.

When I related Judah's news to Bindy, she looked surprised. 'No mention of women among your brother's disciples? Not one? That is peculiar. The Miriame Mourners spoke of no one else.' It was three months later, a warm afternoon on the brink of spring. Gaggles of cyclamen huddled like red and white geese beneath the plane trees. That morning, I had hastened to Deadman's Hill to scatter the last of Mama's leavening in preparation for the coming Passover. When Bindy hailed me on my return, their broad petal faces were pressed towards the sun. The crone shrugged, 'We see what we wish to see, I suppose.'

'Who are the Miriame Mourners? Not those women veiled in white?' Many years earlier, just after Shona was taken to Cana, a flurry of nuns had swept past me at the crossroads of East Nazareth. Broad-boned, apple-cheeked and dressed entirely in white—veils, robes and peculiar cloth slippers—their arms had flown like windmills as they vigorously argued a point.

Bindy's gummy lips bent in a smile at my description. 'Yes, that is them.'

'Why the name, Miriame Mourners?'

'Because they mourn Miriame,' Bindy replied in the tone one reserves for a half-wit. I waited, too accustomed to her ways to be blown off-course, and eventually: 'When Moses died, the People laid him to earth and mourned him for thirty days. His brother Aaron, too, was grieved in this manner when he passed. But not their sister, Miriame. She who had watched over Moses in his papyrus basket; who contrived for her own mother to be chosen by the Pharaoh's daughter to nurse the foundling; who the People of the Exodus hailed as a Prophet. Miriame died in Kadesh, but was never mourned.'

'So?'

Bindy blew air through her lips like a horse to dispatch a hovering fly before continuing. 'So now she is. Every year, as the men prepare to journey to Jerusalem for Passover, the Miriame Mourners make their way to the Egyptian desert. There they perform the mourning rites, as they were done for Moses and Aaron, so that Miriame, too, will be gathered to her people.'

I liked the sound of these women. 'And the slippers?'

'For crossing the desert sands.'

I nodded, but then felt confused. 'Where did the Mourners meet Joshua? He wanders the Galilee, not the Sinai.'

'In the Galilee. Their passage on foot from their home in Antioch near Syria to Kadesh takes time. When I saw them, they had just come from the fishing village of Chorazin,' she gestured to the north. 'Your brother was there. He invited them to share his fire and to break bread with his followers. Mostly female, as I said, and nearly all outcasts: the sick and lame, harlots, widows, lepers. Those plagued by demons.'

'And what does he say? What is it that draws them to him, Bindy?'

Bindy's tongue clicked. 'Some are in love with him. Or with his passion for Maryam. His refusal to give her up.' Her palm pressed to her breast, Bindy cruelly mimed these mooning females, 'Ohhh, if only their own lovers were so gentle and stead-fast!' Then, as if setting a boat to sail, the crone dismissed such foolishness with her hands. 'Others seek forgiveness. Healing.'

'Healing? But Joshua is not a healer.'

'He does not heal as we—as I—do, Rachael. I may channel

215

God's love to ease pain and suffering with the aid of herbs and lore. But I cannot cleanse the sin that causes affliction in the first place. Your brother can. So he says.'

'Joshua forgives sin? Forgives sin like the High Priests at the Temple?'

'Yes. Just like the other one we hear tales of…In the Judaean desert—' Bindy drummed her knobbly chin as she rummaged her memory for the name. 'The Baptiser. Yonaton the Baptiser. Both men forgive trespass as do the priests of the Temple. Lepers, whoremongers, tanners, women destroyed by birthing or the end of their fruitful years, even though their legs be streaked with waste or blood. None are turned back. The Mourners I spoke with swore they had seen both men lay on hands and seek forgiveness for Israelites that the high priests won't touch. And,' Bindy added, like it was an afterthought, 'they do it for free.'

'What?'

Bindy nodded, clearly impressed. 'For nothing. No animals sacrificed or incense burned. No coins exchanged. All they ask is that the sinner truly repent, then go away and sin no more.'

Dread danced at the back of my neck like a spider. 'But to forgive outside the Temple walls is blasphemy, Bindy. It is to claim the healing power of God. If the priests learn of it, Joshua will be in danger.'

'Yes,' Bindy agreed cheerfully. '*Woe to him who threatens the power and pockets of the priests.*'

Stupidly, I leapt to my feet, as if preparing to ride out in rescue. 'We must warn him! Stop him before it's too late!'

Bindy made shushing noises until I returned to sitting. 'He will be safe, Rachael, as long as he is careful. If he forgives only the poor and outcast and keeps far from Jerusalem—it is not the tithes of outcasts that heat the priests' floors, and Rome's arm of friendship only shelters Judaea. It does not reach to the Galilee.'

Just then the door burst open and a girl bustled in, her arms heaped with fresh herbs, her lips spilling words as if continuing a conversation. 'You were right, Bindy.' She pressed her back against the door to close it. 'The meadow was overflowing, though if you can believe it, I was foolish enough to forget a basket and so had to use my hands—' She disappeared towards the hearth, only to return moments later, relieved of her burden, but still chattering like a coney. 'Cows had been through, too. I used both mud and grass to clean them but still you can see that I stepped in the most immense pile of—oh!' She spied me at last.

'This is Rachael,' Bindy said.

'Oh,' the girl said again. Then, as if trying for something better, 'And upon you be peace, Rachael.' This being the manner in which one replied to a greeting, not offered one, she clapped a hand across her mouth in embarrassment. The hand, like the rest of her, was oddly fashioned. Broad and flat, as were her feet, while the long curve of her back ended in a generous mound of flesh from beneath which two bowed legs extended. I recalled the name Sarai had given Bindy's new apprentice while gossiping by the well: Duck.

She would not have had more than twelve years. I tried to smile but my face decided otherwise, my cheeks and lips as stiff as dried clay. 'Peace and blessings be upon you,' I managed at last. 'God keeps you well, I pray?'

'Yes,' she replied hesitantly, squaring her shoulders to issue the required reply: *Yes, thanks be. God is good and great.* 'Yes—' she stuttered. 'God...I mean, yes—' Until Bindy, having had her fill of it, waved the girl from the room towards the hearth. Duck stumbled from view and the crone and I were alone.

'She knows who I am,' I said at last.

'Of course.'

'What did you tell her?' I fumbled in my belt for a rag and blew my nose, determined not to cry.

'That you are good and pure of heart. And the cleverest woman I know.'

I looked away. Feigned interest in the shelves. Finally I said, 'I will be a mother soon.'

'Yes,' Bindy said, as if accepting milk for her tea. 'I can see. When are you due?'

I shrugged, but I knew. Had known the moment the coupling was done and Judah lay panting on his back beside me, a leg thrown across my body in the manner of a conqueror planting a standard. 'At the start of the rainy season. Before Dedication.'

Bindy reckoned with her fingers, 'Seven months.'

'Yes.'

'So there is time.' She rose stiffly. 'Hagar has filled the jars.'

Hagar. So that was Duck's name. 'She is a comfort to you,' I said.

Bindy set out the linen squares. 'I shall prepare two doses, just in case,' she said.

'There is no need.'

She heard me but continued building piles on the cloth: roots, bark, berries, the skeletal dust of dried leaves. 'Take them. You never know.'

'It is not necessary.'

'Go on. What can it hurt?'

'No thank you.'

'Take them, Rachael! Take!'

'No!'

'Do not be so bull-headed, Rachael. Just do—'

'Why should I?' I shouted. 'There is nothing else now!'

Silence, except for skittering footsteps from the hearth—Hagar coming to investigate—that pattered away again. Bindy finished assembling the cure and, tying the rags in two resolute knots, held them out to me. I understood the concession. My former teacher was saying she had not given up hope. That despite my marriage and dismissal from her hearth, I still had a chance to find—or make—myself a place; that there was still hope for a kink or fortuitous detour in my slated path. 'It is your decision, Rachael, but please take them with you,' was what the crone said, 'because you may change your mind.'

I did not reach for the bundles. 'How do you know, Bindy? You do not read stars or divine waters. You said so yourself.'

She nodded her head in agreement but kept her arm outstretched to me; determined to prove she believed in me still. It trembled with the effort, but she would not let it drop. 'I feel it,' she said. 'In my bones.'

When my monthly flows returned Judah was disappointed, but his hope never flagged. As the wet ended and spring began, he continued to conform to the elders' demand that he return home each week to sow new life in my womb. My pleasure in his presence warred with guilt at its cause. In an attempt to ease my throbbing conscience, I buried the second of the cloth bundles Bindy had given me under the box bush behind Mama's house.

Soon, it would be but mould and dust, and the decision would be gone from my hands.

I was reminded of this resolution two months later, when Judah and I passed the spot while gathering kindling for Olivia's hearth. It was Sabbath eve, just past Pentecost and the grain-harvest was drawing to a close. The previous week, the Esdraelons had climbed from the valley with Nazareth's portion strapped to their back. This was Mama's cue to dispatch me to the plains to glean what remained as her widow's wage. The day, in the well-sown fields of vetch and barley, had not gone well.

'We were climbing up from the valley,' I set the scene for my husband as I stacked another branch on the unwieldy tangle in his arms. 'Our robes all covered in chaff and shoulders stooped from the day's labours.'

'It has been hot,' agreed Judah companionably before I went on.

'There was scant grain remaining, but what we'd found was strapped to our backs. We were hot and tired and sticky when who should be there to greet us at the gates of the village but Sarai—'

Judah groaned.

'—with belly to here,' I indicated her generous girth. 'Her time must be close now. She looks like she's eaten a cauldron.'

With considerable effort, Judah shifted his burden to one arm so he might stroke my cheek with a finger. His eyes were wet with sympathy for what he imagined was my envy of a more fertile rival.

Avoiding his eyes, I pretended not to notice. 'So she says all the usual things,' I said, bending to the earth for another stick to add to Judah's pile. '"Oh, the shame of it," and "How low have the mighty fallen. Miriame of Nazareth on the widow's wage!" and—' I pressed my finger to my chin, hoping my expression matched the one of showy contemplation on Sarai's face, '"Do you think it was Shona's sin or Rachael's that made Miriame's sons so feckless?"'

'The sour-breathed heifer!' Judah swore.

'But wait! The best bit comes next.' I smiled just to recall it. 'Ateesha, that's the Phoenician woman I told you about—cast out with her daughters to please the new wife. Well, Ateesha steps between the two of us, belly to belly with Sarai, though because Sarai is so enormous their noses are still close to a cubit apart, and begins cursing Sarai in Phoenician.'

Judah began laughing.

'She curses Sarai's mother, and Sarai's mother's mother, and the mothers of her line all the way back to the first woman, Chavah. Ateesha curses them all. She beseeches Kathirat to ensure that when Sarai's time comes, her eyes cross with the pain and remain so for eternity. She pleads with the Goddess to forever bless Sarai with the belly and breasts of a bearing woman, long after the last of Sarai's children have slipped from between her thighs. She pleads for Sarai's wine to turn to vinegar, for every cake and loaf she bakes to fall flat, for her daughters to be sold as slaves—'

Judah's laughter had given way to silence. Now he cut across me, looking bewildered. 'How do you know, Rachael?'

'What?'

'How do you know what Ateesha said?'

'Because I was there! Standing right beside her, I told you—'

'But she was speaking Phoenician. You said this yourself, Rachael. Cursing Sarai in Phoenician.'

It was my turn to be silent.

'How do you know Phoenician, Rachael? No one in Nazareth speaks it and Ateesha and her daughters are the first Phoenicians to pass through in years.'

Still I said nothing, the wind of my breath held captive in my throat. I felt as I had all those years ago at the Passover Seder beneath Papa's questioning gaze. Innocent of the source of my talents, but worried that their revelation could only mean punishment, and the loss of love.

'I heard them speak it,' I mumbled at last. 'Ateesha and her children, while they reaped, moving up and down the rows with winnowing forks, me with a basket in their wake.'

'But you could not have been listening for long. The People's harvest has only just ended! The in-gathering for outcasts declared just last week!'

'Yesterday,' I whispered.

It is astounding what one hears in the stillness. The wring and smack of clothes at the washing point, the lilt of psalms from the square as the elders prepared for the Sabbath, the drifting whine of a biting insect. The anxious throb of one's heart.

At last, Judah stirred. Throwing the bundle of kindling aside, he beckoned me close, the scent of his skin, the wrap of his arms, as sheltering as a tent.

'My sweet Rachael,' he whispered. 'My tender bloom.'

Then, sounding strangely like Mama that long-ago day when Papa killed my lamb, 'How hard the world must be for you.'

When morning came, Judah murmured his farewells to Olivia and left her at the hearth sacrificing twists of bread for his safe return. As was our habit, we traversed the square together, as close as we could get without touching, to bid one another goodbye at the foot of the northern trail.

Usually, he was gone in a trice. With the graze of his lips still on my skin and the echo of his words in my ear, I would watch as he strode away, thoughts already consumed by political plots and battle plans. But today was different. Having scanned the square for prying eyes and found none, he pulled me into the wood for what I imagined would be a last embrace. Trailing him, I allowed my headscarf to fall to my shoulders and loosened my belt. When he turned at last to face me, I let my lips fall open for his kiss.

But my husband had other matters on his mind. 'There is something I must ask you,' he said. His hand gripped my arms urgently. 'Rachael, you are truly barren, yes? The curse on your womb is God's will not...not your own?'

He knew. Bile and relief flooded my mouth in equal measures. I felt the ropes of my throat move as I swallowed. When I spoke, the words in my ear were too loud. 'I am not barren. It is I who stopped life from taking root in my womb. Not God.'

Judah looked as if he had been slapped. With clumsy paws he rubbed at his eyes, as if seeking clearer sight. 'Why?' he whispered. 'Why would you do such a thing?'

'You know. You know why I did it.'

But it seemed he did not. As if all he knew about me, all he had learned from my brother, and since we were married, and from our talk the previous evening while gathering wood, had flown from his mind.

'You accepted my seed, then poisoned it?' His voice was hoarse. 'Brought shame on my name, on our house? Dishonoured my mother and father? Claimed to love me, yet denied me sons?'

'Or daughters,' I snapped. 'It was not lack of love that moved me to do it, Judah. I love you and you know it. It has nothing to do with you—' I broke off, the incredulous expression on his face assuring me I was only making matters worse.

'I have forsaken it, Judah,' I said quietly. 'This is what matters now. I have relented. Given the cure away. Accepted my fate.'

But such assurances seemed to hit my husband like a rock between the eyes. 'Your fate? Your *fate*? Most women pray to the Almighty for a fate like yours! A mother like Olivia. A husband who spares the rod. A womb that grows quick with child. But plainly this is not enough for you! Not enough for Rachael of Nazareth! So tell me what it is you pray for, Rachael? What is it that you want?'

He was shaking me now, the limpid sheen on his eyes flying loose as tears. 'Tell me! Tell me!'

'To die more than a mile from where I was born!' I shouted. 'To have done more than bake and bear and clean in the years between!'

There was a beat. Loud, like a cymbal, or a new moon drum. Judah released me. Staggered back in the crouch of a beaten dog. 'But what of me?' he said at last. 'Am I not enough?'

'Oh!' Enraged, I flew at him. Pummelled with both fists on his barrel chest. Drubbed and beat and pounded until, somehow, we both began to laugh. There, in the shade of the fir trees, the dry summer earth dusting our feet like flour, we laughed and snorted and gasped.

'Yes,' Judah said as we wiped our eyes. 'Yes, I think I see now. I think I understand.'

Understand? Perhaps he did. But as the moon waxed and waned three times and Judah did not return home I began to harbour doubts. Doubts about my husband's capacity to comprehend my deepest longings and his willingness to pardon my betrayal.

The elders, astonished at his defiance of their edict, flounced about the square muttering darkly, until Simeon sent so many baskets of pomegranates to their houses on the hill—the freshest bounty from his groves—that a grudging harmony was restored.

But from Gamla, where Judah was stationed, the messages continued to come, arriving each day before the Sabbath around noon, to proclaim Judah's regret for another week of absence and its purported cause: a visiting delegation of Essenes; a raid by the Romans; the demands of new recruits. And, as the Tabernacles Feast approached, a new excuse: an attempted insurrection by the Davids.

Then, one lazy afternoon at the end of Elul, a day crawling with tedium and insects and a dry, heartless heat, a message arrived from Gamla that I was not expecting. Scratched on a shard of pottery, it was passed to me by Bindy who, alone among the living—with the exception of Joshua and Judah—knew I could read.

'What does it say, Rachael?' the crone inquired, clamouring at my elbow. She had been guarding the fragment since the previous evening, when a messenger from the north had relinquished it to her keeping, and was now half-frantic with curiosity.

I read it, then turned to her, my eyes wide with astonishment. 'It is from Judah. Joshua has sent word. Maryam has been found.'

Maryam had been found. In the weeks that followed Judah's message my thoughts grew restless with unanswered questions. Where had she been all these years? Was she safe? Was she well? When would she and my brother be coming back home? So certain was I that the answer to this last question must be 'soon', I began falling to sleep each night with a smile on my face. Confident that the following day or the one after that, my eldest brother would burst through the gates of Nazareth astride a donkey colt, his beloved Maryam perched triumphantly behind.

But as the autumn feasts of New Year and Atonement and then Tabernacles came and went with no sign of Joshua, my optimism waned. I began to suspect the worst. To wonder about my husband's decision to send word of Maryam's recovery to me only, and in writing, rather than through the usual sing-song chant of a herald in the square: to fear that after four long years, Maryam's reappearance might not be good news. That whatever had befallen her and my brother, as he sought so desperately to find her, might have altered each of them—and the trajectory of the life they had planned together—forever. I began to fear that she and Joshua might never find their way back home.

If only I could have asked Judah! Surely he knew more than he had revealed in his cryptic missive. And if he did not, perhaps he might finally be willing to depart Gamla for the not-so-distant Sea of Galilee to discover the details of my brother's fate. To see Joshua and his long-lost love with his own eyes, and hear their story himself. But here, too, my hopes fell on barren ground. My husband remained hidden like a worm from the light in the hillside caves of northern Galilee, emerging each week just long enough to dispatch yet another excuse—the delegations, the recruits or, his favourite, the Davids—for his failure to return home. Or so my bitter thoughts went.

Outwardly, and much to Sarai's disappointment, I accepted Judah's regret-filled communications, delivered in the square by a fellow soldier en route to his own village, with equanimity. I even varied my performance some weeks to profess my pride in being married to a man consumed by such important matters of state. In response to Olivia's pitying looks and anxious inquiries, I wore a similarly courageous face.

'Next week for certain, Gazelle,' she would say after the miserable, mumbling comrade chosen by Judah to deliver the bad news finished his piece and raced, with cheeks still burning, towards the town gates to continue his own journey. 'Next week we will see my son descend the northern trail.'

'Perhaps,' I would reply, attempting to sound both cheerful and enigmatic. 'He will come when he can, of this I am certain.'

Only at night, alone in the room Judah and I sometimes shared, did my doubts spring up, unbidden and fully formed, like Chavah from Adam's rib. Were new recruits and Davids really the cause of Judah's prolonged absence? Or was the truth that my husband had yet to forgive my sin? That, despite his claim to have understood me, he had yet to pardon my rebellion or the deception with which I had shrouded it?

Throughout the cold months of the winter wet, I debated the question with myself, lying stiff and wide-eyed before descending to a catacomb of fitful dreams. There I wandered until dawn, searching dark alleyways and serpentine paths for my husband and a swaddled infant that I had somehow mislaid. At the first sounds of Olivia by the hearth, I started to wakefulness and rose to work, eager to shed the sense of foreboding left by my dreams and pursue the peace of mind the Almighty lends, however briefly, to those with busy hands.

But at long last the winter shifted, sighed and began its slow retreat. In the mornings the air was still crisp but men returned from work each afternoon with cloaks in hand. The waters at the washing point rose as the snow melted on the faraway mountains of Lebanon and, in the valley, the first shoots of grain breached the soil and blanketed the plains in green.

And in the wake of the thaw came Judah, stampeding down the trail from Sepphoris late one afternoon a week before Passover. He bounded across the square like a ram outpacing a lion, flung the door open and burst into the room where Olivia and I were kneeling on the mat, shelling almonds.

'Son!' Olivia exclaimed, leaping to her feet so quickly that the empty husks in her lap scattered across the floor. 'What ails you? Is everything all right?'

My husband's chest was heaving, his face and body wet with sweat. He shook his head, but then we were forced to wait as he paced and panted, trying to recover his breath. 'Joshua,' he said at last, mopping his brow with the cool linen cloth Olivia had handed him. 'Joshua is in trouble.'

'What? What do you mean? What trouble?' I was on my feet now, too.

'I do not. Know. He sent a message from. Jerusalem.' Judah was still panting, his broad hands resting on his knees to take the weight of his body. I strained to make sense of his broken phrases. 'It said, *Friend, come quickly. I need your help.*'

'Jerusalem?' I was lost. 'What is Joshua doing in Jerusalem? I thought he was in the Galilee.'

Judah shrugged. I watched him signal Olivia for water. Then, both of us waited, watching the rhythmic movements of his throat as he swallowed. Finally, he returned the dipper to Olivia and wiped his mouth. When he spoke again it was to list his travel requirements on the fingers of one hand. 'Blankets, clean robes, food, water,' he said. Turning towards the open door, he squinted at the sinking sun. 'We shall not leave today. The day is too old, but all must be ready for departure at first light.' Olivia nodded dutifully. She bent to retrieve Judah's travel bag and moved towards the hearth to unpack it. Then, as though it were an afterthought, my husband banged his brow with the heel of his hand exclaiming, 'Oh! Papa's tent.' Olivia looked up, her dark eyes round with attention. 'You must prepare this as well,' Judah told her. 'The one large enough to fit two within.'

For the first time since he had entered the room, Judah's eyes found mine. *Two? Does that mean…Are you intending to…?* I lifted my brow in a silent query. He nodded, grinning. *Yes.*

I did not mean to shout so loudly; did not mean to shout at all. But my joy and relief simply bubbled over. I was loved, not lost; pardoned, not reviled; brimming with promise, not rotting on the vine. Motherhood still loomed on the horizon but the boat in which I was drifting had yet to reach her shore. The news I had planned to tell Judah would keep. By some miracle, I had been granted one more chance to prove myself and be of use: to show myself worthy before God. I threw myself into Judah's open arms.

And so it was that Olivia shuffled about, readying us for the journey to the tune of our coupling. Frantic, forgiving, grasping, we reached for one another again and again.

As if somehow we knew there was little time left.

But there was no sense of foreboding about the next day's dawn, which blossomed to a sky the translucent blue-white of thin milk. Above us, crested larks twittered like mice, while from each den and hollow came the musky scent of new life. As Judah and I set off through the square, daffodils and buttercups sought the sun's warmth through the gaps in the paving stones. Our mothers trailed behind, Olivia waving both tambourine and tongue in a farewell psalm while Mama nagged, reminding us for what seemed like the seventy-seventh time to stop at her ancestral home of Bethany on our way to the Holy City to pass greetings to her sister, my Aunt Malcah. As we picked our way down the steep trail their pleas and farewells continued to fill our ears until at last we reached the plains, where they were blessedly replaced by the soughing of wheat in the breeze.

Finally, Judah and I were free to exchange words. Unhurried words and jesting ones: words unburdened by the run of the hourglass sands and the prospect of imminent separation. We chatted and teased and laughed. We sang, too. Marching psalms and the songs known to all Nazarene youth, many of which Shona had sung to me when I was a girl. About a rat that becomes trapped in a well and another, concerning a duck that unearths a hidden store of grain.

My husband and I strolled side by side, though we remained alert for voices, or the irregular clap of livestock bells that signalled the approach of others. These would send us scurrying—playful with exaggerated modesty—to observe custom: he striding ahead and me trailing three paces behind. Such gestures towards propriety did little to stem the opprobrium of those who passed. Our reckless exuberance spilled over, knitting brows and calling forth wagging fingers from passing priests and goatherds, though we were favoured with a wistful smile from a veiled, bent-backed crone. I imagined she had once been as I was now: a woman in love.

Fortunately, our encounters with other Israelites of either high or low status were limited. The appointed time for the Galilean hordes to commence the three-day journey to Jerusalem for the Passover feast was now just days away and those in the villages were absorbed with preparations, leaving the trail largely deserted.

By afternoon, our talk turned serious. Resting on a sunwarmed rock beside a brook so clear we could observe a shoal of soft-eyed water turtles feeding their young, we slipped dried dates between one another's lips and wondered aloud about the nature of Joshua's plight. Judah told me how my brother's plea for help had immediately prompted him to action. Less than an hour after receiving Joshua's summons, my husband's goatskin was filled, his excuses made and he was gone, hurrying down the trail towards Nazareth. But now he wondered at the depth of his alarm. His first thought had been that Joshua had got himself into trouble in Jerusalem with his preaching. Now, he dismissed this possibility. Only a fool would provoke the Romans by healing and forgiving at Passover, when the gathering of Jews from all parts of the empire at the Temple had the Roman occupiers on edge. And Joshua was no fool.

'So you no longer fear for him?' I asked. Having tossed my sandals aside, I was now dangling my feet in the water. 'You believe he is safe and well?'

'No,' Judah shook his head impatiently. 'Something frightened him, and frightened him enough to summon me away from Gamla, where he knows I am needed. But I do not know what.' He shrugged his massive shoulders, bending absently to scoop up pebbles to skip across the water's surface. 'Your brother is not fond of danger,' he continued, in the manner of one speaking to himself. 'Perhaps he has sensed it in the wind, as a deer scents the hungry lion. This is why he wants me beside him, to stand guard, to ward off disaster, as I have always done. Or, should it prove necessary, to follow him over the edge,' Judah's hand mimed the arc of an object falling from a roof.

'And this you would do? Be my brother's keeper?'

'Of course!' Judah looked offended. A caterpillar had fallen to his chest from the willow tree overhead and he flicked it roughly away. 'Joshua is kin and clan. No man on earth is dearer to my heart! I would kill for him, if it were necessary. I say only that it may *not* have been necessary for me to go out from Gamla like the demon possessed. That I might have taken more time to consider my responsibilities, and set things in order before I left.'

'To have thought before you acted? Looked before you leapt? You?' I mimed horror. Grinning, he grabbed my shoulders and made as if to cast me into the water.

But I shook him off with a shriek. A scorpion the size of Judah's hand had suddenly appeared from beneath the rock on which we were resting. We both watched, open-mouthed, as it scuttled up the stone's face, across my thigh and into my lap.

It all happened at once. My wail of terror, Judah's reflex to bat the creature into the water and, when it clambered back to shore, flip his knife with skilled precision to section it in two. The creature's still-flexing body pinioned to the embankment, the curved, venomous tail fell, splashing in to the waters below. We watched the ripples disperse.

'Perhaps it is just as well,' I said, still breathing hard, 'that you don't stop to think too much.'

It was not until that night, in the scarcely populated caravanserai on the Samarian border, having pitched our tent as far from the others as we dared and made the blankets dance with our love-making, that we finally spoke of the rift between us.

At first Judah swore that I was wrong. That his prolonged absence from Nazareth had not been provoked by anger, nor an unwillingness to forgive me for spurning his seed. Rather, he insisted, the claims he had made by messenger were true: in particular those describing the threat posed by the Davids.

'I could not leave, Rachael. Could not risk it,' he explained as we lay in the dark, a breeze sweetened by almond blossoms from a nearby grove playing across our faces. 'The Davids have banded together and are now casting stones. They say that God is filled with righteous fury. That his anger is the cause of our failure to recapture our land from Rome.'

'God's anger? At what?' We lay side by side like rib bones: close but not touching.

'At our flouting of his commands. The rules of inheritance, of blood,' he continued in response to my silence. 'The rules that stipulate priests come from the house of Aaron, and warriors descend from David. Whereas I, indeed many of our best officers, have no name. No claim to lead an army of God.'

'And how have these sages, these scholars of the sword,' I asked scornfully, 'come to know such truths?'

'Dreams. Well, one of them had a dream, but the others attest to it. They accept his vision as a message from God.' Judah sounded deflated. Like a tired schoolboy repeating a lesson.

I was incensed. I sat bolt upright and sputtered with rage. 'How dare they question your worth? Your place? After all your dedication, everything you have sacrificed to deliver them the throne of Israel. They should be anointing your feet. Praising your name. Falling at your feet like scythed wheat—'

'Perhaps,' Judah said softly, 'but they think otherwise. They have…demands.'

'Demands! Such as?'

'That I, and all other officers with impure blood, accept a lesser rank. That in all matters military it is we who must submit to their commands, the commands of a David, no matter what that man's wit or skill.'

I felt a rise of resentful anger, sharing the stab of humiliation this would have inflicted on Judah. He continued, 'I do not accept this, of course. All of us low-born have vowed to resist.

But this is war, Rachael and I must sleep with one eye open, or risk losing everything. My rank. My post. My men.'

Rolling to my side, I felt in the darkness for Judah's face, let my fingers know his eyes, nose, lips. My hand came to rest in the comforting tangle of hair on his chest, shame covering me like a blanket. 'I beg your pardon, husband,' I whispered. 'Forgive me for doubting you.'

He lifted my hand, sweeping his lips meditatively across the knuckles. 'Do not be sorry,' he said at last. 'You had reason to doubt.'

Eyes wide in the darkness, I waited.

He took my fingers one by one, into his mouth, sucking gently, the words of his confession spaced between digits. 'I could have come home more often. I could have, but I didn't.'

'Why not?' I whispered. The warmth and pull of his mouth on my fingers was inspiring similar sensations between my legs. Turning on his side, he allowed his hand to traverse the hills and dales of my hips and waist, up and back, several times, before slipping it between my thighs.

He said. 'I needed time to think. To decide. To decide what to do about you.'

'I told you! I stopped taking the cure and now I am—'

Judah blocked my mouth with a kiss. The sort of kiss that involved him sucking my lower lip until my breasts heaved and my skin seemed to sparkle like stars. The sort of kiss where I might forgive him almost anything.

'Yes, you said you gave the cure away,' he continued when we surfaced for breath. 'But because you lacked hope. This is not what I want for you. Not how I want you to accept me. To accept this,' he placed my hand on his hardness. 'Then Joshua's message came, and suddenly I knew the answer.'

'What?' I began moving my hand in the manner he liked and he settled on to his back to enjoy my caresses.

'This journey, this is the answer. Taking you with me. So you can see your brother and hear of his adventures yourself. So you can enjoy a respite, however brief, from the pattern of life in Nazareth. So when the voyage is complete, you might return home fat and full. Satisfied. And we can move forward with our lives.' His chest was now heaving, his breath sawing from between parted lips.

I was in no doubt as to what moving forward with our lives meant for me. 'And what will you do, husband?' I whispered, nibbling his ear. 'How will you advance your case?' Beneath the blanket, my hand moved firmly until, on sudden impulse, I decided to use my mouth. I slid down quickly as my husband startled, drew a sharp breath, and began squirming.

'By returning to Gamla,' his words were short and roughly cut, as if he were forcing them from his mouth. 'As soon as I can. To keep the Davids from the gate. It is not safe to stay away for long.' He sat up suddenly and lifted the cover to peer at me. 'My God! Where did you learn to do that?' And for the rest of that evening further discussion of the matter was closed.

In the morning we woke to sounds of unrest. A tight circle of Israelite men were breast-beating and shouting while women knelt keening by the stream. The babes tied to their backs, frightened by their mothers' frenzied lamentations, added their shrieks to the chorus. Even the beasts tethered by the trail were bucking and braying. Drawing his knife, Judah ordered me to pack and went to discover the cause.

The news was grim. 'They have murdered him,' Judah reported when he returned a few moments later to find me wrestling blankets into our bags. 'Word has come that Yonaton the Baptiser is dead.'

The Baptiser: the Israelite Papa and Bindy admired for sanctifying souls in the desert. 'Why? Who?' I sputtered.

'Rome,' Judah replied, and spat in disgust. 'Through the hand of that slavering Greek puppet, Herod.'

I lifted my hands, preparing to rend my robe, but Judah stopped me. 'There is no time for mourning, Rachael. We must travel swiftly. The Baptiser's death is an ill-omen, a clear warning from Rome that healing and forgiving beyond the Temple walls is blasphemy, and will be punished as such. We must find Joshua, and warn him.'

'But why is Rome punishing blasphemy? Surely their concern is to sanction those who threaten the Empire, not the Temple?'

Despite his worry, Judah's features showed pride at my alacrity. 'But with Rome and the Temple, one hand washes the other.' He began dismantling the tent. 'To the Temple, Rome grants the power to tithe and to worship the One God. In turn, the priests teach our people that rebellion offends God, and demonstrate it by collecting their sacred vestments from Jerusalem's governor Pilate each morning before prayers.' Judah spat again.

'The Baptiser was a fool!' I persisted desperately. 'He must have provoked Rome with his healing and promises of forgiveness. You said Joshua would not be so unwise as to kindle unrest by questioning the power of the priests during the Passover Feast.'

Busy lashing the hastily rolled canvas to our bags, Judah replied without looking up. 'I did say it, and hope I am right. But now I am like Joshua, sniffing danger in the wind. And like you,' he knotted the last tether and threw the entire pack across his back as if it were fish bones, 'wanting to see and hear with my own eyes and ears that, in such restless times, Joshua will not be courting trouble.'

We arrived in Bethany the following afternoon intending to make a short stop. We could not stay long, Judah said. We must find Aunt Malcah, discover what, if anything, she knew about Joshua's whereabouts, then depart directly. My aunt, however, had other plans.

Mama's cryptic mutterings and resentful asides about life in Nazareth had led me to expect that her own ancestral home would be more impressive. But Bethany was a pit. So tiny that it lacked walls and a gate; its small, narrow dwellings spattered with bird droppings and clustered like ruins. The only beauty was in the barley fields that edged the settlement on all sides and, at the far side of the grain rows to the south, the olive branches that over-reached the crumbling wall of the garden of Gethsemane.

When my aunt opened the door, her rust-coloured eyes passed over Judah and me as if we were last week's vegetables. She looked as frowsy as usual, her hair unkempt and pointing in all directions, her robe littered with unspecified fragments and stains. 'Finally!' was all she said, as she hurried us inside. She cast a quick glance along the lane for onlookers before throwing the door shut and banging the lock into place. 'What took you so long?'

Judah and I trailed her to the hearth. She offered us nothing, neither water for our goatskins nor food for our bellies. Instead, fluffing her backside like a pillow, she settled herself on a woven mat beside a half-filled bowl of shelled walnuts and hoisted a cracking mallet. The failure to offer hospitality made me flush with shame as I cleared my throat to deliver my mother's formal greetings. 'Peace be with you, esteemed aunt. I come bearing grace and goodwill from your sister—'

Malcah brought the mallet down, sending shell and nut-meat skittering across the floor. 'Yes, yes.' She flicked her eyes at me, an instruction to pick up the debris. 'Peace and goodwill to her, too.'

Judah grasped his opportunity in the gap formed by my distraction and my aunt's lack of social graces. 'Aunt Malcah,' he said briskly, 'I am Judah of Iscariot, Rachael's husband. We are grateful for your hospitality,' he bowed his chin in an attempt at humility, 'but regret we cannot stay long. Indeed, we are eager to return to the road once we learn if you have seen your sister Miriame's eldest son Joshua. Has he passed by here? Do you know where he is now?'

Malcah examined Judah as though he were an insect. 'He has, and I do.' The mallet came crashing down on another shell. Expression unaltered, she indicated the space opposite her on the mat. 'Sit. Sit.'

Judah remained standing. I brushed the nut fragments I had managed to collect into the bowl by my aunt's side and retreated to one of the soiled cushions towards which Malcah was gesturing. My aunt marked Judah's obstinacy and chose to ignore it. Sighing lustily, she set the mallet aside and pressed her hand to her brow. 'Where to begin?' she mused.

Judah looked past the grimy ledge of Malcah's uncovered window at the downward arc of the sun. 'With Joshua,' he replied. 'Where is he?'

'He was here,' Malcah began, 'right here in Bethany. By day, preaching sermons by the well. By night, cuddled up with that harlot Maryam on this very floor.'

Harlot? Maryam? I looked at Judah but he stilled me with his hand, his gaze remaining on Malcah. 'And now he is…?'

But my aunt was not to be rushed. 'At first, most were with him,' my aunt recounted in the hushed and leisurely tones of the story-teller. 'The villagers and labourers in the field, the sick and lame arriving back from the Bethesda pools in Jerusalem where they had sought to cleanse their shame. Outcasts in Bethany and beyond praised him when he said that the last would be first, and the first would be last. They nodded their heads when he claimed that the poor and hungry, even the reviled, were blessed.' Resigning himself, Judah sighed and flopped down beside me.

'But it was not to continue.' Malcah paused dramatically.

'What happened?' I breathed, ignoring the hard look Judah shot at me.

'What happened? What happened?' My aunt was outraged. 'He overstepped himself, that's what happened. They gave him an inch and he took a mile. His mother,' she corrected herself, '*your* mother was the same.'

Joshua like my mother? Judah laid a warning arm on mine, his eyes speaking as loudly as words. *Do not encourage her*. I bit my tongue.

Malcah cleared her throat to regain the floor. 'What happened was that Joshua raised Lazarus from the dead.'

'What?' Judah barked.

'Oh, yes,' Malcah tossed her head and preened. She had known this was a story worth telling. 'Joshua gave life to a dead man. Only weeks ago in Bethany we buried a man, a weaver by the name of Lazarus. Entombed him in the cave at the far end of the field.' Her hand gestured towards the east. 'But the misfortune of his sisters, Martha and Mary, was the greater, for he was the last living male in the family and they could not cleanse death's stain. They remained shunned, reviled, with no male kin to sprinkle them clean.'

'So Joshua forgave the sisters, yes?' Judah said impatiently. 'He performed the rituals that removed the taint of death, so they might lift their heads again, and be returned to the fold.'

'That was his plan,' Malcah conceded frostily. 'But the disciples had other ideas.'

'Disciples?' I prompted.

'Yes. Those fisher fools and a tax collector,' she listed on her fingers. 'And a new one, an albino, they call the twin.'

'So? Then what?' Now Judah was impatient for Malcah to carry on, but she would not be rushed. She must fish in her belt for a rag and noisily blow her nose. She must use a piece of straw to clean between her rotting teeth. Finally, with a last lofty glance at my husband, she picked up the tale. 'The disciples goaded Joshua. Remonstrated with him. Debated and argued from sun-up to sundown until at last, he relented. Agreed to heal Lazarus. To forgive the dead man so he might return to the circle of God's concern; so he might rise and walk again.'

Judah was like a Greek statue, the muscled lines of his body stilled, his mouth open as if he had been slapped. 'Forgive a dead man? Forgive a man that's dead?' he said stupidly. 'How? Why?'

But I understood. 'The dead are the most unclean of all,' I said slowly. 'Cast out forever from the bounds of the village, and God's loving light. If Joshua can forgive a dead man, then who among the living cannot be healed, and saved? And—' I frowned, the significance of my brother's gesture revealing itself as I spoke. 'And if God does not strike Joshua down for forgiving the dead, then He must love him for it, and this makes Joshua more potent than the priests. A saviour.' I looked up. 'The most powerful man in the land.'

Judah looked as I felt. Sick. To behave like this, whether willingly or under duress, was not the conduct of a man looking to avoid trouble. It was that of one pursuing self-slaughter. Malcah was still talking. '...Rolled back the rock and, oh the stench! You could have smelled it for miles. All the desert creatures were driven off by it, even the jackals. But the People stayed. The whole village was there and all of Joshua's disciples. Waiting. Watching. Wanting to see for themselves.'

'See him enter the pit? Actually lay his—' Judah mimed a healer's pose, both hands flat on the earthen floor as if it were a body, his face twisted with disgust.

'Oh, yes,' Malcah confirmed. 'Both hands. He went into that cave and laid hands on that rotting, God-forsaken corpse and mumbled some prayers and then he emerged. Claimed that Lazarus was now forgiven and that, despite having touched him, Joshua remained pure himself. "Lazarus lives!" he shouted. "He is forgiven! God smiles upon him, and he walks in the light again!"'

Judah could bear no more. Leaping to his feet, his hand seeking the reassurance of his dagger hilt, he began gathering up our belongings. 'We must leave now, Rachael. We must find

Joshua at once. The situation is far worse then I had imagined. There is no time to spare. Aunt Malcah, for the last time, please, I beg you. Where is Joshua?'

'Gone!' she squawked. 'Run out of town. The elders banished him and all those with faith in his mission. They would not accept such blasphemy, such flouting of the priests. Oh no! So Joshua scuttled off. Took that harlot with him, and his low-life followers and all the villagers who had sworn their devotion by Lazarus's tomb, in awe of the miracle he'd performed. Nearly half the village gone, trailing after him through the barley rows towards Gethsemane like he was royalty. I have never seen such a show of collective stupidity, not since—'

'Where?' Judah shouted. 'Where did Joshua go?'

Aunt Malcah drew herself up with pride. 'There is no call for rudeness. To the home of the one called Nicodemus. Nico-demus of—' Malcah paused, eyes skywards as she considered before, with a wave of her hand, dismissing all hope of recol-lection, '…something. But the house stands beneath a flowering tree. He said to tell you this when you came calling. A tree of the sort from which you have sighted danger to my nephew before.' Malcah rose, wiped her hands of dust and crossed towards the door. Judah and I trotted after her. 'You must stop him,' she remarked casually over her shoulder. 'Stop him entering the Temple.'

Judah's pace slackened. 'The Temple,' he said weakly.

'Yes, that is where they are going tomorrow. To preach the good news on the cream-coloured steps. The good news that God loves all outcasts and that he has worked through Joshua to forgive them and to raise Lazarus from the dead.'

We were back in the lane with only a few hours of daylight

left. 'Tell him to step with caution,' my aunt continued. 'Remind him that he has brought shame enough on his Aunt Malcah and she wants no more.' The door began closing and we heard her add, 'His mother brought me enough of that already.'

⌒

The clues that Joshua left with Malcah were easy for Judah to fathom. My husband knew Nicodemus. He had lived in Nazareth and gone to school with Joshua and Judah when all of them were boys.

'Why do I not know him?' We had gone out from Bethany to the south, passed swiftly through the rows of barley and now, having crossed the garden of Gethsemane, were winding our way down Olive Mountain towards the Golden Gates.

'Because his father's brother died when you were an infant,' Judah explained. 'He was a wealthy man and left no heirs. So Nicodemus's papa strapped the family's few possessions to a mule and took them to Jerusalem to lay claim to the fortune: more than a talent of gold and a splendid dwelling in the Holy City.' The house was in Cheesemaker's Quarter, Judah continued— nearly grunting with the effort of dredging his memory—in the shadow of King Herod's castle. 'That is what I recall, in any event, though one thing is certain,' he said, with a finger flourish and wry smile. 'We will find it beneath the spreading arms of an apricot tree.'

This I knew already, remembering well the story of Judah's thwarting of the bully, Ruchel. 'Where is Cheesemaker's Quarter?'

We were fast approaching the Golden Gates. From my place several steps behind my husband I saw his broad arm fling towards the south. 'Most of the city's curd is made there,' he flung the words over his shoulder as he barrelled ahead. 'The air is so rich one dines just by breathing.'

Suddenly, my husband cursed beneath his breath, and abruptly changed direction. Passover was still days away, yet the golden doors were already crawling with surly-looking Romans and Levite police. 'We'll enter at Dung Gate instead,' Judah muttered, as he galloped ahead, 'at the south end of the city. The Romans will pay less mind to those entering from this direction.' Soon, we were making our way beside the high stone wall that surrounded Jerusalem, gaze averted from the Valley of Death, the deep gorge housing generations of the city's dead that fell away to one side. The air was thick with the stink and smoke of Gehenna, the rubbish tip that burned without remit, all day and night, just outside the city's southern wall.

We almost did not find my brother. Having entered Jerusalem without incident, past a lone centurion stinking of wine and snoring at his post, we proceeded to wander through its sinuous lanes, searching for the home of Nicodemus. But none of the blossoms on overhead branches looked right and no one we asked knew of a rich man's home sheltered by the gnarled arms of the apricot tree. With night falling, and buffeted by the wind of so many shaking heads, we resigned ourselves to passing the night in an inn and resuming the search on the morrow.

It was a woman who saved us. A woman who recognised the distinctive profile of my nose as I scanned the rooflines for apricot blooms; who knew the coiled mass of Judah's hair. 'Peace be with you, Rachael of Nazareth,' she said and I turned to find a slight figure clothed entirely in black, her face covered by the dropped veil of a harlot. Yoked to her back were two buckets of milk.

'Maryam?' I stuttered. Judah moved to relieve her burdens but she refused, politely, to give them over. Instead she said, 'Joshua will rejoice to see you. He knew you would find him. Please, follow me. I shall take you to him directly.'

From the outside, the house of Nicodemus was little different from the other large dwellings on the street. Built from limestone, it was all hard-edged lines and angles. Date palms sprouted through cracks in the mortar. But once within, we found the cool and hush of a holy place. Paradise wood, used to build the Jerusalem Temple, lined the walls of the entranceway, its glossy finish reflecting movement and scenting the air pleasantly. Maryam led us into a central room where the sparse furnishings—an altar inlaid with ivory and a carved chest—were hewn from the same timber. In the far corner stood a low granite table surrounded by men reclining on fat cushions darted with scarlet thread. They were debating loudly. Nicodemus was in Egypt, Maryam told us, and had left his home in Joshua's care.

When my brother saw Judah, his face split into a huge grin and his shoulders slumped with relief. He leapt from the tight circle of men to wrap my husband in an embrace, before holding him out for fond examination. Joshua's hands seemed childlike as they gripped the trunks of Judah's arms. 'My trusted friend,' he said solemnly. 'I knew you would come. I knew it.' He turned to me warmly, 'Sister, how sweet it is to see you. Welcome.'

As Maryam headed towards the hearth, Joshua presented us to the huddled assemblage of men. Many had visible afflictions: club feet, leprous limbs, the milk-eyes of the blind. Two were already on their feet, their faces long and hard. 'This is Cephas,' said Joshua, pointing to the larger of the two, a giant slab of a man with pitted cheeks. The other, Joshua said, was Cephas's brother, Ananias. 'This is my oldest and dearest friend Judah of Iscariot and his wife, my sister, Rachael.'

Judah bowed his head respectfully. 'The fishermen,' he said. 'Your names are known throughout the north.'

There was no light in the giant's eyes, nor warmth in his expression. He accepted Judah's praise with a slow blink and made no reply. His brother took note of the lead and followed it. They were both standing too close to Joshua, as if they owned him. I saw Judah stiffen, but Joshua was quick to intervene. 'Leave us,' he told the brothers. He waved a hand at those on the floor. 'All of you. Enough has been said. The plans have been laid and we are ready. Tomorrow, the tree we have nurtured these many months will bear fruit. For now I bid you pray and rest. Maryam is busy at the hearth. Soon, we will eat.'

Reluctantly, sullenly, the outcasts got to their feet. Amid the groans and curses of the infirm among them they made their way towards the narrow flight of steps set beside the room's arched entrance. But Cephas and Ananias remained planted, their arms folded across their chests, their expressions impassive. 'Leave,' Joshua commanded them, his voice low but firm. And then, as they hesitated, 'Go.'

When eventually they withdrew—Cephas fixing Judah with one last fish-eyed glare before stomping up the steps—Joshua sighed with relief. 'Wine,' he declared, pointing Judah towards the cushions surrounding the table. 'We must salute this great reunion. Maryam!' he called and, through a chattering hang of beads at the room's far end, she emerged, her face still veiled, a wine vessel and two goblets in hand. These she set before the men and filled, before passing back through the doorway. Joshua used his eyes to indicate that I should follow. Weary from the journey and wanting nothing more than to collapse to the pillows and hear my brother's news from his own lips, I hesitated. But when neither man showed any sign of relenting, I sighed and went in search of Maryam. As I passed through the beaded curtain I heard Judah say, 'So, my friend, what plans have you set in place?'

Maryam was in a cloud of flour, kneading dough for the loaves. The milk she had been carrying was now warming on the most elaborate hearth I had ever seen. It had three pits for roasting and behind these, cross-hatched bars on which two large cauldrons gurgled and hissed. Sacks of grain slumped against the smoothly plastered walls and, beside these rested several basket of figs and two stone jars of wine. She was feeding a crowd, this much was clear. In the rooms overhead we could hear their rodent scuffles and murmurs of complaint.

We were strangers. Maryam was closer to Shona's age than mine. I had begun observing her carefully when Joshua's passion became known—how she tied her headscarf, whom she spoke with at the well—but had never said more to her than *shalom*. Now, she was hidden beneath a tent of dark cloth that concealed her eyes and expression. The distance between us seemed vast; the means to cross it, unknowable.

Handing over two lemons, she indicated a giant mortar set on a woven mat beneath the room's lone window. The bowl was filled with sesame seeds. I knelt there and began grinding tahina. We toiled in silence, the only sounds the press of the pestle, the slam of Maryam's fist against the oven and the steam and sigh of the loaves as they settled atop one another on the platter. But somehow the familiar music of the work—the grind and squelch, the thump and scrape, the whisper of cloth and the heave of breath as we moved about—made things easy between us, so that when Maryam began to speak, she seemed only to be continuing a conversation already begun by joining words to sound.

'He said I was good, my papa. A good girl. Always he would say this. To the wine-maker. The baker. When I came through the door he would sing my praises. *Sweeter than honey, my sweet Maryam.*' Her voice snagged on the memory. She coughed, forced herself to swallow, and pressed on. 'So I thought that in this matter, the only thing that I had ever asked of him, begged of him, that he would give way. But I was mistaken.'

Her confusion was familiar, akin to what I had felt when Shona was forced to marry Boaz: the bewilderment of women when obedience fails to find reward. Maryam threw a cloth around the bread to warm it, tucking and fussing as if cosseting a baby.

'You were with child,' I said, more statement than question. Maryam nodded. 'Joshua's child,' I continued. 'And you sought your Papa's blessing so the two of you could wed?'

The ends of her veil swirled like a midnight tide about her shoulders as she inclined her head. 'But he said no.' She had a unique way of shaping and stringing words: each pronounced distinctly and kept separate from the next. 'He called me a harlot, and said I must pack. Ordered Mama not to interfere. He said we would all be going away. Far from Nazareth and the man who had caused my shame. In the morning, we were on our way. The oxen sold, the grain tipped into baskets, my lips sealed shut—then and thereafter—by the vengeance he swore on Joshua's head should he ever see or hear of him again.'

So that explained her silence. Why she had neither left word for Joshua nor sent it afterwards. She had feared for my brother's life. My heart welled with sympathy. 'Oh Maryam!' I exclaimed.

She shrugged my pity aside. Motioned me over to help her heave the cauldron of steaming milk from the hearth and pour it into two flat trays. Dropping a spoon of yoghurt into each to begin the fermentation, Maryam covered the trays with porous cloth and set them aside.

'Papa took me to Bethlehem,' she continued, 'and sold me for thirty silver pieces to a Pharisee, a scribe from the tribe of Aaron more ancient than Methuselah.' The deal done, Abraham of Magdalene departed, driving Maryam's weeping mother before him. She had neither seen nor heard from them since.

But Maryam's marriage was destined to fail. Her husband was years past his prime and when he came to her mat at night, could only sniff at her and whine like a wounded dog before slinking away. The blooming of her belly not four months later sealed her fate. Disavowing her in the village square with the thrice-repeated phrase, 'I divorce you,' the old man tossed her out, beyond the village gate, with nothing but the clothes in which she stood.

The freshly scrubbed cauldron sizzled with oil. I looked up, my eyes streaming, from chopping onions. Maryam was working a garlic clove free from its papery skin but her fingers stilled and fell, empty, to her lap. 'I did not know what to do, Rachael,' she said quietly. 'I cared little for my own life but for the one quick inside me, Joshua's child, my love knew no bounds. So I hid in the woods, eating sorrel and scavenging for wild dates, and waited for guidance. Passover was still a month away, so the days were cool but the nights still bitter.'

She paused, her eyes far away. 'Have you ever been really hungry, Rachael?' She darted a glance at me. 'One afternoon, more than a week from my banishment, I saw a woman—a *gentile*—feeding scraps to her swine. Bread rinds, sour milk, gristle from a long-dead fowl.' A deep shuddering breath; she let herself go on. 'And when she went inside I fought with those loathsome creatures for each disgusting crumb. When I was done, when I had wiped my slobbering lips and stepped from the pen covered in bristles and foul-smelling mud, I cried. Cried and mourned, scratching and pulling out fistfuls of hair. Something turned in me then, Rachael. Turned and shifted and set, and I vowed before God that I would never behave like a beast, nor allow others to treat me like one again.'

My eyes were so wide I imagined them springing from their sockets and rolling across the floor like acorns.

Maryam went on. 'I looked to God for guidance, and he gave my feet direction. Soon I was on the road to Jerusalem. Journeying to the Temple to beg mercy from the priests.'

'What?' I shrieked, far too loudly. I clapped my hand across my mouth.

Maryam reached for one of the naked garlic cloves, piled in front of her like creamy white stones, and began slicing. 'Yes. I determined to beg the priests for mercy,' she repeated stubbornly, 'and for refuge. But by the time I arrived in the Holy City, it was late afternoon and the golden doors were shut. The start of the Passover Feast was still days away and no one was about. Neither pilgrims nor police nor soldiers.'

'What did you do?' The knife had fallen slack in my grip.

'Knocked, then pounded on the gate with my fists until, at

last, someone answered. Two men: a scribe and a Levite guard. I told them of my misfortune and pleaded for sanctuary. Displayed my swollen belly in hope of moving their hearts to pity.' She shrugged, her clever hands a blur of motion as she reduced the garlic mountain to a molehill. 'But to no avail. "Give me water, then," I begged, "and a morsel of food, for I have come a great distance and have had nothing today." They told me to wait, and went away, locking the gate behind them. I heard the bar drop loudly into place. I knew they would not return. The life inside me squirmed and fitted and, suddenly, I was overcome with weariness and despair. My legs buckled and gave way. I fainted.

'When I woke it was dark. I was sprawled on the marble steps, my brow wet with blood and tongue wasted by thirst. All was silent. Within the borders of the Temple and across the hills and valleys that cradle Jerusalem, nothing stirred. At that moment, even the sight of a Roman soldier pacing the city walls would have been welcome, but there was no one. I was alone.'

It was a long and terrible night and Maryam was insensible for much of it. She resolved that, should she live to see the dawn, she would make her way through the Valley of Death in search of water at the spring of Gihon. But when the sounds of roosting birds summoned her before first light, this proved unnecessary. Beside her were a pot of water and a freshly baked loaf.

'A miracle,' I breathed, suddenly aware I sounded like Papa. 'Do you know who left it?'

Maryam shook her head. 'No, I saw neither figure nor face. But from that day forth when I woke in the morning, I found enough food and drink to last the day. So I remained in my place, sitting or reclining on the steps before the Temple Gate, pleading for mercy whenever the priests and scribes came past.

But they would not relent. The holy men looked past me, or brushed me away like a nettle. But I was not invisible. Others saw me and marked my plight. Shepherds, merchants, tax collectors, harlots; the poor who shift in and out of the city in search of work. Many began hailing me in the morning and again on their return to their villages at night. Some took to having their meals near the Temple steps, in clear view of my vigil. They would jeer and clap at the guards and holy men, and any pilgrims who misused me on their way in or out of the gates. I continued to wake to food and water and, one morning, with the first sign of winter dampening the air, to a folded woollen blanket. Some days, there was even wine.

'As my blessings multiplied, so did the fears of the priests. They pleaded with the Romans to detain me, or at least chase me from the steps.' She dealt a hand of clay dishes about her like betting tokens and spooned olives into each from a crock of seasoned brine. She shrugged. 'I was never arrested. The Romans are no fools and could clearly see that biding their time would soon see mine at hand.'

Maryam's time came just before Pentecost. Drenched in the waters of birth and clasping about her shoulders the stiff grey blanket she had been given, she staggered up the winding path towards the Gethsemane garden in the spare light of a crescent moon, sharing her agony with the whispering branches of the olive trees and the endless, ebony sky.

'The tom cats yowled down at me in reply,' she said, trying to laugh. 'They must have thought I was one of them.' Maryam paused. 'Women were not meant to give birth alone,' she said quietly.

But she was very much alone when she eventually came

to squat at the foot of a mulberry tree, her hands wringing its slim trunk like a neck, and pushed the child, then the afterbirth, into the world. Sobbing with relief that the pain was finished, that she had survived, she suddenly remembered the baby. She severed the cord with her teeth before gathering the infant to her breast: a girl, greased in white and deathly still. But at her touch the baby coughed, spluttered and began to mewl. Wrapping the two of them as best she could in the gory blanket, Maryam fell to the ground and into a dark, dreamless sleep.

She woke in the morning. Beside her was a clean cloth on which a meal had been laid to suit a king: dried figs and dates, bread still hot from the oven and spread thickly with hummus, a bowl of yoghurt sprinkled with nuts. There was water in one stone jar and wine in another. Maryam sat up on her elbows, a smile tipping the ends of her lips. But then she peered beneath the blanket.

Her breasts were full but her arms were empty. The child was gone.

When Maryam and I emerged from the hearth with a covered platter of bread, a bowl of tahina and one of olives, Joshua and Judah fell silent. Joshua was reclining by the low table at the room's far end, his head resting on one hand, the other holding a goblet of wine. Judah was upright, his legs crossed and his back held at an awkward angle, as if he had swallowed a knife and feared any sudden move might eviscerate him.

My brother smiled up at Maryam tenderly, his eyes full of wonder as if she were a fawn taking her first steps. 'The evening meal,' he proclaimed, in the manner of one unveiling the king's new chariot. He sniffed the air with relish. To Judah he said, 'So we are agreed.'

Stiffly, Judah nodded. 'Yes. Since I cannot convince you to abandon your plans, I will support them. You must have help gaining entry to the Temple if you are to get out alive. But I must speak to the others after the meal tonight, Joshua, to the men and the women both, about how best to avoid capture.'

'Yes.' My brother was quick to agree. 'It is a clever plan, to surprise them by running through rather than away from the Temple. Overturning the merchants' tables, freeing the beasts from their stalls to impede pursuit. It could work, even with this rag-tag army.' My brother gazed at Judah with the look of a man spared the noose. 'It is good to have you here, my friend.'

As I unrolled my sleeping mat later that night, Judah outlined the plan. We were alone, though just barely, having set up camp in the wood-panelled entranceway. My toes grazed the front door and only a ragged blanket slung across the doorway arch separated us from Joshua and Maryam, asleep in the main room.

The disciples would leave Nicodemus's house at sunrise, lining the path from Cheesemaker's Quarter to the southernmost gate of the Temple. Joshua would follow a little later, flanked by Judah and the hard-eyed fishermen and bearing a whip. As they strode past, the disciples, posing as Jerusalemites going about their daily toil, would cheer them and shout praises to the Lord before falling in behind and, hopefully, inspiring others to do the same. It was the passion and pressure of this mob that Judah was depending upon to get Joshua past the Levite guards and inside the Temple walls. Once within, my brother would mount the scribes' steps and reveal the good news of Lazarus's rise and the love and forgiveness the One God proffered all, while Judah and the other strong men would keep at bay the Levites, priests and others incited by his claims.

When they could hold the mob back no longer, Judah

would give the sign and the disciples would run to the top of the steps and fan out across the gentile marketplace, weaving through the blue-draped tables on their way towards Benjamin Gate in the hope of escape. To those among Joshua's followers too lame or infirm for such exertions, other tasks were assigned. Mattitiayu would proceed directly to Benjamin Gate and position himself just outside it, armed with a bucket of nails. Following our descent into the city streets he would upset the bucket at the feet of our pursuers in hope of bringing them down. The lepers would eschew the outing altogether and remain at Nicodemus's, ready with food and comfort on the troupe's return.

The skin on my arms twitched with excitement. 'Can you imagine the fury of the Levites,' I exclaimed as Judah, done with words, threw himself down beside me, 'when we force them to stand aside and allow outcasts to enter the Temple gates? I can hardly wait to see the look of surprise on the faces of the scribes when Joshua points his finger at the high priests and charges them with corruption and abuse of the Law!'

Judah gave no reply. Even lying down, he maintained the awkward knife-swallowing pose he had struck earlier that day. His breath came in short, harsh pants while the light from the flickering oil lamp revealed the strain disfiguring his handsome face. I shook his arm. 'What ails you, Judah? Are you all right? Speak!'

'I cannot permit you to go tomorrow, Rachael.'

'What? Not permit me? Why? All the women are going!'

'Yes, but only because they are widows or divorced. Or whores. Women without men to watch over them, to know where to draw the line.'

'But...I...you cannot!'

'I can, Rachael, and I must. Perhaps Joshua is correct that tomorrow's assault on the Temple will catch the police and the priests unawares. If so, we may avoid arrest or a fate far worse. But surprise is our only weapon. We lack numbers, training, discipline,' he tried to grin, 'even a full complement of limbs. Some of those men can barely walk!'

I did not smile. I found it hard to imagine I would ever find anything funny again. 'But this does not matter,' I protested. 'We have you. You will watch over us and guard against harm.' My hand reached out to caress his face but he turned away.

'I am a man, not a miracle worker,' he said, the words squeezing through gritted teeth. 'I will have both hands full just getting us into the Temple and defending Joshua from harm when he stands to challenge the priests.' Judah was muttering now. 'Then the disciples must be borne safely from the Temple and back to this house. I will have no time, no time, to watch over you.'

'I can watch over myself!'

Silently, I gave thanks for my decision to delay telling Judah my secret. If he knew of my condition, I would stand no chance of persuading him now. As it was, I was failing to persuade. My husband's head was shaking, *No*. On the wall behind him, his black shadow did the same.

'But this is why I am here, Judah.' I said quietly, praying for the eloquence to press my case. 'This is why you brought me to Jerusalem. To stand arm in arm with my people and raise the call for justice. To allow me a role in events that matter.' My voice quavered, but I did not cry. 'I saw your face when Joshua drew the disciples to his side tonight. When he spoke of God's willingness to forgive every sinner, no matter our disfigurement or affliction or sex or low rank of birth. When he promised that our hunger and thirst for righteousness would see us blessed. Joshua's quest is no different from yours, Judah. No different from the mission of the brigands. He, too, yearns to topple those with no right to rule. To obey no Lord but God.'

I searched his eyes, bottomless pools in the gloomy light. 'Ask and it will be given you. Seek and you shall find. This is the counsel Joshua offers his men. And this is also your way, Judah. You have always sought what is good and right for yourself and your fellows. When denied it, have you worn sackcloth and ashes? Torn your hair and abandoned hope? No! You have risen to the challenge, gathering your wits and plucking up your sword to fight. This is what I seek. The freedom to fight for a cause that is just and true. Let me march with you and Joshua to the Temple tomorrow. Let me stand shoulder to shoulder with the righteous. Because this is not just your battle, Judah, it is mine, too.'

I had moved him. That much was plain. I heard it in his swallow and the quaver of his sigh. He came towards me, moved over me, nuzzling and kissing the tears from my cheeks, pushing my knees apart with his own and entering me with the force and intensity of one abandoning the cloak of his own skin so he might fully enter mine. Afterwards, as we lay in each other's arms, he said, 'Yes.'

I rose on my elbow and gave him my thanks with a passionate kiss on the lips. Then, settling back in the crook of his arm, I said, 'It is love that spurs Joshua's mission, isn't it? Love for Shona and Papa, but most of all for Maryam. Love and compassion and pure outrage at the injustice she has endured. That is why Joshua goes to the Temple tomorrow. Not for the tanners or tax collectors, the sick and lame or those hard-eyed fishermen, though each would be convinced that their liberation is his only desire. He goes to point the finger at the priests: the holy men who abandoned Maryam in her hour of need. Who stood by while their child was stolen from her arms and, later, when she was forced to sell herself to survive. You know this is what befell Maryam, don't you, Judah? Joshua told you, did he not...?'

But it had been a long day and Judah, mouth wide and leaking drool, had closed his eyes and abandoned himself to sleep.

In the morning, it was he who woke first. With moist brow and eyes sprung wide, Judah hurried me and the other women through the morning meal and out the door. The day had dawned still and warm as the sun rose towards a cloudless sky. Even at this early hour, the noise of cloven hooves was loud. Passover goats and lambs clattered through the city's cobbled lanes, driven by merchants loudly reminding Israelites that the feast began that eve. Across the city, Israelite women were hard at work as tradition demanded: sweeping, scrubbing and candling their homes free of leavening. As I took up my post to await Joshua's passing, I prayed that today a new tradition might be born.

All went to plan. Better than planned, if measured against Judah's fretful predictions. By the time Joshua approached the southern gate of the Temple, the crowd trailing him was many times greater than when the morning began. It was easily large enough for us to push our way past the guards and into the precinct, where Joshua hurried up the marble steps, we women flying after him. As we assembled ourselves about his feet, Judah and the other men formed a protective ring around us: chests thrust out, jaws jutting and daggers drawn. My brother began to speak.

Joshua said that God blessed all those whom the priests condemned as outcasts, and that the holy men were robbers and thieves for selling forgiveness to the poor. 'The meek shall inherit the earth,' he assured the rapt sea of female faces gazing up at him adoringly. 'The Kingdom of Heaven is yours.'

I was transfixed. Not only by the reasoned urgency of my brother's tone or the sense of his words, or even the dearly remembered flicker of bronze in his beard as he stood in the sun, turning his head this way and that. It was the way Joshua's dark eyes sought Maryam's even as his voice rose and fell and, when they alighted on her, shimmered with love.

But the rest of the crowd, having recovered from the audacity of our caper, began to rumble and sway. Pilgrims turned to one another with elaborate expressions of surprise while scribes and sages wagged their fingers and jeered. The priests, their cheeks flushed with rage, began shouting orders across the complex and Levites abandoned their posts, hurrying towards us with knives unsheathed. Soon, we would be overrun. My heart raced.

'Now!' Judah shouted as the first stones hurtled towards our heads, and we were off, springing to the top of the steps like wolves before dodging through the blue-clothed tables in the Gentiles' Court, overturning as many as we could on the way past. The air filled with the clang of scales, the shiver of rolling coins, the shriek of birds and the smash of pots and flagons. When we arrived at the stables where the beasts for sacrifice were caged, we kept to Judah's plans. Maryam grabbed the brass ring on one door while I gripped the other. We dragged the gates ajar and rushed in, shouting and stamping, clapping our hands, driving the beasts into the mayhem, the thunder of stampeding hooves rivalling the cacophony of collapsing tables and the thud of my heart.

A hand fell on my arm. Judah. 'We must get out of here. Now!' he shouted. He was right. Our efforts had slowed them, but the raised fists and bobbing heads of the holy men were now gaining. Soon we would be overrun. 'To Benjamin Gate,' Judah cried and, grabbing Maryam's hand, I ran, my husband falling in behind us, his broad arms outstretched protectively like a falcon's wings.

Benjamin Gate. Benjamin Gate. Judah's words hammered in my ears as we raced across the courtyard, through the appointed door and into the city's northern quarter, skittering down one narrow lane, then the next, turning this way and that to escape our pursuers.

But Benjamin Gate was not the last thing Judah said before we flew through the doors of the Temple. The last word that came from my husband's lips as he glanced up to see the crowd of Roman soldiers peering down from Antonia's Tower at the mayhem below sounded a good deal like *shit*.

By late afternoon, most of the troops had straggled back to Nicodemus's house, covered in grime and sweat. Lame Mattitiayu was missing and a widow clutched a broken arm and wept while I folded linen for a sling and whispered words of comfort. For everyone else there were merely aches and bruises. We were elated. Men hugged and slapped one another on the back while Judah and I were deluged with praise. He for his brilliant battle plans and me for being his wife.

Cephas was charged with Joshua's welfare during the siege

and, when the riot started, took no chances. Tossing my brother's slight form across his shoulders, the giant had charged directly towards Benjamin Gate, keeping clear of the market rampage altogether. This meant Joshua was the first to return to the house, though Judah, Maryam and I burst in a short time later. As subsequent disciples came through the door, my brother rose graciously to greet them, blessing and thanking all in the same way. 'Your place awaits in the Kingdom of Heaven,' he repeated throughout the afternoon, solicitously proffering cups of cool well water and rounds of bread smeared with sesame paste, before touring the room once again, praising God and each of his warriors, a jubilant smile on his face.

Judah refused to add his voice to the celebratory din, or to reply to the tributes being heaped on his head. Soon, it was more than he could do to remain upright. He sank to the floor and sprawled there on his back, his massive limbs thrown across the wooden boards where they settled like dough. He was in the way, though the others did not complain. They just stepped around him, smiling good-naturedly.

I was not so tolerant. 'Sit up,' I hissed.

He did, though not before heaving an enormous sigh, his bleary gaze taking in the babbling assembly as if they were speaking a foreign tongue. 'I am just pleased it is over,' he said to no one in particular, 'and we can go home.'

'Home!' I exclaimed. The word was like a pail of cold water. 'But we have only just arrived.'

'Yes, but the work is done. Joshua has been found. He's done what he needed to do and has not come to harm. You have made your journey from Nazareth and found the adventure you sought. It is now time for me to return north and take up my duties there.' This recitation had a hard, unyielding edge, lacking all chinks and soft spots where pressure might be brought to bear. I felt a rise of despair.

But Joshua interrupted us. Stepping up on to the low stone table, my brother tapped a wooden pestle against a costly looking vase to draw attention. 'Friends, followers, kin and clan. We have been delivered a great victory today. Given it by God, and by a man blessed with both wit and heart.' My brother nodded at Judah, 'My dearest friend and most trusted comrade, Judah of Iscariot.' The women ululated while the men made rumbling noises deep in their chests and raised their fists. Except for Cephas and Ananias, who exchanged sour looks. 'Bathe now, and rest,' my brother told the assemblage, stepping down from his make-shift stage and moving in the direction of the steps. 'Tonight we shall feast.'

Judah got to his feet. 'Say your farewells to Maryam and your brother,' he grunted as he moved to follow Joshua. 'Tomorrow we leave at first light.'

Before I could reply, Maryam was at my elbow, frantically listing supplies we would need from the market to prepare the celebration. Reluctantly, I gave her my full attention. With just a few hours of daylight left, there was much work to do.

❧

'Maryam, come! We need more wine.' My brother's voice was slurred. I heard the bang of the empty jar on the table.

The men had been feasting for hours. Having taken our meal and prepared food for the morning, the women sat by the hearth, jumping up to the men's occasional summons and, in between, chatting listlessly, wishing we might go to bed.

'Maryam!' Joshua bellowed again and Maryam, a full jar of wine already in hand, commanded me to bring another before passing hastily through the beaded door.

The table was crowded with men at various states of drunkenness and angles of recline. As Maryam bent to set the jar down, Joshua reached out to pat her, his face slack with love. But custom forbade women and men to touch in plain sight and, fearing disapproval, Maryam stiffened. She intercepted Joshua's hand and returned it to him.

Joshua pouted. I had never seen my brother behave in this manner, though it was also the first time I had seen him affected by drink. He reached for his beloved again, 'I only wanted to—' This time, Maryam dodged his grasp, or tried to. Instead, she tripped, stumbled and, with a hare's cry of terror, fell. She landed on Cephas, who was lying supine beside my brother in the rigid manner of a corpse.

The giant's reaction was immediate and untutored. Jerking up in surprise his slab-like features wrinkled to express the only emotion I had yet seen cross his face: disgust. Bucking and thrashing as if Maryam were a scorpion, he threw her aside, sending her head crashing into the wood-panelled walls, where she dropped to the floor like an anchor. The revellers fell silent.

Joshua was quick to his feet. Angrily, he nudged Cephas's ribs with his bare foot. 'What are you doing? What do you think you are doing?' He looked to the other disciples, clearly expecting sympathy, but their eyes were narrow, giving nothing away. Ananias scrubbed frantically at an imaginary stain on his robe caused by the brush of Maryam's veil as she careened towards the wall, while Judah warily observed the black form now huddled and shaking with sobs, as if Maryam might suddenly sprout wings that would send her polluted form flying in his direction.

'No.' Joshua said, his head shaking. His expression was a fast-moving sunset of rage, disappointment and despair. 'No, no, no!' He lifted his chin and complained to the heavens. 'They see, Father, but do not believe. They listen, but fail to hear. They claim to love me, but they have no idea who I am.' My brother spoke quietly, as if engaged in a private discussion with God before lifting his ear to tune into the Lord's reply. Nodding his assent, Joshua stepped onto the table. He kicked aside the baskets and goblets in his path and strode to the centre, ignoring the protests of the disciples. He pointed a stiff finger at the albino.

'It is not just for you,' he thundered, 'that I have come. Or you, or you, or you,' he continued, hurling his wrath in quick succession at a mute, the tax collector and a man with the ragged limbs of a leper. His fury appeared to have sobered him, though I saw that he was not entirely steady on his feet. His words, however, were as clear and fierce as rain. 'I have also come for her,' he said, pointing at his beloved's weeping form. 'And my sister,' he said, turning to me. 'And all the women,' he gestured towards the kitchen, 'huddled by the hearth.'

He went on quietly as though, once more, speaking only to God. 'How can I tear down the Temple and build it up again, if even those who follow me, who swear fealty to my mission, cannot comprehend my purpose?'

Then, suddenly, Joshua seemed to know what to do. His eyes scanned the ravaged table and alighted on an upright bowl of salted water. Earlier that evening, during the meal, the men had used it to dip their boiled eggs and vegetables. Now my brother snatched it and stepped carefully to the floor. Placing the bowl at his feet, he whipped his tunic over his head and knotted it, slave style, about his waist. Turning, he beckoned the weeping Maryam. 'Maryam,' he said. 'Come to me. Come, my flower, please don't cry. Maryam, I beg of you. Rise up, Maryam. Rise up!'

I had no inkling of his plan but Maryam, having lifted her head to find my brother's eyes, seemed to know. She shook her head, and began backing away on hands and knees in the direction of the hearth.

'No, Maryam, please. Please do not, my love,' Joshua's tone was urgent, but he did not move towards her. Instead, half-naked, he sought to restrain her with his words, and the strength of the plan they had shaped. 'I have prepared the way, Maryam, but only you can tread the path. It is you who must find the courage and self-love to make your way to the kingdom. The kingdom God promised all of us. To the kingdom at last.' His voice was that of a snake charmer. Maryam stopped backing away and sat up on her heels to listen.

Joshua continued his entreaty. 'If not now, Maryam, then when? If not you, then who? You are deserving, my love. As worthy as the rest. But you must reach for it, Maryam. If not for yourself, then do it for the others. For my sisters and the widows and harlots and the aliens. For our lost little girl, our daughter, and the generations of women to come after.' He took a single step towards her, his eyes wet with emotion. 'Demand your dignity, Maryam. Demand it! In the name of God.'

Everyone seemed to be holding his breath. Slowly, creaking with pain, Maryam rose to her feet and padded in Joshua's direction. The look in her eyes was fearful but resolute. He reached out his hand and, when she gave it, manoeuvred her to a sitting position on the table. Then, with the gentleness of a mother unwrapping her baby, he helped her shed her veil. Since the previous afternoon, when she found Judah and me on the street, I had wondered why she wore it. For whatever she had been, it was clear that, since finding Joshua, Maryam was whoring no more. But now I knew. Joshua, having thrown the ebony cloth aside, was tracing the scars on each cheek, as red and regular as brands, that the scarf had disguised.

Then my brother knelt and, to the gasps of the men, placed Maryam's feet in the bowl of salt water and began to clean them. The men cried out in disgust and in protest ('You are the Messiah,' Cephas kept repeating stupidly, 'You must not lower yourself this way'), but Joshua paid them no heed. Instead, he called for a towel. He worked the cloth carefully between each of Maryam's toes before anointing both feet with fragrant oil. When it was done, he sat back on his heels, satisfied. Helping Maryam to her feet, he clung tightly to her hand as he found the eyes of each man in turn.

'Humble yourselves,' he told them. 'Humble yourselves before one another as I have done before Maryam. Then might you remember that all of us are equal before God.'

An idea came to Joshua in the middle of the night. He crouched by our sleeping mats, trying to shake my sleeping husband to life. 'You have sworn to quit the city at first light, friend,' Joshua said. 'But please, hear me first, so I might persuade you to stay.' Judah did not stir. From somewhere outside, a cockerel crowed. Sighing, my brother lifted the lamp to shine in Judah's eyes.

They took their argument out through the front door and

I fell back to sleep, dreaming fitfully about being trapped in a hissing nest full of venomous snakes. Only when Judah's furious whisper rose to a shout did I start to waking. 'This is not the point!' my husband raged and I heard the familiar sound of his fist smacking his palm. The front door flew open and the two men stormed inside, Judah first and Joshua pacing after him. My husband was ranting, 'The point is that it cannot be done without your capture. Your capture, my capture and the arrest of Rachael, Maryam and every other person fool enough to enter with you!'

Joshua was angry, too. As the two men crashed through the hanging blanket and into the central room, his reply cracked like a whip, though I did not hear his words. Only Judah's, as my husband cut across him impatiently. 'We were fortunate yesterday, lucky! Nothing more. They were not expecting us, nor the tactics we used to avoid being taken. We shall not have that advantage again.' Wide awake now, I shuffled towards the door arch on my belly and lifted a corner of the blanket to observe the dispute. Judah was standing by the table, shaking his hands in dismay in front of Joshua's face. 'You must not return to the Temple today, Joshua. You cannot. You will be recognised! We shall all be recognised! Even walking the streets of this city we are at risk of being denounced and hauled off to Antonia's Fortress. If we march right up to the Temple gates and ask to come in, our fate is certain!'

'But Judah, a soldier of your talents can surely—'

'No!' Judah bellowed. He thumped his chest in anguish. The entire household was awake now and silently eavesdropping from various perches: the women peeking from behind the beaded door to the hearth, the men spilling from the steps to lean against the walls. 'Your plan is suicide, Joshua. It can never succeed. You are a good man, a great one even, but you are not divine! Only God himself could avoid capture on a day like today.' My brother's chin still wooden, Judah's tone turned pleading. 'You told me yesterday you wished only to complete your mission. To attend the Temple and speak the truth on the steps. You promised me you would leave the city when this was done. Go out from Jerusalem and from Judaea all together, until the fire you have been stoking since Lazarus was raised had burned low. That you would return to the Galilee and continue as you were—teaching, forgiving outcasts, exposing the greed of the priests—without provoking Rome. You gave me your word.'

'But I thought I was finished,' Joshua countered. 'That my mission at the Temple was complete. I did not realise that they,' he flipped a dismissive hand at the assemblage of men, 'had yet to comprehend. That they still do not know me, and do not understand why, and for whom, I have come. This is why I must go back to the Temple. With Maryam, so I can bow low before her and bathe her feet where everyone can see. So there can be no doubt left.'

Hearing the plan again only stoked Judah's frenzy. He began to pace, holding his head in his hands. 'It is suicide, suicide!' Cephas and Ananias, observing my husband from the steps, ribbed one another and grinned. Judah began to make a list on his fingers. 'Entering the Temple is suicide. Proclaiming oneself chosen by God to heal and forgive is suicide. Demeaning oneself by bending low to wash the feet of a whore?' Judah seized handfuls of his curly hair and pulled outwards. 'Madness!'

At the word 'whore' my brother flinched, then stiffened.

He drew himself tall and addressed his old friend coldly. 'My mission is not yet finished. Before going out from Jerusalem, I must complete it so that there can be no doubt. I will go to the Temple today and there, on the steps, I shall bow low before Maryam and wash and oil her feet. I will do this with your help and blessing, Judah,' he paused, eyes flashing, 'or without.' And with head held high, Joshua grasped Maryam's hand and strode from the room.

Judah stormed off, too. Not up the steps after Joshua, but out the front door, having first snatched a *keffiyeh* from a hook in the entranceway to wrap about his head. I raced after him. 'Judah!'

His pace did not slacken. 'Leave me be, Rachael.'

'But where are you going?' I cried. Too loudly. He winced and turned, his eyes roving the street to see who might be watching. Moving towards me briskly, he dragged my veil forward to cover more of my face.

'Nowhere,' he said quietly. 'For a walk. Go back inside. I will not be long and you are not safe in the open.'

'But what is to happen?' I whispered. 'Are we departing the city today, as you said? What about Joshua and his plan?'

Judah looked pained. He had an animal's nose for danger and his impulse to flee Jerusalem, with Joshua and me tucked one beneath each arm if necessary, was palpable. But if Joshua would not leave, if my brother insisted on putting himself in harm's way by returning to the Temple, what was he to do?

'I do not know, Rachael,' he said truthfully. 'But the decision will wait until I return. I need to leave now, to get out, move. Clear my head. And *no*,' he said, knowing me all too well, 'you cannot come with me. It is too dangerous. Go back inside.'

His massive hands turned me around and pushed me gently in the direction of Nicodemus's door. 'Go quickly, now. I shall return for you, soon.' And settling himself more deeply in the folds of his black and white scarf, he strode off, heading south along the cobbled way towards the rising smoke of Gehenna.

The sun was low by the time he returned. The house had been cloaked in silence for much of the day. Joshua and Maryam had remained upstairs, whence only the occasional curse on Judah's head could be heard—usually in Cephas's flat tenor—before voices fell to a mumble again. Not knowing what else to do, I had set our belongings in readiness for the return trip north, rolling up Judah's and my sleeping mats, filling our goatskins and packing bread, olives and dried fruit into our bags before tying them closed. Then, still at a loss, I began chopping dates and dried grapes for the harosset paste required for the evening's Seder meal. When I looked up, it was to find two women observing me in silence. They nodded curtly before making their way to the hearth. There they assembled bowls of yoghurt, nuts and olives and placed them on a tray before withdrawing to their lair, leaving me to prepare and consume my meal alone. It seemed that despite being Joshua's sister, in this divided house I was first and foremost Judah's wife: tarred with the same brush both by my husband's achievements and, now, by his sin of doubt.

By late afternoon I was close to gnawing off my own arm from idleness when Judah burst through the door, whistling through his teeth. I ran to his side, desperate for company and news. 'Where were you?'

He removed his scarf and pegged it on the hook before turning to me. His brow was smooth and eyes clear. He was

Judah again: vigorous, confident, in charge. 'Nowhere,' he boomed cheerfully, then changed his mind: 'Buying a lamb for sacrifice. I have tied it in the lane.' He looked around then gathered me for a passionate kiss, one hand gripping a breast. When we separated he gazed in the direction of the hearth. 'Is there anything to eat?'

But before he wolfed down the meal I hurried off to prepare, he went through the house making amends with the others. He bellowed his change of heart up the stairs and, when Joshua descended with tentative steps, he seized my brother and threw his arms around him in a passionate embrace. As my brother's followers filed into the room, Judah hugged each of them in turn until Cephas and Ananias appeared. As if cued by the same gavel, all three men turned away.

Then Joshua and Judah strolled to the dining table, arms slung about one another's shoulders. 'I knew you would return, I knew it,' my brother enthused. 'No man as long on passion and courage as my friend Judah would shirk this fight for justice.' They embraced, slapping one another's backs heartily and pinching and patting each other's cheeks.

Night fell. Joshua and Judah slaughtered the lamb Judah had left mewling in the lane and dashed its blood on the lintel. At the hearth, the women baked flatbread and ferried bowls of bitter herbs and eggs to the table. Joshua reclined at the table's head, in the place I still thought of as Papa's, and told the Passover tale. It was only when the Seder was finished, several hours later, that Joshua filled the men's cups with wine once again. Then Judah reclined beside my brother, who was filling his mouth with grapes, and set forth the battle plan.

The road to Golgotha. We had just taken our first step.

Joshua liked the sound of Judah's plan. Especially the proposal that he enter the Temple through the Golden Gates on a donkey colt. 'This is how the Prophets foretold the Messiah would enter Jerusalem,' Joshua told the men. 'It will lend weight to my message.'

But Judah's demand that my brother depart Jerusalem immediately, that very evening, to pass the night in Bethany so that he could approach the Temple from Olive Mountain at dawn, pleased Joshua less.

'It's perfect,' Judah enthused. 'The disciples will arise at first light and steal across the city, lining the trail from the Gethsemane garden to the Golden Gates. When you come over the hill they will shout *Hosanna*, and herald your ascent to the Holy City. It's a stroke of luck that this is the first eve of Passover. We should find it easy to escape the city undetected.'

'Why?' Cephas sniffed suspiciously.

'Because the streets are full of pilgrims, and will remain so long into the night, making their way to and from the Temple and concluding the bonfire rites in the streets. We should find it easy to melt into the crowd and pass through the gates without drawing notice.'

But it was the 'we' that Judah had in mind, the men and women he had picked to escort Joshua from the city that night, that sparked the strongest outcry from Cephas.

'Just you!' I heard the giant bark from my place by the hearth, where I had been mindlessly passing a broom over the same patch of floor. The women stationed by the hanging curtain of beads to relay the unfolding debate to the rest of us jumped at

274

the harshness of the sound. 'Just you, and two women, to help him flee? What use will women be,' Cephas said contemptuously, 'if you run into trouble?'

'The plan has been designed to avoid trouble,' Judah returned, restraining the 'you blockhead' I knew would have been on the tip of his tongue. 'Two men and their wives making their way towards Bethany will command less notice than one man with an entourage of cripples.'

At this, the disciples shifted and muttered rebelliously, but Judah ignored their ruffled feathers. Instead, he turned his attention to Maryam who was moving about the room refilling the oil lamps. 'You must change your robe,' he commanded her. 'Wear a different veil if you must to cover your…your—' he cleared his throat, before concluding gruffly, 'You are far too recognisable in black.' He turned back to the men.

'The rest of you will pass the night here, at the home of Nicodemus. At first light, you will take the women and go out from the city to line the trail from Gethsemane to the golden doors. Do just as Cephas and Ananias command. They are in charge.' I was clearing the last of the bowls from the table when Judah made this announcement and I saw how he let his gaze remained fixed on the assemblage, as if unconcerned about how this casually tossed bone would be received. Having started at the news, both Cephas and Ananias proceeded to swallow it whole. They preened and cleared their throats, exchanging smug looks. *Clever, Judah*, I thought. *That should keep those wolves at bay.*

My husband was still issuing instructions. 'All of you must take palm fronds with you in the morning to shake at Joshua as he comes past.' He glanced at my brother. 'Another Messianic sign.' I was halfway back to the hearth with hands full, but now

275

turned to look at my husband. He cared little for Joshua's new mission and remained scathing of those who hailed Joshua as the saviour. Yet now he had done it himself. He shifted beneath the weight of my gaze, but would not meet my eyes.

The meal finished and the plans were agreed. The women moved towards the hearth while the fishermen issued the first dictate of their new command: ordering the men into the city streets to burn the ragged bones of the Passover lamb.

The moment the door closed behind them, Judah began harrying Maryam and me to collect our belongings so we could leave for Bethany at once. His sudden turnabout and strange behaviour stoked my unease. 'Are you certain of yourself, Judah?' I whispered each time we crossed paths. 'Sure of your plan?' But he was too busy finding a whet-stone for his knife or dropping beside Joshua to pray or seeking out the owner of the *keffiyeh* he had donned that morning so he could ask to borrow it again, to reply.

Soon, all four of us were on our way, drawing the door of the house closed behind us and hurrying south towards Dung Gate. It was now late at night, and our way was lit by jagged flames and sparks from the Passover fires burning across the city. With Joshua and Judah in the lead and Maryam and me scurrying behind, we hurried past pious men clapping their hands and dancing in circles, and open windows from which wafted lyre music and the fervent chant of Passover psalms.

But beyond the city's ramparts, all turned dark and still. The hills and valleys that cradled Jerusalem yawned in the dull glow of the clouded moon, and from somewhere in the shadows, an owl hooted. Following Judah, our backs pressed against the cool stones of the city walls, we edged towards the golden doors near where we would pick up the trail to Bethany. Judah mimed silence, his finger directing our gaze to the soldiers pacing the rampart overhead. This was the riskiest leg of the journey. We were close enough to hear the bored chatter of the legionnaires as they patrolled the walls: on the other side, the narrow path fell off precipitously to the Valley of Death. What if we tripped and fell, breaking a foot or leg? What if the soldiers heard us and, raising their torches as one, knew us for who we were?

Only when we moved past the still-bustling Temple and onto the winding path up Olive Mountain was I able to draw breath, to relax enough to realise how thirsty I was and to hear the sounds of the world again: the shrill of crickets, the scatter of ground creatures startled by our footfalls, the chatter of olive boughs in the breeze. When we entered Gethsemane, I stopped to rest. Joshua, crouched beside me, mopped sweat from his brow. I drank greedily from my goatskin then held it out to Judah, but my husband's attention was elsewhere. He was reaching into his bag. Pulling out the folded *keffiyeh*, he shook out the patterned scarf with a noisy snap. He wiped his face with it, then reached across me to offer the cloth to my brother.

As Joshua accepted it, the trees and shrubs around us rustled, then exploded into life. There were shouts from all directions, orders barked in Latin and, in the light of the moon, helmeted men like birds assuming formation and turning towards their prey.

'Joshua!' I screamed.

Judah stepped in front of me. 'Get down!' he shouted, just as something fell on him from the trees and sent the knife I'd seen glinting in his fist spinning out towards the grassy darkness. He thudded to the earth and the carrion birds descended, whips whistling, boots thudding sickeningly into flesh. My husband grunted and moaned and a woman's voice, much like mine, shrieked and pleaded with them to stop. *Stand back! Stand back! Have mercy, in the name of God, stand back!*

Somewhere behind me, Maryam was begging: *What are you doing? What are you doing to him? Put him down! Put him down!* Her plaintive wail retreated into the distance, becoming fainter and fainter. *Where are you taking him? Where are you taking him? Where are you taking him?* Until a brutal *crack* filled the air, the sound of metal splintering bone, and I turned to see her sway. With a billowy exhale, Maryam of Magdalene collapsed like a tent.

The soldiers continued their retreat. 'Joshua!' I shouted. But even as my brother's name left my lips, my feet were already moving, driving me towards the brutal vultures that had beaten Judah and rendered Maryam silent in the grass and were now marching away in the direction of the city with something still and limp on their backs. Something I felt sure was my brother.

I invaded their ranks like a battering ram, catching them off guard. They scattered, roaring and cursing. Staggering back, I prepared to charge again, my lips drawn back and teeth gnashing like a rabid dog. But as I launched myself forward once more, a wall of iron barred my way. My head struck the shield, the impact sending waves of pain through my body. I fell to earth and was swallowed by black.

I woke to Judah dabbing at something painful on my brow. I winced and threw his hand away; tried to sit up. The musty-smelling room was familiar. We were at my aunt's house in Bethany. Malcah, her eyes crusted with sleep, was scratching absently at her backside, her wayward hair like straw. A sudden gust of memory blew through me: Joshua's plan to bow low before Maryam at the Temple, our secretive departure from the Holy City, the soldiers who overcame us on Olive Mountain.

'Joshua! Is he all right?' I asked. Or tried to. My tongue was like a plank, stiff and unmoving in my mouth. I took stock of the room's inhabitants. 'Where's Maryam?' I rasped.

Judah made no reply, but continued to dab at my wounds. He swished the rag in the bucket beside him, squeezed it, then came at my face again. I scowled and pushed him away. 'What day is it?'

I was slurring but Malcah took my meaning 'Day!' she squawked indignantly. 'It is not day, girl. It is night. The first night of Passover.'

The first night of Passover. The night we had fled Jerusalem; I had not been insensible for long. I made to rise. 'We must go,' I said, trying to coordinate my limbs to rise from my mat, but feeling as if I were moving through water. 'Find Joshua,' I insisted. My head ached, too. 'They took him,' I staggered towards the door.

Judah dragged me back. With shushing noises, he lowered me back to the mat, shaking his head ruefully. He looked well for someone who had been so brutally beaten. His arms and legs appeared unmarked by the scrapes and bruises that even the dim light of the oil lamp showed were blooming on mine. 'You are not going anywhere, Rachael,' he said. 'Not tonight. Your brother is safe. Herod's soldiers have taken him to the priests. They will question and judge him and then set him free.'

Joshua was safe. Safe and well with King Herod and the priests. I would see him tomorrow. My mind was as slow as a crone's. Though, something was tapping at it—a question—but one I could not grasp. Judah offered me water and I accepted it eagerly, draining the dipper in one gulp. I wiped my hand across my mouth and shook my head in hope of clearing it. The reward was a bolt of pain. I stopped, panting, to gather myself. 'Maryam,' I said at last. 'She was hurt, too. I saw her fall. Where is she? Where is Maryam?'

Judah shrugged, looking vexed. 'I do not know, Rachael. I was knocked senseless, too. When I woke, I only heard you: your whimpering and cries, the shallow wheeze of your breath. I thought of nothing but getting you safely from that garden to Malcah's house where I knew I could tend to you.' He glanced in the direction of my aunt, who acknowledged the tribute with a martyred sigh. 'Drink some more water, my love, and let me dress your wounds.'

He loved me, that was nice. But something was not right. If only my head would stop throbbing long enough for me to puzzle it out. I wanted to believe Judah's words were true. That all was right with the world so I could let my eyes close and…

'Sleep,' Judah said, knowing as he always did the yearnings of my heart. He moved to our sleeping mats, already laid out by the hearth and beckoned me into his arms. 'Sleep while I watch over you. In the morning, we'll attend the chamber where the Council of Priests meets and learn the verdict, then take your brother home. Sleep now. All will be well.'

But it was not. When the cock's crow heralded the morning, I shook Judah but he refused to wake. 'No hurry,' he yawned in reply to my urgent whispers, turning over to resume sleep. 'The Council won't adjourn before noon.'

My head was still throbbing, and this made it worse. How

did he know these things—indeed, know anything for certain—about Joshua's fate? I shook him again, more rudely this time. 'Let us go now. To ensure we are there in attendance when word does come.' He grunted and rolled over but Malcah, woken by our whispers, came to the rescue. Grumpily throwing her blanket aside, she picked up an unwashed clay cup and hurled it at Judah's prone form. 'Get moving, you lump. You'll not use my floor to lie about.'

The journey to the city took longer than expected. Having swallowed the mean mouthfuls my aunt set before us and expressed gratitude for her hospitality with bows and scrapes, Judah and I set forth through the barley fields.

We entered and crossed the garden, where only a few snapped branches and a grassy patch of blood testified to the previous night's violence, but there found Joshua's disciples. They were armed with palm fronds and posted along the route Judah had laid down for Joshua's return to the city. They greeted us with excited cries that turned to dismay when they marked my brother's absence and learned its cause.

As we continued towards the city, our numbers grew. We rehearsed again and again the cause of my brother's absence—a tale that grew increasingly unwieldy as ever more voices chimed in for the telling. It was mid-morning before our motley caravan moved past the fitful Passover crowds seeking entry to the Temple and approached the chamber of hewn stone where the high priests met.

But as we drew close, we could see that the chamber was empty. The stone doors were thrown wide, revealing nothing within but darkness and echoes. Doves, escaped from the nearby Temple, strutted and flapped before the gate. For the first time since the day began, Judah looked worried. He mopped his eyes and stared.

Just outside the gates, a man dressed in an artisan's headdress and a crisply pressed saffron robe was pacing. As we poured into the courtyard, he had stared aghast at the diversity of our group's defects. But now the Pharisee's gaze fell on Judah. To my surprise, he seemed to know him. He rushed towards my husband and dragged him aside, the rise and fall of his well-groomed hands of a piece with the rapid movements of his mouth.

I saw Judah recoil, eyes wide. He shook his head wildly, mashing his hands to his ears. But the man grabbed them away and continued to speak until Judah bent over double, clutching his belly in anguish. Then, Judah struck out. Grabbing fistfuls of the fine yellow robe, he shook the man to and fro. When the Pharisee protested, Judah let him go, but my husband remained staggered by horror: his brows flaring and tongue stuttering in despair. 'But that cannot be, it cannot be! You must be mistaken,' I heard him shout.

It would be hours before I learned the whole story; discovered the terrible truth of what had befallen Joshua. But at that moment, the gorge rising in my throat, I knew one thing for certain. That for my beloved brother Joshua, all was already lost.

My heart spoke to me clearly about Joshua's fate. However, Judah's was less willing to admit anything to him. At least not yet. Standing outside the empty stone chamber, faced with the unwelcome revelations of the Pharisee, Judah still believed that he could halt the disaster unfolding; return the chaos he had instigated to order. Judah of Iscariot was a man who believed he could bend fate and history to his will. That he could set aside all that was base and unworthy in this world and put things to right. And I believed this of him, too, a fact I freely admit, even now that the tragic cost of our conviction is well known.

But while Judah and I suffered for this faith, it was Joshua who paid most dearly. Thwarted in his attempt to return to the Temple to insist that Israelite women walked in the light of God, the Pharisee told us, my brother spent the night at

Antonia's Fortress. There, flagellation being Governor Pilate's preferred means of torture, the Governor's men raked Joshua's skin with a whip tied with lead and fragments of bone.

Then Joshua was taken outside to the parade ground. It was Governor Pilate's tradition at Passover to favour the Jews, the subjects he so despised, by releasing one of their number from prison. On that terrible morning, while the manicured hands of the Pharisee were describing Judah's fatal miscalculations, Pilate was toying with his Israelite prisoners. With Joshua on one side and a murdering renegade named Barabbas to his right, the governor pointed at each man in turn, trying to adjudicate which he might free, and which condemn to death. The crowd joined in the carnival atmosphere, delivering their verdict with claps and shouts. But because all my brother's disciples were still at the Council Chambers, there was no one to cheer him. Barabbas took the prize and the order for Joshua's crucifixion was signed.

Much has been made since of my brother's composure throughout his ordeal. During his flaying, and the interrogations interspersed between. It is said that he stood by the accusations of corruption he levelled at the Temple priests despite his torturers' insistence that he recant. That no matter the weight or number of the lashes, Joshua continued to affirm the claims made by others that he was the Messiah, the King of the Jews. That when the end came Joshua welcomed it, believing his mission would be fulfilled by his death as a martyr.

Perhaps. Like the many who attest to these tales, I was not present during the long night of my brother's trial. But I say to you now that I doubt it.

I knew Joshua well. We slept in the same room for most of

our lives and, during those few clandestine years in Papa's shop, he was my teacher, too. And I knew my father. Papa and Joshua were opposites in appearance but they shared the same character. Both were men of stubborn principle who felt the pain of others like a knife in the heart; men who heard the whisper of God in their ears and strove to obey it; men who were good and pure of heart. But they were real men. Not Gods nor saints nor angels. Real men who, because they are made of flesh and blood, will find their tongues quickened by torture.

This I do know: that just as Judah never intended to hurt my brother, far less kill him, Joshua had no desire to die. If my brother, broken, bleeding and in pain, had known what to say to turn the blows of his torturers aside, he would have said it. Joshua would have done whatever it took to be the one Pilate chose for freedom that day, because Joshua loved his life and wanted to live. He wanted to live because, like all Israelites, he saw life as God's only gift, and sought redemption in this world, not an imaginary world to come. He wanted to live because he knew this was the only way to ensure that his disciples, those self-absorbed listeners who failed to hear, spread his good news—not a gospel of their own.

And he wanted to live because he and his beloved Maryam had plans. Maryam had confided these to me the night we huddled about the hearth with the other women as the men feasted and drank too much wine. They would search for the child taken from them, stolen from Maryam's arms while she slept.

By the time Judah, I, and the rest of the disciples had skidded into the courtyard of Antonia's Fortress, the life-and-death

285

draw was complete. The square was deserted save clumps of hair left by mourners, piles of fly-strewn food scraps and a quietly rejoicing huddle of Barabbas's kin. When the saved man realised who we were, he fell to his knees and pleaded for forgiveness. He was sorry. They were all sorry. The ragged clan bowed and scraped, their faces made long by pity and by astonishment at the random workings of fate.

But it was the kaleidoscope of sentiment in Judah's eyes that compelled my attention. Standing before the Priestly Council, he had been obstinate and angry, resisting the truth and refusing to countenance its consequences. Now, forced to confront the immensity and remorselessness of the tragedy that had befallen my brother, he passed swiftly from denial into states of bewilderment and fury, before arriving at despair. Throwing his hands to the heavens, Judah collapsed to his knees on the cobblestones and began beating his breast in mourning. The Barabbas clan threw dust on their heads and joined in too, followed by the disciples who fell about weeping and wailing.

Time slowed, then seemed to stop. Everyone around me appeared drained of will. Judah keeled over on the stones and curled himself into an inert ball while the disciples staggered around aimlessly, their eyes glazed. I stared at them aghast. There would be time for mourning later. Now we needed to act.

Crouching beside Judah's motionless form I hissed into his ear. 'I do not know what you have done, husband, but I *will* know it. Not now, however. Now there is someone else to whom you must confess.'

The sudden change in his manner was startling. Judah gazed up at me with dazzled eyes. 'Joshua,' he breathed. 'I must confess to Joshua.' But then, just as abruptly, he sagged, his chin falling to his chest like a wilted flower. 'If he has not...If they have not—' Judah's swallow was audible, the word, the thought, too terrible to voice.

'Yes,' I said grimly. 'If Joshua is still among the living. Let us make haste, and find out.'

Golgotha is a rocky outcrop beyond the gates of the holy city. In Aramaic it means 'place of the skull.' Nothing grows there. Instead, the fluids that spill from the body at the end of life, and can be dragged from the body to bring life to an end, pool in strange shapes in the dust. Golgotha was the place where, on a crossbar nailed to the beheaded stump of an olive tree, the Romans hung my brother naked and left him to writhe in the sun. Above his head a crude sign declared his crime in Hebrew, Greek and Latin: 'Joshua of Nazareth, King of the Jews.'

At a run, the journey to Golgotha from Joshua's place of sentencing at Antonia's Fortress took just moments. Despite this, when Judah and I arrived we were alone. The rest of the disciples had vanished, evaporating like water in the desert, most never to be seen again. Were they fearful of arrest? Of sharing my brother's fate at the hands of the Romans? Eager to distance themselves, perhaps, from a man whose ignominious death by crucifixion proved, to the satisfaction of the godly, that his prophetic claims were untrue? I will leave them to tell their own tales. To you I say only that at the foot of my brother's cross, there were but three souls: Maryam of Magdalene, Judah and me.

Maryam was there when Judah and I arrived at a run and stood for a moment, trying to collect our breath. She was crying: sharp, pointed wails that seemed both to describe each of my brother's miseries, and to mourn them: the weeping gouges and livid bruise marks on his skin; the bloody tearing of wrists and feet where he had been nailed to the boards; each pain-filled, laboured breath. She wept in shame at the powerlessness of her love, and her loss of hope in her own future, draining away with the blood that streamed from Joshua's ears and the gaping flap in his side. And she wept because she was being beaten. Whipped, more precisely, by the lone Roman centurion assigned to oversee my brother's death, along with those of two other gasping, leaking men nailed to crosses beside him, one dying on each side.

For reasons known best to himself the soldier, not more than a boy really with his narrow shoulders and hairless chin, was determined to keep Maryam away from the rocks clustered at the base of my brother's tree. This, of course, was the precise spot where Maryam sought to be. Here was where she could sit and, reaching up, lay hands on Joshua. Anoint his feet with oil. Where she could bear witness to his whispers of pain and whimpered pleas to God for release. But each time she started forward, the boy would flick his whip, its tail grazing her legs or opening another bloody bite on her face. Wailing with fury and pain she would retreat but, moved again by Joshua's agony and her own longing to touch and comfort him in the brief time they had left, she would creep forth again.

'Rachael!' she bawled when she saw me. She was near hysteria, her sobs catching in her throat before shuddering forth in waves. With an accusing finger she jabbed the air in the soldier's direction as his crimes spilled forth from her lips: each act of hard-heartedness, every venal sin.

At the start of this tongue-lashing, the boy's cheeks, visible beneath the sculpted sides of his metal helmet, flushed with shame. Studiously avoiding my gaze, he looked to keep himself busy: snapping his whip on the ground to draw dust, examining the riven stumps on which the dying men were impaled as if considering their potential for lumber.

Grabbing hold of Maryam, I shook her. Hard. 'Maryam, you must listen to me. Joshua's time is at hand. If you stop plaguing this young man, he might act so as to ease his way.' I lifted my voice so the Roman might hear. 'He might have mercy on Joshua and give him some gall: to wet his mouth and relieve the pain.' I returned the full force of my gaze to Maryam. 'That is all we can do for him now, Maryam. All we can offer. This most tender of mercies. Do you understand?'

She nodded dumbly.

'So you will be still?' Maryam nodded again.

I turned my attention to the Roman. 'Hey you, boy! That man is dying. Can you not give him something? I have her,' I continued, visibly tightening my grip on Maryam's arm in reply to his hostile look. 'She is with me. Can you not ease his misery? Minister to his thirst? The gods of every nation smile on the merciful.'

The boy considered, his mouth hanging open dumbly. Then, slowly and sullenly, he reached into his belt. With-drawing the furred bulb of a cattail, he squirted it with amber liquid from one of his goatskins, holding it above his mouth as he did so to catch the excess. His gaze returned to Maryam. I took a step back, dragging her with me and nodding encourage-ment. Planting the tail of his spear on the camel-coloured earth, he staked the sponge on its tip and extended it towards Joshua.

Since we had got to the killing grounds my brother, whether through pain, or shame at his body's vulnerability and nakedness, had kept his eyes shut. They remained closed now, but from between his cracked lips, a tentative tongue emerged. Weakly it explored the damp presence. Finding moisture and tasting relief, the tongue withdrew and my brother embraced the sponge with his lips. He drank.

It had been foolish of me to hope that Joshua would spend the last minutes of his life hearing Judah's sins. That he would grant his old friend absolution. Foolish and selfish; and yet, I had wished it. Because despite my ignorance of the precise dimensions of Judah's transgression, I knew that unless Joshua could forgive my husband, I would battle to do so myself. That I would struggle to absolve Judah of a crime so terrible that, when my husband looked up to see Joshua hanging on the cross, he had been felled where he stood. As I was working to resolve the dispute between Maryam and the soldier, Judah had collapsed in the dirt, wailing his plea to Joshua across the distance between them, 'Friend! I am sorry. I have sinned against you. Forgive me, friend. Forgive me!'

But Joshua's last words were not for Judah, nor for me nor even for Maryam. They were for God; though whether they were the first words of a hymn in praise of Him, or a despairing accusation of abandonment, I cannot say.

Eloi, Eloi, lama sabachtani was what my brother whispered in Aramaic, though in any language the meaning is the same.

My God, my God. Why have you forsaken me?

⁓

Darkness loomed. Without speaking, Judah and I agreed to return to Malcah's house for the night. But Maryam would not be moved. She had been shrieking and keening for hours, clawing viciously at her face and arms, sobbing and shuddering through prayer after prayer.

Judah and I did everything to persuade her to come with us, pleading and tugging at her arm, but she would not relent. Ignoring us or slapping us away, she continued in her place at the mouth of the cave where the boy soldier, having freed all three dead bodies with hammer and claw, had hurled them before rolling the covering stone back into place. Eventually, reluctantly, we left her and trudged towards Bethany, with the promise to return for her in the morning: a promise that, in the event, we were unable to keep.

We started towards Gethsemane, following the ragged trail just beyond the northern walls of the city, past the limbless penitents in the Bethesda pools and towards the road to Jericho, before turning east. I led while Judah lagged several paces behind, skulking like a cur.

My eyes leaked tears like an over-filled cup, but I did not cry out. Not yet. It was only when we moved through the garden, past the small rough patch of blood beneath the rustling olive trees where Joshua had been taken that my grief exploded, spilling from my lips in ragged sobs. I pushed on, staggering through the gap in the crumbling retaining wall into the barley fields at Bethany's southern end. There my will failed me: my feet slowed, then stilled, by despair. Bent and broken, I stood among the golden stalks, a pining trunk of immoveable grief.

Then came Judah. As we passed through Gethsemane he had abandoned his shamed silence and begun to mourn aloud. He shouted Joshua's name and mine and beat his broad chest, yanking at his hair, tearing it out in bloody clumps. 'Joshua!

Joshua! Rachael! Rachael!' He keened at the top of his voice, proclaiming to the world his anguish, his pleas for comfort and forgiveness.

The arrogance of it! My heart raced and life returned to my limbs. I whirled on my heels and went for him like a fury. 'How dare you. *How dare you.*' Slamming into the barrel of his chest, I pounded it with my fists. 'After all you have done. You filthy dog! You treacherous swine!'

He neither cowered to avoid me nor offered reply to the arrows of my tongue. Instead, he seemed to welcome my outrage, to accept it as punishment due. Nodding his assent to the curses that flew from my lips, he let his arms hang limp at his side as he accepted each blow. Only when my rage was spent and I stood beside him, gasping for breath, did he offer up his truth.

'It was a mistake, Rachael. A terrible mistake. I was trying to defend him, to shield him from harm, not hurt him. I would never deliberately harm Joshua. But he was courting disaster, Rachael,' he said quietly. 'You could see this as clearly as I. Something had to be done. A decision had to be taken.'

Yes, I had thought this but...still! Setting this internal concession to one side, I poked his chest with my finger. 'But you! What did you decide to do, on your own, with none but God as your witness? What did you *do*?'

'When in Jerusalem, I happened past Joseph of Arimathea and—'

'What? Who is Joseph of Arimathea?'

'The Pharisee you saw this morning. The artisan in the yellow robe who was at the council gates.'

He reached out to touch me, to enfold me in his embrace. Hissing like a cat, I wrapped my arms around my chest and pulled away. But I had to hear the rest. With my eyes, I granted him leave to go on.

Judah swallowed, then continued. 'He is King Herod's steward, and a secret supporter of the brigands. I have known him for years and he knows me: that I am Nazareth-born and a friend of the travelling Galilean preacher. He told me what had come of our day at the Temple, the political tempest whipped up when Joshua breached the walls to preach on the steps, the destruction of the Gentile marketplace.'

'What?'

'What I had said would come of it! That the priests and the Herods and the empire were as one in their outrage. He said they were stalking Joshua like a pack of wild dogs, and that when they found him he would share the fate of Yonaton the Baptiser.' Judah drew his finger across his neck. 'He said I must tell Joshua to flee the city at once.'

I waited.

'I confessed to the Pharisee, Rachael. This may have been wrong but I was so burdened with worry that my troubles just spilled out.'

'Confessed what?'

'That Joshua was beyond my reach. That I could not influence him.' Judah took a shaky breath, then coughed up the rest. 'That your brother sought to return to the Temple the following day. With all his disciples, to bathe the feet of a whore.'

'You told him *what*?' Turning my head, I spat in disgust at the betrayal. The remains of the day were now pink and crowded at the earth's edges, but I would not flee the encroaching dark. I would not soften my stance, nor ease the pain of Judah's admissions in any manner. 'So?' I prompted in a cold voice.

'So Joseph agreed to help. Agreed that Joshua had lost his senses and that such a move as he was planning would see him arrested and worse. He said he would help me get Joshua out of Jerusalem before he was found and—' my husband's face seemed to collapse and his voice dropped to a whisper. 'Found and killed.'

I suppressed the urge to slap the stricken expression from my husband's face. 'Then what?'

'The plan was simple. It should have worked! King Herod's men were to arrest Joshua and take him to the priests. It is they whose power he most threatens and they who loathe him most. Though of course, they are all in it together—'

I dismissed this familiar detour with an impatient wave of my hand as comprehension dawned. 'But the soldiers did not hand Joshua to the priests,' I said slowly, recalling Judah's expression as he discovered the story of the empty council room through the rise and fall of the Pharisee's hands.

'They did! He was given over. But the priests did not keep their end of the bargain. Herod's conditions for handing over your brother were arranged by Joseph of Arimathea himself, and they were clear. Joshua could be threatened, shamed and detained for the duration of the Passover Feast, or even longer as an example to others who might follow him, but he was not to be harmed. And when the priests were finished with him, he was to be dumped over the border. Let go, with a stern warning not to set food in Judaea again. Instead,' he swallowed loudly, 'the priests betrayed Herod. The Council questioned him, then turned him over to Pilate.'

I scoffed. 'Or so goes the story of Joseph of Arimathea. But he would tell you this, would he not? He would warrant that it was the priests who betrayed Herod, not he who betrayed you!' All was blackness in the grain field now. I could see little of Judah now but the whites of his eyes and the flash of his teeth. Somewhere in Gethsemane, a hyena laughed.

'No! Well, yes. You are right, Rachael. We may never know the truth of what happened, and who broke faith with whom. But what, in the end, does it matter? They killed him,' I heard Judah's breath shiver as it filled his chest. 'They killed him.'

There was a thud, then a rustle, as Judah's knees hit the dirt and he began crawling towards me. His bowed head pressed into my thighs. 'Rachael, I beg you to forgive me. I have been arrogant. Have dealt treacherously and done an unspeakable wrong. Overreached myself with every step—' he broke off, his voice fractured by sobs, then forced himself to speak again. 'I have no cause to ask for your pity. No right to your mercy. No grounds to keep your heart. Yet I ask it of you, Rachael. I plead for your pardon because I do not know how to live without it. I cannot go on without your love.'

That moment. For years afterwards, in the faraway land I would come to call home I would pause—while tending to my daughter or correcting a pupil's work—and find myself there. Transported back to the darkness and the whispering ears of barley, my arms folded and chin granite as I stood, judging Judah. For a moment, I hesitated, my hand reaching into the blackness to touch his head, twine my fingers through the torn and bloodied coils of his hair. Reaching across the distance between us; but then, suddenly, drawing back. Stopping myself from running aground on his flesh and by so doing, sacrificing my righteousness, my irreproachability, my well-deserved wrath. Oh, how young I was, and how foolish! Young enough to think harsh words could be retracted. Foolish enough to think that a love like that would come again.

So I withdrew my hand, and placed it at my side. Hardened my heart against him. Reached down to remove Judah's arms from around my legs and stepped back to get clear of him. Said the words I cannot stop remembering: 'I will never forgive you, Judah of Iscariot. Never.'

'Please, Rachael.' He scrambled after me on all fours, then bowed his head again. 'Rachael, I beg you! I beg you, Rachael. I have already lost Joshua. Do not say I must lose you as well.'

But I was already gone, striding up the rows of grain, fearless in my footing despite the dark, on my way to Malcah's. Believing the truth of the last words I ever said to him. 'It is too late, Judah. You already have.'

⌒

That night, for the first time in many months, I dreamed of my sister.

> We are in Nazareth. Shona stands on one side of the washing stream, while I am caught on the other. The current is fierce, the channel deeper and wider than it has ever been. Howling and raging, it forces us away from the banks and away from each other.
>
> Behind my sister stands a man, his face as blank as clean linen. His grip is rough as he pulls at Shona's arm, dragging her back from the river's growling edge. She fights his intentions, shakes him loose, pulls her arm free, her gaze fixed on my face. She has no intention of letting me out of her sight.
>
> Then the man sprouts a wolf's head. Through the mist of the rising water I see the winking fangs, the pink and black gums. Hear

the snarls as he bends to Shona and tears off her face. He lunges at her throat to finish it. I hear my sister screaming. Screaming. Screaming. Screaming.

I woke sitting upright, my hair and robe both drenched in sweat. First light. The sky through Malcah's window was the delicate pink of a shell. But while the dream had faded, the screams went on: not Shona's voice, but another woman's. A woman who sounded as if she had simply tipped her head back and opened her throat so that one long cry, with neither beginning nor end, could pour out.

The villagers were already stampeding towards the sound, yelping and shouting as they sprinted towards the east. I wiped the sleep from my eyes and threw the door wide to run after them. Malcah came after me, cursing and heaving. We ran past the well and the mill and the press, and through the grain fields to the east towards a lone tree perched on a hill of dirt. The tree was covered with blossoms of pink and, even in the hooded light of dawn, something could be seen hanging from it. Hanging and swinging.

It was a man. A man with a rope around his neck. And a tatty mane of black curly hair. The woman was still screaming.

I remember how my feet slowed to a walk. The way my thighs felt suddenly filled with lead. I remember how the crowd parted to let me pass, then closed again with the sea's soft chatter.

Having noted my arrival, the screaming woman closed her throat. The rigid pose of her body—back arched, finger pointing —relaxed, as if her role in the tragedy was now at an end and I would carry on from here. A knife was produced and the rope was slashed. The body that had once been Judah fell to the dirt.

For Israelites, there is nothing more reviled than a suicide: a man who wilfully turns his face from God. The crowd drew breath and stepped back. They suddenly remembered their fasting bellies and untended flocks. Tongues clucking, they withdrew, turning back towards the village. Leaving me alone to commit my husband's broken body to the earth.

But the screaming woman stayed. Eyes moist, lashes fluttering with pity, she dropped beside the corpse and pressed her brow to the mound of stiffening flesh. While Malcah looked on open-mouthed, the screaming woman's lips parted, and she began to pray.

Magnified and sanctified may His great name be!
In the world that He created as He wills!
May His kingdom come in your lives and…

The mourning prayer: its peaks and troughs as familiar as my hand. I heard the rasp of my breath in my ears, but felt nothing. As if I had no heart.

The screaming woman grabbed my hand and pulled me down beside her and suddenly, I heard my voice chime in with hers, felt my lips shape the familiar prayer.

Amen! May His great name be blessed forever,
Blessed and glorified and raised and exalted and honoured and uplifted and lauded.
Always and forever, Amen!

Malcah had slunk away, leaving the screaming woman and me to prostrate and praise. Our vows of faith hung in the air for only a moment, then drifted across the field like smoke.

I wanted to die too. My mouth full of dirt, my throat swollen with grief and guilt, my mind branded with unspeakable images: the hump of bone at the back of Judah's neck, his forever-mask of despair. I hauled him into the shallow grave that was all I could scratch with my nails. Grappled in my belt for the tiny cloth scapegoat Mama had gifted me that long-ago day in Nazareth. Pressing it into Judah's palm, I closed his cold fingers around it. 'Forgive me,' I whispered.

Then, having covered his body with dust, I dragged myself back to Malcah's house. Ignoring her accusing finger and carping cries—*The shame of it, Rachael, the shame on our name! Just like your mother! Just like your mother!*—I collapsed into a thick and dreamless sleep from which I could barely be roused.

But these were dangerous times to sleep through. In the hours and days after Judah's death, my brother's male followers—the women were suddenly scarce—began drifting back to Bethany. Greeting one another circumspectly, they clustered by the well to speak in heated whispers, sharing tales of my brother's final hours and canvassing the reasons for Judah's demise.

During what Malcah would later say were her countless attempts to coax me towards consciousness, my aunt filled my ears with news of what each claimed to know of Joshua's arrest and murder.

It seemed they knew it all. Each had been there when the bushes parted in Gethsemane and the might of King Herod was felt; each had lurked outside the hewn stone chamber when the priests questioned Joshua, then gave him over to Pilate; each had witnessed Joshua's flogging at Antonia's Fortress and his last moments of agony on the cross.

Now, with arms waving and fingers brandished like weapons, they vied to have their version of events accepted.

Driving the contest was the need to explain how Joshua could possibly be the Messiah when God had betrayed him so cruelly: allowing him to be crucified and to die in indignity and gore. Even in Bethany, where Joshua had inspired so much devotion in raising Lazarus, my brother's doubters were many.

Malcah was among them, and I should be too, she informed me, her jabbing finger a provocation on my upper arm as she knelt by my mat. 'You had best pray the people forsake Joshua, Rachael. That they judge him a false prophet and cast his memory aside. Because betraying the Messiah, as everyone says your husband Judah did,' she snorted, though even through the haze of my stupor I heard the fear in her voice, 'is a crime worthy of death. And do not think they will let go their vengeance just because he is dead already. Oh no! They will find another scapegoat. And you and I, his kin and clan, will do very well. Especially you, with a belly full of his child.'

My aunt flapped about, moaning in terror. 'Oh, the shame of it, the shame. Just like your mother. Just like your mother!'

I had tried to open my eyes during this speech; to be sensible long enough to check whether the awl in my chest and the twisting blade in my gut were still an inseparable part of living. They were, so I turned back to the dark. But my aunt's claims pecked at me, like a chick at its shell. *Just like my mother.* Whatever could she mean?

Fortunately, when Malcah had a gripe, she did not leave one guessing. She carried on. 'They will find out the truth,' she hissed. 'And if not, I shall reveal it to them. Before it's too late.'

Reveal what? Cocooned in the dark, I felt my throat close around the words, too weak to expel them.

'The truth about my sister,' my aunt snapped, as if I had spoken. 'And her son.'

This was too much. Creaking and groaning like a hibernating bear, I threw the blanket aside and forced myself upright, scrubbing at my eyes. Made myself concentrate. 'What. Truth?' Each word was an effort, as if I were shaping them for the first time.

My aunt looked into my glazed eyes. 'That your brother is not the Messiah. He cannot be.'

'Cannot be? Why not?'

'Because he is not a David.'

I shook my head, trying to clear it. 'Not a David?'

'No,' my aunt replied, seemingly pleased to offer what came next. 'Joshua was not Yosef's son.'

The story was simple and ancient, yet hard to believe. My mother, betrothed to Papa and just turned woman, had lain with a Roman soldier and came to be with child. Joshua was not Papa's firstborn son. That honour went to Jacob. No wonder the next-in-line had been so resentful. As though he'd known the truth all along.

It was Malcah, just ten and seven years herself at the time, who had faced the facts first. Who had shouted and pointed accusingly at Mama's belly, as the older women rushed about the hearth, readying Miriame for Yosef's arrival in Bethlehem to claim his bride.

'Bethlehem?'

'Yes, we did not come of age in this pit,' Malcah's arm waved Bethany aside, her nose wrinkled with disdain. 'We were forced to flee here. After Miriame's fall. We ran from the mob for our lives. We lost everything. Our land and flocks. Our good name and with that,' Malcah laid her brow on her arm and sobbed, 'my own chance to marry.'

Ignoring the play for pity, I continued asking questions. 'And Mama?'

'Oh, Miriame,' Malcah's bitterness soured the air. Lifting her head she scrubbed at her eyes, though no tears were there. It was late afternoon and through the window, Bethany's villagers could be heard trading greetings on their return from the fields. 'Miriame landed on her feet. Like a cat, that girl. Always was. Acts the harlot, then slides away from the consequences. Escapes to a new life with a gentle husband in a foreign place, leaving the rest of us to wear her shame.'

Mama was a bad girl. Not a saint but a sinner who refused to reap as she'd sown. I struggled to take it in. But had my mother truly escaped judgment? Then or afterwards? I recalled Shona's sentencing and the mob's assault afterwards. *Submit! Submit!* The terror on Mama's face, and her pleas for Papa to abandon Shona, and give in to the throng. *You shall not prevail again, Yosef! Relent! Relent!* First Mama, then her beloved daughter: the same sin, the same consequence. 'The people came for Mama,' I said aloud, knowing I was right.

'Yes.' Malcah shrugged, as if such detail were of little consequence. 'They learned the truth and came seeking justice. To pass judgment on Miriame and ensure she paid the price. But Yosef stood to speak for her and turned the men away.'

'Papa did?'

'Yes. He said he would keep her. Make her his wife. He swore she was innocent.'

My eyes asked the question.

'Yes; innocent, Rachael. Your mother, of all women!' Malcah's laugh was mirthless. She plucked a nit from her scalp and crushed it between thumb and forefinger. 'He said that Miriame was pure, that an angel had whispered in his ear to tell him the life in her womb had been stirred there by God.'

I felt my brows draw tight, trying to understand. But Malcah was away; her version of those long-ago events running freely from her mouth. 'Yosef said the men must free her, and allow them to go on their way. He warned them of the price if his bride should be harmed. "What man takes up stones against a consort of God!" That is what he said.'

I had heard of fallen women being described in such ways. Pagan girls in the Decapolis, unmarried but full of child, naming Zeus or Apollo as the father of their babes. What better way for a woman to rescue her reputation and the future of her name-less spawn than to insist she was the consort of a god? But pagan myths were one thing. Mama was an Israelite and the astonishing claim Papa had made on her behalf was not just against any god, but the god of the Jews. 'And the villagers believed?'

Malcah rolled her eyes. 'They believed. Yosef was a right-eous and honourable man. So they believed him, and let them pass. Your parents did not look back. Out the village gates they hurried with naught but the clothes on their backs, never to return.'

Papa had stood by Mama, just as he would stand by Shona years later. Had refused to cast her to the dogs like spoiled meat. My heart swelled with pride. Small wonder my brother had become the man he turned out to—my thoughts fell away suddenly, and I drew a sharp breath. 'Did Joshua know? About

Papa? That he was not Papa's son?'

Malcah was indifferent—my brother was dead, so who cared?—but she doubted it. 'Your mother spent her whole life hiding the truth, Rachael. Remaking her character so that no one would suspect. But you know this better than anyone,' my aunt's smile was small and mean. 'You were at the blunt end of the whip she used to flay herself.'

I gazed at her dumbly.

'Joshua's story is the reason for yours. The reason Miriame was so cold to you. Because you are as she was once, Rachael. The stubborn wit, the readiness to anger. You recalled to her the self she was fleeing, and she hated you for it. And so also did she fear for you and seek,' my aunt conceded gruffly, 'to protect you from her fate.' Malcah's eyes fell to my belly and she threw her hands in the air. 'But she has failed. Failed! Look at you! Just like her! Just like her!'

Following her gaze, I looked down at my belly despairingly. She was right. I was now just as my mother had been: fat and full with the wrong man's child.

My aunt's eyes narrowed. She leaned forward to wag a finger beneath my nose. 'You listen well, Rachael of Nazareth. Bethany is my home now, and I won't be cast from it. Not for your sins or the treachery of your husband. I will speak the truth about your brother; I will pour doubt on claims that he is the Messiah. I will make sure Joshua's memory is washed away. This time,' her hard gaze grew harder and her lips pressed together in a determined line, 'someone else will take the fall.'

The disciples, however, had other plans. Unlike Malcah and me, their interests lay in demonstrating Joshua *was* the Messiah. How

304

else could they vindicate their past dedication to my brother's cause or make future bids for power in his name?

The remnants of Joshua's followers were now assembled in Bethany, the doubters having melted into the countryside, or resurfaced in their own villages, denying three times before the cock even crowed that they knew Joshua's name. Chief among the loyalists were Cephas, Ananias—the fisher fools, as Malcah still called them—and the albino twin.

I woke from another grief-drugged sleep to hear them clustered near the bulbous trunk of a sycamore tree. They were speaking in hushed tones as they combed and carded my brother's legacy, searching for signs and wonders; for proof that God had anointed Joshua as the Messiah despite the inescapable— and for some unbelievable—truth that the Lord had allowed his chosen saviour to die.

'Death can be a good sign, a sign of God's blessing,' Cephas kept repeating as he paced, his body held upright in the manner of a tree trunk, pulling at his chin.

'Yes, yes, a sign of God's blessing,' Ananias would agree in the obsequious tone of a servant to his master, but then calling his older brother over to whisper, 'But how exactly, brother? How?'

In the wake of my aunt's revelations about Mama and Joshua, I had succumbed to insensibility once more, taking refuge in sleep from the truths and sorrows I'd been left alone to bear. Thankfully, Malcah was to hand, kneeling by my mat several times a day with faithful reports of the developing contest.

'The disciples are a rabble, Rachael. They bicker and carp without cease, sifting through the Law and the wisdom of the prophets for ways to sustain their claim. Oh, they are desperate to prove your brother's humiliation at the hands of the Romans showed his teachings were true. How they hope to do *that* is a riddle. How could anyone believe that a man slaughtered like a lamb was blessed—blessed!—by God?' She waved the ridiculous notion away with both hands.

Her voice was a rasp: the ample detail about the contest in our midst more than I could bear. Eyes closed, I swished my arm like a cow's tail in her direction, trying to chase her away so I might return to the mercy of sleep. But she would not be silenced. She continued, 'They only band close when the elders draw near and determine to lay down the truth.' My aunt's tone was fretful. She needed the elders to prevail. Yet despite her threats to reveal the truth about Joshua's birth to all who would listen, she had yet to wade into the circle of disciples, stand beneath the sycamore tree with all eyes on her, and make her case against my brother. I could hardly blame her. Every mention of the cold-eyed fishermen, Cephas and Ananias, made me shiver in my sleep. Who would wish to be the woman who stood alone before them to speak against their faith?

In the end, however, it was a woman who proffered the key to the kingdom my brother's followers sought to build. It was several weeks later, a warm day late in the month of Iyar, when Maryam staggered towards the well. The harvest had begun in the browning wheat fields and the air was stiff as a sun-dried sheet. The approach of my brother's beloved dissolved a nose-to-nose disagreement between a Bethanian elder and the albino, both men joining the rest in a hasty retreat from the harlot's putrid presence. The men formed a large ring around her, their faces querulous with disgust.

'I saw him!' Maryam announced to the circle of hostile faces. There was a long pause, as if the men might simply ignore her.

At last, however, Cephas asked, in his usual flat manner, 'Saw who?' I was huddled at the rim of the crowd at this point, damp and dazed. When Malcah had seen Maryam emerge from the grain fields to Bethany's south, she rushed to my mat in a desperate bid to wake me. 'Arise, Rachael! Arise at once! Maryam is here! In Bethany! Get up and warn her away from our gate; tell her she will not be granted hospitality at this house.' When I failed to stir, my aunt emptied a pitcher of water on my head.

'Joshua,' Maryam said in answer to Cephas, her eyes misting at the mention of my brother's name. 'I saw my beloved in a dream.'

The men snorted and turned to walk away. Yes, dreams were a way of knowing God's will, but a woman's dreams? Worth less than a speck of meal.

Maryam, impervious to their scorn, began relaying her tale anyway. Her hands were like a drunken painter's—blotting, wiping, smearing—as she described the cave she had seen while she slept. It was Joshua's burial cave, she said, and its round stone door had been pushed aside by none other than the hand of God himself.

'God rolled the stone away and entered the cave, just as Joshua did that day with Lazarus,' Maryam recounted. 'There my beloved lay, unswathed and unanointed, and God forgave him. He healed my beloved so that he might walk in the light again.'

The elders continued their retreat but, at the mention of Lazarus, all the disciples who had been with my brother when he had raised the man—Cephas, Ananias, the twin and most of the villagers—came to a halt. They turned slowly to listen.

'There was music,' Maryam continued, her unfocused gaze passing across the faraway landscape of her vision. 'Psalms.' She began to hum, a tune that was unfamiliar though when the words reached my ears from her dry, flayed lips I recognised them. *My God, my God, why have you forsaken me?* These were Joshua's last words from the cross. Words, I now realised, as Maryam continued to lilt the psalm, that she saw as an affirmation of the One God's mercy. *Yet you are holy, enthroned on Israel's praises. In you we have trusted and have not known shame.*

'Joshua did not give up hope,' Maryam said, spinning around, searching the sea of hostile faces for a glimmer of compassion or understanding. 'He believed in God's love to the very end. This is what he came to tell me. That God did not abandon him to the Romans, did not leave him to die unloved. The Almighty was testing Joshua, his willingness to submit to God's will, just as He tested Abraham by Isaac's sacrifice. Was Joshua willing to suffer and die for our sins? This is what the Almighty demanded he prove. And the answer was yes. Joshua prevailed! He triumphed! That is what my beloved wanted me to know, to accept, from my dreams: that he never lost faith in God, and that with such unyielding faith, the Lord is greatly pleased. And now, he shall have his reward.'

'Reward?' Cephas asked, grunting with the effort of inflection. 'What reward?'

'The reward of life everlasting!' Maryam continued rapturously, giving no sign she had even heard him. 'God has forgiven him! Forgiven and healed Joshua so that he, like Lazarus, can rise and walk again. This is what I have come to tell you. That I have seen him! *I have seen Joshua! My beloved lives!*'

There it was. The solution to the quandary that had been exercising the dusty circle of disciples since they had first returned to Bethany. The solution that Joshua had prefigured in the days preceding his death but, in the event, had required a woman—a sun-crazed, sleep-starved harlot, no less—to comprehend. The solution that pointed away from the lessons of Joshua's life and towards his brutal death and resurrection as proof that his vision of a loving, forgiving God was correct.

Cephas recognised the breakthrough and Ananias's bobbing chin suggested he did too, but no light shone in the twin's colourless eyes. The rest of the men looked blank, too. The black tat of Maryam's robe, the stink of her unwashed body distracting them from the possibilities offered up by her vision. Something else, simpler and more easily grasped, would be required to unify them; to knit the bickering remnants of Joshua's disciples into a single piece of cloth.

Cephas knew this, too. I saw the spark in his eyes, the understanding available only to those who knew exclusion. Cephas knew the strength of the bonds that could be forged among men simply by opening a gate that only some might pass through. He understood that, for a community to be born, someone must be left out: that sometimes a scapegoat was required. He cleared his throat and lurched into speech.

'Even the harlot knows!' he said, gesturing woodenly at Maryam as he manoeuvred his enormous frame into the centre of the crowd that surrounded her. 'She knows what you of little faith have refused to believe: that Joshua died for our sins, not his own. That Joshua is the Messiah. This dream, her dream,' he shaped his lips around the female pronoun as if it were poison, 'says it is so.'

Maryam's expression was a study of conflict. She had flinched at the giant's use of the word 'harlot'; now she appeared grateful at his exaltation of her vision. Her tongue, perhaps considering reproof, darted between her dry lips, then withdrew. She held her peace. Cephas continued. 'God has returned life to Joshua. And we, Joshua's loyal followers, still have work to do.' His cold eye roamed the crowd. 'Wrongs to right,' he added. The men waited.

'The murder of the Messiah must be avenged!' Cephas's fist rose towards the sky. The men rubbed their hands together and grunted their assent. Revenge! For the life of their leader, their own lost honour. Here was something they understood! But how to confront the might of Rome, both author and agent of the deed? Cephas, hearing the rumblings, had a ready reply.

'The centurions arrested Joshua and oversaw his murder. Pilate called for the execution. This much is true,' he said ponderously. 'But was it Rome that betrayed Joshua the Messiah? I say no. No: Rome has been true to herself, as she always is.' He was as inspiring as a block of wood. 'Tell us harlot,' the giant grated, turning stiffly to Maryam. She jumped as the hard eyes of the mob fell on her.

It was then that I saw it, the quality that made Cephas's bearing so thick and strange. His neck and shoulders did not move independently but as though they were welded together. 'Tell us,' he invited Maryam, 'about the betrayal.'

The betrayal. I saw the words enter Maryam's head as if

I were inside it. Watched them slither like eels around the architecture of her tired, addled mind, seeking purchase. Watched as she listed, passing her parched tongue across her lips in a fruitless search for moisture. In the pit of my own belly, a crab-scuttle of fear.

'Betrayal?' Maryam of Magdalene said slowly. 'What betrayal?'

It was as though someone had thrown all the pieces of a wooden puzzle into the air and, somehow, as they rose, peaked, and began their descent—still disconnected from their fellows in space and time—I could see how they would all fit together. How the picture would look, how the tale would be told, when each block was locked into place.

Cephas had never had any love for Judah, and what he wanted, needed, from Maryam was now abundantly clear. And one look at Maryam's dazed, sun-baked countenance was enough to know that when the giant finally got her to water, she would drink.

Once the rabid, rancid men who had followed Joshua accepted that Judah was a more convenient target of blame for my brother's death, and had faced up to the disappointing fact that the betrayer could not be killed for his crime because he was already dead, they would look for someone else to pay. Someone whose kinship with the betrayer demonstrated her guilt and put beyond question the rectitude of exacting payment from her in blood. In this way would the mob affirm who they were becoming—disciples of Joshua the Messiah—by whom they reviled.

Moments later, I was off and running, tearing towards the east, a hastily rolled sleeping mat tucked beneath my arm and an empty goatskin flapping from my fist. Pounding through the shaven rows of barley with the bays of the mob sounding distantly in my ears.

Running for my life.

It was the Miriame Mourners who rescued me, the white-robed nuns on their way home to Antioch from their annual descent to the Egyptian desert where they performed the mourning rites for Moses' sister. The Miriame Mourners who heard me keening—back hunched around my swelling belly, sobs torn from me as if hauled by a hook—in a cave on the eastern edge of Bethany.

This was the cave of rotting bones from which Joshua had raised Lazarus, and where I had spent a sleepless night. The desert air had surprised me with its chill and a pack of slavering jackals, drawn from miles away by my scent, had kept vigil until dawn at the slim gap between cave and covering stone.

When at last daylight scattered the beasts, I determined to set forth. Whatever the chance of being discovered by my brother's marauding disciples or of wandering lost in the desert and expiring in a drift of sand, I preferred to close around my fate with both hands, rather than wait passively for it to seize my throat.

But where should I go? I could not return to Nazareth, for by now my pursuers would have posted sentinels at the gates and at the foot of the trail from the plains. I considered turning east, towards the Salty Sea and into the land of the Nabateans… Or perhaps better to go south, through Idumea and on to Alexandria in Egypt? Then again, maybe north was best, to the Decapolis, the constellation of Greek and Roman towns at the spur of the Galilee Sea, where the pagan population would care little for Joshua's life and death, and the curse on my head as the wife of his betrayer.

Wringing my hands, I paced in circles as if one foot were nailed to the dirt, uncertain which of these destinations might offer a pregnant, penniless widow with a secret past the best chance of life. Had the Miriame Mourners not been in receipt of a message that their ailing leader, left behind in Antioch, was now at death's door, and replied to the summons by cutting short their *hejira* to return to her side, I might have perished in that cave from indecision.

But I did not perish. It was a woman's voice that delivered me from death; a woman's words that stilled my step, hushed my lips and turned my gaze towards a cleft in the rocks. A freckled hand at the end of a white-robed arm—a scrawny arm for a woman who would turn out to be so ample-breasted—reached through the fissure and beckoned.

'Come, child,' she said, over and again, first in Greek and then, when that drew no reply, in Aramaic. 'Come child, come.

My name is Julia, I am an Israelite nun. We are women of God, child, you have nothing to fear from us. Come child, come.' Until, as if bound by a trance, I did move towards her, while the other nuns made haste to roll away the covering stone so I might pass from the darkness back towards the light.

⌒

The lies began at once. Lies about my name, my kin and clan, my excuse for cowering alone in a pit of death with no man in sight and a belly swollen with child. I had spent the sleepless night past concocting such tales and now they rolled smoothly from my tongue. I was Yael of Mo'din, a hamlet of artisans and snake-charmers on the road from Jericho. Yael, whose village had fallen victim to a column of centurions seeking revenge after the elders complained of them to the Roman governor. For the soldiers' crimes, I drew on the usual range of Jewish complaints: extortion, sacrilege and its sweet-faced cousin, syncretism. But this time, I explained, it had been different. The occupiers had taken our side and made the soldiers pay for their crimes.

'When the soldiers returned to Mo'din, they were thirsting for vengeance. A vengeance that spelled doom not just for my kin and clan, but every man, woman and child in the village.' They were all dead, I extemporised tearfully—everyone! Dead or scattered to the wind like seed! Virgins raped and taken as slaves, men and children stabbed or speared. Houses and holy places plundered then left to burn. I explained how my own life was owed to the child growing within me for I had been beyond the village gate during the raid, visiting the midwife. It was on my return, humming to myself and planning the evening meal,

315

that I saw the flames and heard the screams of terror. Running to a hidden lookout point, I saw my husband fight and fall.

My body shook with sobs, my unspent guilt and sorrow at Joshua's murder and Judah's death finding release in Yael's tears. Julia fluttered around me like a broody hen while the untied ends of her white veil, draped atop her head and held in place by a curved fillet of bone, undulated across her narrow shoulders. 'Oh, no! Oh dear! Oh my!'

She looked to be my mother's age but, unlike Mama, seemed animated by some inner warmth. Her amber eyes were attentive but devoid of all judgment; her cheeks aglow like polished wood. The other nuns followed her lead, exchanging looks and murmuring sympathetically. None, I realised, had treated me as polluted; none had taken even one step back, when I emerged from the cave, to avoid my touch. For the first time since I'd scratched a place for Judah's broken body in the dirt, I felt something stir in my heart.

I had nowhere to go and the women, with their leader at death's door, no time to waste. 'The Miriame Mourners,' Julia reassured me, looking around at her nodding train of followers, 'will not abandon you here.' So it was decided. I would join the nuns on the three-hundred-mile journey north to the third-largest city in the Roman Empire. Their home of Antioch.

❦

What do I recall of the passage, of the land's curves and textures, the variously toned skin and draped robes of its people, the bloom and buzz of new life as spring proceeded to summer? The truth is, very little.

We left the Galilean hills, trudged across the fertile plains of Lebanon—the golden wheat glistening in the sun like the snow on the surrounding ridges—and picked up the trail of the River Orontes, which roamed the land as if caressing a woman's curves.

But I had been dragged out of a pit of corpses and remained alert to danger, my pulse still blazing, my sense of smell animal-sharp. Pulling my veil low to hide my eyes, I kept my gaze on the nuns: the women on whom my own life, and that of the child inside me, now depended.

I attended to the stream of chatter and endless argument, quickly gaining proficiency in Greek, a language of which I'd previously had just passing knowledge. I employed childish tricks to commit the women's odd-sounding names to memory. There was Aphia the ancient, Thyatra the tubby, prissy Prisca, regal Rhoda and a woman of elfish appearance whose hands shaped messages only Julia seemed able to parse. 'Mute Minna,' I whispered to myself.

I soon discovered that most of the nuns were divorced, or widows estranged from their sons and therefore alone in the world. A handful had children, either strapped to their backs or running like brushfires between the bell-shaped billows of their skirts. A few had been with the Mourners always, rescued at birth from exposure in the desert due to a harelip or an absent finger, or the crime of being born female.

I learned that Julia, clearly in line to lead the group should the ailing ruler fail, was adored and respected. The other nuns strove relentlessly to please her, bustling forward importantly with a new nugget of knowledge gathered at a caravanserai, or to proffer a posy of wild flowers. They vied to walk with her, sharing confidences or just holding her hand, until someone sang out her name and, with an apologetic smile, Julia would beetle away.

For it seemed that only Julia knew where a required provision could be located among the many baskets the Mourners carried on their backs. Only she could intuit when two women needed separating before pawed earth and flaring nostrils turned to open warfare. Only she understood the flavouring requirements of one or another stew, and how to ensure that every woman and child blossomed and thrived in her care.

⁓

It took nearly a month of travel for us to arrive on the outskirts of Antioch. After so many days on the dusty road, the pagan suburb of Daphne, just outside the southern wall, seemed a paradise: leafy and prosperous, the air damp with waterfall spray, the many stone paths leading to large dwellings freshly limed in white. Vendors hawked bread filled with meat, plum sauce and a fish-scented paste, while bare-chested slaves wove in and about the crowds, toting faggots of wood or hurrying ahead to herald the arrival of their masters at gymnasium or bathhouse. Bronze statues were everywhere, of gods and the Roman kings the pagans worshipped as gods. There were even casts of women, patrons of the city's various cults. The babble of Greek was everywhere, woven through with Latin, and once or twice I even heard my own native tongue of Aramaic.

In the late afternoon, the city was bathed in the shade of Mount Silpios. The walls of the city were high, and as thick as a child is tall. They bridged the Orontes to the west and snaked their way across the mountain's lower ramparts to the east. But the gates were swung wide and casually attended, a condition I judged to be usual from the demeanour of the nuns, who did not even look up from their verbal duels and raucous chatter as they swept through.

During the journey north, the nuns had spoken often of their city's splendour. 'There are many Antiochs,' they had told me breathlessly. 'Over fifteen sites in the Roman Empire bear the name. But only one is a morning's walk to the sea, and scented by bay trees all year round. Only one is known as Antioch the Beautiful.'

Now I understood their boast. At Antioch's centre, visible in the distance as my eyes followed the colonnaded marble walkway down which the nuns were fast disappearing, was the forum, the covered market fringed by triumphal arches around which all Roman cities were built. To the east stood an amphitheatre and to the west a basilica from which men streamed, clad in togas bespeaking their standing as citizens, their arms full of parchment stamped with official-looking seals. There was an elaborate Israelite temple, too, festooned with the gold-plated cherubim said to stand watch at the gates of Paradise. Overhead, on the terraced peak, circular white temples glittered like stars.

I darted through the crowd to catch up with the Miriame Mourners, whose flapping white veils made them look like herons. They had left the marble path for a humbler one, made of broken and missing cobblestones, and entered an older section of city. The winding lanes and ramshackle dwellings wordlessly recounted life in Syria before the arrival of the Greeks three hundred years ago.

Suddenly, the procession ground to a halt. The flock came

to rest before a Greek-style dwelling in desperate need of white-wash and marked by the One God's sign. Julia fished a key from her miraculous bosom while the women pressed tightly around to shield her from scrutiny. When the door fell open, the group surged into a narrow corridor, shooing children before them and shouting their ailing leader's name as they shrugged their burdens to the floor.

Slowly, tentatively, I followed them into the hall, taking in the dwelling's unfamiliar dimensions: the sofa and battery of looms in the central room; the open-mouthed roof and the receptacle for water beneath it, filled with lotus flowers and fish; a glimpse of a vegetable garden out the back. The paint-peeling door, still open behind me, swung slowly shut. Inside my blossoming belly the child swished and flipped in time with my hammering heart.

The journey was at an end. Although for me, of course, it was just the start.

Epilogue

The house is still for the first time in weeks. The nuns, my sisters, have set off for Kadesh to mourn Miriame. Pleading illness, I have been allowed to remain alone in Antioch this year.

Since coming to live with the Mourners, I have been creeping towards forgiveness in the manner of a thief. Circling it, approaching now as one who might grant and also receive it. I have been waiting for a moment to offer it to the world in the way one releases a bird from a cage, in a spirit of grace as much as rebellion.

Now that moment has come. The house echoes with emptiness but I tend the garden, feed the fish, and bask in the rare solitude. I review with care the details of the ceremony I am planning, each act of penance and propitiation.

Just two days after the nuns have left the city, I am ready to begin. I fast for a day and spend the hours after noon in a ritual bath to purify myself. Emerging at dusk, I dot my breast and brow with sacred oil, then settle myself on the sofa in the weaving room. I sew three tiny scapegoats, just like the one my mother gave me so many years ago.

At midnight I shuffle to the altar at the far end of the Mourners' house. I light the lamp resting on the ledge and fall to my knees. I bow my head.

I open my heart first to Mama. It is more than ten years since I came to this city and I know she must be dead now: dead or dying. I consider, not for the first time, how hard it is to believe that I will never see her again. I address her thus:

I understand you now Mama, just as you said I would when I was no longer just a daughter, but had birthed a daughter of my own. The losses you suffered and overcame, the terrible choices you faced—you and all the mothers of daughters born in harsh and unforgiving times. I know that you only wronged me in the ways you too were wronged, Mama; that you reared me in the manner you thought necessary for me to survive.

I rise and pluck one of the newly stitched scapegoats from my belt. I place it on the ledge. I signal its arrival by the toll of a bell, which makes the lamplight dance and sputter. Bowing my head, I sink to my knees again.

Judah, my beloved. Not a day goes by that I don't think of you. I rejoice in the short time we had together, and berate myself for the failings of character, the youthful arrogance that allowed me to harden my heart against you—to cast you out from the shelter of my love. The pardon I ask of you is larger than that which you sought from me and which I offer now—so many years too late—without reservation. I forgive you Judah. I know now that it was what I loved in you, the force of your character, the impulse to action occasioned by youth, that caused your downfall, too.

Another scapegoat deposited on the ledge and the bell sounds again. I feel lighter now, and cleaner. My lips twitch and threaten to part in song.

Then, reflexively—it is like scratching an itch—I think of Shona. I wonder where she is and what she might be doing right now. If she is safe and free.

Clutching the last scapegoat in my hand, I start to kneel again and suddenly it is as if her spirit has entered the room. I know the room, the house, is empty, but the warm, cinnamon-scented presence remains by my side. It envelops me, stays my fall to the floor, prevents my repentant prostration like a strong, gentle hug.

I close my eyes and melt into its embrace, basking in the sweetest balm of forgiveness: that for which one need not even ask.

A salty breeze flows in from the sea; in its wake sandalwood, the scent of my daughter's hair, is everywhere. And though she is many miles from this place, safe in the care of Julia and the other nuns, I cannot escape the sense that she has joined my sister, and is here with me now, too. That her twelve-year-old self is present in the room, offering me the same steadfast gifts as my sister always did. Love, acceptance—and forgiveness, even for the wrongs I have not yet done her.

I swoon and stagger, and the spell is broken. When I raise my eyes, the room is truly empty, not just of people but of presence.

The flame has burned low. The gusts through the window are cold, penetrating the thin, Greek-style robe I now wear and stippling my skin with goosebumps. I move to the window to drop the blind, smiling to myself.

Whatever the trials of my life, I have also known blessings. I have never been cast out or deemed beyond pardon; I have managed to find love and healing, somehow, at every turn. Love and forgiveness. Everyone should be so fortunate. At least, that is what Joshua always said.

Author's Note

The impulse behind *The Book of Rachael* was born many years ago. I was in my loungeroom, spellbound by a BBC documentary series called *Son of God*. The programs were about Jesus the man—not the religious figure—a poor Jewish peasant about whom I knew next to nothing. I certainly hadn't known he had four brothers whose names and life journeys had been carefully recorded for posterity.

The names of Jesus's sisters, in contrast, were not known. Nor, indeed, was the basic fact of whether he even had any. Back then, not even the most basic information about the female relatives of a man who at that time already had a whiff of notoriety about him was deemed important enough to record. It would have been like a reporter today profiling a famous farmer and including the names of all his sheep.

Gall quickly turned to resolution—I would write the story of the forgotten sisters!—but just as quickly to despair. I was a columnist and a published non-fiction writer but there were no facts about the sisters on which to base even an article, let alone a book. That's OK, I remember thinking, I'll just write a novel instead. Seven years later, that novel is the one you now hold in your hands.

I wonder now whether it really makes sense to call this sort of writing historical fiction. Can setting entirely fictional characters to roam in the landscape of a multi-authored, oft-redacted religious tale really be described as historical? Not if the criteria include scholarly examination of verifiable, chronologically ordered events. So I don't think of *The Book of Rachael* as historical fiction. I think of it as the bringing to life of a fictional character by evoking the time and place in which the character's story is set. In *The Book of Rachael* I have set the fictional sisters to roam across the historicised terrain of the gospels.

To help me evoke that time and place I read many things. Among the most helpful were *Jesus: an Unconventional Biography* by Jacques Duquesne, *The Jews in the Time of Jesus* by Stephen M. Wylen, *In Memory of Her* by Elisabeth Schussler Fiorenza, *Women and Religion in the First Christian Centuries* by Deborah F. Sawyer, *Son of God* by Angela Tilby and the Jewish Museum of Australia's exhibit program *Women in the Bible: Tricksters, Victors and (M)others*. I also consulted *The Natural History of the Bible* by H. B. Tristram, Winifred Walker's *All the Plants of the Bible* and Allan Swenson's trilogy on the plants, flowers and herbs of the bible. The Nazareth Village Research website was also very helpful.

Acknowledgments

First and foremost I want to thank my partner who is too important to leave to last. We have shared the last eighteen years and together have raised two beautiful sons. Yet he still pursues my happiness with the same fervour he did on the day we met, proving beyond doubt that my grandmother was—as is often the case—absolutely right. I did indeed pick a good one. Without Adam Clarke, there would never have been a book about Rachael or a newly minted fiction writer, which is what he insists I must now call myself. Love you, sweet.

My children lived the latter part of their childhood and early teenage years in the shadow of my fitful and only-eventually-successful efforts to write a novel. They never tired of asking when I was going to finish it, and still occasionally inquire as to when it's going to make our fortune. When I laugh and say, 'Don't count on it,' they give me a hug and say they are proud of me. What more could a mother possibly want?

Tracey Aitken never doubted. I wish she wasn't already my best friend so I could appoint her to the task.

Sophie Cunningham, Richard Freadman and the Rev. Anne Amos deserve medals for reading early drafts and making encouraging noises. So does Olga Lorenzo, whose uncompromising vision of what the book had the potential to be was inspirational, if not occasionally terrifying. Ben, John, Saralinda,

Dave, Daniel and Emily helped smooth the edges and made it fun. RMIT's Professional Writing and Editing course in Melbourne deserves plaudits. One day we'll find a way to stop the government's repeated and inexplicable attempts to kill it off.

I am also grateful to the Victorian Writers' Centre for renting me a room of my own for one fabulous year at the beautiful Glenfern, and to Mena Meyerowitz and the wonderful folks at La Café who advised on things Hebrew and Israeli.

In my darkest moments with the manuscript, I would fantasise about how one day it would all be behind me. One day, I would finish the damn book and it would be accepted for publication by Text. I still can't believe this particular dream has come true. With Mandy Brett as my editor and Jane Novak to hold my hand while we market the thing, my cup truly runneth over.